HE LIVED BY THE INDIAN'S RULES . . .

"Listen, or thine own tongue will keep thee deaf.
Have one door to thy lodge and sleep across it.
Women, war and horses can always break loose.
Shouting at eagles brings out the wolves.
Unbelt carefully and keep thy moccasins tied on.
Two loves to become one."

YET HE DREAMED OF THE WHITE MAN'S WORLD.

That stubborn, disinherited loner, The American . . . hero of Hervey Allen's epic novel,

THE FOREST AND THE FORT

"a vast song of the building of America."
—*Atlanta Journal*

Also by
Hervey Allen

Anthony Adverse Part 1: THE ROOTS OF THE TREE

Anthony Adverse Part 2: THE OTHER BRONZE BOY

Anthony Adverse Part 3: THE LONELY TWIN

Published by
WARNER BOOKS

Hervey Allen

THE FOREST AND THE FORT

**Turkeyfoot Reading Center
Confluence, PA 15424**

WARNER BOOKS

A Warner Communications Company

WARNER BOOKS EDITION

ISBN 0-446-81437-7

This Warner Books Edition is published by
arrangement with Holt, Rinehart and Winston Inc.

Cover art by Jim Dietz

Warner Books, Inc., 75 Rockefeller Plaza, New York, N.Y. 10019

Ⓦ A Warner Communications Company

Printed in the United States of America

Not associated with Warner Press, Inc., of Anderson, Indiana

First Printing: July, 1978

10 9 8 7 6 5 4 3 2 1

TABLE OF CONTENTS

PART ONE: *The Forest*

PART TWO: *The Fort*

PART THREE: *The Mountain Road*

The Forest
and the Fort

PART ONE

The Forest

1

Genesis

IN THE BEGINNING was the forest. God made it and no man knew the end of it. It was not new. It was old; ancient as the hills it covered. Those who first entered it saw it had been there since the beginning of habitable time. There were rivers in it and distant mountains; birds, beasts, and the mysterious villages of red men. The trees were vast, round, and countless; columns of the roof of heaven. The place beneath was endlessly aisled. There were green glades where the deer fed and looked at the buffalo; trails that went back into the animal time. There were valleys where the clouds lay and no man came there; caves where the wolves mated; peaks where the panther screamed.

But the forest itself was silent. It slept and dreamed of something in a perpetual grey-green shadow in the summer. The lightning flashed at evening and the thunder echo rolled. In the fall the leaves fell and the stars looked down through a roof of sticks. The snow sifted and glittered. Winds heavy with the silver breath of winter smoked on the mountains. The trees burgeoned. Red flashed into the green flame of spring. The grey-green shadow brooded in the forest again, gestating sunlight.

Birds, those free spirits of the weather, were the only beings who saw the spectacle entire. As the earth rocked, every spring and autumn their blood burned. They rose, trillions of them, feathered nations with innumerable tongues and various languages, and took to the air. Their nests and their love songs followed the tilting ecliptic like a pæan of time. They also sang the praises of the Almighty One with innocent, unthinking hearts. High in cold atmospheres, they beheld the grandeur and beauty of His thought.

Northward a necklace of great lakes glittered across the breast of the continent. Eastward the tabled plains of the Atlantic flashed lonely to the unbroken water rim. Not a sail gleamed. Only the steam clouds over the warm river in the ocean cliffed towering into heaven. The moon rose out of them at the full and looked at the sun setting beyond the Appalachians into a sea of western grass. Between lay the forest, green, gladed, unbroken, beautiful; riding the still waves of the long mountains, stretching from ice blink to palms.

The fingers of innumerable days trailed across the roof of the forest, while spring and autumn ran up and down it countless thousands of times. The stars shifted in their houses. Eastward over the waters the wings of gulls wheeled; gleamed and vanished; vanished and gleamed— prophetically. Until in the fullness of time something whiter glinted there; held the sunlight steadily; discovered the tracery of sails. Man-made thunder saluted the land.

Then harbours reflected the lights of ships' lanterns; the windows of gabled houses gleamed orange in the dusk. Broad plumes of smoke arose from capes and along the estuaries by day. Fire and steel axes ate the forest away, thinning it westward. Field patches and road scars began to show among the trees. The haze of wood smoke gathered over towns.

Generation after generation the ships kept coming. From one century into another the white man increased his town bases behind him. The tentacles and network of roads began reaching out for the hills. Vainly the silent stone-tipped arrows flitted from the forest at twilight. The flash and roar of musketry replied. Manitou and Jehovah wrestled in the valleys together—and the tasseled corn-god lost. Death like a mist out of lethal nowhere fell upon the red man until he vanished. The forefathers he left behind him slept in quiet mounds beside the east-running rivers. Only tobacco smoke lingered like a memorial incense scenting the breeze.

Beyond the cloudy rampart of the mountains the Indian gathered his surviving tribes. In the years numbered 1700 he and the forest stood at bay together. And for a while the forest prevailed. In the quarrel between the two houses of the Great White Fathers lay the Indian's chief hope of continuing to exist. Now on one side, now on the other his hatchet rose and fell. What he fought for was to preserve the forest beyond the Alleghenies. If the trees and the game went, if the white man came there, the Indian must go, too.

He knew that. His great men and prophets arose by the secret council fire and said so. The wampum strings of alliance flitted from tribe to tribe. Many laid hands upon them and promised never to let go. Meanwhile, with sonorous oratory, he smoked the peace pipe or exchanged the war belt with the French or English—always on the side of the trees.

And for a while, for a long time, the forest stood there. It stemmed the onrush of the colonists of Europe. The frontier ceased to flow westward majestically. It blundered against the barrier of the trees, the tribes, and the mountains. It recoiled. The inflow of its peoples pooled like the trickle of waters rising slowly behind a dam head; fanned out northward; flowed notably south.

Beyond the mountains lay the Valleys of Eden. But to go there was to slip one's finger out of the handclasp of mankind. To go there was to go lonely; to defy the forest, the Indians, and the lawful king. To go there was to move westward without the baggage or the impedimenta of the past. It was to drop everything, except God, language itself, and the memory of simple numbers. It was to begin all over again, to become a something new and unique in time.

But that was the fascination of it. That was the lure. That was at once the refuge, the opportunity, and the goal.

13

The American did not begin by overthrowing society, by reorganizing an old civilization. He left all that completely behind him. He disinherited himself. He reinvented and reincarnated society. For the first time in memorized history man was free to act entirely on his own responsibility. He was back in the forest again. He had nothing but himself, the animals, and the trees to contend with. There liberty was not a dream and an idea to die for; it was a state of nature to be successfully lived in. In the Valleys of Eden, west of the Alleghenies, that was where and how new America began. The seeds of it were scattered in lonely cabins, lost apparently in an ocean of trees.

Out of them genesis.

2

A Scriptural Prelude

ANCESTRALLY it is sometimes, although not always, well to go back as far as one can. In North America the Atlantic usually provides your easy eastern limit of the past. And that is convenient even when it is not actually final.

All that it is necessary to know here, then, is that in the next to the last year of the seventeenth century there appeared in the vicinity of Norwalk, Connecticut, a forceful individual by the name of Abijah Albine. He came from England. He was a doctor of divinity out of some university, a disciple of St. Augustine through Calvin, and a mighty preacher of the word of God. In the course of a decade he gathered about him a scared, troublesome, gossiping, but withal faithful flock. He died in 1742. And that is about all that can be known with rigid certainty about the Reverend Abijah Albine. Naturally, a number of doubts remain.

And there are more than a few doubts about the Reverend Abijah. However, it is the doubts about him that are the more interesting.

Actually, not even his name is an absolute certainty. It glimmers a bit phosphorescently since it has faded from his mossy tombstone. It may originally have been Aldine. To tell the truth, there is a hushed and yellow rumour now close-mouthed for over two hundred years that his name *was* Aldine, and that he changed it when he came to America, because:

(a) It was advisable to do so (debts). (b) He had quarrelled bitterly with his father. (c) He foresaw possible clerical errors even in the golden list of predestination, and wished for no avoidable confusion on the last day as to who was among the elect.

From a certain source it appears that some other Aldines believed in the efficacy of good works—at least about Norwalk. They were in a parlous state there, one gathers. So perhaps eternity was worth a consonant. If so, it was at least a new way of sidling into heaven by a sort of crablike shifting backward from "d" to "b."

All this and much besides, but alack, only a few more facts or credible rumours about the Reverend Abijah remain now perilously near oblivion. They are dimly translated through time, as it were, by some quirk of happenstance extant in the faded brown, but still gossiping handwriting of one Mistress Preserved Pickerel, erstwhile of Norwalk, and a "female pillar of Doctor Albine's flock," if the evidence of her own complacence and mixed imagery are to be credited. Albeit, a shifting and somewhat salty pillar it would also appear.

For her letters—there are seven and a half of them, something just a little over the holy number, the last forever torn—are written from New York back to Norwalk to the wife, later the relict, of Abijah, and in the comparatively golden old age of Mrs. Pickerel. The Preserved Pickerels it appears had removed to New York to collect customs for our sovereign lord the king sometime in the early thirties.

And Mrs. Pickerel's letters from New York do abound in the most saline, when not entirely feline, comments, asides, and personalities, upon the then present and recent past in Norwalk; and in a belated, senile revelling in the elegant fleshpots of the provincial metropolis, calculated no doubt to quicken the sin of envy in the soul of any woman in Norwalk, but in a clergyman's relict particularly.

16

Indeed, no small part of Mrs. Pickerel's correspondence is devoted to an almost, but not quite openly scandalous discussion of the pious merits and natural failings of the incumbents of various city pulpits, with now and then a kittenish slap backward over her shoulder by way of comparison with the Reverend Abijah Albine, her former pastor.

What the wife, and later the widow, of the Reverend Abijah thought of *that* is hard to tell now, for only her naked epitaph remains and that, properly enough, is purely formal:

> He and She
> Rejoice
> Around the Glassy Sea

Of these backward glancing blows into time, mostly at the expense of the Reverend Abijah, more hereafter.

Suffice it now to say that in her maturer age, and as a consort of one of the collectors of the Port of New York, Mistress Pickerel seems to have enthusiastically abandoned many of the more rigid and pious prejudices of her virginal days in Norwalk and to have indulged herself in laces, in fripperies and furbelows, a black servant in livery, and a coach. All of which she describes, doubtless for the edification of former and less fortunate friends in Norwalk, with an ecstatic minuteness and a glow of sunset satisfaction that goes far toward cancelling her occasional epistolary sighs that, "all here is vanity, vanity —and the ways of the Lord seldom trod."

One thing is certain, over the course of only a few years, every congregation and sect in New York which had even the remotest burden of worldly prestige to explain away saw Mrs. Pickerel, the Preserved Collector, the respectable servant, and the genteel coach present themselves for worship, sometimes for several Sabbaths or Sundays, as the case might be, in succession.

One is at least inferentially aware here of a certain ladder-ascending process in these pious peregrinations from one chapel or church to another. Let us hope, charitably, that it was a ladder aimed at heaven, a kind of ethereal progress. But whether worldly or not, there can be no doubt that the last state of Mrs. Pickerel was that of a complete latitudinarian, and that she ended, for she says so, sitting at the feet of the incumbent Gamaliel preaching at Holy Trinity, according to the Church of England. And no doubt she sat in one of the more expensive pews. According to her, the rector there had been ordained by *both* the bishops of Bath and Wells." Perhaps she felt thus doubly assured of any benefits which might accrue from the apostolic succession.

But one can never know, never be sure. For her last letter, the torn one, ends with a panegyric on the amazing tall coiffure of Madame Schuyler, the vanities of patroons' wives in general, and directions how to make night packing for spit curls. The tear then irrevocably intervenes. It may be that, fired by this missive, Abijah's widow suddenly went in for curl papers herself.

She might well have, for, poor lady, most of the rewards of virtue seem to have been reserved for her by Abijah in that other world to which he had inadvertently preceded her. One gleans this all along in these almost apostolic epistles to Norwalk, straws here and there pickupable amidst the rich harvest of gossip garnered by the pious pen of Mrs. Pickerel, especially when she discourses upon and compares sermons of this and that divine. And from these straws, pertinent here to the record, we do inevitably learn that—

The Reverend Abijah Albine, "that ram of God," had first made sheep's eyes, or at least *baa-ed* sheepishly, at Mistress Pickerel—long before she was preserved as a Pickerel, of course—when, so she states, "no man had as yet even laid hands upon my stainless fleece."

For some reason, not vouchsafed, this mild method of approach by her minister had failed, although the flock was fluttered, and the Reverend Abijah had eventually solaced himself with one Abby, or Abigail, Belding, undoubtedly the "dear Ab" to whom the Pickerel ad-

18

dresses her letters. Abigail's brother, by the way, was postmaster at Norwalk, and probably her sole support in her widowed old age.

This mutual share in the same divine romance must have been a bond between the two women, and an open-sesame to intimacies in correspondence which, one can hazard, even Mrs. Pickerel might not otherwise have ventured upon. She, of course, could have had no idea that she was leaving a casement at least half open into the past.

Improving this view only a little, it is still possible to glance through that window into the study of the Reverend Dr. Albine at Norwalk early in the eighteenth century, and to see that the Lord had blessed him and his Abigail, and that they had two sons. One, Benjamin, the older, was small, slight, but with great burning eyes and the hectic face of a young seraph; and the other, Lemuel, was tall, well built even as a boy, and later on dangerously powerful, for he took after his father, who was a huge man with a great golden beard and arms like flails.

And it would also be possible to see, since it was very notable and much remarked upon, that the Reverend Abijah yearned over his delicate older boy, whose mind was as remarkable as his body was sickly, and that he laboured with him and prayed over him and taught him so well, or so ill, that at the age of eight Benjamin not only could read from the Greek testament, but could also expound it movingly, and with a kind of abject winsomeness that made most people, who came to hear him, weep and go away marvelling contritely.

Now, this was all well enough for Benjamin, though it turned out *not* so well later on. But it was misery itself for the younger child, Lemuel, and for his mother. For the good doctor lavished all his attention and affection on his first-born. And he was so proud of him, and so crotchety about him, and so absorbed in preparing him to be the wonder of the coming age in the ministry, that there was nothing left over for Abigail or Lemuel, except

19

perhaps cautions to be quiet and cold bursts of rage that they were there at all.

And as time went on it grew even worse.

For Lemuel was a lad of spirit and stood up to his father, comforting his mother as well as he could secretly, and fetching and hewing wood and drawing water for her and the others. As a result of which he grew tall, active, silent and strong. And his father hated him, saying that Benjamin was of the elect and a child of God, while Lemuel was a child of the Devil and born to be damned. And thus the days went on while Mistress Abigail's heart was nigh to breaking. She taught Lemuel his A B C from her own hornbook, and how to read and figure a little. This was all the education he ever got, since his father would have none of him, and took him into the study only to admonish, or even to whip him.

This state of affairs was well understood in the congregation and the village, where it began to be whispered about that young Benjamin might not be altogether divinely inspired. That sceptical rumour coming to the ears of Abijah Albine made life even harder than before for Abigail, upon whose family her husband laid the blame for the talk.

Yet he acquiesced readily enough in allowing Lemuel's uncle Belding to arrange to apprentice him to the blacksmith on the square at Norwalk when the boy was only fifteen years old, though already growing rapidly into a great lout of a young man.

And so Lemuel left home and began toiling over the anvil just across the village square from his father's meetinghouse. And he throve at it, and grew mightier every day. But Mistress Albine was left alone at the manse, her only music the distant clinking of the iron under the hammer of Lemuel and the memory of what he was like when a child.

Now, this outcome was quite in keeping, insists Mrs. Pickerel in one of her letters. For what was Abijah but a smith of God, who beat the living word out of the

Bible every sermon with his fists and his windmill arms, until the windows of the chapel rattled? In the course of his ministry the great leather-covered Book on the pulpit was thrice rebound. What wonder, then, that Lemuel took naturally to beating a worldly anvil across the square on weekdays? Though this is one of Mistress Pickerel's prettiest similitudes, one can be sure it carried small comfort to the mind of Abigail, whose heart was also laid upon an anvil to be flattened out. She saw no end to it, and tried only to possess her soul in patience. But the ways of the Lord are wonderful—and unexpected.

The Angel of Death came through the green lanes of the village of Norwalk, looking for pious young souls and bestowing the gift of smallpox. Perhaps the bruit of Benjamin had reached even to Paradise on the wings of his father's prayers. Certainly it had travelled as far as Guilford and New Haven, where we hear the lad had often been taken by his father to talk with the elders in Israel. Yet despite that, and in the deep nighttime, the Dark Angel touched him and he arose and left his body behind.

Then the eyes of the Reverend Abijah Albine were opened for a while. In his unbearable sorrow he bowed himself down, and poured ashes on his head, and saw the pride and the bitter error of his ways. His wife comforted him, and he wept with her until they were together again in spirit for a time. And he sent for his son Lemuel and humbled himself before him also, begging him, for his mother's sake at least, to come back again under the roof.

But Lemuel was a grown man now, although a young one, mighty in body and firm in mind. His thoughts had run on many a day as he laboured over the anvil. So he looked about his father's study, where he had always been called to be punished heretofore; he looked at the books in Hebrew, in Greek, and in Latin that lined the walls. He smiled slowly, and turned over in his mind how he could speak to his father so they should understand each other. Finally he rolled up the sleeve of his huge right arm, pointed to it, and said quite simply:

"You and my uncle and the Almighty have conspired together to make me a blacksmith. I am already a good one. I have only one more year to serve. That is your bargain I shall keep. When I am free I shall find me a woman, follow my trade, and go west. I hear there is both land and freedom to be had in Pennsylvania."

"It is a nest of malignants," said his father. "I am told that every error is at liberty to flourish there."

"So I have heard," said Lemuel. He pulled down his sleeve, pondering awhile, and tied the wristbands slowly. Abijah and his wife Abigail sat waiting.

"I have a mind to go there," said Lemuel, and stalked out, leaving them alone.

Which might have been the end of him, so far as we would ever know, had it not been that he got himself into a rather notable scrape soon thereafter. Or rather his father got him into it. And that Mrs. Pickerel has a good deal of advice about the affair and some comfort to offer in her letters to Mrs. Albine even some years afterward. The incident was sufficiently grave and tragic to be mentioned in passing elsewhere as well.

Whether Lemuel found his woman before he served out his last year as an apprentice is not clear. The exact timing of events is more than difficult to make out, since Lemuel's doings are merely alluded to by Mrs. Pickerel in passing and in reply to Mrs. Albine's letters, which we do not have. But the sequence of happenings is fairly plain.

It seems probable that Lemuel did complete his year as an apprentice. And that afterward he continued with his employer. Or else he took his place and set up for himself as the blacksmith at Norwalk in the same smithy on the square. Also he found his girl. That Mrs. Albine extensively disapproved of her in writing is probably the only reason we know anything about her at all.

"For," says Mrs. Pickerel, evidently in reply to a

sorrowful and indignant letter from Lemuel's mother, "it is quite plain that the girl you pour out the vials of your wrath upon can't be such an hussy, or I should have heard of her myself, long before this. There is not much goes on between here and Norwalk but that Old Herd, the rider, who stops in at our kitchen frequent for small beer and cheese whenever he has a post up, doesn't hint at as broad as your own behind. And a shilling under his plate is ile to his memory. Tower Hill is in the Rhode Island borders. But I'll write to Cousin Usher at Westerly. His new, new wife will be brought to bed soon and I shall send her a wine jelly and an India kerchief with my duty, and ask."

And later:

"Old Herd rid into town tonight with the letter from Cousin Usher. He charged me six province shillings for it, the thief, and it cost me five more to get the rest of the story out of him. Laws me, Ab, you'll have the vapours if the old rascal charges you as much for this letter of mine—and with such news!

"The news, *your* news, is that Lem married the O'Moore girl two months ago come New Year's. There's not a jot or tittle in that tailor's bundling story, and the governor's son rides to a lass in Bristol. So compose yourself, you dear old fool.

"It's true that she's dark, Irish, and of the Romish persuasion. That'll be like the juice of seven galls to Abijah, but let him drink it. He's bitter enough himself to settle such a draught. And do you take *my* advice and get a piece of the cake, if there be any, and put it under your pillow and sleep on it like a lamb. These O'Moores are cousins to the Desmonds. And the head of that fine house, the governor's lady tells me, is a colonel in the service of France himself, and owns a hul regiment of household guards at the palace in Paris. Your blacksmith might have done worse, madam. And besides that he went out of town.

"Cousin Usher's infant strangled bornin'. There's no

23

wisewoman worth her salt north o' Guilford. But we're both well over that ourselves, I hopes.

"Tell me if Lem tries to bring her to Norwalk. I'll, too, if I do hear. She's at Tower Hill still keep'n quiet at Mr. Sand's ordinary there. Common sense that. No telling what Abijah might do. Persuade your brother the postmaster to put the fear of the Lord upon Old Herd and the other two carriers, Mumford and Peat. They're jay birds for talk. But Lemuel is a powerful man and shoes their horses. Need I say more?"

She might have, one thinks. Since we do not even know the given name of Lemuel's dark, Irish O'Moore, or whether he ever brought her to Norwalk or not. Probably not, one can guess. He was not there long after his marriage, to judge by what followed. And the cause of his sudden leaving was notable.

One beautiful Easter morning in the year 1740 a party of British officers and provincial gentlemen rode into Norwalk, going "down east." What their errand was and who they were, there is now no way of telling. They appeared. And the disturbance they made in the town was considerable.

Every soul in the place whose body was not either that of an infant or bedridden was at church. Everyone, that is, except Lemuel. He was the only comfort the strangers appear to have found. The road they had just passed over was one of the worst in the king's dominions, outside of Ireland, and what they all wanted was two things: liquor, and a blacksmith to get their nags reshod.

There being no drink to be had for love or money until church was over, and that might be hours yet, the whole party, after having thundered at half the doors in town and disturbed every watchdog into a foaming delirium, gathered before the forge across the square from the chapel and began to clamour for the smith.

The Reverend Abijah Albine was just entering upon "secondly" under the third head in his sermon on the Resurrection, much moved thereto by the thought of Benjamin in Paradise, when this clamour, like the gathering of a hunt from hell, arose across the square and came rolling in through the open doors of the meeting-house, for it was a warm spring day.

The spell the minister had laid on his congregation was lost, and with it the fruits of many weeks' work on his Easter sermon. He stopped, prayed silently, and then went on again. Finally, he began to beat the Bible frantically and to roar sonorously, because that was the only practical defence he had against his rivals for attention, those devil's minions across the square.

The effect he produced was notable. It caused even the most urgent and strident of the gentlemen gathered around the blacksmith shop to look across at the little white building with the steeple, which seemed to be a church but was apparently the stable of a lion. A moment's silence fell on them, produced by sheer astonishment.

The Reverend Abijah smiled grimly in his pulpit and reversed the hourglass. It looked, after all, as though he were going to be able to go on. Then there was a sudden burst of laughter across the square, and immediately afterward the mellow clink of his son's hammer on hot iron.

Now, this was more than the minister could bear. He felt that his own flesh and blood was defying him openly. His eyes burned in his head. He closed the great Book with a bang, and sailed down the aisle with his gown flapping behind him. Most of those in the chapel crowded to the door to see.

The minister strode furiously across the square, and there was that in his face which caused the gentlemen who were crowded about the smithy door to step aside hastily and give him room. Although one of them did laugh, and would have tripped "the damned Whig" up as he passed, if one of his companions had not prevented him. Perhaps it might have been better if he had succeeded, since the path was now cleared to all of the mischief which followed.

25

Abijah found himself confronting, or confronted by, his son Lemuel, who stood with his leather apron on, hammering away merrily over the anvil at a red-hot horseshoe with a *clink* and a *clang*. The horse for which the shoe was being readied was standing close by in the shed, held by her owner, a calm, middle-aged man in the gorgeous scarlet and gold lace of a colonel of Royal Light Infantry. Abijah was not so possessed but that he recognized the officer's rank and breeding instinctively, and it gave his native English heart to pause. Lemuel, however, went ahead working at the horseshoe.

"I forbid you!" cried his father at last, standing and pointing a long arm and finger at him imperatively. "Cease! Would you profane the Sabbath in the presence of God's minister and your own father?"

And at that Lemuel did cease working the iron and looked across the anvil at his father, while several of the gentlemen crowded into the shed to see whether they would be getting their horses shod now or not.

Seeing the iron was turning cold, the colonel spoke up, hoping to save the day.

"My dear sir," said he to Abijah, "here is no question of profaning the Sabbath. We are a party of travellers in need of assistance. We are bound for Boston on government business. I have demanded your son's help to shoe the horses in the king's name."

"No king rules here save Jesus," replied Abijah sullenly.

"I take it you are mistaken, sir," said the colonel coldly. "This is part of his Majesty's dominions, and I opine he reigns even in Connecticut by the grace of God."

Someone outside laughed. Abijah went black in the face and towered up to his full height. He pointed upward.

"I forbid it," he said. "In God's name."

By this time the shoe on the anvil had gone cold. The issue had been put squarely to Lemuel, and all stood waiting tensely to see what the big smith would do.

He turned and thrust the iron back into the fire. It was the colonel who worked the bellows. Finally the shoe came out white-hot again with little sparks flashing along it. Lemuel laid it on the anvil and looked calmly at his father, who still stood there. Then he raised his hammer to strike.

The Reverend Abijah Albine rushed forward and caught the hammer arm of his son Lemuel in mid-air. The hammer crashed.

Then something quite astonishing happened to the Reverend Abijah.

He found his own hands pinioned behind his back in the iron grasp of the mighty blacksmith he had fathered, and he found himself lifted into the air and being carried across the common like so much lumber on the shoulder of Lemuel.

The minister was a hulk of a man himself. It was a great feat of strength on the part of Lemuel, discussed for miles around for many a year. But across the square Abijah went, despite his struggles and hoarse shouts. The amazed congregation stood aghast on the chapel steps, or peered out the door horrified. Not a man moved, not a woman screamed. It was all over in a few seconds.

When he got to the church Lemuel suddenly set his father on his feet again. Then he twisted him about and looked into his face. In the steely eyes of his son, Abijah saw the result of twenty years of tyranny glaring back at him.

"You attend to your trade and I'll attend to mine," shouted Lemuel, so all could hear.

"Back into *your* shop you go!" he roared. And picking up the older man by the arm and knee, he heaved him into the chapel through a window sash, with a violent shattering and rending sound.

The sermon on the Resurrection was never finished.

The Reverend Abijah Albine sat on the floor of his church where he had been pitched by his son. A piece of broken window glass had cut his forehead. He bled freely, but was otherwise bodily uninjured. He sat there groaning for his life in ruins about him, while his wife

27

and some of the faithful tried to comfort him. But in vain, for across the square the sound of the hammer rang triumphantly, shaping the secular iron into horseshoes.

Lemuel finished his work, surrounded by the now silent and entirely respectful gentlemen.

It was an hour at least before the selectmen of Norwalk could meet. What was the outcome of their deliberations, no one knows. Lemuel hitched up his wagon, threw his tools and put the anvil into it and rode off with the strangers. No one suggested following him. Probably the situation was held to have solved itself by his departure, as well as it could.

Lemuel, we know, drove north. The gentlemen were going to Boston. Perhaps Mrs. Lemuel was still at Tower Hill in Rhode Island.

That is all, except that in the penultimate letter from the Pickerel about a year later occurs the following:

"The hand of the Lord, my dear Abby, has been laid heavily upon you. But do, I pray you, cease to reproach yourself as though you were the cause of what are, after all, but natural afflictions. Recollect, it was an imposthume and not the hand of Lemuel that was the final taking off of Abijah. Since you are so bitter against your own flesh and blood, 'tis small wonder that you are now forced to turn to your brother Belding both for comfort and maintenance. I will send you some clothes, some usable things that are no longer fashionable here. I doubt if you hear again from Lem. Nor has his wife much cause to remember you kindly or to pine for your company. Charity begets charity—and contrawise. These are hard sayings, mistress, but they are true. Remember, Abijah is *gone*. You can now return to your better self, if you will. As for your son, I doubt if he is lost as you seem to think—to you possibly—but the Lord can hear prayers even if they be said in Pennsylvania. The small package from me and Mr. Pickerel goes forward to you by Old Herd the first post he rides north. Farewell for the nonce, but let me hear."

And so time slams the door on this little village tragedy with, to quote Mistress Pickerel, "some usable things that are no longer fashionable here."

3

Flight into the Wilderness

THE PAST is the Land of Missing Persons, and it is only by a combination of diligence and good fortune that anyone who is not monumentally remembered can be found there.

As for those in America who wandered beyond the utmost borders of the wilderness, neither their lives nor the resting places of their bones were too often noticed or conveniently marked. Oblivion dogged their steps and ate the last one. The silent trees of the forest finally closed over their heads. They vanished, drowned in a green nowhere, leaving a crumbling cabin, a few stones arranged in the dancing basin of a spring, a cellar hole on a hillside, with an apple tree or a rosebush in ashes to scatter petals in springtime, as though they remembered something lovely, tragic, and secret that no one else knew.

So it would seem almost useless; necessarily a fruitless task to ask where a blacksmith and his wife went, whose trail we have blundered upon in some faded old letters after two centuries have passed. They have wandered out of time; how find them again in space?

One might easily fail in such a self-appointed search. Patience will be needed, and not too much success can be expected. With Lemuel Albine there are some signs still in our favour, however.

He was a blacksmith. He was a huge and remarkably powerful man. He had a peculiar, if not a unique, family name. His character seemed fated to get him into trouble. All or any of these items might have been deliberately or accidentally noticed sometime, somewhere, and set down.

Also the search is narrowed a good deal; that is, it is not hopelessly continental. Mrs. Pickerel had ventured her opinion to the effect that Lemuel's prayers could be or were being heard in Pennsylvania, and he had once told his parents he had a good mind to go there—that he would find him a woman, follow his trade, and go west. All that somehow got itself into the record and, what is more, preserved.

Let us go to Pennsylvania, then, and go west. But how far?

Far enough certainly to find free land and freedom. Probably Lemuel wanted a good deal of both, like a great many other people who had been oppressed and found themselves disinherited both from property and from the past. We know he must have left Norwalk with a disgust for village life, and a burning indignation against tyranny, books, schools, ministers, authority—perhaps even religion. That might carry a young man quite far. And there is something else.

In 1740, at least, one did not heave one's father through his own meetinghouse window just for the sheer, blithe joy of the thing, even if one were a powerful blacksmith. There were bound to be serious mental as well as physical consequences. One would have liked to leave both the scene and the memory of such an act extremely far behind. If one were going west, for example, it might be well to go as far west as the direction held. Especially, when one's still surviving mother was only waiting to get her hands in the hair of one's newly married wife. That is not evidence, of course, but it is fair human and historical reasoning. And the inference in this case is, that if any evidence of Lemuel's whereabouts can be found,

31

it would be as far west in Pennsylvania as he could go—
if not farther!

Now, in 1740, or thereabouts, the farthest west attain-
able in Pennsylvania was by river, and at Harris's Ferry
on the Susquehanna. It is true that some had gone even
beyond there into the Kittatinny Mountains or the far-
flung coves of the hills nearer the Juniata. And there were
traders who went every year over the great ridges as far
as "Allegheny." But it was a question if they were still
in Pennsylvania, because no one knew precisely how far
into the sunset Pennsylvania extended.

There were four or five ponderable opinions about
that: the Penns', the Virginians', the French, the English,
and the Indians'. Even the Quakers finally got into war
about it. World wars, Indian wars, intercolonial and Revo-
lutionary wars.

So those who had been ferried over the river by Mr.
Harris had actually embarked with a sort of Charon for
a trip into the vague and misty beyond. They were so-
journers rather than settlers in a kind of no man's land,
tenants of what landlord no one knew. And if a person
were to be found far west in Pennsylvania, he might either
be at Harris's or he would probably have passed over
the river there into the free beyond.

Let us see, then. How will this do?

Here is an entry on a page of an ancient account book
kept by Esther Say, the able wife of John Harris, trader
and ferryman, early in 1741:

> £1-2s-4d, to ye Smith L'Albine, for forging
> and furbishing ye gun locks of Robin Patterson's
> company, who came here to ride ye Borders,
> this same Patterson having been killed by a bolt
> of thunder whilst watering off against a lone
> tree, owing ye said smith.
>
> Paid

Now, it is impossible not to exclaim immediately over
the severe tax on the renal powers of Mr. Patterson, and

to observe, if a male, how not to behave in a thunderstorm.

As to who Mr. Patterson was, and why his company was riding "ye Borders," it is not now easy to say. There appear to have been seven in the party up until the time Mr. Patterson tried to compete with the storm. For the rest, it looks as though this might be Lemuel. "L'Albine" could be a Frenchman, to be sure, but that is not likely at Harris's in 1741. It also might be, and probably is, meant for "Lemuel Albine," who we know was a smith. That is especially convincing, since any blacksmith would readily enough take to repairing gun-locks on the frontier.

But there's nothing more to go by. Not an item in the whole book, and it covers over a year, that can be fathered upon Lemuel. We do not know for certain whether Lemuel's wife was with him, or exactly what he was doing at Harris's beyond repairing gun-locks.

There is, however, a good deal in these accounts at Harris's about one Garrett Pendergass, or "Pendergrass," —the man probably spelled his own name two or three ways,—and as we hear about Lemuel from him later, and at some length, it is possible to infer that Mrs. Albine was with her husband, that they tarried at Harris's about a year, and that during that time Lemuel plied his hammer whenever he could. We learn he also became interested in trading, largely through his acquaintance with Garrett Pendergass, who, it appears, had his own designs upon him. These, to do Pendergass justice, were quite right and forward-looking for both himself and Lemuel, who might have been better off in the end if he had listened to them.

One can pick up a good deal about this Garrett Pendergass and his family here and there. Some years later he is to be found at Raystown, or Bedford, on the Juniata, running an establishment next to the fort there, a kind of combination inn and trading post, by far the best on that frontier. Where he came from, there is no certain record. Probably from about Colchester in England. But he appears, from a variety of indications and testimony, to have been an able, upright, and educated man.

At the same time he ran across Lemuel Albine at Harris's he seems to have been acting for old John Harris and his wife, as a kind of factor or advance agent with the Shawnees. Probably he transported trade goods from Harris's Ferry, distributed them to the Indians then in the hunting grounds just east of the Allegheny ridge, and gathered up the furs and skins in return. His reward was likely to be allowed to do some trading on his own. Also he was interested in patenting land.

At any rate, about this time he had gone up the "Conedogwainet Branch," past the most outlying cabins there, and settled, or camped, in semi-permanent form in the Path Valley beyond. He even maintained a "lodge" or some kind of trade-meeting place in the Great Cove west of the Blue Mountains, possibly not far from where Fort Lyttleton afterward was. He and his family used to "resort thither in the season"; that is, when the trade was on. Thence it was only a short and fairly good path for horses by the old Indian trace through the water gap of the Juniata to the Shawnee hunting grounds.

In any event, Pendergass's cabin was at the extreme border of things in those days. Only the licensed traders had pushed on farther west. Some of them, in that comparatively quiet and peaceful time, before the Indian and the French troubles broke out, had penetrated to the Allegheny and built cabins in the vicinity of Chartier's Town. But they were itinerants rather than settlers; they came and went with the seasonal trade in furs. So when Garrett Pendergass wrote something in his "diary" in Path Valley beyond the Blue Mountains he was setting down a record of how the days went at the very verge of the world.

His "diary" is a curious old book. Not a diary in the strict sense of the word, rather a commonplace book, the last third frequently blurred by some leak in a long-vanished roof, maybe. It has the smell of dusty leather trunks about it; something of the air of a century's sojourn in a garret. And it is a memorandum of many things: births, deaths, accounts paid and unpaid, moves and removes, who came and went, receipts and simples, the state of trade, and the weather, an occasional piece of hearty male gossip, hints for planting, little plans and sketches for forgotten things, a map of the country about what was later Bedford—what not?

Leaving out Mr. Pendergass's religious worries, what to do for the "murraine," and a host of other matters secular and divine, let us put together certain passages concerning Lemuel, really, when assembled, quite a peephole backward into time. The day dates are not certain, however. Even the months rest frequently upon internal evidence of things done. The "diary" was not kept for our convenience.

This entry is evidently sometime in the spring of 1742. April? Wheat had been planted about a week or so before, and new clearing was going on at the Pendergass cabin in Path Valley:

Mond'y—Set Delaware Joe and the negar boy to burning brambles about the new pasture spring. The negar set the woods afire, which burnt clear to the ridge and driv the deer over the new spelts lot. A horrid burnt scar on the mountain and the negar. But will clear there when new hands are to be had. Powder scarce.

Thursd'y—Came the big Yankee smith and his pretty Irish wife from Harris's. She being made much of by my Rose and both our girls. Is a mighty help about the cookery, and much admired for having rid here on the flat stoneboat and helped con the oxen that drew her and the bar iron over the hills. Had a bull ox about the High Springs of the Conadog' branch mauled bad by a painter. The smith about building the forge tomorrow without loss of

35

time, he hasty in work yet patient. Hope to persuade him in on the trading. These are the first draft cattle came over the ridge into Path Valley. Rose convinced now.

Fri—Albine's mauled ox, mad with the flies, made off today into the woods. Gone beef and all. A sore loss. Rose not convinced, but will be when the wagons roll.

Sab'th—We five to hear the Reverend Jms McArdle at the Conadogwinet log meeting at McComb's in the vale. A pert young minister, he, has a call to preach to the Indians like a mad Moravian. Dissuaded him. Returned to find the little chimney finished and the smith's bellows agoing. His wife, a Catholic, said her prayers in the woods on beads. Rose much put out. I remonstrated working Sabbath. Albine says he is tired of the Christian calendar. A strange, determined man.

Mond'y—Coolness among the women.

Wensd'y—The smith's shed roof on, and the song of the hammer heard in these hills.

Fri—Albine worked on the wagon irons all day, and nigh finished. Horses all shod again. The Lord be praised. Much cheerful chattering amongst the women in the kitchen shed. A famous good dinner tonight. Good day.

Sab'th—Passed through, riding west, six Shawnees in the rain, squaws and young, leaving their Wyoming grounds. No game left there they say. Gave them small rum and some meal. But had no powder to spare. Fear trouble if all our eastern Injuns do go beyond the mountains. Albine very curious about these wild people. Fear he has a secret mind to follow them. Will earnestly dissuade him.

May Day—But go rejoicing here. A pleasant custom forgot in these woods I fear. Ploughed. The oxen a mighty help, and the big share new bent and tempered.

Wensd'y—The poor negar hit by a copperhead sarpent, and half the wool still burnt off him by the woods fire. A miserable specimen. Bought him from Isaac Tiligman, who held with Lord Baltimore's claim. Must persuade Harris to buy the valley from the Penns as they offer, so I can get land warrants. Albine and I to the ferry tomorrow for the trade goods.

Sab'th—At Harris's.

Mond'y—At Harris's—loading all the day.

Thursd'y—Returned with six pack horses and the new wagon loaded down. More in this trip than in three before. Rose convinced now. Harris lent me his man Charlworth, a narrow-eyed fellow, two years to serve. Think he would like to be gone but for the Injuns. Found the negar boy up and around.

Sab'th agin—We all singing hymns together when came Mrs. McQuiston's girl Maggie tapping at the door and in a great way, she having been driv into the woods and about to bear. Her mother won't abide her. Thought it might be my Charlie, he being a big boy now, and she walking nine miles to our cabin, but found out not. Thankful. 'Minds me of the piece I knew once in Colchester, and the trouble I had.

Mond'y—Rounded up the hogs. Mrs. Albine of much

help with the McQuiston girl, who cried out terrible. She and Rose brought her through with a lusty baby girl for their trouble. Albine gone to Harris's again with one wagon.

Wensd'y—The smith returned.

Sab'th—Rode to McQuiston's cabin. Found the girl and James MacTeage's boy spent last summer in the woods together like two Injuns. Lived in grease at the sulphur springs nigh the Juniata crossing. She came home to winter. No sign of him now except his baby. Mrs. McQuiston will not take it on at all, at all. Two more mouths at our cabin, and four hands in time.

Wensd'y—Started the new ell and cook shed on the cabin. Barn roofed in. Folk coming here every day for to get iron worked by Albine, or maybe to hear about the McQuiston trouble. More people about than I knew.

Satd'y—Albine laced Charlworth, Harris's man, till he roared like a bull o' Bashan. This for having a loud mouth and a bawdy tongue. The smith and his wife like our own now. Have persuaded him to stay, I think. Preparing for trade at the lodge in Great Cove. Will leave Monday, weather moderating. Much goods this year, thanks to the new wagons. Winter like to be much more comfortable this time. Plenty on hand.

The following items occur about a year later, apparently about the beginning of summer, 1743:

Sab'th—Long talk with my wife Rose today. She not so averse from my long projected journey as I supposed. Apprehensive I desire to move her to the

Great Cove, and she so comfortable here. Promised not. The time has not come for that yet. Mrs. Albine makes ready. All here cast down at thought of our parting so soon.

Tues'd—Came the western hunter, Tingooqua, or Old Catfish, with his lame squaw and three horses to show us the trace from Great Cove to the crossings, and be fed at our fire. The half-king will let Albine tarry at the Turkey Foot if he trades. Thence about eighteen leagues to the Oio, or to Shirtees. Have a mind to see the new country myself, but Lord the women! Albine gone a week now.

Sat'd'y—The smith back today from Harris's. Has laid out well, and nearly his all. Three pack horses, a brindled ox, and a red one, iron nails aplenty, and some bar iron. Nevertheless, I tried again to dissuade him from going so far, his wife being three months along, Rose says. And the Catfish talking of the French tampering with our Indians at the Allegheny. Did urge him to stay, or set up at the lodge in Great Cove instead. Too many people here he avers. Was rather grim, but thanked me.

Wensd'y—Is as I thought. Nothing will hold Albine here. Says he wishes to be reborn again, but not in the Lord. Asked me to urge him no more. I promised. Owe him more than shillings and pence, or trade goods can repay. He much touched by my Rose's gift of the old cradle from home. Will pack it along, carrying fine meal till the time comes. Trust they be settled by that time. Says he has promised to furbish guns for the half-king for his land at the Turkey Track. A doubtful holding, I fear. They go to the promised land, but among the fierce heathen, and no cities of refuge. The Lord be with them. Great cooking and packing of gear and victuals for

39

what they all call *The Western Ride*. My young ones all agog.

Thursd'y—Leaving young James and Tom, Delaware Joe, Charlworth, the McQuiston girl and her brat, and the useless negar with Harris's new man, Barber, a factor that he lent me for this year's trading. He to live in the house here at Path Valley. Barber an honest and careful man will keep things going. Warned him about Charlworth and the McQuiston. Harris owes me 180£, sterling, due from last trading, which he freely acknowledges. Barber brings a rumour of our king declaring war on the French, but I doubt it. If so, fierce troubles may come here. God forbid. We ride tomorrow through the peacefulest woods where is no man. Albine expects the Shawnee guide at the Juniata crossing. Thence about four days ride to the Turkey Foot of the Yogaginy. Weather and the women permitting, I will go as far as the crossing with him and spy out the land.

Thursd'y—Being the last Thursday in this August, I guess, I like a fool not having writ in this book since June, having left it behind by forgetfulness in the chimney cupboard with my doeskin purse with the rose noble in it. The purse gone and my old lucky piece likewise, together with sundry shillings and halfpence. Much vexed at the loss of this ancient coin which I had from my father, and he likewise, and also at Barber for letting Charlworth and the McQuiston make off with it, and leave the baby. A pretty bargain, by godson! And Rose *pleased* to find the child here and another of her own coming on! It do beat the devil. All else well, and the tobacco got in. Enough for our own pipes this winter, and as good as the Maryland weed, from which it came. Will pick up the day of the month when next at Harris's. Barber has forgot it. Meanwhile—will try to make amends here to my poor journal, which I thank God was not taken, as there are some things in it for my memory alone. Will date back later.

June entry—(going back)—'Twas the last Friday of last June, if I recall rightly, we left to ride with the smith Albine and his wife as far as the Juniata crossings. Of my family along was my wife Rose, my grown son Charlie, and my two big girls, Polly and Bella. Took six pack horses, one loaded with presents for the Shawnees to the tune of £3, 8s. The rest with supplies and gear. Albine and his Mrs. had two pack horses and the two oxen laden, not drawing. The oxen did much delay us as I opined. Tingooqua and his squaw rode with the packs from camp to camp. All in all eight souls along, counting t' Injuns, and as large a cavalcado as any ever seen in these woods, saving the traders' caravans to Allegheny.

Camped in the Branch Gap in the mountains the first night, where a glade for pasture, and on to the lodge at Great Cove. All well there from last winter, but a scaffolding broke down by the bears and the old smoked hog meat et. Albine came up next day, delayed by the oxen. His wife manages his two pack nags beautiful. Rose, to my great comfort, pleased with the prospect and the land here at Great Cove. Two turkeys and a deer shot today. The birds thin yet. Stopped for two weeks about, repairing the lodge with split shingles on the slabs, and a new storehouse up beyond the powers of bears. Some hogs gone wild in the oak woods near by, whose I know not, perhaps from Miller's. Shot two. The smith mended the great kittle. All readied for fall trade at the lodge when Barber brings up the goods in Sept'mb'r.

Off over the old trace to the Juniata, about the middle of July, as I reckon. Trail good, but for one mishap below the water gap where we came near losing Albine's brindled ox. Drew it out of the swamp with three horses and much tugging. Some powder spoiled, which I made up to him, but left me short. The ox lame, but will recover. Through the water gap the fourth day, and on to the Shawanee grounds. A marvellous beautiful valley I covet dwelling in someday, God prospering me. Camped, and made the dale with the stinking spring in it by noon next day.

Spent a good ten days there in that cool vale between the two high hills. Shot no game ourselves for fear of angering the Shawnees, who brought us deer and bear meat for our red cloth, a little flour, and a packet of needles. The Catfish brought in the two chiefs from the village near the crossings, where about twenty huts. Our presents well received, and all most amicable. No French goods here that I can see.

Purged ourselves at the spring on the north side of the Branch. This brought the pains on Mrs. Albine, but she recovered, scared. Did bathe in the stinking spring, too, which proves fine for the hair. All comfortable in bark half-huts, but thank God no rain. Very dry. A great fire in the valley west of the Allegheny ridge set by some wandering Delawares the Shawanees say. They very angry. Smoke blue on the mountains west.

About the first of August, as I reckon, the guides came from the half-king to pilot Albine to the three forks of Yohaginy they call Turkey Foot. Many tears among the women. Albine silent, and I much cast down at our parting now after two good friendly years. Strongly tempted to remonstrate again, but kept my promise. His Mrs. very heavy with child now, and will be her first. A brave pair withal, but he a mite determined. Rode with them as far as the crossing of the Juniata, and the Injuns from the village all with us. They over the river with many calls back and forth of sad farewells, and so off into the woods to the west-running waters. And I doubt we see them again. . . .

4

In Which a Little Boy Turns Turtle

THE FIRST THING he could remember was lying on a pile of soft twigs and looking out over a sea of treetops in early leaf. In the distance the silver vein of a river gleamed, but there was no end to the treetops.

It was somewhere on the side of a steep hill and he was basking in the new warmth of the spring sun beside a tremendous stump with great gnarled roots.

On the top of the stump sat his mother, cross-legged like a Tartar. She was a dark, hawk-faced woman with a tender, smiling mouth. Her smooth raven hair, brushed straight back, was caught about with a snood of some scarlet material in which a sprig of red berries had been thrust. The little boy felt that she was strong, wild, and comfortable. He thought her name was Emma, afterward, because he could remember his father calling her "Em." That, with the memory of her face as she stood there with the strong yellow-green forest sunlight falling on her, and a few tones of her voice, was about all he ever could remember about her.

Curiously enough, he could never recall her face any other way than just as it was at that moment. It must have been about noon, for there were no shadows upon her. She was bathed in spring sunshine that somehow seemed to shine from within rather than to shine upon her. And it must have been one of those rare moments of early childhood, when the eyes open to fix irrevocably and brilliantly a fleeting moment of time in the mind's eternity. He himself was purely passive. It was just after the noon meal, perhaps. For the moment he was completely happy, utterly comfortable, and serene as only a child can be. From the vantage point of complete well-being he looked at his mother.

There she sat on the stump doing some knitting. He could see the long bone needles flash in the sun. There was a rifle gun lying just in front of her across the stump. At times she would stop knitting to listen intently. When she did so, he seemed to hear with her. He could hear the wind in the treetops and an occasional note of lonely bird song. Then his mother would begin to knit again.

On a gentler slope, not far below, his father was ploughing. He could see him, the man in a sweaty deer-skin shirt, striding along behind the plough and the brindled ox. He was a huge, tall man, with a golden beard. It wasn't a field he was ploughing. It was a rough new clearing on the hillside, with blackened tree trunks sticking up all over it like fire-scarred posts. The ox and the plough and the man went on and about and around.

After a long while the man stopped ploughing. It was cooler now. The sun was nearing the western treetops. The man came up the hill carrying the plough, and driving the ox before him. The ox came and breathed in the child's face. He always remembered the wide flare of its horns, the shining brown eyes, the soft wet nostrils, and the sweet hot breath in his face. He cried out, half with terror and half with delight, at being intimately noticed by such a wonderful brute.

"Shut up, boy, or the Injuns will git ya," said his father, laughing.

Then his mother reached down to comfort him, as though out of the clouds. He could hear the reassuring tones of her voice. The vague, soft comfort of her presence always remained, palpable, warm, and physical, even in his dreams, but he could never remember, never hear just what it was she said to him as she reached down. If he could only recall her words, get her to say them again, he knew he would be at peace once more. But it was best not to try to do that, because if he tried to remember too hard, he heard her scream. The scream came from underground, and wakened him. Somehow the comfort of his mother and nightmare were always close together.

But that day, after his father finished ploughing, they all went down to the cabin together quite happily. It was a dark, one-room cabin. It, and the shed where the anvil stood and the ox looked at you, sat in a small valley not far from the running spring that bubbled all night long. The water made a noise like little owls. When you were sleepy you could hardly tell the difference.

It was the great fireplace in the chimney at one end of the cabin by which he chiefly remembered it in years to come. That was necessarily so, for there were no windows in the cabin. Light, warmth, and comfort streamed from the hearth. When the door was open in the summer it made an oblong of light, and the green forest glimmered beyond. Afterward, when he first saw the sea, it reminded him of the forest beyond the door. His mother was like a shadow about the hearth. He could never see her face there even in the firelight. She was always crouching over the fire, cooking, with her back towards him.

In what years had these things happened; how old was he?

He could never tell exactly. It must have been "long, long ago." The cabin was the place where he had come from before his real life began. It was a dim dream of the morning of life, beautiful when he dreamed it again. Beautiful, and always close to nightmare.

All he knew was that he was so young he still thought the fire was alive. It ate the sticks his mother fed it. It cracked them with its yellow teeth as a dog cracks bones. But the fire belonged to his father just as the ox did. His father "made" it. His father had made everything they had. He could make anything.

There was another fire in the shed, by the anvil. It ate little lumps of black things. His father made things

46

out of iron there. Sometimes tall red men with feathers in their hair came and stood by the shed while his father worked on their guns. The hammer rang and sang. The sparks flew. Then the red men would grunt, take their guns, and go back into the forest again. They moved like shadows. They toed in. When they came his mother always closed the cabin door.

He could never entirely recall his father's face. Only the grey-blue eyes under the fur cap, and the yellow beard. Sparks flew into the beard from the iron. Some of the deep tones of his father's voice remained. "Em," he would call, "Em." They were deep and kindly then. "Lem" was his father's name. "Em" and "Lem." Those words were used oftenest about the cabin.

But his father remained chiefly a vast bulk, the sheer height and the width of him, a shadow full of mysterious strength. Out of the shadow came quite clearly, as though thrust from darkness into light, his long, sinewy hands with heavy veins. They made things. They grasped the handle of the hammer, or an axe. He could remember that.

And he could remember those hands making a bow for him with a long knife.

That was after he had been so ill, a terrible stabbing pain under his belt. Hot and cold cloths had been laid on him. He recalled his mother crying out something to his father, and the comforting tones that replied. He had taken new confidence from them himself. They had often called his own name to him then. "Sal, Sal, little Sal—"

When he got up again and was well his father made him the bow and the arrows to shoot with. Then he knew all of his name. He was proud of it. When he wandered too far, shooting arrows at the trees, his mother would call him back. "Sal, Sal—Sal-*athiel* Albine, you come back here. Stay out of the woods." Those were among the few words he could remember his mother saying. She was always saying them. There were painters and bars in the woods. It grew darker as you went farther in among the great trees. There were Injuns there. They'd get ya! Sometimes he could hear his father's gun shoot away off in the woods. That was for meat.

The world was nothing but woods. It was all green and dark; silent, except for the little glade and the clearing where the cabin stood by the spring. He had not yet asked himself how the cabin and the forest came to be there. It was the world as he had found it, and so, natural enough. The snow came in the winter and they lived in the dark by the fire. Winter was like one long, dark night, except that you couldn't sleep all the time. Then, when the warmth came, he would be released again to play in the sunlight near the cabin.

Less and less he went into the woods. His father was away often now and his mother kept him near her. She was lonely, and gradually he became aware that she was afraid. He helped her, doing a thousand small chores. He was a big boy for his age, and strong. He spent hours shooting his arrows at the mark on the big sugar tree near the cabin. The arrows went straight now. The bow twanged. Someday he would have a rifle gun to shoot, his father said.

Once his father came back in the night quietly and mysteriously. He heard him and his mother whispering together. Something in the forest had gone wrong. He felt that. Menace hung about the cabin like an animal. The wind in the nighttime made sinister sounds. The song of the anvil was heard no more. No Indians came to have their guns worked on. His mother and father never laughed together as they used to. They were waiting for something. The boy felt that.

One day a strange white man and an Indian came to the cabin. They emerged into the clearing quite suddenly. The white man wore a white coat and tight breeches. He had a sword, and buttons that twinkled in the sun. There was gold lace on his hat and sleeves. He rode a horse, but the Indian walked. It was the first horse the boy had ever seen. It seemed to hold its head in the sky. It laid hold of a post with its teeth and inhaled wind.

48

"Lem, Lem," called his mother, as though trouble had come.

The white man took off his hat with a plume and gold lace on it and made the boy's mother a bow. He was very pleasant, and smiled. He talked in a strange language that made the boy laugh. It was gibberish. To his great astonishment his mother replied in the same tongue.

His father had come hurrying from the shed with the rifle gun over his arm. His mother was telling his father what the stranger was saying. It was very important. The boy could see that. It made his father angry. His voice boomed when he replied. The stranger shrugged his shoulders so that his epaulets danced.

At last the boy grew tired listening to what he could not understand. He went out to look at the horse. The Indian lifted him into the saddle. He was scared. It was very high up there on the horse, but how fine! He sat with the reins in his hands looking proud. Finally he shouted. The horse stamped. The white stranger looked out of the cabin and laughed.

After a while the Indian picked up the boy's bow and started to show him how to shoot. He said nothing, but he sent the arrows straight. He rearranged the boy's hands on the bow. It went better that way. The Indian knew.

The Indian was a magnificent fellow. A great knife hung down on a thong before his breast, and he had a red turtle painted over his left nipple. When you put your hand on the turtle you could feel the Indian's heart underneath go *thump, bump*. It was not long before the boy was not afraid of the Indian any more. He was not so strange, and he was exciting.

There were long eagle feathers in that Indian's hair. His nose turned in toward his mouth, and his eyes looked out like a hawk's. He smelled of wood smoke and bear's grease. He played with the child roughly. He took him by the hair of his head and almost lifted him by it. His mother called out, but the white stranger laughed again and reassured her.

There was nothing to be afraid of. It was fun to be wrastled with, and lifted up by the hair. The boy wanted to go away with the Indian when he and the stranger left. His mother had to stop him. He stood, watching the Indian loping along beside the horse. Then his father called out something in an angry tone after the white man. It was something about snails and frogs.

The horseman wheeled suddenly and made partway back. Then he stopped and shouted, "You are crazee man. I ride ze woods for tell your wife. She ez couzen mon bon ami Dillon. I say all ze Anglais chez Chartier—" Here he rose in his saddle with excitement and made a circular motion around the top of his head. "You see? C'est la guerre, monsieur. You have bébé là! You go? No?"

In the flaring sunset the long shadows crept across the clearing, pointing from the woods towards the cabin. The boy never forgot that tense moment. His father leaned against the doorpost with his rifle across his breast, muttering. His mother had thrown herself against him and kept hold of the gun. "Lem," she kept saying, "Lem, Lem!" For a minute the Englishman and the Frenchman looked at each other. The brass housings of the officer's harness and his weapons and buttons twinkled and gleamed. At the edge of the hill by the clearing the feathered silhouette of the Indian stood dark and menacing, waiting against an angry sky. The silence spoke.

Then the Frenchman took off his hat, bowed from the saddle and said, "Adieu, madame." He wheeled and rode off into the forest. The Indian was gone.

Not knowing exactly why, the boy rushed into the cabin sobbing. His father hushed him sternly. . . .

They were going to have to move. The French king had said so. It was the king's land. That man had come to tell them. All the English must go back over the mountains. All the land and the woods belonged to the king of France and the Indians. The Indians were the friends of the king of France. They had already killed some English traders and taken their goods. All this was not

50

very clear to a small boy. He heard his father talking.

God lived in the sky. The king of France lived across the great water. The king had said they must go. Sal's father said God didn't want them to move. They would disobey the king. They would ask God to help them. It was now that his mother taught the boy to pray. Every night they said, "Our Father who art in heaven." But a great fear had come to the cabin. Sal's father hunted at night now. Sometimes he brought back only fish. There was another reason why they couldn't go, Sal soon discovered. It was something that was a secret between his father and mother.

The leaves fell from the trees. It began to turn cold. There was a new baby by the fire. It had come in the night while the boy slept. So had the first snow. He looked for the baby's trail in the snow, but it was not there. It couldn't walk. An Indian had brought it. He showed the marks of the moccasins to his father. They came close to the door, and went away again. His father said, "God damn," but he patted the boy on the head.

Afterward, he couldn't remember whether the baby was a boy or a girl, but he could remember the bundle squirming by the fire, and squalling. He remembered a small red hand about his finger. His mother gave the baby milk. The weather was terribly cold now. His father went out only to get meat and feed the ox. He always went out at night. He opened the door carefully and crawled out into the starlight with his rifle gun.

It was the ox that went first. An Injun cut its throat in the night, while his father was away. They heard the ox die, groaning. His mother stood at the door with the gun and shivered.

The boy cried when he saw his friend the ox next day. His father made meat out of it. The ox would never come and smell him friendly any more. He felt sad, and it was dark in the cabin. The winter was long. The snow drifted. They needed salt. Then his father didn't come back.

They waited. His mother prayed. The boy never saw

his father again. He was alone now. He thought about that. His mother had the baby.

Salathiel helped his mother. He knew he must do that. The ox meat and the big logs were gone. He went into the woods and dragged in branches for the fire. It was getting warmer again and they managed. There was only a little meal and some small potatoes left. The boy shot some rabbits and a bird now and then with his bow, when they came into the clearing. He grew skilful and patient. His mother praised him. But she always called him back anxiously. She said, "Salathiel, Salathiel Albine," when he went to the spring to get water. The spring was "far away." He cut branches for his mother with the small axe. The fire looked cheerful at night, but the door was always close barred, and his mother never sang any more. They both missed his father, but said nothing. She sat by the fire and listened. She sat with the gun and the baby. Outside the owls sang. The leaves were coming out again. Soon it would be summer. The boy slept. He dreamed that his friend the ox came and smelled him.

Then one day it was all over.

In the very early morning he went to the spring. A frog jumped into the water. As he reached down to fill his bucket a brown arm with a copper band around it came out of the bushes and grasped him by the hair. He stopped breathing. The arm lifted him up to his feet by the hair, and he found himself looking into the face of the Indian with the turtle on his breast.

The Turtle had a knife in his hand. He looked fierce. His eyes glittered, but the boy hoped it was only fun. He had been lifted up that way by the hair before. He was big now. He wouldn't cry. He managed to grin in the Indian's face, because his hair hurt him. He clicked his teeth together because it hurt. The Turtle grunted and put up his knife.

Then he lifted the boy up and threw him on his horse, which was hidden in the bushes. It was the same horse the French king's man had been riding the summer before, but it was blind in one eye and looked thin now. That was all the boy had time to notice before he heard his mother scream. . . .

He never forgot that scream as long as he lived. Somehow the scream came to live with him on the inside of his head. . . .

Suddenly the little clearing was full of racing forms with blackened faces. They streamed across towards the cabin from the trees, closing in like shadows.

The boy gave one whooping, strangled cry before the Turtle clapped the bucket down over his head, and rode off with him. He held the boy's wrists behind him and put a thong on them. Salathiel Albine knew better than to cry out. He knew what had happened. The Injuns had got him. Inside the bucket the blood roared in his ears. His little heart pounded fearfully.

Presently there was nothing to be heard but the breathing of the horse and the muffled thud of its hoofs on the leafy floor of the forest. The bucket banged Sal's nose, and wore sore furrows on his small shoulders, but he said nothing. He could look down his bleeding nose and see the ground and the horse's feet, under the bucket. They rode on. They forded a large stream. Presently they were passing over some grassland. They rode on until evening, he thought. About twilight the Turtle rode into an Indian village and gave the death helloo twice. A chorus of exultant yells answered him. The Turtle's loot from the raid was an ironbound bucket and a man-child. His squaw, Mawakis, might value the bucket. When he took it off the boy's head, the white child sat with a masklike face. Two ribbons of blood streamed from his nostrils. His heart and brain were frozen with terror. He scarcely breathed. He sat on the horse waiting to be killed.

Some squaws and a crowd of young Indians and children surrounded the horse. It stood with its head drooping. The Turtle had gone off somewhere.

The crowd began to hoot and shout and to poke sticks at the white boy. He said nothing. He sat. A big boy jabbed at him viciously with a pointed stick. The French officer's horse, a present to the Chief Big Turtle, had lost one eye that way not long before. It took the Indian boy's forearm in its teeth and began to crunch the bones. The lad screamed. The horse bit. The squaws and children shrieked with delight.

Just then the Big Turtle came back, seized the horse by the nose, and kicked the Indian boy in the jaw. The crowd scattered.

The Turtle led the horse to the door of his hut, and tied it. It grasped a post with its lips and teeth and began to inflate itself with air. It made a noise like a saw. "Wind Eater" was that horse's name.

Big Turtle lifted Salathiel off the horse, untied his hands, and pushed him before him into the log hut half sunk in the ground. This served the Turtle and his squaw for a lodge in the winter when they stayed to trade with the French.

The Indian woman waddled towards them through the smoke. There was a chimney, but she had built a small fire in the center of the room on the clay floor. Through the reek she peered at the child and the Turtle with brown, thoughtless eyes. She was fat, and she wore a brocaded court gown that, minus its hoops, swathed her in enormous grimy folds through which the original pattern of damasked gold and silver butterflies still glittered here and there. The place stank of Indian, wood smoke, rum, and urine. The white boy choked, and looked about him. He began to feel the blood in his hands and feet again.

The Big Turtle began an angry, guttural discourse to his squaw Mawakis, who swayed and grinned at him. He picked up an empty leather rum bottle and tossed it into the chimney. Then he pointed at the fire and gave Mawakis a hearty kick. At that she began to move. She seemed to realize he was there. She picked up the burning sticks from the floor by their ends and threw them into the chimney, where they began to blaze merrily. The Turtle assisted her by hitting her between the shoulders from time to time with small smouldering chunks. She shrugged them off. Finally she put a kettle of venison and hominy on the new fire to boil.

During this performance the boy stood leaning against the wall by the door, listening to the horse, Wind Eater. He was sick at the stomach and he retched violently. Afterwhile, the smoke began to clear and he felt better. But he slumped down on the floor shivering.

The Big Turtle melted some bear's grease on his hands, and, dragging the boy close to the fire, rubbed him with it. Then he put him under a buffalo robe on a pile of skins in the corner. The boy kept shivering and his teeth chattered, but he gradually grew warmer. His eyes followed Mawakis moving about the room. She was smoking a pipe about three inches long, filled with dried sumach leaves and tobacco. The smoke smelt sweet. Suddenly the boy went to sleep.

It was night when they awakened him. He could hear the owls and night birds. The fire was a heap of glowing coals. The meat and hominy were ready. They gave him a bowl of it, and the hot, thick soup revived him.

In one corner the Big Turtle sat on some dressed deerskins and fed his mouth with a wooden spoon out of a pumpkin bowl. He sucked the marrow out of the deer bones with a *plop,* and tossed them into the chimney. Then he took a long stone pipe out of a deerskin bag. He polished it with his hand. He filled it out of two other bags with the killikinick and tobacco. He lit it with a coal from the fire, and smoked. He blew the smoke out through his nose. The boy watched, fearful and fascinated.

How long the Turtle sat smoking, Salathiel had no idea. He was sure that the Indian was thinking about him. As a consequence he held his breath in order to be completely still and attract no attention. Then he had to breathe again with a long sigh. Now the Turtle really was looking his way! He said something to Mawakis sharply. She built up the fire again till the shadows danced. Then she brought the Turtle a small, copper pot with two sticks in it. When he lifted the sticks they dripped scarlet. There must be blood in the pot. The boy felt himself lost. The Turtle was coming for him now.

It was true.

The Turtle walked over and pulled the boy from under the robe. He stood him up in the middle of the floor. He put his face close to the boy's, looked into his eyes, and scowled at him. The child was certain now that his time had come. He didn't care. He looked at the Indian, and hated him. He scowled back—fiercely.

The Big Turtle laughed.

He pushed the boy to the floor, sat down beside him, and began to stir the pot. Certainly there must be blood in it, it was so red. Salathiel closed his eyes now—the Turtle had taken out his knife.

He began by pricking the boy on the chest with it. The child shuddered. His skin seemed to have dried up. It was sheer terror. He could scarcely feel anything on the surface of his body. Then everything went black, and he thought he heard his mother scream. She had done that for him. There was no use screaming himself.

Presently he became aware of the yellow firelight again. He opened his eyes a glimmer. Now he could see the hands of the Turtle still busy over his breast with the bright knife and one of the red sticks from the pot. He watched, breathing slowly. After a while he saw the picture of a turtle begin to stand out over his left nipple. It was a little turtle. Red. It stood out boldly against his white skin.

The Big Turtle smiled at the Little Turtle. He began to breathe more easily. Mawakis made a consoling noise in her throat. She understood. This child would be counted someday as a warrior she and the Big Turtle had given to the tribe. There had never been any children in their lodge. The Shawnees were a hard-pressed people and needed warriors. Her husband finished and pointed sternly and proudly to the sign on the boy's breast. She saw—and gave a grunt of grateful assent.

56

The Big Turtle motioned to her.

She picked the Little Turtle up and wrapped a fine, new trade blanket about him. She put a warm bone filled with marrow in his mouth. Then she squatted down on the floor beside him and began to rock herself back and forth on her hunkers and croon.

The Big Turtle crawled into the pile of skins and went to sleep. Mawakis continued to croon and rock a little. Outside the door the horse Wind Eater made noises like a pipe organ in pain. The fire died down. The boy gradually grew warmer, content with a full stomach, and an incapacity to feel any more. As he slid into an exhausted sleep, once again and far off, he thought he heard his mother's scream. That sound was still more than he could bear.

He hastened to leave the bad neighbourhood of reality. He seemed by an effortless desire of the will to throw himself backward into the oblivion of darkness. Why not? Why remain Salathiel? The worst had happened. The Injuns had got him. Salathiel had turned into a little turtle. He slept.

Thus, sometime between the ages of five and seven— he never knew exactly how old he was—he had tasted despair. Afterward, it seemed to him that he had died and awakened still living, but in another world. Nothing worse or more final could ever happen to him. The red turtle was at his heart. His opportunities for fear had all been exhausted in advance. In the real world outside he was never afraid of anything animate or inanimate again. What was left of terror remained sealed up in some dark cells of his brain to which only one bad dream had the master key.

Towards morning he half wakened. The fire was low and dim. Yet he could see the figure of Mawakis, leaning against the wall. She still squatted there like a bronze image of Patience, her face maternal and composed in sleep. There was something about her that comforted him. He felt safer. He relaxed and slumbered deeply.

Light was streaming into the lodge through the open door when next he opened his eyes. A wisp of smoke from the fireplace curled slowly across the ceiling. He awakened gladly into life again.

And into a matchless early May morning.

The misty face of the sun peered into the lodge of the Shawnee Chief Kaysinata, known as the Big Turtle, and of Mawakis, his barren squaw. It was in the Indian town of Sacunk, near the junction of the creek called Beaver with the Ohio, or Beautiful River, about a day's journey down from the Great Forks. French militia and fur traders had helped build the huts for their Indian allies and customers only a short while before. They were anxious to keep their enemies, the English and the Iroquois, out of these virgin hunting grounds, and they had been at some pains and expense to induce the wandering Shawnees to settle there when they abandoned Pennsylvania. Kaysinata had already received much gear and finery from his new Great White Father of France. The lodge was piled with miscellaneous gifts and the recent loot of some unfortunate Pennsylvania traders, who had been driven away from the Ohio country or murdered.

The Little Turtle propped himself up on his elbows and let his curious, young eyes slip from an officer's cocked hat with a medal on it, over piles of matchcoats and new blankets, broken rum bottles, flints, a staved-in keg, a bundle of axes and an array of powder horns, to a fine English saddle with the pistols sticking out of its fringed holsters. All this meant little to the boy. He was ravenously hungry.

Beyond the door the sun glittered on a magnificent expanse of the Beautiful River gliding along with sunny streaks in its current between misty islands and towering, forested banks. In the chimney, which the French had so kindly built, the backlog of the night before finally collapsed and burst into flame.

Kaysinata, the Big Turtle, grunted and rumbled. Mawakis rose and began to bestir herself. She put a great dried

58

salmon on a cleft stick before the fire. The Little Turtle, alias Salathiel Albine, sat up abruptly.

A ravishing odour of broiling fish filled the lodge.

5

Of Old Forgotten Things

TIME to a child is heavily alloyed with eternity. And where Salathiel had come to dwell there was nothing but the long flow of the seasons to mark the calendar of earth. Life was like the course of the Beautiful River that came out of the forest, ran through the forest, and disappeared into it forever. What were days and nights to it, or to those whose life flowed away with it along its banks? Their days were like the river, a mysterious and interminable flow. And even the clearest and most vivid reflections make no impression on water; leave no record of the dream.

In another place and century, Salathiel Albine thought he could count at least ten, and perhaps a baker's dozen of winters that the Little Turtle passed in the lodges of Kaysinata as they moved about. But there again he could never be certain. All seasons are not memorable, and in the forest it was the winter without corn, or the summer of the great salmon run on the Allegheny, or the autumn when the raccoons were so ridiculously fat, that blazed notches on the tree of life. Such things were remembered and spoken of.

He was certain, however, that it was spring when Kaysinata first brought him to the cabin at Sacunk, for the days between the time of his advent and the departure of the tribe from the village for their summer hunting were numbered, literally, by the hairs of his head.

Mawakis took a sharp knife, and laying his hair, which was still yellow and hung nearly to his shoulders, on a log, she cut it off as short as she could. Then she dipped her fingers in ashes and began to pluck him bare as a fowl for the pot. She took a few hairs at a time, and she took a long time. Afterwhile he was bald except for one lock that grew from the middle scalp, which Mawakis greased with bear's fat and wrapped about near the base with twine. It looked like a little sheaf of wheat left alone when the field had been gleaned. After that, when the fuzz came, Kaysinata shaved his head. That hurt at first, and so he remembered.

And one thing more about that time or later. Kaysinata put him in a canoe and paddled up the Ohio to Logstown. Logstown was an even bigger village than Sacunk. There were many Indian children there from various tribes and he played with them and swam in the river. They spoke several tribal tongues. Their people had come to get powder and little rolls of lead for the summer hunting from a French half-breed trader named Chartier. But there was an Englishman there, too. His name was Gist. He stayed for two days only. He was afraid. The French would have had him killed or taken prisoner, but he was a messenger come from the governor of the Long Knives, and Kaysinata would have none of it.

Gist spoke secretly to the Little Turtle. The boy was glad to hear his own tongue again. Gist asked him his name, and who his parents were. Salathiel thought awhile and told him. Gist bade him remember them when he said his prayers. He would have ransomed the boy from the Big Turtle, if he had had any goods with him. But he had none. He was on a mission from the governor of Virginia to spy out the land for the Ohio company. He went across the river in a canoe in the night. But Salathiel remembered. It made an impression on him. For a long time he secretly said the prayer his mother had taught him, and told the names of his parents to God. After a long while the words grew dim. They became little more than a noise that he made to himself in his head. At length he thought he forgot.

The Big Turtle was angry when he learned that Gist had talked with his "son." He took him to the river and ducked him. He held him long under the water. Then he had him painted brown, blue, and red. He put a fine new doeskin shirt on him that Mawakis had made, and he showed him at the council fire. All the Indians, and he himself, saw that he was now indeed the Little Turtle, and one of the Sawanos, the people who came from the south. This was after they returned to Sacunk.

Soon after that they went hunting. It was the first time. They hunted beaver that summer. The Little Turtle learned all about beavers. He was badly bitten by a pup. The scar on his thumb remained.

Every summer the tribe scattered. They left their winter cabins in the trading villages by the river and became separate lodges, hunting where they listed, as long as they didn't interfere with one another.

For the most part the Shawnees wandered west, or south into the great empty country south of the Beautiful River, empty of men, but full of game. They sought buffalo and elk there in the bluegrass glades. Even the boys shot deer. Once they were ambushed by Catawbas. Kaysinata killed two of them and took their scalps.

One summer the whole tribe went and camped at the DeTroit. The Little Turtle saw many white men's houses there, and the great barns along the river between the two lakes, like the street of a town. He saw an ox again.

The French officers at the fort kindled the council fire often. Their chief was called de Bienville. There were many speeches, and much rum flowed. There were drinking clubs amongst the lodges, and people ran about screaming. They shot guns off and wounded one another. They fought with knives and several were killed. It was hard for the chiefs to keep the peace among the tribes.

The French were persuading the Shawnees to take up the hatchet against the Dawn Land people. Kaysinata was gloomy and sad. He had once grasped the hand of the

English at the great council fire at Philadelphia. There were too many of them to fight, he said. Let them trade. Their goods were cheaper and better than those of the French. Many gifts were showered upon him by the French to make him change his mind.

That was a bad summer for old people and children at the DeTroit. Mawakis was drunk most of the time. She grew blear-eyed and fat. Her teeth loosened. She beat the Little Turtle often, until the Big Turtle beat her. Kaysinata hated the firewater and the wars that the French would kindle against the English and the six fires of the Long House. He was a hunter. His half-brother Nymwha was a prophet. Nymwha made medicine with tobacco, killikinick, feathers, and the shoulder blades of deer. He foretold disaster to the Shawnees from the wars of the palefaces. He tried to persuade his people to leave the DeTroit, to give up guns and firewater, to hunt with bow and arrow again, and to use the fire sticks.

Powder and shot, flint and steel were accursed, said Nymwha. All the gifts of the paleface were poison to the Indian, he said. They laughed at him.

The tribes from the north across the great lake danced the war dance. They danced all summer, and drank. They often went mad and killed one another. There was no hunting. There would be no food in the fall. The French would have to feed them, and they would have to take up the hatchet for the French.

Kaysinata believed Nymwha. He also saw things with his fathers' eyes. It was a bad summer. Even the children ran wild. The squaws drove them from the lodges. They shifted for themselves, all but the very little ones, whom Father Bonnecamp brought to the fort and baptized.

It never occurred to the Little Turtle to take refuge with the French. He remembered in the back of his mind he was once an Englishman and the French were his enemies, although he now thought of himself as an Indian and was proud of it. He was a big boy, and strong. He spoke the chief's Shawnee well, and he could talk in several other tongues, and the sign language. He and some other youngsters stole a birchbark canoe from the Ottawas, who were drinking brandy from kegs with wooden dippers. There was a hole in the canoe, but they repaired it. They spent the summer fishing and gathering berries. They camped on islands in the lake, and built fires. Rattlesnakes bit two of them and they died. Once the woods burned while they slept and they took to the lake just in time, with their eyebrows burned off. A Huron boy called Speckled Snake was drowned.

Before autumn came Kaysinata and Nymwha took their squaws and lodges away early from the DeTroit. They took the fine clothes, the brass kettles, the paints and vermilion, and the wheat flour and lead they had received from the French, and headed south across country for the Beautiful River. All their furs and skins were gone. The horse, Wind Eater, had died.

They stole horses from the Mingoes, and hunted to lay in food for the winter. There would be no corn that year for hominy. None had been planted. They smoked fish, and dried berries. They took bears and fat raccoons. They worked the squaws hard. They struck the stream called Beaver and followed it south till they came to the Beautiful River again. But that autumn they did not go back to Sacunk. They settled for the winter at Logstown on the banks of the Beautiful River. The French soldiers came soon after and built them log huts and stone chimneys, and they lived there that winter on the bounty of the French.

Kaysinata had at last been persuaded to take up the hatchet against the English. Nemacolin, the Delaware, who lived near the fort of the Old People at Red Stone, came and told him he had shown the English the Old Buffalo trail over the mountains, through the Great and Little Meadows. The English were coming. They had sent horses and soldiers to Red Stone. The Long Knives were already there. Next year they would build a fort at the Great Forks. The Six Nations had sold the English land south of the Ohio.

Kaysinata was very angry at this news. He feared the

English more than the French. When the English came they cut down the trees, made houses, and stayed. Soon the hunting grounds would be full of English all along the Beautiful River. So the Big Turtle listened to the French.

The Little Turtle heard all this talk, sitting in the cabins at Logstown. He filled the pipes of the chiefs. He blew smoke in their faces to be polite. He was growing tall now. He listened with open ears. Mawakis was losing her teeth. She sat in the lodge, and slept often. Soon she would be old.

In the chief's hut there was always much meat, gifts, and food. Kaysinata and Nymwha were the best hunters of all the Shawnees. They remembered most of the old lore of their fathers. They spoke of it together at night. The Little Turtle listened. He grew tall and fierce. His hands and feet were large. He played with Indian boys older than he was. He made them afraid of him. He was the chief's son. The Big Turtle taught him how to wrestle and strike out with both hands and feet, like the half-breed Frenchmen. He taught him how to skin beasts, and how to throw the knife and the hatchet. His bow of arc wood had once been a warrior's. It came from the Illinois. The Little Turtle was the only boy who could bend it. He was taller now than the bow.

That winter, about the time the ice formed, two Englishmen came to Logstown. Shingas, the Delaware chief, brought them. One was a tall, young man with a pink face and his hair tied back in a queue. He was a Long Knife and brought with him an interpreter called "David's son." Four French deserters also arrived, with whom the tall, young man talked. He also sent for Tanacharison, the half-king, who was away hunting. He came and talked with the tall man secretly in his tent.

Then there was a great council of the Delawares, Shawnees, and Mingoes held at the council house. The Little Turtle heard English talked again between David's son and the Long Knife. He told all that passed to Kaysinata, who sat and said nothing. The Long Knife wanted

65

guides and an escort to the French captain at Venango. He had come to warn the French to leave the country. Kaysinata laughed. "It's lead will do the talking," he said to Nymwha. He would not let the Little Turtle speak to the Englishmen. Shingas, Tanacharison, Jeskakake, White Thunder, and the Hunter went with the Long Knife, Wash'ton, and David's son to Venango. They were not seen again.

"There will be war now between the palefaces," said Nymwha. "We will wait till they are weary and then drive them out. One paleface is as bad as another. Let the hatchet bite deep."

In the early spring Kaysinata needed horses. He stole two from the English at their fort near Red Stone. He stole another from an Englishman named Frazier at the mouth of Turtle Creek, on the Monongahela. The Little Turtle lifted that horse. First he went close to the cabin. He heard the man Frazier saying goddamn to his wife. She was angry, and poured water on the fire. Then the Little Turtle caught the horse and just rode away while no one was looking. He was very proud. He said goddamn to the horse, like Mr. Frazier, and it went faster. He named the horse that. The French laughed, but not for long, for Nymwha stole three horses from them at Venango. He cut off their manes and dyed them with walnut juice so that they would not be recognized. The two lodges went far up the Beaver and made sugar from the big maples near its source. Then they all rode west on a great hunting.

They ranged along the Ohio, clear out to the Big Miami. They caught catfish and shot ducks and swans. They ate beaver and buffalo and venison. Kaysinata and his half-brother Nymwha hunted together. They pitched their lodges side by side. There were four squaws in Nymwha's lodge. All his children had been daughters. They were strong. That was why Kaysinata hunted with Nymwha.

Mawakis was no longer much good to Kaysinata. Her front teeth were worn down and loosened from chewing deerskins for his shirts. She could no longer make them soft for him. She was full of miseries, and longed for firewater to feel young again.

Kaysinata wanted much dried fish and jerked buffalo meat. He brought in many animals to skin. There must be dried berries and pemmican for the winter. The corn must be ground, and the hominy stamped. The fires were to be tended. Nymwha's squaws could do the work. He and the Big Turtle still insisted on laying in supplies for the winter. They did not wish to sell themselves to the French and the traders just for a little food. They worked the women hard.

Nymwha watched his squaws carefully. He would not let his daughters marry. He made bad medicine and prophesied they would give birth to snakes. He scared the young men and drove them away. The three big girls bothered the Little Turtle. They once caught him in swimming and found he was not a full man yet and made fun of him. He hated them. When he grew larger he made them afraid of him. He beat them with Nymwha's stick. He never spoke to them again, except to tell them to bring him something. They made moccasins for him, and grunted. They were named after the three winds.

It was different with Mawakis. The Big Turtle did not abuse her. He simply disregarded her as she grew old. She stumbled after him through the forest when they made a march, carrying what she could on her back. Sometimes she was too late to kindle the evening fire for Kaysinata. The Little Turtle would do that. He also brought her things to eat and she gradually became quite dependent upon him. Once he was gone a week and stole a little horse for her from the Twigtees. Nymwha praised him for going far away to steal. Kaysinata said nothing. Sometimes he gave Mawakis tobacco to smoke.

There was an affection between the Little Turtle and Mawakis. She was the only being who loved him for himself. She had tried to be a mother to him. Had it not been for her, he might have forgotten his own mother entirely. Sometimes Mawakis would squat close to him

67

in the half-lodge at evening while Kaysinata smoked and they looked into the fire. She would stroke his cheek with her old, roughened fingers. Then he would think of the fire in the cabin and the old days that were now like a dream.

At such times Nymwha made medicine and talked with his great-grandfathers. Animals looked at them from the trees with red, glowing eyes. The owls sang. Pictures would come upon the white shoulder blades of the deer with which he prophesied. They clicked together in the ancient box of hardwood that had come from the south. There were other things in the box. Once a year Nymwha blew upon the conch shell, which was also there, and burnt tobacco to celebrate the day the Sawanos had come from their far island in the south. All the voices from the past were sad now, he said. He drank the bitter drink, and dreamed dreams. Sometimes he danced and once he frothed at the mouth.

To all this Kaysinata said nothing, but he listened to Nymwha and believed him.

Many evenings Mawakis sat looking into the fire and told the Little Turtle of her girlhood in the happy valley east of the mountains. Those were good times, she said. The paleface was far away in the dawnlight then. The spotted sickness slept. Kaysinata agreed, and told stories himself. He, too, longed to return to the good valley between the long mountains, where his forefathers had hunted by the Juniata. He made the Little Turtle learn by heart the names of the places where his grandfathers slept along the streams in that valley. He taught him the signs of the hills and the stars by which to find them. There was a song about them and their sleeping places which all the squaws sang. It was so old some of the words could no longer be explained. It was old, old medicine.

But for the most part the Little Turtle was lonely in the forest on those western huntings, even when Nymwha's lodge was along. There were no companions for the Little Turtle, no young men or boys in the party.

Kaysinata and Nymwha worked him hard. All day they taught him many things. But they would not let him go to the villages of other tribes alone. Nor would they smoke with him. "Women and tobacco are for men," they said. "You are tall, but you are not yet a man. Hunt. Grow strong. Listen to us and become wise. War is coming."

So, because of that, the forests and the long stretches of the Beautiful River were lonely to the boy. He was grave and sad in the summer. He was glad when they turned back as the first leaves began to fall. They had wandered far. They marched back eastward under the great trees for a score of days. The moon changed from little to full. At night they came out on bottom lands where there was good grass, and there they camped. The trail was made that way. The horses grazed under the stars and the Little Turtle watched them.

All day under the trees the rut of the trace ran eastward through the forest. In some places it was waist-deep, worn by moccasins that had passed going and coming, no one knew how long. At night it usually led out under the stars again. Then it was that they hobbled the horses and camped near running water.

They came back to the Beaver Creek well and strong that year. They had much food and piles of beaver pelts and deerskins. Even Mawakis was better. There had been no firewater.

On the banks of the Beaver Creek the tribe gathered. There were many villages there of several tribes. In the autumn the traders came with goods and rum. And it was then that the fun began, and the trouble too.

Kaysinata, however, would buy no firewater that year. He traded all his deerskins and the beaver pelts for guns, powder, flints, and clothes. Then he took the best horses and went away with six other warriors to raid the English east of the mountains. It was good raiding weather. It was fine Indian summer. And Nymwha's saying had come true. There was war. The French had struck the English and finished the fort at the Great Forks, which the English had begun. They called that fort "Due-kane." They gathered the warriors there. The squaws and youngsters were left alone on the Beaver, except for the old men. And there was much firewater. Mawakis was drunk again.

That was the year the bad trouble began. The tribes began to break up. Many warriors who went to raid never returned. Many more were away loafing at the fort at the Great Forks most of the time. Few cared to hunt while the French fed them. There was small work done in the villages by the squaws. Sometimes even the fires went out. Plunder, firewater, and some captives began to arrive. Everything was plentiful but food. But no one ate much. They drank. When the firewater ran out, a kind of coma succeeded the long delirium. Nothing was as it once had been. Life in the villages of the Mingoes and the Shawnees along the Beaver Creek was haggard and miserable. The squaws sold themselves to strangers and French soldiers for a little food. The chiefs were at the fort talking with the French. They were going to drive the English into the salty lake, they said.

Nymwha had foretold all this. He had seen something like it happen before. He removed from Logstown to the high rocks on the south side of the Beautiful River, just a little downstream from Fort Duquesne. There he camped in an inaccessible gorge which led to the top of the cliff. There was a hill near by that swarmed with turkeys. Only officers could land near the rocks. The commandant issued an order about it. Nymwha would rent his daughters to none but those who wore a sword. He required considerable gifts for them. His daughters were happy, and there was great plenty in the lodge, and no trouble.

Nymwha hid an English trader near the rocks and kept him till he could go east. The man's name was McKee. Nymwha gave McKee wampum to take back to the English and told him consoling speeches to say to their chief men. He saw many bad pictures on the shoulder blades of deer when he made medicine now, but he said nothing about them to the French.

"Let the hatchet fall on many," he said. "Who would be a paleface? They live only to feel themselves. They

70

destroy all that the Manitous have made. They are right when they kill one another. Let the hatchet fall on many of them."

The Little Turtle found life in the village on Beaver Creek difficult while the Big Turtle was away. He took a canoe and went to see his uncle Nymwha, at McKees Rock. He told him that Kaysinata had returned from raiding, but was still at the fort. Mawakis was hungry and there was little game to be had. Life was bad in the villages. At first Nymwha said nothing. He smoked for a long time. He looked at the boy keenly. Then for the first time he passed the pipe to his nephew, the Little Turtle, who also now blew the smoke out through his nose.

"Now," said Nymwha, "listen like a man. These things are but the beginning of wisdom":

Go alone, go with one other, or go with many. Never go with two; one of them will prove an enemy.

Take what is thine and eat it immediately; tomorrow it will spoil or be stolen.

When two arrows strike the same deer, dispute not. Return thine arrow to its place. There are more deer in the forest than arrows in thy quiver.

Loud voices in the lodges proclaim the men are aweary or away.

Paint thine honorable scars with vermilion; to conceal them will arouse suspicion.

Keep thy big medicine in a secret place or it will surely be stolen from thee.

Give gifts to those who do not need them. Those who have nothing will always desire more.

Strike when thou art angry that the blow may have meaning, and last.

Two suck marrow from the same bone with great difficulty.

Slay for thine own necessity. Not for others.

Manitou must be sought in the high, stony mountains; fat buffalo in the valley where the grass grows long.

When the seasons are mild and the hunting easy, old men will rule. Flee then into the high mountains.

Listen, or thine own tongue will keep thee deaf.

Have one door to thy lodge, and sleep across it.

Women, war, and horses can always break loose.

Shouting at eagles brings out the wolves.

Threaten like the thunder, after the lightning falls.

Unbelt carefully and keep thy moccasins tied on.

Two loves to become one.

Three is the number of all that befalls.

Leave the company of the unlucky, or become awkward, too.

Lend a canoe to a fool in the winter. Borrow his horse in the spring.

Look at a man's hands if you would know him, his face is a favored lie.

6

How Nymwha Blew on a Conch Shell in the Moon of Full Leaves

NYMWHA was a man who listened to his own voices. He believed in his medicine whether it promised him good or ill. Through all the great war between the French and English he lived in the high gorge near McKees Rocks in the way his ancestors had lived before him. He hunted. Save for a few French officers who came for a while to visit his daughters, no one else had come there. The country to the south of the Beautiful River was deserted now because of the war.

At the fort at the Great Forks the tribes gathered to help the French meet the English. All the warriors were gone from the Beaver. It was lean times there in the villages of old men, women, and children. Most of the Delawares, the Wyandots, the Twigtees, the Shawnees, and the tribes from the north were gathered at the fort. A great army of the British, Red Coats and Long Knives with cannon, were coming over the mountains. All men, even the Long House, waited to see which way the hatchet would fall. The music played, the cannon were fired often at the fort. The banks of the three rivers there, and the islands, were lined with the watch fires of many warriors. The Little Turtle climbed the high rocks near Nymwha's camp to look at them. At night he could look up-river past an island and see the red glow of the fires of the warriors pictured in the water and the sky.

73

Mawakis and the Little Turtle had come to live with Nymwha while Kaysinata was on the warpath. There was quiet, much food, and contentment at his snug bark lodges in the gorge. Even the French officers did not come any more as battle drew near them. And two of the squaws had babies now. The papooses hung strapped to boards under the trees. They seldom cried. They hung there silent, and looked about them with big brown eyes. They were as fond of honeycomb as young bear cubs. They would suck it from your finger.

Mawakis made much of them. She grew better after she had once been chased by snakes. There was nothing to drink in Nymwha's gorge but cold water from the spring. Many canoes passed up and down the river far below, but none landed to speak with Nymwha. He was content. "They will find trouble both ways," he said. He and the Little Turtle smoked together, while the women chewed deerskins. Nymwha once spoke at night of the far-off past:

Many, many bead strings of moons ago, the Sawanos lived happily in a great island in the broad water in the south. The trees and the animals were different there. The fruits and nuts rained upon the earth constantly, for there were no seasons. The sun stood still in heaven and no winter came. There were great fish in the lake that was salty and lay all along beneath the heaven of stars. Out of it came the sun and moon, and into it the sun went at evening.

The Sawanos were a mighty people in that island. They blew upon conch shells, they fished, and they fought with other Indians who came from the far south to eat them. They conquered in battle. But mostly they were peaceful. They waxed fat; grew old. They died of old age and innocence.

Then in an evil day came the paleface out of the dawnlight. They were Espanioles, the first and fiercest of all the palefaces. They had priests and crosses like the French. They wore coats made of iron, stronger

74

than the shells of nuts. Their canoes drifted under white mountains and had sticks that made the winds to obey them. The Espanioles rode upon horses. They killed with thunder. They brought dogs which barked and ran in packs like wolves. They hunted the Indians. The spitting and spotted sickness slept in the beards of their warriors. Death walked with them from land to land. Soon it was better to die than to live in the same world with them.

Then a great medicine man arose in the tribe of the Sawanos. He was greater and wiser than the chiefs. He was a fisherman. He had a broken back, and a large head. A fish had eaten his foot. But he spoke the truth. "Come," he said. "I will show you a great island across the deep water. I have been there. It is where the sun goes in the night. There are turkeys there, and alligators, but no palefaces. The land is empty except for a few Indians. The deer there are shaggy. The moon sleeps in a cave there all day. Bury your images and carved poles in the mounds with your grandfathers. Leave them sleeping, and come with me."

So the Sawanos followed him. They took white clay and made their canoes the color of moonlight. They paddled after the crookbacked man. After two nights they came to the great island where the alligators roared and there were turkeys and deer. They raised their lodges beside the great water.

Then the fisherman said, "Blow once every summer on this conch shell in the same moon that you have safely landed. Then your grandfathers in the old island will know their children are still here. And forget not to do it, or it will be the end of you. Blow on the conch once in the moon of Full Leaves if all is well. But if the paleface follows you, and you wish the help of your grandfathers, blow three times, and say these words. . . .

". . . In my family," said Nymwha, "the words have

been handed down from mother to son with the conch shell. It was to the totem of the Turtle that the conch and the words were delivered. I have the conch shell. Only I and Kaysinata, my half-brother, know the old words. In my lodge is nothing but daughters. Thou art the only son of the Big Turtle. When thou art a man I will deliver thee the words. It is for this that I prepare thee and make thee wise. It was for this that Kaysinata took thee from the cabin of the gold beard. The clan of the Turtle had no children at all. Now the paleface comes again. Soon it will be the moon of Full Leaves. Kaysinata and I will smoke a pipe and make medicine together. Whether we shall blow once or thrice upon the conch shell, who knows? Our pipes will tell us, and our medicine. We shall see."

Nymwha was very brave when he said this. He touched the Little Turtle on the shoulder with his pipe and looked at him.

"Listen," he said. "From the time the Sawanos landed in the great island in the moon of Full Leaves they became wanderers, and they have wandered ever since. This is the story of their wanderings. Listen and remember":

They left the land of the alligator and the salt-running rivers. They followed the trails of deer and buffalo into the sunset till they came to the great, blue mountains where the smoke stands out from the high hills at morning like an arm with a broad hand on it. There they fought with a fierce people called the Cherokees, who have lived in those hills since the beginning. And they fled before them northward and westward into a fat but empty land.

There was nothing but animals in that country. Only the Old People had lived there long ago. They were giants. It was they who built the forts shaped like serpents out of mud and stones, but no man had seen them. No one remembered who they were.

76

Then the Sawanos fought with the Catawbas, and those battles were also sore.

So they came north again through the great hills into the country where the rain turned white in the winter, and a rumour came that the Espanioles were behind them. They blew upon the conch shell and communed with the ghosts of their grandfathers in the old island. But what the ghosts said no one could now be sure.

So the Sawanos made friends with the Delawares, the First Comers into the land, who were a mighty people in those days. They blew upon the conch shell and told the ghosts of their old grandfathers that now they had new grandfathers in the new island, and their names were those of the Delawares, and they begged their new grandfathers for land to hunt in and to build their lodges in, and be at peace. And that land the Delawares gave them. It was on the rivers that run into the Great Bay.

Yet there was no peace for the Sawanos, whom men now call the Shawnees. The English came. They took the land from the Shawnees and from their grandfathers, the Delawares. They raced the English in a great foot race for the land, and the English cheated. They had many men who ran far. The Shawnees moved into the sunset again.

That was not so long ago, he said. The grandmother of Nymwha had her lodge near the place where the lodges of the Broad Hats stand on the Delaware. Nymwha, himself, had played there when he was a young boy. Now he was hiding in a gorge on the Ohio. The Shawnees were still wanderers. In his lifetime they had fled westward across the mountains into the great forests. The English had followed and built cabins in the valleys of the hills in the Shawnee hunting grounds by the Juniata. It was there that Nymwha would have made his home. He liked that country best. His father slept by the streams there. But now the English were coming again. They were coming into the Ohio country. They would fight with the French for the land. They had done that before. Nymwha could remember all that.

He would say no more. He smoked the pipe, and sat silent. Of the days to come he would say nothing at all. . . .

In the month when the British were cutting a road through the forest over the mountains, and the French and Indians watched for them at Fort Duquesne, Kaysinata came to visit his half-brother Nymwha at the gorge near the high rocks. He came secretly by night in a canoe from the fort, and alone. The Big Turtle was a famous warrior now. The scalp locks of the English hung in fringes from his leggings, and the war paint gleamed on his face.

"Dost thou still exist?" said Nymwha, and held out his hand.

"I do," said Kaysinata, "and here is my hand."

Kaysinata and Nymwha said nothing to the women for fear the bad ghosts of their mothers might follow them when they made medicine. That was man's concern. They fasted for a day, drank the bitter drink, purged themselves, and went into the forest to make medicine where they could not be found out. They bade the Little Turtle keep the squaws tied in the lodges until they returned. They gave him a gun for the first time, and said, "Watch."

After two days they came back.

A deer was then killed. They had venison and roasted the first ears of the young corn for a feast. All by now were very hungry, but the feast was a sign that Nymwha and the Big Turtle had made good medicine. The two chiefs sat together in the same lodge and smoked fine tobacco. They invited the Little Turtle to come and sit with them.

"Does he learn?" asked Kaysinata.

"He does," replied Nymwha.

"It is well," said the Big Turtle. "Let Mawakis fetch him a coal for his pipe. Let him begin."

So the Little Turtle smoked with the two chiefs before

78

all the women, and he was both happy and proud. Nymwha had praised him greatly.

As for Kaysinata, he returned to Fort Duquesne by night as secretly as he had come. And it was high time he came back there, for he found that nearly half the warriors were gone. As the English drew nearer, and the strength of "Bladock's" army became known, canoe after canoe had slipped down the Beautiful River, or up the Allegheny, filled with warriors, with the gifts which the French had given them, with the loot and prisoners from their raids on English settlements. There were a number of white women and children among them who were thus spirited off into the wilderness and were seen no more.

Soon the glow in the sky by night from the watch fires of the tribes was only a small patch on the clouds to what it had been before. Most disconcerting of all, the French themselves could not wholly conceal that they were quietly making certain preparations to leave. Apparently it was not their intention to stay for a siege of the fort, if it came to that.

The Shawnees were no exception to what was going on. Although amongst them the authority of their chiefs was great, many had left while the Big Turtle was away. More were preparing to go. It took all of his persuasion and oratory, the promises and presents of Monsieur de Beaujeu to detain the remainder.

For that purpose Kaysinata held an assembly of the Shawnee warriors. He taunted those who had left, with panic and cowardice. He lauded those who remained. He promised them that when the English approached nigh the fort a messenger should go to Nymwha, who would make medicine just when the battle was about to be joined. Nymwha would blow upon the ancient conch shell three times, said Kaysinata, and ask the help of their grandfathers' ghosts. Kaysinata reminded them that when this had been done before the Shawnees had always prevailed. It was a certain medicine to be used only to drive the paleface from the land. It would be bound to give overwhelming victory. If the host of the English was great, so was the opportunity to strike a blow. Never again would there be so many scalps, guns, and prisoners to be taken. "Bladock" was a fool. The hatchet would surprise him and find him out.

Thus, by arts and promises, the Big Turtle persuaded them to stay.

There was a great war dance at the fort. Their father, the commandant, Monsieur de Contrecœur, sat in his chair and gave his children new guns, lead, blankets, and powder. An English boy named Smith, who had been captured near Raystown, was made to run the gantlet. Afterward the French nursed him back to life in the fort. All was ready. The place of the ambush was decided upon near the lower crossing of the Monongahela. The English were only three marches away. The sound of their cannon could be heard in the forest at sunrise.

At the beginning of the moon of Full Leaves a messenger came down the river to Nymwha. "Make ready," he said, "the time has come. Speak to the grandfathers."

Then Nymwha arose from the lodge where he had been singing and fasting. He put the women in one hut and tied the door fast with wolf gut. He threatened them, and told them not to watch or follow him. He took his box with the medicine in it, his best blankets, his feathers, a copper kettle, and his paint pots. He caught the two best horses out of seven that fed in the long glade at the top of the cliffs, and bidding the Little Turtle to follow at a respectful distance, he set off southward into the forest, singing a powerful song to his grandfathers. After a day the Little Turtle knew that song, for the words went the same way over and over again. He joined in, and Nymwha was pleased.

The trail south was a good one. It was narrow and it led along the crests of the hills. It was the warpath of those who went to fight the Catawbas and the Cherokees. There were signs carved upon the rocks, if one knew where to look for them. There were old pictures painted on the blazes of ancient trees. They told of the passing of many warriors long ago before there were horses.

On the third day Nymwha and the Little Turtle came to a tall hill in the midst of the largest stretch of meadows the Little Turtle had ever seen. Once there must have been cornfields there. He could see that.

On the top of the hill was a fort of the Old People, with a mound in the middle. Inside the fort there grew a kind of fragrant pine tree which the Little Turtle had never seen before, and many of the bitter drink bushes. All these had come from the south, Nymwha said. They camped there and Nymwha watched exactly to see where the sun rose and set. He made a broad mark on the two pine trees to mark the sun's place in the east and the west, and he laid a long deer thong between the two blazed trees.

The next day they made ready to make medicine. They cleansed themselves, and fasted.

First they uncovered an old hearth of stone under the deep pine needles. Nymwha knew exactly where it was. They built a fire on it until the stones were hot. Then they put out the fire, swept the stones clean, and built a frame of saplings over them which they covered with blankets. After the stones cooled somewhat, Nymwha threw upon them dried bundles of herbs which he had brought with him, and the tender end-shoots of the pines gathered on the spot. They packed the floor thick with these, and every cranny of it.

Next they went down to the river together and drew the brass kettle full of water, after washing it clean with sand. Then they took it back slung on a pole between them to the top of the hill. Nymwha now removed all the wire from the long gristle loops of his ears. He took off all his clothes, even his breechclout, and ordered the Little Turtle to do the same. He plucked leaves from the bitter drink bushes and made a strong, brown brew that was rank. They drank this. After a while they became dizzy. They fell down, and vomited.

Then Nymwha dumped the water from the kettle on the hot stones in the hut covered with blankets. He and the Little Turtle crawled in and sat in the aromatic steam. They sat there till the paint and the grease and the sweat ran out of them. Pretty soon balls of wax fell out of their ears. They sat there till Nymwha was through chanting the cleansing song. Then they darted out of the hut and plunged into the river. They drank deeply of the cool water. They felt well. They were clean inside and out.

The Little Turtle saw when he came out on the bank that he was a white man. Only the mark of the red turtle remained very clear over his heart. It was bigger now. It had grown with him. Nymwha looked at how white he was and grunted. Then they went back to the hills, wrapped themselves in their blankets, and slept.

In the nighttime the Little Turtle dreamed. He heard his mother scream. It seemed to come from underground. He remembered again what had happened to him and to her. He awoke shivering. He was very hungry. He had not eaten for two days. The owls sang. He was an Indian again. He said nothing to Nymwha of his dream for fear Nymwha would know the ghost of his mother had followed him. He went to sleep once more. Nymwha awoke him at sunrise. He would not let him eat.

"This is the day," Nymwha said. Then he began to make big medicine.

He painted himself carefully, then he faced south from the deer thong that stretched between the two pine trees. He walked south for as many paces as he had fingers and toes. On the spot where he stopped he built a pile of big stones with a flat one on top. On that he laid dried pine cones, the heart of a deer, and lumps of the sweet gum which had gathered in the marks he had made on the two pine trees. Over these Nymwha laid clean, dry twigs. He sang a loud song, kindled a fire with his fire sticks, and fanned it with a fan made out of eagles' wings.

"O, ho," he said, "O, ho, ho-ho."

The fire burned fiercely and consumed the deer heart and the gum. Nymwha then threw fine tobacco upon it. The good leaf burned slowly. A thick, sweet smoke arose. Nymwha fanned it into the south.

"O, ho," he said, "O, ho, ho-ho.

"Grandfathers in the far island, grandfathers and warriors of the People of the South, listen. All is not well with your children, the Sawanos. The paleface comes again. Today there is a great battle at the Ford of the Monongahela at the lower crossing. I call upon you to keep your promise. I ask you to hasten. I call upon you three times. I have burned the deer heart, gum, and tobacco. Sniff them deeply and awaken. Hasten upon the wings of these eagles that I cast upon the fire. I, Nymwha, of the clan of the Turtle of your children, the Sawanos, I call upon you, I say the old words of the fisherman. I speak to you three times with the loud voice of the shell.

"O, ho. O, ho, ho."

The fan made of the wings of eagles scorched slowly on the fire and poured forth a dense white smoke. Nymwha stood before it, tall and waiting. His blanket drooped from his shoulders to his feet. He raised his hands three times before the fire, saying the secret words.

Suddenly the feathers sublimed in an intense, clear flame. They crackled. Nymwha drew the old conch shell from under his blanket and blew on it.

All the woods echoed back as though a bull buffalo had bellowed.

He blew on the shell a second time.

While he filled his lungs for the final effort, the echo answered back. Nymwha smiled. He seemed to hear the war horns of his grandfathers. He raised the shell and blew on it a third time. Not a sound came forth. Only some white dust and a few grains of sea sand. Shattered by the vibration, the ancient shell fell to pieces in his hand.

The Little Turtle saw that the big medicine of Nymwha had failed. But he was surprised not at that, but at how he felt about it. He was glad. He felt like a white man. He wanted to laugh. When the shell fell apart Nymwha had grunted.

"Hoomph."

A ghost of smoke drifted down into the meadows from the dying fire. On the pile of stones the bones of the eagle wings covered the last embers like the fingers of a skeleton hand.

Nymwha fell forward on his face, groaning. He was a man who had believed in his own medicine.

The return to the camp in the gorge was a quiet one. There were no songs along the way going back. "What you saw, you have not seen," said Nymwha to the Little Turtle, and said no more.

But the Little Turtle turned all these things over in his mind as he rode along. He was glad he had said nothing to Nymwha of his dream. It was no time to remind Nymwha that he was a white man. But the Little Turtle had certainly been reminded of it. He was no longer so content that Kaysinata had stolen him. More than the big medicine had failed. He began to ponder on what his life as a white boy might have been. "Salathiel, Salathiel Albine, you come out of the woods." How she had called him! What had they done to his father! Why was it *he* had never come back? He thought of Kaysinata in a new way, and hated him. He was sorry for his "uncle." Nymwha had cared for him. But Nymwha could care for nothing now that his medicine had failed. Already he rode his horse slumped down like an old man.

What was going to happen? Was it really better to live in the forest than to live like a white man? Kaysinata said so. How did he know? Someday I will talk to some of the captives, he promised himself. I will do so secretly. I will try to remember the words. I will tell them my name is Salathiel—Salathiel Albine. They will be glad to see me. I will ask them.

So he pondered and tried to comfort himself as he rode back to the lodges by the Beautiful River. When they got there they were met by the tremendous news of Braddock's defeat.

Curiously enough, it was that news which confirmed

the Little Turtle in beginning to ponder the ways of being an Indian. He was ashamed. And he was afraid now they would begin to remember he was a white man, after all. He became more than careful for one of his years, although apparently he was reckless. He began to consider carefully the consequences of anything he did. This was partly due to the influence of Nymwha. Nymwha had made him learn many things by heart. Now he said them over and considered them. He found that he had always thought the English must win in the end. It might not be so now. It appeared that the Red Coats were no longer invincible. What then?

Now the youth called Little Turtle or Salathiel Albine— he did not yet know which—was not alone in his predicament.

No battle fought in North America has ever had such far-reaching and permanent effects as Braddock's defeat. Afterward, the battle was largely forgotten, but the effects went on. It was like the tolling of a great bell in time, whose ripple of sound grew less, but ever widened out in eternity. On the sunny afternoon of July 9, 1755, in the ravines of a forest meadow along a river whose name most Englishmen have never heard, General Edward Braddock, a perfect product of the Horse Guards, lost quite definitely and permanently the empire of Marlborough and Queen Anne, in the reign of his Majesty, George II.

It was the first day on the white man's calendar which Salathiel could be absolutely sure of. It was, of course, irrevocably fixed in his memory. Consciously or unconsciously, like most other Americans of his generation and time, he arranged the years of his life as before and after Braddock's defeat, as time wore on.

The French and the Indians at Fort Duquesne went crazy. They could hardly believe themselves. The British Red Coats had been beaten! They had been massacred and stampeded. There was a way to stop them. The Indians and the Americans remembered the way. The

French straightway forgot. Like brave Europeans they could not shake off an habitual preference for being massacred en masse. For them the battle was counted a victory, but it was also the beginning of the end of their empire.

Salathiel remembered to his dying day the fierce red glow in the sky by night above the river gorge about Fort Duquesne after the battle, the constant firing of cannon, and the fusillades of joy that went on day after day; the passing of canoes down the Ohio filled with prisoners with blackened faces, and their Indian captors howling like demons. It was a full week before the place quieted down. Those who had run away before the battle returned to take scalps and trophies from the stricken field. He and Nymwha beheld all this at a distance, from the high rocks above the river. Nymwha would not go to the fort.

"Let them go by," said Nymwha; "this is the end."

It was not until many years later that Salathiel thought he knew what his uncle, the Shawnee, meant.

Seven days after the victory Kaysinata came to see Nymwha. He was still quite drunk. He was still dirty and bloody; covered with fringes of scalps that he had belted about him. He never knew himself how many he had taken. Any chief could have as many as he wanted. The dead lay heaped in the bushes, piled three deep.

Kaysinata boasted himself to Nymwha. He vaunted his brave deeds, and the success of the great medicine.

Then Nymwha laughed. He told Kaysinata what had happened. He showed him the fragments of the broken shell. It was only then that the Big Turtle finally grew silent.

"Listen," said Nymwha, "Kaysinata, my brother, you are a fool. The English and the Long Knives will come back again. The days of our people are numbered. They will be broken even as the shell broke in my hand. The firewater will overpower you. You will lie with your face down in the mud like Mawakis. You will bite the dust.

There is no longer a way to speak with our grandfathers. They have nothing to say to us. We are no longer their children. Go, and take the Little Turtle with you. He also is a paleface. Even your son has been stolen from the white man, and you will have to give him back again. Treat him well, lest his people remember when they ask for him. Remember what I have said. I am Nymwha. I am not the spirit of firewater. I am sober."

Kaysinata listened, but he was furiously angry. He made the Little Turtle and Mawakis leave the lodges of Nymwha. He shouted insults at Nymwha, and boasted. But he was sad and terrified at heart. All that summer he raided the English frontiers to prove that Nymwha was wrong. He brought gifts and spoil—horses, clothes, and weapons—back to Logstown. Soon the villages along the Beaver were full of miserable women and children "captivated" from the settlements. There were only a few men. . . .

Then the English began to come over the mountains again.

Nymwha was right. After only three winters the English were back at the fort at the Great Forks. The General Forbes was a sick man, but he had himself carried in a blanket bed across the mountains. That general died, but the English stayed. The General Stanwix came next and started building a fort at the Great Forks out of brick. They called it Fort Pitt now. The French had gone. They would never come back again. They had given the Indian lands to the English. What was a man with many English prisoners going to do? The times were terrible. Kaysinata raided, and drank. He fell down in the mud and put his face in it with Mawakis. Sometimes there was nothing to eat. Finally he made peace with the English at Fort Pitt.

Meanwhile, the Little Turtle had been forced to shift for himself as best he could. Many Indian lads had to do that in those days. The Little Turtle had become a lone wolf. He was what the older warriors called a "young scalp." He had gone secretly to Nymwha, and taken his advice. It was good advice, well suited to the times. And what times they were could best be known by following the Little Turtle.

7

How They Found Moses in the Bulrushes

THERE were four of them, all about the same age. There was the Little Turtle, Locust Mouth, Whippoorwill Hill, and Black Hawk. They were not quite young braves yet, but old enough to be free of the squaws. When the firewater and the English traders came now they had learned to flee the lodges on the Beaver and live to themselves.

It was usually sometime between the first fall of leaves and the coming of ice on the waters when they stole a canoe and lived on the islands up and down the Beautiful River in the fat season of the year. As time went on, and their tactics improved, they returned only at longer and longer intervals to the village, and they gradually increased the scope of their depredations.

It was a life of complete freedom and irresponsibility, maintained by infinite cunning and stealth. No small animal and not many large ones were safe from them. The islands they haunted at first were long reaches of low forest and flood meadows with high clay banks or an occasional brown sand beach. They stretched for miles along the river in places. They teemed with small life: squirrels, rabbits, coons, possums, waterfowl, and turkeys. The antlered deer swam the river between them, back and forth.

Snapping turtles were their first and by no means most contemptible enemy. Locust Mouth lost a big toe. Despite that, they learned to snare the ducks in the water. They caught enormous bewhiskered catfish, and feasted. One island was a grove of nothing but chestnut trees. The squirrels tasted sweetest there. It became the favourite haunt of the band. A swift current with eddies protected that island's shores. There were mussels and clams on the shoals.

But they moved often. It was partly instinctive precaution and partly restlessness. When they tired of one island they moved to another at night under the stars. The small, black canoe made no noise. They would land, hide out in the rushes to make sure no one was before them, and then settle down for a period. An informal and natural discipline kept them together, and the fear of discovery.

The hand of all men, even the squaws', would be against them. As the strict tribal customs of the Indians began to break up and lapse in the years of war, raids, and no less devastating trade with the English, such freelance and wandering bands of hungry and murderous youngsters were not unusual. Their success depended entirely on what skill they could develop among themselves. They were the crows, or the hawks and eaglets, of the forest, upon whom no one had mercy—if they were caught.

The band of the Little Turtle existed successfully at odd times for several years by the simple strategy of never being seen or heard, and by not stealing from or closely approaching Indian villages. They throve on and in the forest alone. They hunted silently with snares, bow and arrow, tomahawk, and scalp knife. They had one small iron pot under which they lit carefully smokeless fires in hollow clay banks. There were three thin blankets amongst the four of them. That arrangement kept the boy on watch cold, alert, and awake. There was little talking, and shouting was unthinkable. They called themselves the "Shadow Brethren," and acted the parts. For the rest, there were four fine scalping knives, three good, keen English hatchets, and the canoe and paddles. That was all, except for the Little Turtle's flint and steel and his powerful bow of arc wood. He made his own arrows—and he followed Nymwha's advice, whom he visited secretly at the gorge from time to time.

The Little Turtle was now much taller than his bow. He was "high as the head of a horse," and he shot long, straight, and hard. He was not cruel; he simply had no qualms at all. He was like a young male panther in its third year, long, muscular, and lean.

The Shadows wore breechclouts, moccasins, and their hair in knots like little grain sheaves on the top of their heads. The rest of their heads they kept shaved. The Little Turtle had a brown scalp lock. The others were like black horsehair. That, and his grey-blue eyes, his wide, smiling mouth, and long leg bones, were all that marked his English origin.

He was always hawk-nosed, and he was now burned, tanned, and smoked a fine even copper color. As he grew older his frame became larger and more powerful than an Indian's. Fluff appeared on him, which he carefully singed off. It was an embarrassing distinction not to be tolerated. His skin thus became hardened by fire. He promised to be a young giant shortly. His muscles were like fluid oak wood, and the others were rightly afraid of him if it came to a quarrel. He simply lifted them clear of his shoulders and hurled them down with a crash. He used their own strength against them, as Kaysinata had taught him, and among the Shawnees wrestling was an ancient art. His senses were as keen as the others', and his mind gave him a wider and more certain play of thought.

He saw that when one thing happened another must follow. The others did not, unless they had seen things happen together that way before. Then they expected the same thing over and over again. He did not. That was the chief difference between him and the other Shadows, and perhaps, too, he could decide and carry things out more quickly and to a certain result, because he could remember back time and imagine the future more vividly than his brothers. "Now" was enormously

91

complete to them; night was more like the passing of a cloud than the passing of time. The forest was eternity—but not for the Little Turtle. He dreamed of something and somewhere else. He wondered. Gradually the four of them came to have but one will and purpose. It was by mutual, almost by unconscious consent that both were supplied by the Little Turtle. Black Hawk, the son of a chief, was his only rival. But he was the youngest Shadow of all.

The absence of firearms among them they finally came to realize as their chief advantage. Other people betrayed themselves sooner or later by the smoke of careless fires or the firing of guns. They performed silently, and were never out of powder or stopped by the damp.

They learned to take the deer in the water. An exhausted doe about to make a landing found four topknots swimming beside her at twilight, and her throat cut. An unerring stone, a loop in the grass, or a twig trap was the death of any small thing they fixed upon as prey. For birds—an arrow came flitting from the thicket and struck the drumming partridge from the log. They marked down what they needed and took it. There was always something for the pot. On the Isle of Chestnuts in the autumn they were even like to become fat.

They kept coming back there often after the first year, in spite of a difficult landing. The river was narrow on either side, deep and swift. There was a fall not far below. Most people went around, and the place was their own for quiet keeping. That was why and where they caught the Reverend James McArdle.

From a certain point of view the arrival of Mr. McArdle on the Isle of Chestnuts might be regarded as a sheer physical accident. That was the light in which the Shadows looked at it. He came like a fish from the stream. But even accidents are said not to occur in a timeless vacuum. And from the standpoint of Mr. McArdle himself, his sudden advent on an island in the Ohio was a beautifully special act of God. He was left there, like Moses, in the bulrushes.

James McArdle was a self-constituted missionary, Scotch-Irish from Belfast, fanatically learned, and as hard to root out of the land as a dock weed. He insisted that God had called him loudly to preach to the Indians. Some averred he might have heard another noise. But preach he did. He had played apostle to five eastern tribes in three Algonquian dialects in ten years. A sermon to the Munsees on the circumcision must have been misinterpreted by them, for they had removed both his ears instead. He had borne this with patience, however, since his vital organ, the tongue, still remained intact. And with it he had continued to preach his novel doctrine, whenever and wherever he could, to the effect that the Indians were the lost ten tribes of Israel, a remnant of God's chosen people condemned to wander in the wilderness again until the news of their redemption was brought to them.

Mr. McArdle was by no means alone in this opinion. Many of his more discreet, reverend, and regularly licensed brethren concurred—but for the most part in writing. It was only natural, then, that his rather unwelcome news of the alleged partiality of the Deity for Indians, or lost Hebrews, should not be received by the harried and burnt-out laity of the English settlements with a helpful burst of sustaining glee. Quite the contrary. Suffice it to say that even in the coldest winters the Reverend James McArdle had found himself invariably enjoying constant hot water, and many close shaves, on the indignant Pennsylvania frontiers.

Martyr and rebel to the core, no human pressure could straighten out his spiritual eccentricity. Finally, he was carried bodily out of the Conococheague settlement on a fence rail. And he was then forced to look on while some miserable squaws, three little children, and two old men of the Delawares, whom he had harboured and comforted, were quietly knocked on the head in the year of grace 1759.

Earless and disillusioned, sick at heart but indomitable, he set out westward over the new "Glades Road," lately cut by General Forbes, and for some months cobbled for the garrison and teamsters at the new Fort Ligonier on the Loyalhanna. Opportunity serving, he then joined an ammunition convoy, and the late autumn of the same year found him mending shoes on weekdays and souls on the Sabbath at Fort Pitt.

Already there was a considerable settlement at Pittsburgh. There were upward of thirty houses, traders' stores, barracks for the garrison, and a constant stream of Indians who came and went. So the field of redemption there appeared both ample and ripe. But in his hope for a harvest Mr. McArdle was once more given to suffer frustration.

The king's deputy Indian agent, George Croghan, was an Irish Catholic. It was rumoured that on the previous St. Patrick's Day he had openly drunk the health of the Pretender, in the fervour of his cups. However that might be, when sober he looked with a jaundiced eye upon the efforts of Orangemen to evangelize the "king's Indians." Once again Mr. McArdle was prevented. Nor did he fare much better in his efforts among the Welsh, Swiss, and Pennsylvania Germans of the Royal Americans in garrison.

Their commander at the time was also a Swiss, an impoverished officer, but a cultivated gentleman, who had been nourished at the very breast of Calvinism in his native Geneva, as a child. Yet—as he himself put it—when he became a man he thought as a man. He went in for mathematics, and he read Voltaire. Then, too, as a soldier he was inclined to render most things to Cæsar, and he would tolerate no spiritual advisers in the confines of the posts committed to his charge, except those "duly appointed by mundane authority to ration their celestial nonsense to the king's troops."

Thus at the very outset Mr. McArdle's dream of a Theban Legion at Fort Pitt, as well as his hopes of a harvest of souls amongst the lost tribes of Israel, were murdered, as it were, in the cradle like holy twin innocents. And when the Reverend James went in unto Herod

94

to protest—eloquently—he found instead a dapper and dangerous little soldier, who occasionally smelled at a verbena-scented handkerchief, while he rocked the foundations of Mr. McArdle's faith seriously. In short, McArdle was given his day in court, treated as an equal, as a scholar and a gentleman; and lost his case on the flaws in his own cherished argument. It was a terrible, almost a soul-shattering experience for the Reverend James, who was finally dismissed with a glass of neat brandy and the military courtesies of the gate.

And so to pastures new.

That was the only alternative to cobbling. The unknown and unconverted wilderness lay westward before him, where the lost tribes wandered *ad lib*. This was, he felt, the crucial test of his faith. He obtained a "small shallope," as doubtful as the charity which conferred it, and, despite the fact that winter would soon be coming on, he set off down the Ohio, remarking that the Lord would provide. The Beautiful River did all the rest.

It was three days later when necessity and the current drove him ashore at the Isle of Chestnuts. It was twilight, and he was weak and cold from exposure and little food. He caught his foot in a crevice of rock as he stepped ashore, and snapped his ankle painfully. He lay for a moment groaning among the rushes. Instantly four young Indians were upon him like a pack of wolves.

His dugout slowly floated off in an eddy.

Possibly because he lay perfectly still, they did not kill him immediately. They scarcely knew what to do with a perfectly inert "enemy." This was submission itself. So they stood around looking at him curiously in the last grey twilight. He had fainted, more from the pain in his ankle than from the beating they had given him. Then he came to again and said something in the Onondaga tongue. There was no reply. He tried several other dialects, with no result. Then he began to pray, for his pain was great and he thought his time had come. He said, "Our Father."

"My mom say that," said a young voice out of the darkness, with a strange thick accent.

"Who are you, then," demanded McArdle hopefully.

There was a pause. "Sal—Salathi-el Albine," the voice replied presently.

The Little Turtle could remember his name, but it had taken him some time to frame the syllables satisfactorily when he tried to speak them. For him it was a momentous reply, as well as for Mr. McArdle.

The sudden question out of the darkness, "Who are you?" had forced an issue, which, deep in his being, the boy had been asking himself over and over, and getting no answer. Now an instant reply had been demanded from the outside. There was no time to adjust the balance nicely and reconsider. The weight of the stranger's question had unexpectedly been thrown into the scale. The Little Turtle was forced to speak up, and he found it was Salathiel Albine who stood there, after all. He had simply been disguised as the Little Turtle. It was Salathiel who found himself. Now he knew.

As for the Reverend James, he felt that he was saved alive. His prayer had been answered. Hope was like a drink of strong cordial to him. He revived. He sat up, and managed to make a sign of friendship which Nymwha had taught Salathiel. He even made it understood that his dugout was floating away.

Salathiel gave the word and two of the boys plunged in and eventually returned with it. It was a long, cold swim in the darkness, and they almost missed it. McArdle had the presence of mind to reward them with a knife and spoon. Things went better after that. Meanwhile, he had been able to tell something of his predicament to young Albine.

He and the boy called Locust Mouth finally picked up the Reverend James between them and carried him to a hollow behind the bank, where they built up a fire and laid him beside it. Albine wrapped him in his blanket and they gave him some roast squirrel and hot, baked chestnuts. He sent them back to his boat for a little corn

96

meal and salt, and they baked cakes on a stone. McArdle's foot was numb now. He strained every nerve to make himself welcome. Some iron fishhooks from a small box in his pocket brought even the young Black Hawk around. Also he found that by talking slowly, and by using simple words and gestures, he could make himself understood in English by the big boy with the turtle on his breast.

Thus the evening wore away with McArdle as an object of considerable interest. Curiosity and novelty had apparently been substituted for hostility. Nothing, however, finally allayed the pain of a broken ankle, and in spite of the risks the minister was at last forced to do something about it.

He was a man of iron nerves, and after explaining as well as he could to Albine, he gave directions for setting his leg. They hauled and pulled him until he fainted again. Once the "fun" became fast and furious, and if he had groaned or cried out the young savages might have found it too interesting to leave off. But he kept silent, and he finally got them to bind his leg in a piece of heavy bark for a splint—and stop. It was an ill job, of course, and as a souvenir of the occasion Mr. McArdle limped all the rest of his life. His foot turned in.

They remained at the island for nearly a fortnight. A period of lazy Indian summer had set in. McArdle was unable to walk and the Shadows were content enough to linger. A division of spoil had taken place. The "shallope" and all the rest of the captive's small effects were divided amongst Locust Mouth, Black Hawk, and Whippoorwill Hill. McArdle himself fell to the Little Turtle as the share of the leader. He managed to preserve his Bible and watch by giving them to Salathiel, who kept them as the white man's big medicine. In that he was sincere enough, for he soon came to regard McArdle as a Nymwha among the palefaces. McArdle knew many signs of the Old Medicine. He belonged.

Through the long hours of the night the Reverend James talked to the white boy. He talked of the white lodges in the Sunrise Land beyond the mountains, where the people were more numerous than the trees of the forest. The Little Turtle listened while Salathiel within him awakened and dreamed. The glimmering vocabulary of his childhood began to come back. They said their prayers together while the others slept. The Reverend James began secretly to teach Salathiel many things. He began with the watch, which was magic and a speaking thing. For the first time, and suddenly, Salathiel became aware of the audible and visual passage of time. Where was he going, and what would he be? All this was kept private from the three other Shadows, who would never know.

Gradually the boy felt the pride of his race stir within him. It was his people who had made the watch. All that McArdle spoke of belonged to him if he should claim it. Greater than being the son of the Big Turtle was being one of the white men. All these things he kept in his breast and said nothing.

One morning the season changed suddenly and there was a skin of ice on the shallows about the island. It was time to return to the lodge of Kaysinata. They felt confident in the white man's "big canoe." They laid him in it and paddled back two days to the mouth of the Beaver. That year the Shawnees had gone farther up the creek. Near the old huts at Logstown they killed two wolves and took their skins. Every winter there were more wolves now. Wolves followed war.

The Big Turtle was proud of his son for the prisoner he had taken. He let McArdle lie by the fire in the lodge. Mawakis was pleased and happy that the Little Turtle had come back. Things would go better for her with him around. McArdle made himself useful. He made things with his hands and spoke of the Great Spirit. They soon respected and feared him. Sal Albine began to regain the use of his English tongue. Once resumed, it came back, and it went on with a rush. Hitherto, the Little Turtle had felt it beneath him to converse with white captives. But this man was different, and he was his own prisoner. He began quietly to try out his talk on some of the other captives. There were many that year. There was a certain white girl he had noticed. He spoke to her. He liked her, but she was afraid of him. She still thought he was an Indian. It was best not to tell her that he wasn't. Kaysinata might be angered. He was jealous for his son.

Meanwhile, the Reverend James McArdle's leg was slowly healing and he talked at night of many things. Mawakis would go to sleep, wake up again suddenly, and grunt. Then they would laugh, conscious that the difference between her sleeping and waking existence was merely an unpleasant surprise. The fire flickered and smoked as before. But there were new pictures in the embers for Salathiel.

8

Shadows of Indian Summer

THE YEARS were at hand when for all the English frontiers, but especially in Pennsylvania, the terrible expression "Indian summer" took on an even more deeply sinister meaning than it had had before. It was not the gorgeous, dreamful beauty of dying nature through the eastern mountains that made the season so memorable; not the quiet, noble triumph of the year. It was the renewed and extended terror of the delay of winter that made the paleface paler. The Indians were summer fighters. Winter brought surcease to the settlers. Indian summer meant more Indians longer in the fall.

After the French were driven north, and westward down the Beautiful River, there was a brief pause in hostilities. A peace was patched up between the English and the tribes along the Ohio. The hot embers of French resistance smouldered, flared up, and finally died away at Montreal. All men waited to see what the English would do. Would they return again to the Dawn Lands, or would they stay west of the mountains? Even the faithful Iroquois were restive and watchful. The Shawnees and Delawares mourned secretly for their fathers, the French. Who now would help them against the English and the Long House? But for a time they waited. They let the English traders come among them again, and took gifts from the crown. Most of their captives they kept.

When General Stanwix left Fort Pitt in the early

spring of 1760, thirty-five chiefs accompanied him eastward. Kaysinata and Nymwha went along. Some turned back at Raystown, but the half-brothers went clear to Philadelphia, leaving their horses at Lancaster.

In Philadelphia they saw the great town and the endless numbers of the Broad Hats and English. They saw the canoes with cannon that sailed upon the rivers and over the great salt lake. They saw them come from and depart into the sunrise. They saw the streets swarming with people, horses, and wagons. The drums banged, the soldiers marched. The Broad Hats spoke of peace. The church bells kept ringing. They sat in the house of the governor and dined like Manitous. The Governor Hamilton shook hands with them. He called them "my children," and they felt small. The general hung a gold medal around their necks with the English king's face on it. The speaker of the council of the Broad Hats harangued them. The honourable house gave them a few stingy presents. Then they were dressed up like British majors, all but the wig, packed in wagons, and sent off. They were kicked out at Lancaster to get home as best they might. A Broad Hat there had sold their horses to pay for the corn. People laughed at them, or looked at them with sullen hate.

Nymwha and Kaysinata had seen. They understood. When they were very small they had hunted in the forests and fished along the streams where the farms and villages now stood. They saw that the English increased mightily; that nothing could withstand them. They traded their gold medals for horses at Harris's and fled home over the mountains. At Fort Bedford a white man named Garrett Pendergass fed them, warmed them by a huge chimney in his store, and gave them new trading blankets after they had made the sign of amity. He understood the Old Medicine. He belonged. He treated them as chieftains of a great nation. It was the only kindness and real courtesy they received on the way west.

At the foot of the Allegheny ridge, by the ruins of the old Shawnee cabins, Nymwha and Kaysinata burned

101

tobacco at the graves of their fathers. Already large trees grew on the low mounds of the sleepers. They kindled a fire on the old hearth found under the soil and ashes. They saw the stars rise over the mountains in the same places as they had in ancient days. The black mountains twisted like great serpents across the starpath. The dark forests murmured with old voices. They prayed to the dead. They slept by their last fire in the beautiful valley of the land of their boyhood. They sang the song of the hunter who returns no more.

It was early summer when they got back to the Ohio. They avoided the English at Fort Pitt. The place was made strong with brick and stone now. It bristled with cannon that looked into the three rivers and the moat. The English were not going. They had built a strong house to stay in forever. It was folly to withstand them. Nymwha and Kaysinata had seen what they had seen.

They agreed to act secretly together, come what might. Nymwha went back to his lodges in the gorge near the fort. Kaysinata returned to the Beaver.

Kaysinata moved his lodges that summer clear out to the Wabash. He went hunting farther westward than ever before. The belts of Pontiac and his brother, the Prophet, were going around. Many had laid hold of them and promised not to let go. Kaysinata had not yet held one in his hand. He was hunting. He moved often. He took the Little Turtle, McArdle, Mawakis, and three of the "captivated" English women along. Black Hawk and Locust Mouth followed. They were made welcome by the fire.

They camped for a while at the salt lick where the buffalo came trampling a great road, and the huge teeth of the mysterious dead beasts were found. There were countless bones of these great animals only a little way under the earth. McArdle told Salathiel they were the bones of elephants and monsters before the Flood. They ran short of powder here, but there were no traders to go to.

"Arrows will do, as they did for our fathers," said the Big Turtle. The young men shook their heads.

Kaysinata permitted the young men much freedom now. In another summer they would be made braves of the tribe. He also listened to McArdle when he spoke of the Great Spirit. But he smoked his pipe and said nothing. He had heard from the French about Maly's Son. This was another medicine. But the words were good. McArdle was a wise man. He kept peace in the camp. He made it possible for the three captive white women to exist. Kaysinata would permit no one else to speak to them. Kaysinata respected McArdle. He let him come and go as he liked. He was good, and he was harmless. He knew the old signs.

That summer the Little Turtle, the Reverend James, Black Hawk, and Locust Mouth rode westward, clear out of the forest. They came to the prairies that belonged to the Illinois. They rode at last to the place where the trees came to an end. An ocean of grass stretched away into the sunset. Locust Mouth was frightened, heaven was so vast. But McArdle wrote a book about this country on strips of bark. He bound it together with deer sinews, and two slabs for covers. He had taught the Albine boy how to read out of his pocket Bible.

He and the two Indian boys and young Albine hunted buffalo together on the prairies. The Illinois were friendly with them. They were very cleanly, and lived in beautiful villages. Even their dogs were brought to be village broken. It was a good summer. Salathiel learned to make the marks that spoke on the bark. McArdle practised him constantly. He made him write most of the book about the Fox Indians and the prairie. They made pens out of the feathers of wild geese. Salathiel wrote down what McArdle would say. He had to spell every word correctly. They used many strips of long bark.

Out of his Bible McArdle began to demonstrate the meaning of words. He taught God and language at the same time. He explained and explained. He acted and gestured. He even drew rough pictures. In two years he taught Salathiel how to count and cipher.

He began with sticks of wood, stones, fingers and toes, and ended with geometrical figures. Secretly the missionary had great hopes for the boy over whose mind and soul he laboured. He felt that he owed him his life. Salathiel Albine could now speak his native tongue much better than he knew. The Reverend James McArdle was a bigoted enthusiast, but a learned man. He had come to preach to the Indians, but the Lord had shown him another work. More and more his time was taken up with the white captives he came across. There were many of them, even among the Illinois. And there were many more farther east among the Shawnees and Delawares.

In the winters McArdle went from one Indian village to another through the Ohio country, administering to the captives and preaching to them or the Indians whenever he could. He and the Little Turtle wrote the names of these captives and where they came from upon bark tablets and concealed them.

Most of the Indians were in awe of McArdle. They saw that the finger of the Great Spirit had touched his head. There could be no doubt of it. He even gave things away because people needed them. He did kind deeds without asking anything in return. Also he set bones and attempted to treat disease. In this he was not always successful, but many in their own time and way were grateful.

Thus the Reverend James could pass from tribe to tribe, and was welcome. His knowledge of Indian tongues was now astonishing. And many a hopeless white prisoner had cause to bless him. The smallpox came walking through the forest in '61, and in many a village where there had been songs there was silence. McArdle bound the scabs of the spotted sickness on the arm of Sal Albine. The boy was sick, but he soon recovered. It was a light case, and he was never troubled again by the spotted sickness. This "cure" tended to cement the bond between Salathiel and McArdle, when they returned to the Beaver again in the early autumn after the great hunting westward.

That was the last fall that the Shadows hunted together as a free band of young scalps. That year they ranged the forest northward to the great lake called Erie. Raids on the settlements had once again surreptitiously begun. There were many small war parties passing to and fro from the mountains. The Shadows were strong young hunters now, but that autumn it was dangerous work. They stole what they needed from war parties and others, and fled. They became enormously skilful and cunning.

They stole horses and loot from famous warriors returning from the settlements. They grew proud of themselves, and they grew bolder. Near Venango, on the Allegheny, they caught some Indian girls in a river cornfield and lay with them. Most of the girls were pleased and kept quiet, but the Little Turtle had no such luck. He was dead-white under his breechclout, and his girl was afraid of him. She cried out bitterly, and the old men came swarming out of the villages with muskets. The boys had to swim down the river to their horses and ride away with the bullets whistling around them. It was a close thing. After it was over the others, particularly the young Black Hawk, boasted. They were men now. They had proved it. Sal Albine said nothing. He knew he was white, and different from his comrades. He was finally convinced of that. The Indian girl had been afraid of him. He was a stranger. She had screamed.

Kaysinata was very angry when they returned. Ganstax, a Seneca chief, one of the Mingoes, had complained to him. The Shadows had been recognized at Venango. It was time such foolishness was over, said the Big Turtle. Next year they must be received as full warriors, take squaws among the Shawnees, and have their own lodges.

In these days Kaysinata and Nymwha were both much troubled. Secretly, they wished to remain friends with the English. But Kaysinata had been forced to lay hold of the war belt sent by Pontiac. He had sent blue wampum in return. Nymwha was not a great warrior. His actions

105

were not so jealously watched. He promised to make medicine and spy on the English. He was plausible. He left the gorge and moved upriver nearer to the fort on a stream called Sawmill Run. The English had built a lumber mill there and posted soldiers near the mouth of the creek. The place was almost opposite the fort. Nymwha felt safer there. He warned his friend McKee of the trouble to come. The commandant began quietly to prepare. . . .

In the spring all the tribes were to rise as one man and at one time. They were to surprise all the English forts west of the mountains and massacre the garrisons to a man. They were to fall on the settlements at the time of the spring corn planting. That year there would be no harvest but death on the frontier. All the cabins and little villages west of the mountains were to be burned. There was to be no mercy. The hatchet was to speak to the English from the Great Lakes to the Potomac. The silence of the forest was to resume. Even the Six Nations wavered in their loyalty to the English king. Many of the Senecas and all of the Mingoes joined Pontiac. There were many secret councils. All were to act together. There was to be only one enemy, the paleface. The Shawnees and their grandfathers, the Delawares, secretly rejoiced. Wait, wait until the spring!

Unfortunately, some could not wait. The excitement was too great. Raids began, led by individuals, even in the autumn before. Many prisoners, women and children, were brought back for hostages. There were more mouths than ever at a time when there was little food. Sickness came with the white captives. The winter was long, fierce, and bitter. No one had ever seen or heard so many wolves before. They sang at night. "It is the death howl of the land," whispered the squaws. The plans of men, they knew, did not always succeed. White children with the Little Spots had been brought to the villages on the Beaver.

That new trouble ran through the lodges of the Shawnees, the Mingoes, and the Delawares for miles back

106

into the country like fire through a dry pine forest. Few entirely escaped. Many strong old warriors died. Locust Mouth and Whippoorwill Hill were stricken. They built a sweat lodge, and threw water on the hot stones, and sat in the steam. They died the next day, speechless and swollen. The Little Turtle and McArdle buried them. Measles was the English name of that death.

The Little Turtle buried many friends. He was not sick with those spots either. All who crawled into the sweat lodge died, but that made no difference to the others. It was the thing to do. Mawakis died. She also was speechless. She gave the Little Turtle the two gold coins on a bar that hung about her neck, medals that had come from her grandmothers. She patted his hand, and her eyes turned back in her head. The Little Turtle wept. McArdle said it was right he should do so. Black Hawk came and mourned with him. He was the only other Shadow left.

Salathiel grew impatient. He heard of the plans for attacking the English. Many rumours flew about. Salathiel Albine began to think it was time to run away. "Wait," said McArdle, "the time to do that will disclose itself."

Kaysinata sat in his empty lodge and drank firewater. He mourned for Mawakis and for old companions. Now that his squaw was gone, he missed her. He was troubled about the coming war. Nymwha had sent him secret messages. He would not himself come to the Beaver.

Kaysinata was alone in the lodge now with the Little Turtle and the Reverend James McArdle. The fire often went out. He sat with his head leaning against a keg of firewater. He drank from it with a wooden spoon. The snakes came for Kaysinata, and McArdle and the Little Turtle held him down. They put a stick in his mouth and tied it there. In a few hours, they were able to take it out and he talked to them again of things everybody could see.

The traders had been murdered or warned away. Cloth and food and blankets were very scarce. Clothes wore out. That winter many dressed in wolfskins, and all but starved. Many captives died. Spring, it seemed, would

never come. At the fort the English feasted and cele-
brated Christmas, 1762. The commandant kept his
powder dry and handy.

9

Witchcraft and Deep Snow

MARY CALAHAN was a white witch. She was a poor Celtic bogtrotter sold out of Ireland into the plantations by some London snatchers, and later "captivated" by the Indians along with her American mistress and her daughter near Frederick, in the province of Maryland. It was she, and her mistress and *her* daughter, who had gone along to do the squaw work for Kaysinata on the western hunting of the summer before.

"Malycal," as the Indians called her, could neither read, write, nor speak much English. She spoke Erse as though it were a living liturgy, and her life mostly had been bright, age-old misery. But for all that she was a wisewoman from the hills of Munster with half an eye at times into the past or the future. It was a trick she had of cocking her eye into the mist. She foresaw the death of her mistress in detail, and foretold it with tears. But to no avail. For Mistress Jessica Lloyd was a proud, tireless woman, who despised the Irish even more than the Indians. Mary was left behind for her trouble when Mistress Lloyd and Miss Eva tried to escape in a bark canoe to Fort Pitt. They were drowned on the falls in the Beaver, and wolves tore their faces after they were dead.

The next day William Wilson, a trader, came from Maryland and offered to ransom the Lloyds from the Shawnees. Wilson then wanted to take Mary back to Maryland, and offered Kaysinata four hundred blue wampum shells and his tow bag for her, but Mary did not want to go. She had five years to serve yet at Lloyds. She said the work was easier with the Indians, and that she hated the bloody English, who were cruel and cold as the Western Sea. Kaysinata let her have her way and refused to part with her. So she stayed on to make hominy for his lodge and foretell the weather and the hunting and certain select deaths.

That had been in the early fall and Wilson was still able to get back to the fort. He was the last trader to visit the villages on the Beaver till the war was over, and his scalp prickled, for he felt the hatchet raised in the air over his head.

When Mawakis died at the beginning of winter, Malycal had taken her place and did all the chief's work for him, taking better care of the lodge than any squaw, though she would sleep in no man's blanket. Her fleas did their own hopping. She preferred to scratch alone, she said. No one troubled her.

All the other women in the village were afraid of Malycal, both white and Indian. She knew when they were going to die. Sometimes she laughed to herself, and sometimes she told them. She came and went pretty much as she pleased. People gave her tobacco when she needed it, so she would not think ill of them. When she drank she sang long songs in Irish. She sang the "Cattle Drive." She was afraid of McArdle because he spoke Latin like a mass priest. He forbade her to mutter at him. On the whole, and considering, they got along together in the lodge not badly. And it was well they did, for it came on to be one of the worst winters ever known.

Malycal foretold the great snow that lasted nearly a month.

It was her business to inform Kaysinata of the weather and he valued her much for it, because it helped the hunters. She would go out into a clearing, lie down, and look up at the sky for a long time. Presently she would stop winking and her face went dead. In the evening she would come back into the lodge, eat, and speak of the weather.

Salathiel learned to believe her. He wrote down what she had said would happen on certain days, and it came out her way. Even McArdle was half convinced. Before the great snow came they roofed in the lodge of Kaysinata with pine slabs, and Malycal stuffed moss and clay between the logs of the walls like sod in a Munster shebang. She also brought in some coal which she had dug out of the streambank, like peat. It made the first coal fire Salathiel ever saw. It was so hot McArdle had to build a clay and stick chimney to contain it.

Many now came to see the coals glowing, until Malycal began to bid farewell as soon as they poked their heads into the chief's house. Some thought, afterward, she put the *kibosh** on those she said good-bye to then. At last Kaysinata began throwing the hatchet at visitors and they stayed away both day and night.

Then the snow came.

Great black clouds of ducks and other wildfowl from the lake regions, flying south, began to darken the sun the day before. Next the sky came down close to the forest and turned pearl grey. The third day it grew dark as evening. Then it began to snow. It snowed for nineteen days.

Sometimes it stopped at night when the wind died down, and the wolves could be heard howling. They gathered on the tops of the hills to sing. Otherwise the wind came steadily from the north. The forest began to lean towards the south. High trees finally collapsed quietly. At last no one could go out, the snow was so deep. They stayed in the lodges and ate what they had, and waited. The Shawnees did not make snowshoes then like the Ottawas. They were the people of the south and it was not done. Everybody along the Beaver was soon pretty hungry.

There was also an earthquake that winter before the

---

*That is, *the cap of Death*.

snow went. It broke the ice on the river in places. The ground rumbled. Frozen catfish were thrown up out of the mud. It was a great help to those on the Beaver Creek, for no one could hunt in the soft drifts, and the fish saved many from starving. They came alive on the fire. Large, white horned owls came from the far north and sang to the villages till men's blood froze. Some people went to the fort to beg from George Croghan. They got salt beef there, but no powder. The commandant, Captain Ecuyer, said he would give them plenty of powder and shot when they came in the spring. He laughed when he said it.

When a hard crust at last formed on the snow, it was Salathiel and McArdle who did most of the hunting. What little fresh meat there was that winter they brought in. They took sleeping bears out of hollow trees. The deer had gone over the river. Even rabbits were scarce, for the owls and wolves lived on them. They shot grey wolves for their coats, and trapped otters. One day about mid-winter they killed a young elk. It was great luck. But they had ranged far to find him, and it took them two days to get the carcass home over the snow. They hung it on trees at night and stood the wolves off with a leaping fire. At that they were nearly frozen, but the meat was desperately needed. In fact, it came in too late. When they got back to the village they heard Malycal keening, giving the Irish death howl.

Most of the white captives had been done away with in a massacre.

There was nothing for them to eat and they would have died anyway, said Kaysinata. It was a measure well meant, to save trouble. The useful and strong had been saved. Now there would be enough meat to go around. Those who had been done away with were stuffed into the river through a hole in the ice. If anyone came looking for them they would not be found. Kaysinata was anxious the news should not be taken to the fort.

McArdle listened sadly to the chief and then went outside of the lodge to weep. He crossed off eleven names

112

on his bark tablets and put a little hatchet after them. Salathiel saw there was now quite a bundle of these bark tablets with prisoners' names, wrapped in deerskin. It was the record of most of the Indian captives held west of Fort Pitt. McArdle had been at great pains to get the names set down. Salathiel had helped write down many of them himself. He could remember the lists, too. McArdle and he had memorized them together. So many prisoners among the Delawares, so many among the Mingoes, the Shawnees, and the Illinois—so many. The Little Turtle made a singsong of all the names. He was to say nothing of the lists on the bark tablets. They were to go sometime to the fort. McArdle was afraid he would be killed and the names lost. If so, young Albine and the song would remember them. It would be time to take the list to the fort in the spring, McArdle said.

Salathiel had made up his mind to go to the fort in the spring, anyhow. He would tell them that he was English and sing the song of the lists to the captain-commandant. Mawakis was gone now. He was tired of the gloomy life in the lodge. Kaysinata was getting old and demanding. Salathiel would not stay to go on the warpath against his own people. He would leave and go clear back to the inhabitants. Maybe he could find him a girl there. He was beginning to be much troubled under his breechclout. Black Hawk laughed at him. He took the young squaws into the woods and tried them out. He boasted often. He laughed at the Little Turtle for wanting a white girl. "What is the difference?" he asked.

"To me, but not to you," said Salathiel. "You are an Indian."

Black Hawk was surprised.

When the snow finally went there was a great flood. Half the low country along the Beaver was like a lake. But it was better for the Indians that way. The game was driven to take refuge on high ground and hilltops that were now temporary islands. There was a great slaughter and everyone had plenty and to spare.

Kaysinata now sent for rum to Venango. He paid a

great price for it. No regular traders came that year on account of the troubles. There was a scarcity of cloth, powder, and blankets. Many dressed in skins again like their fathers. Few had expected this. The young warriors were now anxious to begin the attack on the English forts in order to plunder the stores. It was hard to restrain them. Kaysinata called in the Shawnees up and down the Beaver. He wished to delay the attack until the time appointed. Two bears were killed, and he gave a feast. He also gave out the firewater. As a consequence nothing was decided. This suited Kaysinata well, for he was a much-perplexed man.

McArdle saw to it that the whites who were still left alive had pickings from the feast. There were still seven of them in the vicinity, four children and three women. They had been afraid to call attention to themselves by asking for food. It was the sight of these captives which finally enabled the Big Turtle to make up his mind what course to take.

He had tried to walk two paths at once, and so he staggered with uncertainty. He wished cautiously to remain friends with his powerful fathers, the English; he longed to rise against them with his brother Pontiac and drive them from the land. Nymwha was partly responsible for this. He pointed out that, since the French and Indians together had failed to drive out the English, it was not likely that the Indians would now succeed alone. Nor would the Six Nations be with Pontiac. About the time the sugar sap began to run, a messenger came from the Long House to Kaysinata saying, "Beware how you play the fool." So the Big Turtle was left on tenterhooks. He saw his son, the Little Turtle, was about to leave him. In his heart Kaysinata was sad. He smoked much. He asked his pipe many questions. But there was no rum left to give him courage to answer them.

Finally, he decided he would use the remaining captives to stay friends with the English by sending them safe and sound back to Fort Pitt. The commandant there, the Captain Ecuyer, was always demanding return of white

114

captives. Now the Big Turtle would return them and so gain favour. And he would send the Little Turtle and McArdle along with the captives to guard them, and to take wampum to the commandant. The Little Turtle could make the speeches to the Captain Ecuyer that would go with each belt of wampum. McArdle could explain away the massacre of the other prisoners, if they asked him. He could say they had been drowned in the flood. He was a man of God, whom the English would believe. Also he was an important prisoner himself.

All this, of course, was to be done quite secretly. If Pontiac or his own people objected, he would explain it as a crafty move to lull the commandant into security before the attack. The more the Big Turtle smoked over the problem the better he liked what his pipe told him. One thing he liked especially. No one could say now that his son, the Little Turtle, had run away to his own people. If he stayed on at the fort, Kaysinata could blame the English. He, himself, would not lose honour.

Kaysinata hoped that the Little Turtle would stay at the fort; that he would return to his own people, and never come back. It was not that in his own way the Big Turtle was not fond of the Little Turtle. He was a good son, he admired him for his courage, wits, and strength. But the ritual reason why Kaysinata had shot the big, yellow-bearded smith in the back, stolen his boy baby and adopted him, had lapsed; it no longer held good. Nymwha's big medicine had failed. The clan of the Turtle could no longer speak with the grandfathers of the Sawanos. The old shell was broken. The words of the fisherman could be forgotten. The way was closed. The Clan of the Turtle could cease.

It was for this, and not for sorrow of personal parting, that Malycal one night saw the tears run down the cheeks of Kaysinata, as the chief sat in his own corner and smoked bitter stems. Now that Mawakis was gone, Kaysinata talked with Malycal alone, or he talked to his grandfathers. It was hard to tell which. He muttered. But Malycal understood. Her people also had been driven west by the English long, long ago. She made medicine in her gloom of the lodge where the coal fire flickered. The medicine of his own people had failed him.

Nymwha agreed that the plan for the captives was a good one. Still it was hard for Kaysinata to come to the point. He began to feel like an old man.

At last he called the Little Turtle and McArdle to him and explained his scheme. He let them see many things for themselves. He put matters so as to save his own face. As for Salathiel and McArdle, if they saw their own opportunity, they also remained silent. And that, too, was understood.

Kaysinata gave the Little Turtle four strings of wampum. These he was to take with him along with the captives to Fort Pitt. Then he was to lay the strings across the knees of the commandant and say his say. The first string was to wipe away the captain's tears, another was to open his eyes, the third was to renew the ancient friendship of Kaysinata and his fathers, the English. The fourth belt was to cause the captain to remember it. Kaysinata made the Little Turtle learn the speeches solemnly. Once more McArdle had to go out of the lodge to hide his emotion, but this time it was to laugh. The pains the good minister had taken with Salathiel Albine would not be in vain, he saw. The youth would be delivered out of the hands of the heathen with his soul and mind alive. "Blessed be the name of the Lord, whose ways are inscrutable."

It was spring now, but there was yet a chill in the air. The great flood had gone down the river leaving ice behind it. Part of the works at Fort Pitt had been caved in along the riverbanks. The commandant laboured desperately to repair them. The Indians gathered their tribes for the attack. Still Kaysinata delayed. Almost a month went by.

One day word came by an Ottawa runner that nearly all the English forts westward had been taken. The hatchet of Pontiac had fallen. The DeTroit was besieged. Niagara was beleaguered, Venango attacked. Soon they, too, would fall. The surprise was disastrous and complete. All the English were cut off from their friends beyond the mountains. There could be no holding back now.

The war belts passed through the forest and the tribes from the west and north closed in on Fort Pitt. The Shawnees rose like one man. Soon the road to the fort would be completely closed. Already the commandant was firing great guns at the canoes that tried to pass up and down the rivers. Kaysinata sent for the Little Turtle and McArdle in frantic haste.

He called the seven captives into his lodge and explained. McArdle made a prayer to the Great Spirit. Kaysinata gave them new blankets and a little parched corn. He also showed them a long canoe concealed in the bushes, and gave a musket and powder to McArdle.

By no means were they to fall into the hands of any passing war parties. They were to go by night and slip secretly past the watchers and into the fort. If necessary, they could stop with Nymwha at his lodges on Sawmill Run until opportunity served. The fort was just across the river. Nymwha understood. He would help. To blunder now might cost the lives of the captives and bring down the wrath of Pontiac upon Kaysinata. Let them hurry, and they still might make it. McArdle was to dress himself as a half-breed Frenchman supposed to be bringing messages from the DeTroit. The Little Turtle was to go as the young brave he seemed to be.

They waited in the lodge till night fell. At the last moment, parting from his son was not so easy for Kaysinata. He gave the Little Turtle a curious thing to remember. He told him never to eat turtle meat of any kind, lest it be the end of him. Then Kaysinata put his hand on the sign on Salathiel's breast and Salathiel's on his own, and made him promise solemnly to return if ever he or Nymwha sent for him. Then he gave him his ancient tomahawk and they shook hands both with the left and the right hand. This was a warrior's dismissal into the world, and Salathiel felt that. Kaysinata had been a great chief. Now he was old. The moment was poignant.

Malycal sat by, crooning. She also understood. She gave Salathiel a crucifix, which she made out of two hazel sticks bound together, and her blessing. She gave them all, the women and children, and even McArdle, "good luck," and a cup of hot fish soup. Then she covered the fire in the lodge with ashes.

They went down quietly as a cloud passes in the darkness to the banks and the black water of the Beaver Creek. The ice had now long passed away. The trees would soon be in full leaf. The owls bubbled and sang. A fish jumped in the water. No one said a word. The scared children had long since learned not to whimper. The women were grim. A young moon looked through the western branches, sinking rapidly. Soon there would be only black darkness in the tunnel of branches that met over the creek. As yet the far ripples of the stream still sparkled.

They began to embark.

10

A Marriage Is Recorded on Slippery Elm Bark

THE THREE WOMEN wrapped the four young children in blankets and put them in the bottom of the canoe. The women sat up. McArdle paddled in the bow; the Little Turtle in the stern. They slid out onto the dark waters of Beaver Creek. For a moment they stayed with paddles poised while the current swung the canoe. The Little Turtle looked back. Kaysinata stood on a high point of land with a single pine tree on it. The eagle feathers in the chief's hair spread out raggedly against the sinking moon. He wrapped his blanket about him with both arms and stood there darkly. The paddles dipped and the canoe slid forward. Presently it glided around a bend into the forest. Kaysinata vanished. Here and there the creek still glittered in the dying moonlight. The whippoorwills cried and answered one another. The moon sank.

The fast, little river ran like a twisting cavern through the forest. Here the water raced swiftly; there it would widen out into shallows under the stars, and the swift impulse of the paddles was necessary as the current slackened. Afterwhile, they began to hear the wolves howling along the bluffs of the Ohio, still many miles ahead of them.

Sal Albine could see the dim figure of the woman who sat facing downstream in the forward part of the big canoe, the silver flash of McArdle's paddle in the bow. But immediately in front of Salathiel was the blanket-draped shadow and dark head of a young girl. Her golden hair was done in braids and he could see the white glimmer of her neck in the V between her pigtails. That winter he had noticed her several times moving about among the lodges, helping one of the squaws dress deerskins. He remembered she had been singing at her work. It was a simple and monotonous little tune, the "Black Joke." He leaned forward between paddle strokes, humming the theme. She looked back at him startled.

"What's your name, girl?" he asked.

"Jane Sligo," she murmured.

"Mine is Salathiel Albine," he whispered.

"I thought you were the Little Turtle, the chief's son," she said.

"I'm white, like you," he replied.

There was a pause while they paddled around the bend. The howling of the wolves was much nearer now.

"Take me with you to the fort," she whispered eagerly. One of the women looked back. They were both silent awhile.

"In my blanket?" he asked in a low tone, between paddle strokes. She did not reply.

"Jane!" he pleaded, whispering her name. The woman in the bow of the canoe looked back again.

"Your mother?" he asked, after the woman had turned and was looking ahead again. She shook her head and made a circular motion about the top of her head. He understood then that her mother had been scalped.

"I'll take you," he promised.

She put her hand behind her back and gripped his. Her hand was warm and soft, with little pads of calluses on it from grinding corn. He leaned forward and kissed her between the braids of her hair. Her hair smelled of pine smoke. They both sat silent now. The woman ahead did not look back again. They were nearing the great river.

The canoe went forward into the night with sweeping strokes. In the bow the Reverend James McArdle began to breathe hard. His young companion in the stern was suddenly setting him a strong pace. Presently the night seemed to open up before them. A great stretch of sky shimmering with milky stars gave them the feeling of floating out into eternity. The stars seemed to blink together at the chorus of wolves answering one another from bank to bank of the great river.

They floated out onto the calm bosom of the Ohio. Here and there the gaunt outline of a great tree with writhing branches drifted by, for the river had recently been in flood. On their right was a long sand spit that ran out like a white leprous finger into the black water that poured from the mouth of Beaver Creek. Five or six wolves were growling over something there. Their eyes dripped like molten coins. It was necessary to pass close by that place in order to avoid an eddy. McArdle and Albine plied the paddles rapidly. The dark bundles on the sand spit that the wolves were dragging about were the bodies of those massacred weeks before. They seemed to have gathered together at the mouth of the river. One of the women moaned.

"Oh, God," said she, "why did we'uns ever leave Lancaster? It's them there now."

The canoe shot by.

They turned its bow into the current and felt the slow drag of the mighty stream against them. McArdle began to repeat the Twenty-third Psalm. The women turned to quiet the children who had been scared by the wolves. Far ahead there was a great wavering red light in the sky. Perhaps the fort was burning. A storm was brewing over in the east. The light of the flames beat up under the thunderheads.

The little company crouched low and wrapped their blankets about them as the chill night wind sang past their ears. There must have been a hailstorm somewhere. Luckily there was no rain. On that reach of the river it was as clear as a new mirror. The dark mass of a forested island began to loom up before them. They would hide there all day and go on the next evening. The lodges of Nymwha were at the sawmill built by the English soldiers just across the river from Fort Pitt. They had agreed to go there first. It was at the mouth of a little stream called Sawmill Run. It would take them at least another night's paddling to get there. The loom of the island seemed to float slowly down upon them.

They beached the canoe and hid it carefully. Albine made sure they were alone on the island. They went inland into the forest under the great elm boughs that hung down over the banks. There was a high bank that leaned forward at an acute angle hollowed out by some ancient flood. It was dry there now and the ledge beneath was deep with half-rotted leaves. They sank down into the leaves thankfully. Dawn began over the river. The exhausted voyageurs slept.

Sal Albine took Jane Sligo by the hand and led her off into the thicket. He knew a deep hollow under the roots of an ancient catalpa that had outweathered more than four hundred seasons. There was no wind now. The morning sun beat into the place gratefully, and bathed the erect column of the tree with pale golden light. The girl stood patiently, hanging her head in confusion while he spread his blanket for both of them. He pulled her down to him. They sank into a great depth of dry leaves that gradually covered them like the sands of time.

It was hours later, and midafternoon, when, quietly raising his head above the surface of his forest covering, the boy beheld the stealthy, alert face of a startled vixen looking at him fixedly over a neighbouring tree root. Her barking had wakened him. Jane was reluctant to leave her bed where the warmth of the sun had penetrated. It was delicious among the fragrant leaves. They rose unwillingly, and shook them off.

They returned through the woods and found McArdle and the two women and young children sitting about a smokeless fire of chestnut burrs in the shelter of the bank. They were picking bare the bones of a wild turkey. Something about them reminded young Albine of the wolves on the sand spit of the night before. He and Jane stopped for a moment, standing hand in hand.

"There they are," said the woman who had kept looking back at them the night before in the canoe. "I told you so! She's nothing but a blanket girl. I heard'm whisperin' last night. Jane Sligo, ye young slut, I'll have the hide off'n yer." She raised a branch angrily.

"What's the matter with the white squaw?" Albine asked McArdle in the Indian tongue. The face of the woman reminded him of the face of the fox that had recently looked at him. "Is she angry because no one has slept with her?"

"Her husband's dead," replied McArdle.

Jane tried to smile at the children and the other women by the fire. "We were only bundlin'," she said apologetically.

"Ye lie!" shrieked the woman, waving the branch threateningly. "Look at your blanket. Ye lie! I know ya!"

She advanced on the girl and would have beaten her, but Albine snatched the branch from her hand and shoved her away. He looked appealingly at McArdle. Meanwhile, the other woman shoved Jane from the fire when she tried to approach it.

"Keep your hands off them children," she said. "There's no place for the likes of you here. I'm a lady. I've got a juty toward them pore innocents whose mar was murdered, and I won't have no trash from the settlements that beds down in a Injun's blanket in the woods tryin' to pretend t' mother 'em."

Jane had turned pale now. She covered her face with her hands and wept.

"The young man is white," said McArdle.

"What!" said both women. "What!"

"His people must have been from Connecticut. They're good old stock there," insisted McArdle.

The women sniffed. "Why don't you make it right then?" said the lady. "You're a minister, ben't ya?"

McArdle nodded. "I'd thought of it," he admitted, "but it seemed sudden."

"Not soon enough," sniffed the lady.

"That's what I say," added the Fox. Jane sobbed. The

123

boy with the Indian topknot stood looking on, puzzled.

"Salathiel," said the Reverend James McArdle suddenly, "you'll be after getting married! Are you willing, Jane?"

The girl rose slowly from beside the fire where she had been crouching. She looked her tormentors in the face.

"I'll not be pushed away from the fire by no old women like you," she said. She came over and stood beside young Albine. McArdle took out his tattered Bible and joined their hands over it.

The Fox took a thin ring from her finger. "Here," she said, and tossed the ring to McArdle. "I'll not be needin' it much longer. I'll never see the settlements agin. I've got a lump in my breast. The crab's eating into my heart." She began to weep. The children looked on, wide-eyed.

Both the women cried while McArdle married Jane and Salathiel. He married them with a broad Scotch-Irish accent, with the Presbyterian service, and the sick woman's ring. The starved children continued to look on like so many gaunt little wolf cubs.

After it was over Jane gave Salathiel a peck on the cheek and went and sat down by the fire. The Fox moved over for her now. She took the girl's hand and fondled it. She looked at the ring on Jane's finger and wept again.

"It brought me good luck oncet. That's why I guv it yer," she choked.

Jane tried to thank her. McArdle sat on the end of a log reading his Bible. He felt he had done a good morning's work. Salathiel busied himself baking some corn-cakes on hot stones. There was no salt, but they broke the marriage bread together thankfully and with friendly smiles. McArdle traced something with his fish-gall ink on a piece of his precious bark. The "lady" signed it, and the Fox made her mark. The minister also signed it and gave it to Jane, who could read. After she spelled it out she put it carefully in her bosom.

What was it all about? wondered Salathiel Albine. What had been wrong with Jane that the women had

124

worried her so? She was a good girl. She had been happy with him. It had all gone very well and easily. He knew he was a man now. He felt contented and satisfied, but not a little puzzled. White ways were curious. He went down and drank his belly full of river water and washed the paint off his face. Let them see he was not an Indian.

Jane was delighted with him when he came back. She put her arms around him and kissed him. He smiled at her and held her hand. She would make him a good squaw.

On the whole, he liked her.

11

Outside Looking In

AT NIGHT, after the moon sank, they launched the canoe and pushed on up the river again. There were not so many wolves now. Miles ahead, as they swept around a bend, came a new sound, distant but unmistakable. It was the barking of European dogs at the fort.

Daylight overtook them before they could reach the fort. It lay only a few miles farther upriver, but beyond an island. In the darkness of the morning hours they heard rifle fire. Once the river gorge echoed to the bellowing of a great gun. The point between the two rivers, where the fort stood, was overlooked by towering cliffs. Another hour of darkness and they might have made it, but there was a clear reach of water ahead and the dawn was upon them. It was plain that if they tried to make a dash for it they would be fired on by the fort. In the fog, before the sun rose, they saw the bright flash of hand grenades being thrown into the ditch on the Monongahela side.

They were also aware now of many canoes making across both rivers away from the fort in the mist as the light grew brighter. All night the Indians crept close to harass the garrison. With the day they retreated to the opposite banks or lay concealed in hollows close under the walls of the fort. There were already hundreds of them concentrated in the country about the Great Forks.

Once a canoe came drifting downriver and quite near

them in the mist. It came near enough to hail, and
Salathiel replied in the Shawnee tongue. It was a scalping
party of Mingoes returning to the Beaver from the
Pennsylvania settlements. Albine knew who they were.
He let them pass without discovering himself. They gave
the death helloo twice and passed triumphantly westward
down the river. It was a close call. The women cowered
down in the canoe. The children whimpered. The mist
had saved them. McArdle encouraged them, telling them
their journey was near its end.

Presently they turned aside toward the south bank and
made their way into a deep creek that came down out
of the hills. A brief distance behind, the land towered up
in a series of cliffs to the plateau above. A short reach
of level bank hereabouts was covered with huge and
ancient trees. It was here that the English had built their
sawmill at the mouth of the creek. It had not been destroyed yet. They could still see its roof rising black
above the fog. The lodges of Nymwha and his squaws lay
a half mile farther upstream on the banks of Sawmill
Run. They arrived at the camp shortly after the sun
began peering into the river valley and licking up the
mists. The guns from the fort spoke. They were firing at
any canoes they could see, and spraying the banks opposite the fort with grapeshot. The commandant was a
careful man. He began each new day with a fusillade
as a matter of routine.

There was no one, besides the chief himself, but the
three squaws and the two papooses at the lodges of
Nymwha. The creek and the gorge of it was now his
winter hunting and camping ground. He received the
message of his half-brother Kaysinata with approval and
regaled the party with dried venison and hoecake. Nymwha also had recently sent wampum to the fort to make
his private peace. The English, he said, would soon be
coming over the mountains with an army to relieve the
fort. Already they were gathering at Carlisle. Of what
use, then, to howl like wolves outside their palisades?
Those who climbed the stockades only fell inside upon

127

bayonets. Their scalps were even now nailed to the gate of the fort. Nymwha and his half-brother saw eye to eye.

It would not be easy to gain admittance to the fort. By day they fired the cannon at canoes that tried to pass it or that approached too near. At night they fired from the ramparts at the slightest noise in the ditch beneath. The Indians all about were lying in wait for refugees trying to gain the fort. Nymwha assured McArdle that the matter of getting their little party into the place would have to be well planned and considered. Nymwha smoked a pipe upon it. He passed the smoke to Salathiel, who also looked thoughtful and blew the smoke in two streams from his nostrils. Nymwha advised Salathiel to go and see the lay of the land about the fort for himself. Also, at the sawmill, he said, there were two English soldiers still hidden in the loft. There was, too, a sunken boat concealed at the mouth of the creek. Nymwha had burned neither the soldiers nor the mill. He had even sent food to the soldiers. Let the Little Turtle tell the Commandant Ecuyer that when he reached the fort. Let him consider well and act. Meanwhile the white captives would be hidden and safe. Nymwha knocked the ashes from his pipe. He had spoken.

Albine went and slept with Jane. He slept all morning, rose, and ate heavily. Then he put the paint of a Shawnee warrior on his face again. That afternoon he and McArdle climbed the hills above Sawmill Run and looked along the three rivers and down on the fort. The place lay nearly a thousand feet below them, spread out like a green map. The Allegheny, or the Aligwissippi, as the Delawares called it, and the Monongahela swept together just below them to make the broad Ohio. The rivers were about half a mile wide.

Just at the point of the Y stood the fort.

The English flag flaunted brightly in the sun from a mastlike flagpole with spars upon it. The bronze and brasses of the cannon glittered. The place swarmed with people. They were driving the cattle out to pasture into the fields east of the fort with strong supporting parties of soldiers scouting before them.

The houses about the fort had all been burned. You could see the fresh scars of the burning upon the river-banks. That had probably been done by the commandant's orders, for in the upper town that stood farther away up the flat at the foot of a high hill, some houses were still left standing. There were cultivated fields there, roads and tracks that led eastward.

Women were going into the fields with sickles, with a company of riflemen before them, to cut spelts. A wagon raised the dust with a small party going out for firewood. Smoke rose from the chimneys of the barracks in the star-shaped fort and hung there like a pall in the still air of the gorge. In a garden along the Allegheny side of the fort the lacy white of appleblossoms stood out against the tender green of the leaves and lay scattered like snowflakes on the ground. Salathiel had never seen fruit trees before. He was greatly surprised by the "snow." It was a warm day.

On an island below the fort, on the other side of the Allegheny River, the skin tepees of an Indian encampment lay hidden from the ramparts, behind a small hill. Canoes were pulled up there on the beach. At a distance they looked like a row of black teeth. All of this, from the top of the cliffs south of the fort, where McArdle and Salathiel were standing, was like looking down on an ant heap. It was a view in miniature of inch-high horses and pea-sized men. But the surrounding country was gigantic.

Along the river gorges, on every side, the ancient leaf-banked forests rolled away northward, eastward, and westward, like folds of solid dark-green velvet draped along the cliffs. And the white man was down there in the fields and houses that huddled near his star-shaped fort dark in the middle of its flashing moat! His hateful, but magic activities lay spread out before the eyes of the Indians watching from the high hills along the gorges. You could see him in his bright scarlet clothes, his houses, and his glittering weapons. You could hear his dogs bark. The thunder of his cannon made the land quake.

The heart of young Albine leaped within him. The fort at the end of the long point seemed to be aimed like the head of an arrow, pointing straight westward at the heart of the Indian lands. What would happen when the great king across the water loosed that arrow from his string?

Salathiel laughed. He despised his savage childhood now. Spread before him at his feet was the scene in which his manhood should begin. Down there was his white heritage. All he had to do was to cross the river and enter into it. Indeed and indeed, Kaysinata and Nymwha were right. They were wise in their own way and time. Well, he would take their wampum to the fort, deliver their message, and have done with them. He would take Jane there, too. Later, when the siege was over, they would go back over the mountains to the settlements. All this came into the boy's mind with a rush and an invincible determination.

McArdle was excited, too. It was many years now since he had seen a white settlement. He explained, and talked, and answered a thousand questions. Secretly he was sad. He also longed to return but his conscience, he knew, would force him to stay with the Indians and the captives.

So they stood together, well hidden, in a thicket at the top of the cliff. Salathiel watched, fascinated, until evening came. The bland, smooth song of the bugles rose, echoing up out of the gorge. The sunset gun crashed. The flag came down. The dogs in the fort howled. Twilight descended. The fires of the fort, its yellow windows and little lights, began to shine and twinkle. The cressets along the parapets flared. Finally, Salathiel turned away reluctantly to follow McArdle back to the lodges of Nymwha.

Later that evening they went down the stream together to the sawmill and conferred with the soldiers. At the mill they found an English sergeant by the name of Jobson, and one Murphy, an Irish recruit. McArdle talked long with them both. He and Salathiel had a good plan to get into the fort. So they raised the sunken boat by moonlight and bailed her out to be ready to start.

Salathiel was to go alone with the soldiers when the moon sank. He was to take the Big Turtle's wampum, and McArdle's bark tablets with the names of the white captives on them, and give them carefully to the commandant.

It was finally agreed to make a dash for it after the moon went down, row across the river, and get into the outer ditch on the Monongahela side. Then they would carefully crawl up the glacis and call out. They would have to take their chances of being fired on in the dark or of meeting hostile parties of Indians prowling about the fort. It would be an advantage to have the two soldiers from the mill along. Their voices would both be known to the sentries.

The commandant was to be asked to send back as soon as opportunity served for the women and children left at Nymwha's lodges. A green flag was to be hoisted at the fort the day of the night before the commandant would send to fetch them. McArdle promised to stay until the boats came. Then he would go westward again into the Indian lands, he said. There were still many captives to see to. His release was not yet.

Salathiel saw it was no use to argue with McArdle where his conscience was involved. Instead, he went back to the lodges to say good-bye to Jane. She took the parting calmly.

"I'm a married woman now," she said. "I can wait." She showed him the bark writing with the marriage record and signatures on it, proudly. She rubbed her wedding ring for good luck.

Salathiel kissed her, and returned to the mill.

While he had been gone, the soldiers had been busy muffling the oarlocks. When full darkness came they intended to row up an eddy in the Monongahela and cross over to the fort along a sand bar that choked the river near its southern side.

Slowly the moon dropped towards the western hills. The soldiers chewed tobacco and spat into the water. As darkness became more complete, a chorus of wolves began farther down the Ohio. At the fort the dogs barked and barked.

The evening wore on.

PART TWO

The Fort

12

Inside Looking Out

SIMEON ECUYER, gentleman, captain in his Brittanic Majesty's 60th Regiment of foot, the Royal Americans, and commandant of Fort Pitt, sat near the door of his quarters and contemplated, not without military interest and a Gallic eye for the picturesque, the scene in the interior of the fort that lay before him.

He had moved that day into the "Governor's Quarters," as it was called. It was the new brick building near the southwest bastion, which Colonel Bouquet had occupied some months ago, and reserved for his use, if and when he should return. The colonel had even left his camp bed behind, with a good mattress. But, as there seemed small chance that Colonel Bouquet would be able to return from the eastern settlements and lead the remnants of his sickly West Indian regiments over the Alleghenies to the relief of Fort Pitt for some time to come, Captain Ecuyer had taken advantage of a state of siege, and the excuse of necessity, to move into his colonel's quarters.

The captain was a professional soldier and therefore an adept at judging when such necessities arose. But he was also careful, and to salve his nice military conscience he had dispatched the colonel's lame mare, now nearly well, fattened and newly shod, back to the colonel's farm in Maryland, with nothing but a burden of her own oats and a letter. God alone knew whether she and the mes-

135

senger who went with her would ever arrive at Fort Bedford. Between the prowling Indians and the wild Scotch-Irish on the frontiers, the king's property and that of his officers in western Pennsylvania was ever of uncertain tenure. Even the dispatches were frequently stopped and opened.

The good captain was tired of America. He was a native of Geneva. His mother had been a Frenchwoman of the impoverished Huguenot nobility, who had married a Swiss advocate, and Simeon, their only son, had been brought up on law, theology, the classics, and military history. As a curious consequence, he had become a soldier of fortune, a sceptic, and an officer whose native abilities could be appreciated only by brilliant superiors. They being few, his fortunes had languished. In the course of years and several services, he had grown patiently tired of unremarked success and unrewarded energy.

Now he would have liked nothing better than to sell out his commission in the Royal Americans and retire to spend the remainder of his days enjoying the excellent wines and the no less cultivated and elegant conversation for which the shores of Lake Geneva and his native city were so noted.

But he was still a mere captain, and as yet too young to retire. Only thirty-six, in fact, although he looked much older. And there was small chance of his being able to sell out. No one with money, and the influence that went with it, wanted to buy a commission in the Royal American regiment. It was all work and small pay in that service, and ungrateful work at that.

Colonel Henri Bouquet, whom the captain had first met when in the service of the king of Sardinia, had lured his friend Ecuyer from a minor but promising post in the electoral household troops at Munich, by tales of the opportunities for active service and swift promotion to be had with the Royal Americans. They were to be a new corps with new blood and new tactics suited to warfare in the New World. Ecuyer had finally succumbed. He trusted and admired the genius of his friend Bouquet.

136

They had been together at the battle of Coni, and besides that, the colonel was a Swiss himself, a native of Rolle in the canton of Vaud.

Only part of the colonel's great expectations for America had come true, however. There had been a great deal of active service in the bitter school of Indian warfare, and little more. Promotion, apparently pay itself, had all but ceased. Nevertheless, it was still a distinction and a joy to serve under Colonel Bouquet. He succeeded where "great generals" had awfully failed. Indeed, he was the prime reason why Ecuyer still employed his own not inconsiderable talents in the service of King George, despite wounds, hope deferred, and growing poverty. One was constantly learning from the colonel. There at least one advanced in one's own mind and profession, one grew. And what a rare sensation was that in any army!

For the rest of the officers in the Royal Americans the captain did not care—particularly. They were well enough. Some were professional soldiers like himself, foreigners in a foreign service. They at least obeyed orders carefully for the sake of professional reputation. But it was not always so with the bulk of the English officers who had come out to America with visions of easy garrison duty on a colonial post, only to find an Indian war on their hands. That was the worst kind of war in the world; little honour, savage and merciless fighting, incredible hardships, and fearful personal risk. A certain lack of enthusiasm among the older English officers was therefore understandable, but to Ecuyer's professional mind none the less exasperating. The subalterns alone he regarded as the grand hope of the regiment. They came from good families both in England and in America. They were the most promising material for soldiers the captain had ever seen. And in his time Ecuyer had seen a good deal of promising young material from East Prussia to Sicily.

As for the rank and file, they had been raised as the act of Parliament forming the regiment had required— in America. As it so happened, mostly in the province of

Pennsylvania. They were made up mainly of immigrant Swiss, Welsh, Pennsylvania "Dutch," Irish, Scotch-Irish, Germans, renegade Quakers, a few frontier riflemen, escaped servants, and quite a number of mariners picked up along the water front at Philadelphia, men who would rather fight Indians and be scalped than linger to be flogged to death in the king's floating hells.

In this "Militia of Babel," as the captain called it, the orders were given in English, and all by enlistment were made subjects of the British crown. That, the Mutiny Act, the hope of sometime being paid, and fear of the officers and the enemy, kept the regiment together—and one thing more. Something which it amused the captain to think all the historians he had read, except Cæsar, had contrived completely to overlook. Yet it was one of the strongest and most patent characteristics of man: loyalty to one's own military legion, *esprit de corps*. It was the only principle, so far as the captain could see, that was stronger even than self-preservation, religion, or patriotism.

Now, there were a great many unfavorable things that could be said about the Royal Americans. The English officers and the War Department constantly said them, but there was one thing that outweighed all the rest. The Royal Americans had *esprit de corps*. Thanks to Colonel Bouquet, Captain Ecuyer, and a few others, they were at that moment the hope of the frontier, and of Fort Pitt in particular. In a sea of chaos, in the welter of disaster and confusion which had followed the onslaught of the hosts of Pontiac, they stood like a ribbed fortress on an island of rock.

There was an exceedingly simple, personal reason for this then vital military fact. In times of great crisis the "administration of events" tends to fall into the hands of a certain few persons. In the month of May, 1763, it so happened that the defence, in fact the very existence, of the western frontiers in America, depended upon two individuals primarily: Colonel Henri Bouquet and Captain Simeon Ecuyer. They met the situation, of which they were aware, not only zealously but ingeniously, and they were followed and obeyed even by rascals and masterless characters, because by no means could either of them be bought, cajoled, flattered, frightened, or betrayed into doing anything less than his whole duty at any moment. They were in fact, as well as by law, the superiors of those they commanded.

All this was more or less in the nature of things. For even if his mother had been a French noblewoman and left him a small pension in the public funds, Captain Ecuyer was a thorough Swiss, a professional soldier of fortune from Switzerland. Born a republican, he served the monarch to whom he had sworn allegiance with skill, honour, and a professional zeal that might have touched King George to the heart, if he had ever heard of it. But there was small chance of that, or of promotion, and the captain knew it. He accepted what fate had thrust upon him, but he had his personal feelings just the same. And he cursed quietly and fluently, but resignedly, as he ran his professional eye over the barbarous scene before him. Pittsburgh, as the settlers now called it, was indeed a long way from Geneva.

Also the captain's claret had given out. The last bottle was gone. He was now reduced to native, Monongahela corn whiskey. Even the issue and the trade rum was exhausted. He took a reluctant sip of the perfectly white, slightly oily liquid from the glass poised on the arm of his chair, and shuddered. No wonder the Indians rose against the English! This was a drink fit only for some hostelry in inferno. It seared the throat and caused the eyeballs to start out of their sockets like ships' cannon from a porthole. Reduced to this potable lava, Captain Ecuyer nevertheless still wiped his brow with a fine cambric handkerchief nicely laundered.

Thanks to the allegedly triune God, he still had Johnson! Johnson, that invaluable combination armourer, valet, barber, cook, washerman, and groom. And to think that they were going to hang Johnson in England for stealing a pearl-set pin! Surely a gentle offence at worst!

But also, thank God, they had transported him instead to the colonies. What life on the frontiers would have been like without Johnson, Captain Ecuyer shivered to think.

For the captain was now quite literally at the end of the world. Just over the Ohio bastion on the point, and across the Ohio River, began the pathless forests. No one really knew where they ended. They extended west, into the sunset, probably into China or Russia. Some geographers claimed they extended to the South Sea. Apparently, they were inhabited illimitably by the same kind of merciless devils as now surrounded Fort Pitt.

To the mind of Captain Ecuyer, a thoroughly cultivated and European mind, the Indians constituted a ponderous problem in extermination.

Personally, they annoyed him. Their manners were bad. Also they were the enemies of the sovereign he served, and, as a good soldier, he was being thoroughly practical about doing away with them, individually or in such numbers as might from time to time try to fall upon him. In this policy General Amherst himself concurred. In fact, he had already written Colonel Bouquet suggesting the use of Cuban bloodhounds, if they could be obtained, and the introduction of smallpox-infected clothing amongst the tribes.

In any event, Fort Pitt was not going to be surprised or easily taken by the savages. Captain Ecuyer was the warrant for that assumption. Even with a mathematical mind, a military education, and a longing to return to Geneva, a keen and obstinate sense of the importance of his command was constantly present in the captain's thoughts.

Should Fort Pitt fall, the English might well be rolled back to the eastern seaboard. The post at the DeTroit, already in desperate straits, would be cut off beyond hope, and the country west of the mountains lost, perhaps permanently. It would lapse back into the wandering keep of devil hordes with stone axes. The captain was taking several stone axes home, along with a collection of arrowheads and scalps. He foresaw the day when it would be convenient to have some tangible evidence of what would be, at Geneva, an otherwise incredible past.

Meanwhile, the hope of English advance and perhaps the fate of an empire lay in the hands of Colonel Bouquet, who was gathering his expedition at Carlisle, and in Ecuyer's hands at Fort Pitt. Both the colonel and the captain were keen enough to know that. They were also Gallic enough to laugh wryly in their letters to each other over the fact that the English empery in America depended, for the time being, upon two Swiss gentlemen whom King George had hired to fight for him, and that no one in London would ever know it unless they lost.

The restrained grin of their painfully official correspondence had something horribly factual about it that conveyed itself in the same way that the grim geniality and toothsomely sardonic expression of a skull comments in the darkness upon both the past and the future. The passions, the wild contrary resolves, the terrors, and the conflicting interests of the harried frontiers, which made the task of these two Swiss officers so difficult, would someday drop away like flesh from the skull, leaving the bare bone of fact to make its own comment. Here, as elsewhere, the sword would decide.

Night after night Captain Ecuyer poured out his thoughts in such letters to Colonel Bouquet at Carlisle and Fort Bedford, and the colonel in like manner replied.

On the rough pine desk in the headquarters room behind Captain Ecuyer the papers, pen, and wax had already been laid out by Johnson, and a well-snuffed candle lit. A bright fire of large lumps of soft coal glowed incandescent in the chimney. Nights in the deep river valley were often chilly and damp. Johnson himself, a middle-aged man with a sleek bag wig, the bulging contours of an old servant, and a kindly face rendered expressionless by suffering, was starching and ironing his master's lace jabots, spreading them upon an ingenious little rack placed before the fire.

To look into the log-walled room was thus to behold

a delicate, lacy film of butterflies spread out against the glow of the coal fire. A greasy cloud of coal and wood smoke hung over the fort continually. Soot fell in flakes. Consequently, the process of laundering the captain's linens, lace cuffs, and stocks was continuous; the polishing of his boots, buttons, and weapons, endless. And Captain Ecuyer had three wigs.

To these labours Johnson devoted himself, and to the grooming of his own equally immaculate exterior. The captain, or rather his physical appearance, had become religion with Johnson. It was the last check of duty, devotion, and responsibility which still held him to the European world from which, in reality, the current of events was sweeping him farther away every day. Events had achieved and were achieving a new personality for Johnson in spite of himself. He was, in short, being made over from an Englishman into an American, rapidly.

To one who had been bred in London as a porter of sedan chairs, later a lackey, and eventually as the chief valet in a noble and ecclesiastical establishment in Exeter, the process of becoming a frontiersman, both mentally and physically, was an unexpected nervous strain.

Who would have thought that the bishop would have transported him merely for borrowing her ladyship's pin? A lamb covered with pearls! It was only for a servant's ball. He had only been detected in returning it. But her ladyship had been all for having him hanged. Possibly he should have been more grateful to his Lordship for merely transporting him as an act of Christian charity. But Johnson was beginning to doubt that. The new country was putting new ideas into his head. The bishop of Exeter and his ilk seemed unnecessary and far away. Johnson was beginning to become an individual instead of a mere member of a class. He had been forced to do so, because in the New World there were occasions when he had to act for himself in situations where there were no rules made by man, no precedents to follow.

Already he was thinking of acquiring land and settling

142

down. He was engaged to a young woman of property, Amelia Hart, a Pittsburgh trader's daughter.

But he had been most proper in his advances. Too proper, in fact. The Reverend Charles Frederick Post, a missionary, had published the banns of Mr. Johnson and Miss Hart in three sundry places, on three separate occasions, which made the people to stare, it being such a strange and unheard-of thing. Then Mr. Post had departed down the Ohio before the ceremony was performed, leaving Mr. Johnson to consummate his own union. The enthusiastic co-operation of the putative Mrs. Johnson had, however, greatly encouraged her triply banned husband. As a consequence, he had led a sort of double life, that of an accomplished European servant in the service of Captain Ecuyer at the fort; that of an American in the log store of Mr. Hart and his daughter, until lately situated on the banks of the Monongahela just beyond the glacis of Fort Pitt.

If and when Johnson could find someone to take his place, he had made up his mind to retire from the fort. But, under the circumstances, a satisfactory substitute was not likely to turn up. Johnson had been one of the best valets in England and the captain was fully conscious of his good luck in having retained him. He had paid his passage money when he arrived at Philadelphia, and thus saved Johnson from five years of indentured slavery. And Johnson was grateful for that. He found himself in a predicament between a comfortable servitude and the prospects of a fearful but fascinating freedom. Meanwhile, Amelia was having a child. Meanwhile, Mr. Johnson relieved his peculiar state of mental anxiety with nothing less than a fanatical attention to the details of Captain Ecuyer's service and outfit, for much the same reason that solitary prisoners sometimes carve meticulous baskets out of peach stones.

That was the reason Captain Ecuyer was able to sit on the edge of the Western world dressed with all the precision and attention to immaculate detail that would have admitted him to a levy at St. James's. That was the reason his boots shone, his gorget glittered, his wig had the mould of the metropolis, and his frill with a small diamond pin in it was stiff, but not too stiff, with starch. The gold buttons on his scarlet coat blinked in the firelight, and the Val lace from his cuffs dropped over his capable masculine hands.

All this was not without its effect on the garrison. It gave the captain the right prestige and appearance of an officer of the line. It was an example to some of the slovenly colonial officers, and it set the captain apart as a being from another world quite properly endowed with authority amidst the dirt, grime, and impudence of the barbarous frontier population. Since the captain had nothing of the macaroni or the martinet about him, but was just and kindly without being either weak or vain, his outer appearance, thanks partly to Johnson, expressed nicely his clean and precise, his logical and capable mind.

The fact that he was a gentleman of steadfast courage and shrewd policy had already been made abundantly plain to both the traders and the Indians. Perhaps the final element which implicated his successful defence of Fort Pitt was a tact which arose from an understanding of certain democratic principles then in actual practice in Switzerland alone.

By accident of birth the captain was without the blind arrogance of social class. Perhaps it would have been better if King George had hired more gentlemen from the vicinity of Geneva. At any rate, for once, by sheer accident and good fortune, that sovereign was being ably served on the frontiers of his empire by a civilized man.

Nor was this a trivial and personal fact. For in the extremely neat gentleman who sat smoking a cigar in front of headquarters at Fort Pitt was temporarily personified the hope of endowing with the life of reality the colonial charters that ran, in theory, from sea to sea. The fort and hovels in his charge was the only gate through which Englishmen and Americans could then pass to get to the Indian hunting grounds westward.

At that moment the official guardian of the gate, gold

144

buttons and all, was being carefully and fearfully observed by three little girls in pigtails, who held hands and whispered. A smile from the captain was sufficient to send them scampering back, scared but happy, to the bedlam of a casemate near the flag bastion which then constituted their home.

"Scared but happy" might, indeed, be said to describe the general spirit abroad in the fort. Rather happy tonight, for after a cold spell and a flood the weather was unusually pleasant. More important matters than the weather were about to engage the attention of the garrison, however.

13

A Stone Souvenir Descends from Heaven

CAPTAIN ECUYER had permitted his coat to slip down off his shoulders, and across the back of his chair. The moon, whose setting young Albine and his companion, at a distance of only a mile or two, were awaiting so eagerly, still obstinately poured its feeble light over the Ohio bastion. The interior of the fort was illuminated by it with a kind of unearthly grey light.

Leave out the presence of firearms, and the scene of the captain's cogitations might almost have been taken from a page in the *Germania* of Tacitus. In fact, the Germanic peoples *were* back in the forest again and the Celts were still with them. The five-sided enclosure of the fort resounded with a cacophony of English, Welsh, German, and Irish. The captain thought in French.

There was really nothing so unique about America, he told himself. The frontier of Western civilization had moved from the Rhine to the Ohio in about two thousand years. Meanwhile, to be sure, Europeans had forgotten what primeval forests and a barbarous frontier were like. Yet they plunged back into them as though they had an ancestral memory of what were the original conditions of their home. It must have been something like this once along the *limes* between the Rhine and the Vistula.

The captain's memory was a classical one, but for that very reason he thought in natural terms. Much of the old texts was illuminated by his own experience. It was

146

the military angle, of course, that interested him most.

It was a mistake, for instance, to try to conduct campaigns with garrison troops. That was always ineffectual against barbarians. What the English needed were field armies, ably led. And there should be plenty of effective auxiliaries. The Royal Americans were, in fact, a sort of vexillation, if you cared to look at it that way. The English generals were unfortunate in despising the colonials. Braddock had been the Varus of George II. Probably the English would never recover from that campaign. It might be that there had been a natural and fatal wound for the dream of empire that day on the banks of the Monongahela. Their prestige, in North America at least, had gone. Snobbery in generals was the chief nemesis of empire. In the end, history is nothing but the tragedy of manners, thought the captain. The manners best suited to reality prevailed. In America, west of the mountains at least, people had been forced to become realists again. There manners must once more be suited to the demands of nature instead of man. But London would probably never understand that. It was two millenniums away.

Here in Pennsylvania or Virginia, no one yet knew which, one could again read *Cæsar* with a genuine understanding. The man was full of excellent hints for Indian warfare. The captain, for instance, had just filled the ditch of Fort Pitt with small caltrops and beaver traps. They were excellent things for a moccasined foot to step on, or into. All the howls that rose from the ditch now at night were not ones of defiance. The fort was surprising its would-be surprisers. A Rhine bridge across the Ohio glimmered in the captain's mind. There was plenty of timber to make one. He was going to suggest it to Colonel Bouquet. All the towns and settlements should be surrounded by stockades. Tiles or slate should be put on the roofs to turn aside the fire arrows.

But how could anyone ever persuade the provincial assembly to appropriate money for such things as that? He looked uneasily at his own shingle roofs on the barracks of the fort. They projected temptingly above the ramparts. Their many chimneys threw off thick curls of oily coal smoke. The soot fell upon the captain where he sat. A low hum of life, conversation, the cries of children, the lowing of cattle, the constant and infernal barking of dogs, and the stench of squealing swine saluted the sinking moon and the captain's ears and nostrils alike.

There were five hundred and forty "mouths," men, women, and children, including the garrison and the refugee population of Pittsburgh, crowded into the fort. Every casemate in the walls was occupied and glimmering with candles, torches, or lanthorns. The square windows of the barracks looked at him from all sides with rows of yellow eyes. Now and then a door opened, revealing a scene of crowded confusion within, and a glimpse of glowing coal fires. These fires went day and night, summer and winter. They were both the curse and the comfort of the place. Its inhabitants were almost fanatically prodigal with fuel. People took coal out of the hill across the river and used it like madmen. There was no end to the coal.

A military forge across from the gate was also in full blast. The hammers of the smiths and the muted ring of glowing iron on anvils seemed to fill the place with a clashing of harsh bells. Stacks of hay and provender rose everywhere like little hillocks, furnishing at once a perfect fire menace and the assembly points for cows, horses, and poultry. The loud flapping of cow dung on the flagstones, the pissing of cattle, the interminable trumpeting of geese, and crowing of cocks provided merely the comparatively hushed monotone accompaniment for the constant staccato of humanity that arose from the casemates where the families of the unfortunate settlers of burnt Pittsburgh now sheltered themselves.

Somewhere an Irishman was apparently beating his wife to death. Babies squalled. Mothers screamed the names of their strayed offspring. Little boys played leapfrog. Lines of people were waiting to get corn meal and whisky from the storehouses turned over to the traders. From the commissary rations were being issued to the garrison. There seemed to be no sign that sleep was in order at night. Against the silent loom of the dark forests across the river the Americans were unconsciously raising a defiant human shout. It was almost a shriek. It was the outstanding characteristic of the inhabitants, a constant disorderly and complaining noise. Not infrequently it became surly in tone. The garrison of Fort Pitt boomed and yelled at the moon.

It would be better when the planet sank. Darkness would come and some of them would *have* to go to sleep then, thought the captain. In the early morning the Indians would creep in upon them. They attacked with fire arrows and hysteria. Guns, with them, were largely something with which to make a noise. Most of them were vile shots, even worse than the English regulars. Only the Americans could use a rifle. They always fired it at something or someone in particular. The Europeans had not learned to do that yet. The Indians fought with hatchets and knives. Hence, a stockade stopped them. The captain re-arranged his stock, and sighed audibly. It was his task, with only a modicum of authority, to bring order into all this chaos. The inhabitants had come into the fort only a few days before. Up until that time it had at least resembled a military post. Now it was the parade ground of pandemonium.

"Tomorrow," said the captain, *"allons nous en!"*

The reforms of administration which the captain had been turning over in his mind while he sat looking at the confusion before him now began taking shape in his thoughts in the diction of the orders to be written that night. Only in the clear area immediately in front of head-quarters upon which he was looking, about the gate, and on the walls and outer stockade was order visible.

On the walls the cannoneers stood with smoking lin-stocks beside their loaded cannon. He could see the glow of their matches in the gloom of the bastions. Beyond, over the moat, the sentries of the Royal Americans walked to and fro along the platform of the stockade which Captain Ecuyer had had built all about the glacis. Just at that moment he listened somewhat sceptically to the announcement that all was well, repeated twenty-seven times, one after the other by each sentry. The consoling thought was thus enunciated clear around the walls. At least the sentries were alert. The captain counted the voices. He stood there, and finally crushed the fire out of his cigar while he leaned forward listening intently.

The moon sank, and the shades of night engulfed the pentagon of Fort Pitt. The place gradually became quieter. The dogs no longer howled. Now and then, in the alleys behind the barracks, they growled. The captain rose and wrapped his coat about him.

Inside, Johnson finished and folded up the little mangle he had brought from Philadelphia, to put it into the chest which held his valet's kit. The starch on the jabots was dry. He began to fold them neatly and put them into a small drawer in the captain's military chest. Then he stopped, standing for a moment as though suddenly frozen. Captain Ecuyer also was still standing just as he had risen with his coat wrapped about him. For at that moment a curious and demoniacal wailing began in the fields beyond the fort.

The women camping in the casemates and lean-to huts arranged against the walls clutched their children to their breasts. It sounded as though a pack of wolves was being slowly burned to death out there. A graveyard chill crept along the spines of the sentries, who stood transfixed, peering over the pointed stakes of the parapet about the glacis.

Ghostly glimmers of fire twinkled amidst the grass in the meadows about the fort. From these points, soaring up like rockets, streaks of flame mounted into the sky. Some of the sentries shouted. Captain Ecuyer saw the fire arrows fall like shooting stars into the fort. They plunged, hissing faintly. Instantly the shingle roofs of the barracks were alight with little spluttering tongues of flame. Pentecost had come with a vengeance. A babble rose from the fort. Captain Ecuyer roared. The deep roll of drums began to thunder, echoing from bank to bank of the three rivers.

Under the penthouse roof, by the gate, the captain could see the drummers in dim silhouette against the lanthorns, moving their arms like automatons. The garrison turned out. Ladders were rushed to the roofs. Women formed a line and began passing buckets from the wells. The swish of water on the roofs became rhythmic. The tongues of flame spluttered and went out.

A pile of hay burst into lurid smoky flame, and was quenched. A crackle of rifle fire began from the opposite banks of the rivers. The bullets whizzed and moaned into the fort. Here and there wood splintered. The tinkle of a smashed window light sounded ominous. Three wounded men plunged, with sickening crashes, from the roofs. The Indians wailed like lost souls. The fire arrows finally became fewer. Now and then from the stockade the sullen bump of a musket thudded into the night. The Royal Americans were being careful of their precious powder. The crack of the settlers' rifles was more frequent.

Captain Ecuyer mounted the ramparts and took his stand by the cannon on the flag bastion. To the eastward, on rising ground near Grant's Hill, a house had burst into flame. A crowd of Indians could be seen about it capering against the fire, and driving off cattle. They were nearly a mile away.

The captain gave an order. Twice, under his direction, the matross corrected the elevation of his piece. Its thundering explosion shook the fort. At the foot of Grant's Hill, the house, the Indians, and the cattle disappeared in an intense white flash and a rocking shell explosion that re-echoed from the woods. The burning timbers of the house hurtled into a near-by thicket and set it on fire. The red glow, framed by the frowning forests, threw a kind of infernal dawn over the valley. From the parapets of the fort several cannon began to spray the country about with grapeshot. The rifle firing and demoniacal yelling died away. The cannon ceased. Over the fort hung a low, dun-coloured cloud of choking powder and coal smoke.

Except for the dismal bellowing of some wounded cattle, and the disconsolate lapping of water in the flooded moat, silence settled down as if it had sneaked back in the enveloping velvet darkness of a foggy midnight. The night and the stars above marched on.

The captain made his rounds. Finally he stood watching the dark lines of the forests across the rivers that swept away, rocking along the clifftops into the slowly paling eastern sky. There must be nearly a thousand savages concealed there. He had estimated their rifles—hundreds of them. The prospect of a long siege was by no means a delightful one. He hoped Colonel Bouquet at Carlisle would hurry. Perhaps by this time he had been able to advance to Fort Bedford. Perhaps? There were only a few weeks' provisions left at Fort Pitt. The captain stood pondering that solemn thought. A retreat through the forest would mean almost certain death for all. An arrow from the nowhere above suddenly plunged viciously into the muscle of the calf of his left leg.

It was exceedingly painful, and the wound bled profusely. It was a nasty gash. He retired to his quarters to be bandaged. The men on the stockades began to throw hand grenades down the glacis as morning approached. They exploded in the ditch with a crimson splash and a bump. The captain tensely watched Johnson and the surgeon cut a stone arrowhead out of the calf of his left leg. That arrowhead would be the most cherished item in his souvenir collection, he reflected painfully.

Suddenly he could see himself at Geneva, exhibiting it to his neighbours. The faces of many people he had forgotten surrounded him. He was sitting in a small summerhouse near the lake. The vision was extremely clear. He began to hear familiar old voices. Then he fainted.

Johnson completed the work of the surgeon, who had been called hastily elsewhere. He poured *eau de Cologne* into the wound. The smarting brought the captain to again. Johnson wrapped his master in a cloak and laid him upon Colonel Bouquet's camp bed. He poured the blood out of his boot, washed it, wiped it, and lay down himself on the floor. After a while Johnson began to snore. The captain shuddered feverishly now and then. It seemed to him he could see the future in the dark. Finally he slept exhaustedly. Outside an occasional hand grenade viciously punctuated the early morning hours.

14

Portrait in Oils of a Young Scalp

THE ARROW which struck the captain was also like to have been the death of young Albine and his two soldier companions. It was plain to the garrison that considerable numbers of Indians must have crept into the ditch and be lurking in the shadow of the palisade. The news of Captain Ecuyer's being wounded caused them to keep a doubly sharp and vengeful watch from the platform. The slightest sound from the riverbank, or the least suspicion of something moving in the shadow of the glacis, brought spurts of rifle fire from the loopholes, or the earth-shaking splash of a grenade.

It was nearly morning, therefore, before the little party of three dared even to leave the cover of the deep overhung riverbank by the point, where they had landed and taken shelter about midnight.

There had been no trouble in crossing the river after the moon had gone down. They had simply rowed up an eddy to the bar, and then poled across. One could wade across at low water in the summer from the south side of the Monongahela to the point. It was just their bad luck to have chosen a night when an attack was on to try to enter the fort. When they were halfway across, the Indian rifle fire had broken out viciously from the cliffs on the banks above them. Also they were afraid they might be seen in a cannon flash from the fort. For that reason they abandoned the boat, and crouching low, waded in on the bar that ran out from the point.

Under the deep bank it was safe enough till dawn came. With daylight, however, they would inevitably be seen by the Indians on the opposite bank, and picked off. Yet if they stuck their heads above the bank now they would be killed by the sentries on the parapet. So it was the devil and the deep sea. They stood shivering in the mud for two hours, occasionally conferring in whispers. Jobson, the sergeant, eventually decided to try to make the foot of the parapet by crawling around the point into the "King's Artillery Garden" on the Allegheny side of the fort.

They started, having to swim once, and proceeded with infinite caution, for as they wormed their way through the rows of lettuce and red cabbages toward the deeper loom of the slope of the glacis they became aware of other forms crouching here and there in the darkness. Once Albine whispered something in Shawnee as a crawling Indian overtook them from behind. A low grunt replied. The Indian crawled on. Presently a shot rang from the palisade and the Indian sprang into the air and crashed into the ditch. That was warning enough. After that they kept still for an hour. Murphy, the other soldier, stuffed himself with parsley, like a rabbit. It was his last meal.

The sky began to turn grey. The lurking forms on the glacis slipped back through the bushes to the riverbank. They heard canoes being quietly launched. Presently the three white men felt they were alone. Morning was coming on fast now. They could occasionally see the head of a sentry sliding, like a dark bead, along the pointed stakes of the palisade. Between them and it lay the slope of the glacis, and the ditch. It was still pitch-dark in the ditch. They were on the western side of the fort. Jobson wriggled up the slope without being seen, and called out. Young Albine and Murphy followed more slowly.

"Don't shoot!" cried the sergeant. "It's me, Sergeant

155

Jobson, from the sawmill. Is that you, Leftenant Francis? I know your voice. For God's sake, call your men off!"

A cultivated young English voice replied. The lieutenant assured himself he was really talking with Sergeant Jobson. He took a terrible time doing so. Then he sent for a rope. It was a terrible time coming.

The three men on the glacis could now be seen from the parapet. "Hi, Murphy," said a soldier from the platform, "have you still got your har? Who's that wid ye?"

"It's a young white bhoy tryin' to escape from thim red divils, and mind ye don't tike him for one. An' fer Christ's sake, git that rope or we'll all be moithered out here entirely, you with yer blatherin' mouth in there."

"Shut your own," growled Sergeant Jobson, "and get you ready to make a rush. Here's the rope now."

It came wriggling over the parapet, and fell into the ditch with a splash. The sergeant went first. He picked his way through the ditch, tied the rope under his arms, and was drawn up, not without a good deal of difficulty. The rope came dangling down again.

"It's your turn me bhoy," said Murphy. "You're a spalpeen. I'll tarry."

A couple of bullets droned across the river and splashed against the parapet. Someone had brought a lanthorn onto the platform. Everyone on the palisade ducked, and cursed the man with the light. It went out.

Sal Albine rose clutching his bundle of bark leaves to his breast. He put the thong that held them together in his mouth, and rushed for the rope. Out of one corner of his eye he saw the Indian in the ditch, wriggling, but he couldn't call out. He had the thong in his mouth, and he mustn't drop that precious list. He went up the rope hand over hand, bracing his feet against the wall of the palisade. He stood on the platform and began to shout a warning to Murphy.

"Good for you, young'un," said Jobson, clapping him on the back. Then they heard Murphy scream.

"Jasus! Jasus! I've caught me fut in a baver trap. Howly

156

Mither of God!" The party of ten soldiers on the parapet stood looking down at him helplessly.

"I'll go back," said Albine, and started. But it was too late.

A form, painted black and green, with animallike red stripes on its face, rose out of the shadow of the ditch. It rushed upon Murphy where he was struggling helpless in the trap, and gripped him by the hair. A knife flashed. A horrible floundering and moaning followed while the Irishman's scalp was torn from his head. He shrieked. The Indian rushed down the glacis and the death helloo rose triumphantly from under the riverbank. It was answered and reanswered eerily from the opposite bank. On the parapet Salathiel Albine, Sergeant Jobson, Lieutenant Francis, and eight soldiers of the Royal American regiment dressed in scarlet coats and white leather cross belts, stood shivering in the lethal dawn. They seemed stunned. It had not been possible to fire at the Indian without killing Murphy. Then someone threw a hand grenade. It blew Murphy to pieces.

"You God-damned idjit!" replied the lieutenant. A young soldier began to vomit. "Git back to yer posts," roared the sergeant. "Do you think it's a quiltin' bee?" The men scattered.

Young Albine stood on the platform and looked out over the inner moat and roofs of Fort Pitt. In his nostrils for the first time was the faintly fecal odour of civilization mixed with coal and powder smoke. He was never to grow quite used to it. His nostrils expanded with astonishment and disgust.

"Come on, me lad," said the lieutenant. "I'll have to enter all this in the orderly book."

They walked along the stockade platform in the growing daylight, and descended a ladder opposite the music bastion. The musicians were gathering there and the cannoneers preparing to fire the sunrise gun. They crossed a hand bridge over the fosse that fed the moat from the Allegheny, and found themselves at the guardhouse at the outer gate of the fort.

The guard was already drawn up awaiting the morning relief. In the increasing morning light their burnished arms and scarlet coats gleamed cheerfully. The water of the moat reflected impressively the frowning dark ramparts and cannon looking out from the embrasures of the wall. The place seemed armed to the teeth. From fifty chimneys the black coal smoke announcing breakfast rolled threateningly into the air, and drifted down the Ohio. The sun peeked over the eastern hills, its first beams saluted by the thunder of the morning gun, and a ruffle of fifes, drums, and trumpets. The echoes rolled grandly up the river canyons as the Union Jack rose over Fort Pitt.

The heart of the young man dressed in muddy wolfskins, with the bark bundle under his arm, expanded with pride, hope, and astonishment. To the young from the wilderness this bare outpost of civilization, the ragged panoply of European war thrust into his native forests, had the effect of an explosion in his imagination. His white heritage fell upon him at one swoop; left him dizzy. He rallied to it with the phlegm of the savages he had been raised among. Inwardly he was amazed and excited; outwardly he was calm and apparently contemptuous.

"Can you speak English?" asked Lieutenant Francis, for so far Salathiel had made no reply to anything he had said.

"Better than you," replied Albine proudly. "I can even repeat all the psalms by heart."

"Every Scotch rebel in these mountains can," said the lieutenant wryly. Most of the people, he noticed, had the accent and manners of the former age. They were all Covenanters except the Catholic Irish, and they were nearly all runaway servants.

"What's that under your arm, a Bible?" the lieutenant asked.

"It's a list of white captives now in the western woods," replied Salathiel, "and it's for the chief here. How do you call him?"

"The commandant," said Francis. He looked at the youth in wolfskins now with more curiosity and respect.

"I have wampum from the chiefs for him too," added Salathiel.

The lieutenant nodded. In these parts you could never tell who or what a man was. There were no certain signs of class distinction. He thought it best to take Salathiel to his quarters and give him some clothes and breakfast. There would be some wild tales of the forest in him at least. The lieutenant was bored. He missed the excitement of routs at Bristol, and you couldn't bed with a girl in America without catching fleas at least. Eventually they gathered under one's wig. He scratched thoughtfully.

They were waiting for the drawbridge to fall. It soon came down with a crash, and the relief in the scarlet of the Royal Americans marched across. The drums banged. The lieutenant saluted and dismissed. Then he led the way onto the little island barbican in the moat and across the second drawbridge into the fort. The smell of corn mush, frying bacon, boiling pork, humanity, and cattle filled the air. The fumes from the chimney caused Salathiel to choke. Astonishment once more filled his mind.

It had never occurred to him that buildings could be built of anything but logs. He had never seen anything but a log cabin or an Indian hut. The fort was a mass of solid dirty grey brick and stone. There seemed to be enormous numbers of people in it. The cattle also were amazing. He remembered his father's ox that had once breathed in his face. All these animals looked monstrous. And the chief sound that marked the presence of the white man was the crowing of cocks. It sounded delirious.

The lieutenant paused to unlock the door of his quarters. Salathiel stood lost in admiration over the ingenious contrivance of lock and key. He even stooped to examine it.

"Come in, come in," said the young officer impatiently.

For the first time in his life young Albine entered a civilized room.

It was a simple enough place—a mere plastered cubicle of the single officers' quarters, but to Salathiel it conveyed the impression of immense and inexhaustible wealth, prodigally displayed. There were three deal chairs, a bed, an officer's chest of polished wood with a brass lock, and a painted table. A shelfful of books, containing nearly a dozen volumes, hung on the wall. Across from it a small cupboard displayed some pewter and a few pieces of china and crockery. There was a ragged woollen rug on the floor. Into this place, through a spotlessly clean window, poured the level rays of the newly risen sun, which seemed to Salathiel to gild the apartment with a kind of palatial splendour. He stood obviously lost in wonder and admiration until the lieutenant laughed.

Lieutenant Francis was a young gentleman of talent and small income. The second son of a rich and titled English family, his commission in the Royal Americans had been bought for him in lieu of a lean living in the Irish church. Baggage, even some effects of elegance, had accompanied him. He actually painted a little. Two oil landscapes and a portrait of his sister, by no means despicable, adorned the walls. There were iron candlesticks, long clay pipes, and bottles on the mantelpiece. A white cloth with a set of military silver and steel knives was laid out on the table, and his servant just at that moment knocked on the door, entered, and began to prepare breakfast over a bright coal fire in the little chimney place. To cap the climax, the walls were plastered and a ray of sunshine, focused by one of the bottle panes, illuminated charmingly the white face of the young lady in court dress smirking at them all.

All this at once assaulted the sense of Salathiel. He felt as though he had been suddenly translated into the lodge of Manitou. The young man in gold lace and scarlet, hanging his gilt-hilted sword on a peg in the wall, might have been the sultan of Golconda, or the king of England. It had never occurred to Salathiel that a room could be smooth and white inside. He ran his fingers along the plaster in amazement, and left a smudge on the wall.

"Sit down," said the lieutenant, laughing. "No, no, in the chair!"

So that was what they were for!

"Hawkins," continued the lieutenant, addressing his servant, "set another place for my guest." The soldier grinned and coughed. They settled down to tea, rashers of bacon, corn bread, and eggs.

It was now that young Albine, perhaps by sheer native shrewdness, hit upon a scheme which was to lead him to whatever modicum of success he achieved in life. Imitation was his only hope and defence. He began to copy the actions of Lieutenant Francis' eating. He mimicked him precisely. He poured his tea into his saucer, blew upon it carefully, and swallowed it. It was to him a nauseous dose, but he downed it. He watched every move the lieutenant made with his knife, fork, and spoon. He managed not to spill anything. He thought butter was wonderful. He ate six eggs and a half pound of bacon.

"That's all we have, sir," said Hawkins, rising, with his face a beet color, from before the fire. "It's the week's supply."

"Buy some more," said the lieutenant, tossing him a coin *en grand seigneur*.

Salathiel blushed under his paint and mud. But what did these English live on? Eggs? The lieutenant made some hot toddy. He plied his guest, and both their tongues were loosened.

They began to talk with instead of at each other. In the half-Biblical, half-learned jargon of the Reverend James McArdle, mixed with the idiom of the frontier and some Indian words, Salathiel began to reconstruct his life in the forest in reply to the amused, but searching, questions of Lieutenant Francis. He did surprisingly well. Then he began to ask questions, too. A feeling of friendliness sprang up between them as the toddy neared the bottom of the bowl. The young Englishman began to tell

161

Salathiel about Bristol and Bath. Francis grew enthusiastic about Bath. "It would do you good to take a plunge in the hot springs there," he said. "I believe you'd come out a white man. Lord, I'd like to spend the morning in the bath myself!" He scratched his wig dolefully. "Now then," said he, "if you're going to the commandant, you will simply have to have some decent clothes. Ecuyer dresses like a courtier. He's the only man on the frontier who's not hoppin' with fleas. But before you dress up, I'd like to catch you just as you are. Do you mind?"

Albine, of course, hadn't the faintest idea what he meant.

"Sit over there in that streak of sunlight," continued the lieutenant. "Here, try a pipe." Although he was still completely puzzled, Salathiel complied. The tobacco was excellent. The lieutenant took out his palette, a small piece of old tent canvas stretched on a frame, and some oil paints. He began to daub rapidly. The sunbeam shifted slowly down the wall. Outside, a trumpet sounded, making his subject jump, and the tramp of marching men passed the door. The lieutenant painted on. This fellow, he knew, would never look like that again. And he *was* a specimen, a type!

He sketched in the head against a tangled background of dim forest and branches. Across it fell streaks of sunlight, high-lighting the big shaved head with its prominent ears, the topknot with an eagle feather tied to it. The face he did rather from the side. The large, piercing grey eyes, wide apart, the nose that swept down and finally curved in a little at the mouth. That was the really astonishing feature. Or was it the hatchetlike lines of the lower jaw that gave him so much character? It would have been a grim face if it were not for the mouth, the fine, big, white teeth, slightly pouting lips parted in a happy, manly young smile. That smile was ingratiating, whether it was unconscious or not. Certainly it was natural.

On the costume Lieutenant Francis let himself go. He draped the wolfskin over one shoulder and put in the little red turtle over the heart. "And we will suppose it is summer," he said. "The background shows it." He put a rifle gun in his subject's hand. The lieutenant drew guns well. And he seated his subject on a stump whose roots wreathed themselves into the base of the picture.

"No chairs down the Ohio?" he asked.

Salathiel shook his head, and laughed.

"Hold that," said Francis. He worked rapidly.

A general enthusiasm glowed through him and seemed to animate his brush. His hand seemed to have a life of its own. This was, by far, the best thing he had ever done. The skin colour was the hardest. It had a copper tinge under the grime. Perhaps he painted it too red. He put in the three white marks on the cheekbones, of the Shawnee tribe, and last of all the pipe with its curling wreath of smoke.

On a stump in the forest his young hunter sat, smoking between shots. "Rest in the wilderness," said the lieutenant. All that was needed was a wild turkey lying at his hunter's feet. He would put that in later. He stopped, rather breathless and tired. A fit of coughing shook him.

Salathiel could not admire the picture enough. He kept going backward and forward between it and a bit of looking glass on the chest. The picture, he saw, was how he looked to the young Englishman.

"I like your likeness better," he said.

Francis laughed. "I see you will probably get on in this world," said he. The lieutenant was pleased.

"But I will have to stop looking like that if I do," Salathiel added.

The lieutenant laughed again.

"I opine you will," he admitted. "Perhaps you had better begin the metamorphosis now."

"What?" said Albine, looking puzzled.

Francis did not explain. He gave his new-found friend a piece of soap and poured out a basin of hot water. He showed him how to use the soap, and persuaded him to wash his face. The paint, the mud, the smoke of many

163

campfires, and the bear's grease came off. The lieutenant sat back enjoying all this immensely. His friend was white, after all. Looking in the glass again Albine could scarcely recognize himself. He looked at the picture half regretfully. That was me, he thought.

Just then Hawkins came back with some clothes from the quartermaster, where the lieutenant had sent him. All this reminded young Francis of amateur play acting at home. Nothing had amused him so much for a long time. It made him a bit homesick, but he liked it all the better for that. He now contributed an old linen shirt, tied at the wrists.

Salathiel then stepped out behind the quarters and had Hawkins dash several buckets of water over him. He left the muddy wolfskin lying on the ground and returned to dress in the new clothes: a pair of soldier's boots, knitted socks, half-leather breeches, and the lieutenant's shirt. An old green coat, provided by the province of Pennsylvania for its militia, completed the costume. Only the boots were unbearable. He finally took them off and put on his moccasins again.

"That's better. They go with the topknot. But I'd let my hair grow," said Francis, who never cracked a smile. "Put the feather on again. It gives you a more respectable look."

Hawkins would have guffawed but, even in his moccasins, the young man stood six feet four, with narrow hips and broad shoulders. The muscles in his arms were pantherlike. Also he looked intensely grave. It might be a mistake to guffaw. Anyway, at that moment the lieutenant sent Hawkins along with a message to headquarters. He returned shortly with the desired answer.

Salathiel picked up the bundle of bark and his pouch with the wampum in it. Then he and the lieutenant set out together to see the commandant. Lieutenant Francis was filled with a kind of schoolboy curiosity, bordering on mirth. He wanted to see Captain Simeon Ecuyer confronted by young Albine. It would be something to tell at mess, where his reputation as a wit had suffered somewhat of late for lack of new material to embroider upon.

15

Shaving as a Fine Art

ECUYER was in a back room of headquarters, where he slept. There was a large window there. There was also the largest mirror west of the mountains. It had been sent by Governor John Penn to General Stanwix when, for a brief time, the English commander in chief had been at Pittsburgh planning the building of the fort. Despite the window, there was a candle burning in a sconce on each side of the mirror, and Johnson was shaving the captain in a chair placed before it. The captain's wig was off. His wounded leg lay stretched out on a stool. The lather covered his face, and his eyes were closed.

"Come in, gentlemen," said he. He spoke with a clear voice and scarcely a trace of accent. "Do sit down, please."

They took the bench by the door.

The lieutenant began to relate the events of the night before, while Johnson continued to shave the captain. He shaved slowly with short, brief strokes. Young Albine watched him, fascinated. He had never seen anyone shaved that way before. Shaving an Indian's head was quite a different process. The captain did not open his eyes even when Lieutenant Francis recounted the incident of Murphy's death.

"Arrange to punish the man who threw that grenade," he finally said. "The men must learn to think before they throw grenades, and to aim at what they shoot at with

166

a rifle. What is the message the newcomer you speak of brought?"

Francis nudged Salathiel. He stepped out into the middle of the floor and drew the wampum strings from his pouch.

"Father," said he. Johnson stopped shaving.

The lieutenant put his hand over his mouth. This was going to be magnificent.

Captain Ecuyer opened his eyes.

A strange, tall, hawk-eyed young man was standing before him holding out strips of wampum that wriggled on his wrists like snakes. Captain Ecuyer wiped some lather away from the region of his mouth. A small ironical smile was revealed under the lather.

"Go on," he said, without sitting up.

"Father, I am the mouth of Kaysinata, the Big Turtle, and the tongue of the half-chief Nymwha," continued Salathiel. "The mouth opens and the tongue in it speaks for your children, the Shawnees. Father, the commanding officer, by this string of wampum we open your ears, wipe the tears from your eyes, and remove everything that is bad from your heart." He laid a string upon the knee of Captain Ecuyer, and went on:

"Father, with this string we renew the ancient chain of friendship with Our Great Father, the king across the seas. We would bury the hatchet and ask that his gifts be renewed; that powder and shot, horses, and white flour be sent to us. We have listened to lying tongues. Our hearts are sore. The children of the English who tarry in our lodges we will return to our father . . ."

"Enough!" said Ecuyer, sitting up. Even with lather on his face he looked impressive. His eyes shone with indignation.

"Go back to your friends and tell them when they deliver their captives and come here themselves to ask peace, we will smoke the calumet with them. Do not lay any more strings on my knees, young man. I accept those you have given me to open my eyes. My eyes are open.

Go back and say so. Here, Johnson, take these trinkets and put them in the chest where we keep the rest of this stuff." He sank back in the chair. Johnson took the belts of wampum and went out.

"Go back"—the words rang in the ears of Salathiel with a doleful sound. The forests seemed to be closing around him again.

"But, captain, the commandant, I don't want to go back," he said.

"What!" exclaimed the captain. "What! Then why do you come here?"

Salathiel began to explain as best he could. The fervour of forest oratory, that had sustained him and made him stand up to deliver the wampum with savage bravado, deserted him. The mouth and tongue of the Indian chief was silent. It was with his own voice and for himself that he pleaded now.

The captain opened his eyes again, very wide indeed. From a mouthpiece the young man before him had suddenly turned into an individual. The captain would listen to such a man. With mouthpieces he had little patience. His leg hurt him, but it was a young white man speaking to him now, and he was sympathetic and patient.

The story Salathiel poured out interested him. "Good!" he exclaimed when he heard about McArdle's list of captives. Then he lapsed into silence. From time to time he raised his hand in assent. Otherwise, Salathiel soon seemed to be speaking to a man asleep. The captain had closed his eyes again. The lather dried on his cheeks. Finally he opened his eyes and looked at the speaker.

"I would advise you to stay here. You might even enlist," he said. "Lieutenant Francis, look after this fellow for me. See that he is started in right. He seems to have brought valuable information. Also go and tell Captain-lieutenant Shay to take the guard mount for me today. I can't get about now. My leg's horrid stiff. Tell Johnson to hurry back. The lather's drying. Damn it, where's that rascal gone to? As for the prisoners on Sawmill Run," he added, as though they were an afterthought, while he glanced at Albine, "I'll send for them as soon as I can. Now sit down, young man, I want to ask you certain questions about those captives."

Lieutenant Francis departed. Salathiel sat waiting.

He could hear a watch ticking in the captain's vest, but Ecuyer said nothing. He was very tired. Johnson did not return, for some reason. The captain lay with his eyes closed, waiting for him. The wound in his leg crawled. He felt faint, and Fort Pitt seemed far away. Five or six minutes passed.

It was then that young Albine made the most important move of his career. He rose quietly on his moccasins. There was something fascinating about the captain's half-shaved face; something alluring about the little brush that made the foam.

The soap cup and the brush lay beside a case with seven razors marked with the days of the week. The one for Tuesday was open. Johnson had been using it. Salathiel picked the one for Wednesday. It looked keen. He began to stir the soap with the brush. The lather creamed anew. That settled it.

Copying Johnson, he began to spread the lather carefully on the captain's cheeks. Ecuyer threw back his head, thinking Johnson had returned.

Very carefully, just as Johnson had done, with quick, careful strokes, Albine began to shave Captain Ecuyer. It was just like carefully scraping a fine, thin doe's hide. He finished the cheeks and under the nostrils. Captain Ecuyer had a long upper lip that he stiffened against the razor. The chin Salathiel was most careful about, and he ran the razor over it lightly. But he had the hang of it now. The captain threw back his head even farther, exposing his throat. The shaving went on. Johnson stepped into the room, and gasped.

The captain opened his eyes.

He saw a young savage with a feather in his hair, standing above him, with a razor resting at his throat. He said nothing. Neither did Johnson.

169

Salathiel Albine finished shaving the commandant of Fort Pitt. . . .

The captain sat up and felt his face critically. He ran his hand over his cheeks, and especially his throat, thoughtfully. Then he began to laugh.

"There you are, Johnson," said he. "You've found an assistant, and a damned good one. What's your name, young man? Are you honest? At least you didn't cut my throat, and I've never been sure that Johnson wasn't going to do that, ever since I paid his passage money."

The scandalized Johnson protested loudly.

"Tut, tut!" said the captain. "You've been talkin' about leavin' me ever since you got sweet on that trader's daughter and married her. I know! And now here's a natural from the forests, with a sartorial gift. What more can you ask in this howling country? It's a special act of grace!"

For a moment Johnson had been angry and jealous. But now the captain's suggestion seemed to pull a trigger in his brain. He *had* been thinking of leaving the captain —next year. Maybe there was something in what the captain said. Johnson looked at young Albine keenly.

"Come," said the captain, "help me over into that camp bed. It's Colonel Bouquet's. But he isn't here, and I am. God help me," he added, and touched his leg ruefully.

Johnson and Albine together lifted the commandant into the cot.

Johnson began to curl the captain's wig. He gave directions to Salathiel how to put away the shaving things, and watched him closely. Pretty soon Salathiel was washing one of the captain's shirts at the fireplace. He was most careful. He did everything exactly as he was told. He moved quietly on his moccasins, and said nothing. Johnson nodded.

An obedient assistant would make life easier for him, anyway. The idea *might* work. The captain had a good eye for a man. Of course, he would have to show this young savage everything. But it was easier to teach than to work. Anybody knew that.

Salathiel went back for supper to Lieutenant Francis' quarters. Johnson had told him to report again in the morning. The young Englishman congratulated him.

"You're on the way up," said the lieutenant. "But I can't have you eating here at the table with me any more if you are going to be the captain's servant. That won't do, you know."

"Why not?" asked Salathiel.

"Oh, afterwhile you'll find out," replied the Englishman. "But in this country that doesn't need to prevent us being friends quietly on the side. We will go hunting when the woods are safe again." They shook hands on it.

"I'll need a gun," said Salathiel wistfully. A gun was something he had never been able to obtain, even from Nymwha.

Lieutenant Francis looked at the picture of his new friend on the mantelpiece, where he sat with a nice shooting-iron in his hand, and pondered.

"*I'll* give you one!" he said impulsively.

He rose and gave him his own fowling piece. It was a double-barrelled hunting gun of small caliber, and quite beautifully chased. "Wilson, London, 1752" was under the mark.

"My God, she's a fair beauty," exclaimed Salathiel, flushing with pleasure.

"She's all that," said the lieutenant. "But that piece belonged to my older brother, and I never liked him, or anything he owned. Maybe it will bring down good fortune if I give it away. Anyway, keep it, and go shooting!"

"Thank you with all my heart," replied Salathiel.

"Well, well, good luck," said the lieutenant, almost as though he were glad to be rid of the gun. Then he smiled.

Salathiel understood it was time to go.

He stepped out into the night and the confines of the

171

crowded fort. He had no idea where he was going to sleep. Overhead was a pall of coal smoke, but he could see the stars through it. They winked at him blindly.

16

How Salathiel Slept
with a Widow

SALATHIEL stood before the door of Lieutenant Francis' quarters with his blanket and his new gun over his arm, but in a quandary. No one had said anything about where he was going to sleep. As far as he could see, every nook and cranny in the fort was preempted, and he still had a feeling of faint hostility to all the noisy crowds of whites gathered about the fires and those swarming in and out of various buildings. There seemed to be something indecent about so many people being crowded together in one place. He hesitated.

An occasional shot from the parapet confirmed the state of siege. He wondered what Jane was doing over in the lodges of Nymwha on Sawmill Run. It would be cold sleeping without her. He was alone again! This was the first night of his new life—and there was no place to sleep unless he found one.

He began to walk about quietly, looking for a bit of shelter or a soft place to lie down. The only result was to disturb a number of people, who complained. Evidently his accent and appearance were not reassuring, either. He enquired for his friend, Sergeant Jobson, only to find he was on duty at the outer barbican. He persisted. But growls, surly replies, a blast of profanity or ironic abuse was all he got from those he approached on the subject of a place to sleep.

He was wary, anyway. He was a very strange stranger

in a strange land. No trees, nothing but brick and stone—not a pile of leaves to lie down in. Even the ground was covered with cobbles.

At last he found himself in one corner of the fort near a line of casemates. Unlike the other casemates, these were not occupied by people. They looked like caves in the wall. It was dark under them. He entered one, thrusting his hands out before him. That casemate was full of hay. Some officers' horses were being stabled there. There was also a sentry on duty, he discovered, who warned him away.

The hay belonged to the king. No, he couldn't sleep on it. It was orders.

He sat down nonplussed and weary on a wagon tongue. The sentry passed on. His back was turned. Albine slipped noiselessly into the shadow of the casemate and climbed over the pile of hay that went up nearly to the roof. It smelled sweet. It was the new "English grass." He had never smelled grass like that before. There was a space of a couple of feet between the top of the hay and the arch of the casemate. He crawled through. Behind, at the far end, was a hollow. He discovered it by sliding down. It was warm, silent, and dark back there. A grille in the rear wall let in a little moonlight and air. A few mice rustled. He sat quiet, listening to the futile tramp of the sentry outside. Then he heard someone breathing. Whoever it was seemed to be asleep. He settled himself in a soft spot, dug in deep, and wrapped his blanket about him.

It seemed that no time at all had passed when the clamour of the reveille wakened him. The cold light of early day was coming in dimly over the top of the hay and through the barred grille behind. Outside there was a great bellowing of cattle and a distant popping of rifles. At first he could not recall where he was. Then he remembered, and stretched himself luxuriously. He had had an elegant sleep on the king's hay.

"Whist!" said a voice in a half-whisper. "Who be ye?"

He sat up and brushed the hair out of his eyes. Not

174

ten feet away, sitting where the ray of light fell upon her from the grille was a redheaded girl looking at him with wide-eyed surprise. As the light from the slanting ray grew more intense, her hair flared. There were dried leaves and wisps of grass in it. She was chewing a straw quizzically and squatting cross-legged.

"Arre ye a man or a kelpie?" said she. It was probably only his topknot she saw, as his head alone stuck up out of the hay.

"Kelpie?" said he. "Kelpie?"

"Aye, I thought so," she continued. "No man would leave a young widow like meself to perish of cold the night, and him with a blanket. It's not Christian."

"You're a widow!" he said. He looked at her now closely.

He had never seen a widow, he thought. He remembered they were mentioned in the Bible. There was the Widow of Nain, for example. What he saw now was a handsome girl apparently about sixteen, a magnificent head of auburn hair, freckles, a sprightly turned-up nose, and large grey eyes. She was dressed in ragged linsey-woolsey with a bedraggled shawl wrapped about her firm young body and shoulders. She had neither shoes nor stockings.

"I'm a married man, myself," he said at last. Certain things had reminded him of that.

"You're not tired of it, are you?" she asked.

"No, no," he replied. "I'm not tired of it! I was only married a few days ago. I've left her with the Indians across the river at Sawmill Run."

"That was hasty of you. You'll never seen her again," she said.

"I'll fetch her as soon as I can cross over to git to her," he retorted.

She shook her head. "Me husband was moithered at Toitle Creek a month come Tuesday. Injuns. It was only a little stream and he was tryin' to cross that to fetch me. But he was just a bhoy, and I never got much good from him. So I buried him and came on to the fort my-

175

selt. I ain't got nobody to do for me. I'm alone. Gawd, I wisht you wasn't married!" She looked as if she were going to cry.

"I'll get you something to eat this morning," he replied. His own stomach reminded him. "Stay here till I come back."

"Mind the sintry," she whispered. He nodded. The light was coming over the top and through the hay now. He wriggled through it and peered out cautiously.

There was no sentry in the daytime. Anyone stealing hay would be seen from the ramparts. He stepped out and brushed himself off. Now for breakfast.

That was not so easy. He passed down the line of settlers huddled against the wall, camping and cooking in the open. Once or twice he stopped. A family was gathered about a kettle, eating mush.

"You're a lone wolf, aren't you?" said one old woman, eyeing him suspiciously. "Be off."

A lone wolf! That was it. Somehow that tickled him. But there was no place for him by that fire. He went on to one of the barracks and asked for Sergeant Jobson. In the barracks there were long tables, and a great smouldering coal fire in the end chimney. They roared for Jobson, who came looking sleepy.

"It's the boy I was telling you of. Make a place for him," said he. He seemed glad to see Salathiel.

"It's rations you want, I suppose," he added. Salathiel nodded and smiled with relief. Some of the men were still eating at the table near the fire where Jobson led him.

"It's not regular rations, but it will do," said the sergeant.

Salathiel sat down and filled himself up with bacon and fried mush. There was plenty. The soldiers at least had that. He began to put aside something on a plate surreptitiously.

"So you've got someone you're feedin' already," said Jobson, and clapped him on the back. "You're a fast

176

worker, me lad. Sure, you can have it, if you bring back the pannikin."

A few minutes later he was back in the casemate behind the hay, watching the girl wolf her food. She sighed with satisfaction and lay back on his blanket. Already she had appropriated that.

"Will you be here tonight?" he asked.

"I'll wait for you," she assured him. "Don't forget me. You're the only friend I've got."

"I'll be here, sartin," he promised. He gave her a tentative kiss. She made no objection. "What's your name?" he demanded.

"Bustle—Bustle McQuiston. Missis," she added. "It's me married name." She threw one arm sleepily about his neck.

"All right, Mistress McQuiston," said Salathiel. "But I've got to go now. They promised me work at headquarters."

She didn't believe him, of course, but he didn't care. He crawled back through the hay and made for Captain Ecuyer's quarters.

All the troubles at Fort Pitt, at least for young Albine, were now on the outside of the walls. He felt like a young panther in the spring, trying out its claws on new bark.

17

A Nice Bundling Arrangement

AT HEADQUARTERS Salathiel found the captain out and Johnson fuming. After this, he was told, he was to report early, immediately before reveille. He was to make up the captain's fire, start his breakfast, and lay out his boots and clothes for the day. Also, he was to be damned quiet about it. If he didn't care to show up on time, there were lots of other young fellows who would be glad of the place.

Johnson grumbled on.

Actually, the cause of his being disgruntled was that he had come to the decision only the day before to train young Albine to take his place. Once the siege was over, Johnson had finally decided to cast his lot with his wife's family, to go entirely American. The cloak of valet and general factotum was then to fall on Salathiel. When the young fellow had not come on time, Johnson had been anxious. Yet it would never do to let Salathiel see that.

As a matter of fact, there was no one else to take Johnson's place, if young Albine would not. The personnel of the Royal Americans was such that only the roughest kind of orderly or officer's servant could be had from them at best. That might do for the subalterns, but not for the commandant. And among the frontiersmen, farmers, traders, and workmen of Pittsburgh, now crowded into the fort, Johnson could think of no promising candidates for the post of valet to Captain Ecuyer.

He had been quick to realize, however, that in young Albine fresh from the forest, raw though he was, lay a virgin field for cultivation free from the tares of any civilized prejudices. He determined to reap his own harvest from that field even though he would have to clear the ground and dig out the primeval stumps. In fact, for various reasons he preferred it that way. He wanted to have a faithful and competent successor.

For in deciding to set up for himself as a trader or farmer, Johnson could not bear to see the captain left neglected. Both a professional pride and a personal obligation to Ecuyer forbade. Indeed, he had rather a poor conscience about leaving the captain at all. But he couldn't go back to England and a break would have to come. He intended to trade or take up land. Everything grew out of land. The shaving incident of the day before had, as though by a natural mandate, appointed the person of his necessary substitute. To Johnson, young Albine now seemed to have been indicated as though he had been chosen by lot.

Of all this Salathiel, of course, had no inkling. In drawing the line about eating with a servant, Lieutenant Francis had merely puzzled him. Salathiel regarded his chance of being useful to Captain Ecuyer as both good luck and an honour. In his eyes it was as honourable to brush the captain's shoes as it would have been to fill the pipe of Pontiac. In fact he was complimented, and he therefore took his lecture from Johnson seriously and in good part. Johnson was encouraged by that and brightened considerably. As a consequence they got down to work the very first morning.

Not until years afterward did it even occur to Salathiel to think there was anything incongruous in having begun his experience of civilization by being taught by one of the best of English valets the intricate mysteries of the European male toilet in a frontier fort besieged by howling Indians. On the contrary, at the time it seemed not only natural, but inevitable.

So he began that morning on the captain's boots, shoes,

straps, saddles, and other leather accoutrements. On the care of leather, on the nature of saddle soap, on the mixing of polishes, on lampblack, pipe clay, and their application, Johnson enlarged, demonstrated, and put his pupil to work.

As a teacher Johnson had the essentials. He was enthusiastic, he was patient, and he knew much more than he taught. He did not smile, therefore, when Albine polished the sole of one of the captain's boots. He merely explained. And both time and the brushes flew. Salathiel was fascinated by a glimpse into the chests and the complicated valet kit. To his eyes it had the fascination that trade goods and a mechanical toy have for the savage. And, in addition, he could see that it was ingeniously made for its intended use. He asked questions, but Johnson insisted on one thing at a time.

"It's leather now," said he. "Next we'll take up the care of clothes and the linens."

There was also the horse, but he said nothing of that yet. It had always hurt him that in America he had had to be a stableboy too. He had lost caste with himself there. So the morning flew.

Pretty soon the captain's leatherwork was impeccable. All his boots, his holsters and saddles shone.

It was then that Johnson began to show his pupil how to go to work on himself. In half an hour Salathiel was a changed man. He looked at himself in the glass, amazed. There was only one thing he would not do. He would not wear a wig. With one on he did not know himself at all. Indeed, in Johnson's third best wig he did look ridiculous. Johnson sighed. He plaited a pigtail onto the boy's topknot. He felt that was as far as he dared to go.

"When your hair grows," said he, "we can powder it."

Salathiel shook his head.

"But you *will* let it grow?" asked Johnson anxiously. He agreed to that.

"It will take months," said Johnson. "Until then you'll look like a sailor."

"What's a sailor?" asked his pupil.

"Oh, Lord!" said Johnson. But just then Captain Ecuyer came in.

The captain, despite his stiff leg, was in an affable mood. An express with encouraging news from Fort Bedford had crept in only the night before with tidings of Bouquet's advance to that place. The captain himself had made unexpected progress that morning in reorganizing the affairs of the garrison. He therefore sat down, removed his wig, and leaned back contentedly. Secretly, he was not a little pleased to find his domestic arrangements already on so comfortable a basis. Ecuyer was not an altogether well man. He had received a wound at Quebec some years before which had never healed satisfactorily, and he needed to recruit all the energy he could in the comfort of his own quarters. Albine shaved him under the direction of Johnson, while the latter rebandaged the new wound in his leg.

The new wound from the stone arrowhead had already begun to heal. That, too, was an immense relief. One could never tell. He was good enough to praise the new barber and to commend him for having brought in the lists of white captives on the bark tablets. He enquired about McArdle and for some reason, not evident to Salathiel, seemed amused. But he was also obviously pleased. Those lists were going to be of immense help. He told Albine he had already written to Colonel Bouquet about them. The tribes would no longer be able to fool them. He and the colonel could now name the captives whom they demanded. The chiefs would think they must be mystically informed. A complete copy of the lists should be forwarded to Colonel Bouquet that very night, if a messenger could be found willing to take the risk.

Albine volunteered to go.

"No, no," said the captain, "that was not what I meant, decidedly not." And then, "Can you write?"

"Not very well," Salathiel replied truthfully.

"But well enough, no doubt," insisted Ecuyer. "No, no, we shall keep you here, by all means. A secretary-orderly and a valet-apprentice," he continued, winking at

181

Johnson, "that, and all in one, *parvus sed aptus!* It is not lightly to be sent out to be scalped." He leaned back luxuriously while Johnson sparingly applied some precious cologne water. There was not much left of it. An odour of verbena filled the room. Salathiel sniffed audibly, and the others laughed at him.

Striking while the iron was in so pleasantly glowing a condition, Johnson suggested the terms of Salathiel's hire. He was not to enlist. He was to remain as the captain's personal attendant. He was to have tuppence a day, his food and clothes. If they moved, the captain would provide a mount. To this, Salathiel eagerly agreed and Ecuyer consented.

"But *le bon Dieu* only knows when you will be paid, young man," he said ruefully. "I have only ten shillings left in my purse now. I haven't been paid for a year myself, and I had to borrow fifty guineas for my journey here from Quebec. You'll touch no coin until we get back over the mountains. If we ever do," he added, drumming on the arms of his chair.

But to young Albine this was perfect. Money meant nothing to him. He had never seen any coin except the two guineas of Charles II long treasured by Mawakis and now in his pouch. They were soldered on a silver bar and chain black from a century of wear by Indian squaws.

"You can sleep in the back room here," said Johnson to clinch the bargain.

"Oh, I don't think I'll want to do that," he replied. Both the captain and Johnson grinned.

"No?" said the captain. "Why, I thought your wife was across the river!"

"She is," said Salathiel, and wondered why they laughed at him.

"Very well," said Ecuyer, "but I'll want you any evening now to help copy. We'll see if you'll do as well with the quill as the razor."

Johnson nodded significantly. It was a bargain.

Johnson himself clinched it later by presenting his apprentice with an old, but as he said, respectable coat. It had tails and was to be worn only about headquarters. It could be altered to fit.

The captain lay back for his midday nap. He slept soundly from twelve to one. Then he ate. It was his invariable custom. It was one of the secrets of his success. Only a pitched battle could prevent his nap.

Johnson began to lay the table for lunch in the next room. There were four places. The table furnishings came out of a separate kit. A stream of whispered instruction from Johnson kept seeping into Salathiel's ears. He tried to memorize the process. The little bowls in the big bowls, cup and saucer. The round dishes, soup plates. The knife, fork, and spoon. The napkins remained a mystery until he saw them used. The cloth-covered, neatly set table looked magic. Great chiefs would eat there! At first he regarded setting places as pure ritual. He learned the movements and arrangements by rote. In the beginning it was without meaning. One did certain things in a certain way. That was why he did so well. He took over Johnson's technique as a mimic. Later he saw the meaning of his acts, the end in view. But he was never able to improve on Johnson.

That day at one o'clock precisely the captain stood beside his chair. The three invited officers arrived. Ecuyer drank to the king, apologizing for the whisky. They sat down, and the meal proceeded. Salathiel watched, sitting in a corner. Johnson made occasional explanatory gestures. He cooked at the open fire and served.

There was soup, cabbage and chicken, a plum duff with lighted brandy. Salathiel thought it had caught fire by mistake. Then he was lost in admiration. The white chiefs ate fire, he thought, and smiled at his own lingo. The discharge of a cannon outside, in reality fired at a canoe attempting to pass downriver, nevertheless seemed to the boy from the forest a fitting close to the meal.

The meal, however, continued. The whisky of the three officers was replenished. It was really a council of war. Ecuyer was planning to incorporate all of the militia in the regular companies. The discussion was lively. The boy listened. Then he began to think of Bustle McQuiston. Presently Johnson used him to help wash the dishes. The officers had departed. That was how his period of service began.

Immediately after lunch there was a great blowing of bugles and banging of drums. The entire male population in the fort, except those on actual watch, was assembled. The captain even made a short speech. During the siege he was going to draft all of the militia, and that was every able-bodied man, into the regular garrison. Heads were counted and the men were divided equally amongst the various companies. Those who would not fight should not eat. This applied to Quakers too. Captain Ecuyer was not very patient with Quakers.

"Thou shalt not number my people," muttered one of them.

"Then thou shalt not be numbered among those eating," was the reply.

Necessity and not Scripture was now the basis of authority.

Albine and Johnson found themselves tolled off to the company of Lieutenant Francis. They went on guard that afternoon. There would be drill every morning thereafter. All those under arms were to draw pay and the king's rations. Arms and accoutrements were issued. Many found themselves in boots for the first time. Among them was Salathiel.

A particularly vicious attack on the Monongahela side of the fort, followed by the driving off of some of the cattle still pasturing near Grant's Hill, amply proved the necessity of Captain Ecuyer's strict measures and stiffened the backbone of discipline.

Confident of general consent now, the commandant began to clear up the mess which the interior of the fort presented. Hay and powder were moved under shelter. Families were consigned to regular quarters. Cattle pens were hastily erected. Traders were moved into casemates with all of their goods while boards were laid across the doors for counters. The amount of provisions, particularly the meal and dried meat in private possession, was carefully registered. All the liquor was piled in one shed and put under guard, despite the protests of Mr. Croghan, the Indian agent. Mr. Croghan's remonstrances threatening to become violent, he was put under guard with the liquor, thus becoming at once the object of envy, disciplinary example, and repartee.

Salathiel found himself stationed on the platform of the stockade nearest the point where the two rivers met. From there he could look directly across the Ohio to the mouth of Sawmill Run. There was no activity there whatever. The firing came from the cliffs along the Monongahela south of the fort. The sharpshooters replied. Salathiel longed to be able to use his new gun instead of a musket. It would carry across the river, he was sure.

The rifles of the Pennsylvanians were relied upon for long-distance work. They were uncannily accurate. He watched these riflemen crouching here and there along the ramparts, waiting for the telltale puff of smoke that advertised the position of their enemies. Then they would draw a bead on the spot, wait—wait quietly with the long patience of the hunter—and shoot. But they shot only when they saw something.

Captain Ecuyer came walking along the ramparts commending them for that. He insisted that the Royal Americans should follow the example of the Pennsylvanians. He had a cane and hobbled a little.

Salathiel watched this display of skill with the rifle gun and a desire was born in his heart to be a fine shot. It was like the desire of a musician to have and to master a fine instrument. The Pennsylvanians treated their rifles as though they were fancy girls. They cherished them and pampered them. The long bows of their ancestors had at last found an adequate and a more powerful successor. Their rifles, each made separately by a cunning smith, were individual works of art. They were the most deadly weapons in the world.

Just before twilight a hail of lead descended upon the fort from the heights to the south. There was only one reply from the fort. A rifle cracked. From the top of the high cliff on Coal Hill an Indian sprang into the air and hurtled downward. They heard the crash of his body in the thicket below. A roar went up from the flag bastion. Somebody gave the death helloo. Soldiers could be seen pounding the fortunate marksman on the back. The shooting from the cliffs had suddenly ceased.

The bugles called to mess. Fires leaped in the twilight, suddenly turning a golden colour as darkness fell. The relief appeared, marching along the rampart. A few minutes later Johnson and Salathiel were back at headquarters, preparing supper for Captain Ecuyer.

Afterward the desk candles were lit, and, for the first time, Salathiel sat down that evening to copy out dispatches. He wrote in a long flowing hand with wide gaps between words. It was like a lesson set by the Reverend James, only he was writing on paper now. Captain Ecuyer looked at the copy and was satisfied with suggesting a closer space between words. Paper was scarce. The candles burned low. Johnson snuffed them twice. Then he nodded to Albine. "Tomorrow," said he, "on time, you know." Salathiel promised, and once more found himself outside headquarters and alone.

He longed suddenly for the quiet of the forests, the noise of the night wind through the trees. A guard was going about gathering up the innumerable loose dogs. There were lamentations and argument from their owners. Presently the dogs were all thrust together into a closed lean-to against the wall. They began to eat one another with hideous clamour.

Pressing his hands to his ears, Salathiel made his way to the casemate and crawled through the hay. It was quiet and dark in there. The place still smelled sweetly of fragrant grasses. A couple of horses stabled at the front could be heard crunching away. They were eating their way inward. But their threat of disturbance was extremely remote. Now and then the steps of the sentry could be

186

heard slowly passing. Salathiel laughed and stretched out. Someone giggled.

"Are you there, McQuiston?" said he.

"I am," whispered the girl. "Did you bring me my fixin's?"

"I did," he said. "Come on over and we'll eat." He undid a cloth around some fragments from the captain's table he had put aside.

Bustle sat leaning against him, picking a chicken bone. She sighed with contentment. His arm went about her and she laid her head against his shoulder. They talked on in low tones. She had been out only briefly that day, she said. The women about the fires had seemed rather hostile. "I didn't belong to no family," she explained. "I washed up, and I borrowed a comb off a lil gal, and a Mrs. McKee give me somethin' to eat. Then I come back in here. 'Pears more homelike back in the hay with the horses munchin'. Hit's like Pendergasses' old barn back to Raystown. Ain't you goin' fer yer gal?" she enquired with a catch in her voice.

"Soon as can be," he replied. "She's safest acrost at the sawmill now. When I can git a boat acrost, I'll go. There's more Injuns around the fort than you think, and the captain says he won't risk it yet. If I went myself, happen I couldn't get back again. There's other women and children with her, you know. It wouldn't do to jes get 'em scalped. It's best to wait."

Bustle considered this for some time. "I reckon you're right," she said doubtfully.

"If we're agoin' to keep house in here," she said after a while, " 'pears thar's somethin' I oughter tell yer."

He waited.

"I'm agoin' to have a baby, and you'll have to leave me alone. It ain't that I don't like yer," she went on breathlessly. "I know how men are. I'd like to play 'Gallop the Mare to Shappinstown' with you right well. But I've been athinkin' it over, and that don't seem right. He's just daid. And I think I ought to hev me baby before I take me a new man. Anyway," she said clutching him

187

tightly, "ef you're agoin' to sleep here, you've got to promise to let me alone. I thought I'd be fair and tell you fust off. Maybe you'll go for Jane now?"

"I tell you I *can't* go for Jane now without getting her or me, and maybe a lot of others, to have their hair lifted," he said vehemently. "It ain't you that's keepin' me from goin'. Hit's common sense. Ef'n you don't want me to sleep with you, I'll promise to let you alone. I'm no renegade. I'm jes lonely. I never had no folks sence I was little. It was nice findin' you here. I'll take keer of you ef'n you'll let *me* alone," he said, trying to gain some moral prestige.

She giggled.

"Hit's a bargain then," she said. "I'll try to look after myself in the day. You bring me some fixin's here at night, and we'll not tell nobody. It's nice here," she added after a while. "I hope them horses don't eat their way through from the front. There's no tellin' how long this yere siege is agoin' to last."

"It can't last after the hay and grub gives out," he said. "Bouquet's men will be here from Fort Bedford long before that."

"Aye," she said, "ef'n the Injuns don't stop 'em."

"They're comin'," he said softly but with a kind of doubtful assurance. "Captain Ecuyer says so." They arranged their blankets and lay down together.

"Mind," said she, "hit's only a bundlin' arrangement.

"Jes bundlin'," he said.

She gave him a peck on the mouth. He laughed and they were soon asleep.

A furious fusillade from the Ohio bastion roused him about four in the morning. The whole garrison stood to arms. There were many moccasin tracks seen in the ditch next morning. One of the sentries was dead, shot clean through the heart.

Salathiel and Johnson served the captain's breakfast. The work of the day went on. It was absolutely quiet. The Indians seemed to have withdrawn. Johnson began to show his pupil how to launder linens.

In the afternoon Salathiel had a talk with one of the gunsmiths. He showed him the fowling piece Lieutenant Francis had given him. It was beautifully chased. "Mighty purty fer shootin' lil birds," said the gunsmith. "I *could* fix it fer business, maybe," he admitted after a while. "It's Spanish steel by the look of it. I ain't never seed a gun with two barrels afore," he added. Then they brought four of the king's horses in to be shod, and he returned to the bellows.

Salathiel began to ponder about the gun. "It could be fixed." He remembered that. For the first time the desirability of money occurred to him. How much would it cost? he wondered.

18

A Mercenary View of Affairs

CAPTAIN ECUYER was a Swiss mercenary—but to suppose that that phrase was adequately descriptive of this Homeric little man would be an ignorant indictment of language. Ecuyer, indeed, was not to be caught up or understood in any phrase, title, or epithet arbitrarily attached to his name. He was naturally addressed as "your Honour" by discerning men of virtue and paid the compliment of being called a son of a bitch by villains.

But even that gamut was insufficient, for he was not so easily tagable or to be had in a word.

To both his superiors and his inferiors there was never anything elusive, but there was always something mysterious about the man; the impact of his personality seemed invariably to produce an effect greater than its visible cause. And it was that, plus a kind of radiation of invincible courage, which awed savages and made even the sophisticated respectful.

The peculiar tang of his character enlivened headquarters and pervaded the entire post under his command. His will acted as a solvent upon difficulties, but not acidulously. He drove constantly, but never with a whip. As every good officer should, he seemed impersonally to personify a higher and legitimate authority. And he conveyed an impression easily, by some personal art of gesture, carriage, and expression, that to resist that authority would be like trying to make a river flow backward by rowing it with a spoon. If he desired, he could even confirm the inevitable by the stern tones of his voice. But there again, he seldom found it necessary to do so.

Those who came in contact with him at all intimately sensed in the indescribable flavour of the man's presence and the pleasantly ironical pitch of his talk a humorous ripeness of experience, a poised consideration and affability, combined with a latent capacity for anger which it might be terrible to evoke.

All this, if there had been a touch of pomposity about him, would have been funny. Combined with a sick ego or priggishness, tyranny or a martinet might have been the result.

But Ecuyer possessed an immediate sense of the ridiculous in both himself and others, and he was almost ambitionless, except for a natural, professional desire for advancement in rank. In short, he was a professional soldier, a military bachelor, and a cultivated man. Honour was his motto and Patience his watchword.

Both he and Colonel Henri Bouquet looked forward to retirement, when the wars were over, to cultivate their own gardens in neighbourly companionship. And for that purpose they had together secured adjacent plantations on the borders of Maryland near Frederick, situated in some extremely pleasantly wooded and kindly watered land.

Now, the strange thing about this plantation where the captain expected to pass an amiable old age was that it did not, at least in his own mind, interfere at all with his equally cherished plan of spending his old age in Geneva. Apparently the captain was going to have two old ages to spend. He was not unaware of this little difficulty ahead, he even regarded it whimsically. But he was not at all unwilling to have two strings to the rainbow of his future, and there was also the consideration, always present in the mind of the soldier, that he might not have any old age to spend anywhere. The captain's nice balancing of this matter was, indeed, somewhat complex.

It was a good thing to have land. Everybody who was anybody, even nobodies in America, took up land. Johnson, the valet, was going in for land. Colonel Bouquet had finally persuaded Ecuyer into the arrangement of the plantation. It was an intimate arrangement, helpful even now. The prospect of being neighbours and veteran friends in the future made his association with the colonel more pleasantly personal in the present. And if Ecuyer could once "seat himself" on his plantation, if he became the master of a house, servants, and acres, he could write "esquire" after his name with a good conscience. And that was a consideration not to be sneezed at even in the colonies. Major Simeon Ecuyer, Esquire, was the style he looked forward to and fancied. Possibly colonel, if he had luck. Of all this, naturally enough, he said nothing except to Bouquet, who always encouraged him. But the mere prospect of thus solidly settling down tended to enhance the captain's prestige in his own eyes. This was not mere vanity. It seemed to promise some tangible reward and comfort for years of hazard and barbaric hardships innumerable.

As for Geneva—that was another matter. There was a lady there. Lucille was her name. The captain had been formally betrothed to her as a youth, an arrangement by families, of course. His father's prospects had been brilliant then for a city advocate, particularly after the ancient suit about the city wall had been settled, and the family of Lucille had condescended only a little for substantial reasons and because of friendship in betrothing Lucille to Simeon. The tragedy was that the young people had actually fallen in love with each other later on.

There had been one wonderful winter in Palermo, where Lucille's mother had gone for her health, accompanied by Lucille and the Ecuyers. The odour of orange or lemon blossoms was still moonlight and music to the captain when he thought of that time. He and Lucille! It would have been a marriage of the soul! Then reverses had come. His father had died suddenly. His mother was left with nothing but a small pension secured in the English funds. And Simeon had gone for a soldier of fortune to fight for the king of Sardinia, like so many other Swiss before him. In the end, he comforted himself by thinking it was not Lucille but her parents who proved unfaithful.

Lucille had promised. She said she would wait. She loved him. But the campaign in Piedmont and the Islands had been long. Letters at best were difficult, and the lustre of foreign laurels doubtful. When he had returned after nearly four years to Geneva on a lieutenant's stipend, Lucille was married to the richest and most eloquent minister of the largest church in the canton of Vaud. They lived in a beautiful chalet by the lake in the summer. And Ecüyer had seen her once there, a distant view from a boat, walking in her garden. And he had seen her once again in church, where she had got up precipitately and walked out when he gazed earnestly at her. And that was all.

That was all, except for a small, ebony box which the captain cherished. In it was a miniature set with small brilliants, a withered spray of lemon blossoms, and a wisp of straw-coloured hair. If these had once been too frequently bedewed by the tears of anguish of a young soldier, they were now looked upon dry-eyed by an older one only semi-occasionally—yet still, as the years went on, with a growing sense and maturer realization of the loss of what might have been. If sentimentality be an emotion without a sufficient cause, it would be unjust to attribute that state to the captain's feelings. His disappointment was abysmal, his affection final, and a small ebony box, far from being the childish keepsake of a shallow sorrow, was in reality the coffin in which reposed the still darling image of his stolen love.

Dreams that arise from, that hover about the fountain of life, and are forever forbidden, die at best but lingering deaths. And it was some compensation to the captain to garb his little tragedy with at least a consoling cerecloth of hope—hope that the doctor of God who had married

Lucille might be called by his Maker to an accounting in heaven, which, on account of his cloth, the captain had been unable to demand on earth. Many an accomplished soldier has married a widow after the battles of both are over. The hope was not an impossible one, however improbable. And even the thin probability of it was balm of Gilead, recalled forcefully to Ecuyer's memory by the scent of verbena in his nostrils, and to his anticipation by the word "Geneva" on his lips.

For the rest, Ecuyer was content—even if he was not fully satisfied. He had not been soured even by so bitter an experience. He was too essentially strong and clear in nature for that. He had his profession, his mind, and his honour. On that tripod he fixed and supported himself. He solaced his loneliness by a certain well-concealed sympathy with others, which brought him companionship. An experience of deep trouble made him reluctant to confer pain. He was prone to relent, sometimes at the last moment, from inflicting extreme penalties. And he had gradually discovered that to agree suddenly with an obstinate opponent is quite frequently to take him at the unexpected disadvantage of his own terms.

As for the rest?—Well, the rest was not silence. For the living it was something more salutary. The rest was conversation and routine.

All the captain's conversations, however, were not held aloud. He had his mind and his books. There was a small chest of the latter, well filled, and a large library in the former arranged conveniently for reference. Both accompanied him wherever he went.

Fully to understand the captain's wide opportunities for silent conversation, to glimpse his intimate routine, and to appreciate why he was always a bit mysterious even to his friends, could best be accomplished, perhaps, by stepping into the small bedroom back of headquarters at Fort Pitt some evening when the captain was alone. There was a certain military and personal ritual about the captain's evenings.

At Fort Pitt it was his habit, events and the state of

siege permitting, to retire fairly early whenever he could. After young Albine had finished copying out the last orders and dispatches and left, Johnson would light the large brass, sperm lamp in front of headquarters, lock up the desk, chests, and cupboards, and rid up. He would then help the captain pull off his boots, bring his small shoes, and build up a brief fire in the bedroom to take off the chill. He would leave one candle burning by Ecuyer's bed, snuff out all the others, and say good night. Ecuyer would hear him go sedately to the door and walk a few steps beyond headquarters. Then Johnson would begin to run as though he were leaving trouble behind him.

The officer of the day, seeing headquarters darkening, would immediately report to receive his instructions and the parole and countersign. Ecuyer prided himself in always referring in these countersigns to something loyal and English, and in never writing them out until the last thing at night. Thus there was no means of learning them in advance by anybody, and for that reason the officer reporting always found the captain standing by his bedroom fireplace at headquarters with the orderly book in his hand, and one candle burning, ready to undress for bed.

On Friday, June 3, 1763, Lieutenant Francis reported a little after ten o'clock and found the captain in a cheerful mood with the prospect of a possible night's sleep before him, since there had been a lull of two days in any attacks in force.

Tomorrow would be the new king's birthday and Ecuyer gave orders that the men were to receive a dram that evening for their good behaviour, and another the following day to mark the royal anniversary. Since all the rum was exhausted, it was understood that the drams would have to be whisky. That, to tell the truth, worried Ecuyer more than it did Lieutenant Francis.

"And," said the captain opening and reading directly from the orderly book, as he often did—

". . . the commanding officer desires his thanks to be given to the garrison in general for their assiduity in carrying on this work with such good spirit and dispatch, and for the future orders that but one-half of the garrison off duty be ordered for work in the forenoon and to be relieved by the other half in the afternoon."

The lieutenant looked pleased, and the captain nodded, for they both understood that this curtailing of constant labour would be even better news to the garrison than the extra drams.

Ecuyer then remarked that the parole for tomorrow would be "the king" and the countersign "George," that it was still strangely cold for this time of year, *but fine clear weather and no excuse for a surprise*. To which proposition the lieutenant carefully agreed, saluted, received the commanding officer's hearty good night—and retired.

Ecuyer then locked the door, a precaution he always took against possible surprises and massacre, mutiny, or a madman with a grievance. It gave him one more, even if a last chance, he opined. He wiped the flints and renewed the priming in his pistols lying in the case by the bed, laid his wig on a frame, undressed, anointed his old wound in the groin with *Dr. Pfaff's Emollient Elixir,* used the jordan painfully, washed, and got into bed.

It was the first time in three weeks that he had not had to sleep in most of his clothes. He wrapped his flannel gown closely about him. So far there had been no summer to speak of this year. It was still downright chill at nights in the deep river valley and his old wound received in Quebec, more than the new one, troubled him. At times he felt feverish and his leg swelled. He shivered a little and lay still a moment to get warm.

The face on the pillow under the yellow light of the single candle showed a finely cut, almost a delicate profile, a clear olive complexion, a decidedly Latin cast to the skull under the finely cropped, black hair, and a red mark on the forehead from the drawstring of his wig. The features would have been those of an ascetic if it had not been for the full mouth, and the flash of intensely white teeth which were always showing, even when he was alone, in a constantly amused and half-ironical smile that unconsciously followed the rapid play of his thought.

Having tasted for a minute or two, with closed eyes, the delights of warmth, seclusion, and relaxation, the captain groped with his hand under his bed and laid hold of a small, fat volume, one of two which had been laid there awaiting the occasion when he could read.

This, to tell the truth, was the most enjoyable hour of Ecuyer's day. He breathed contentedly, and opened the book to a marked place; to the account of the siege of Amida, by the historian Ammianus. Both the style and the narrative pleased him. Presently he read how the fire arrows of the Persians had been quenched by pouring wet sand on them at Amida. It was a suggestion worth following, one which brought his mind back to his own state of siege on another frontier.

He laid the book on his breast, still opened, and listened to the growing noises outside. The fort was noisier than usual tonight. Evidently the loyal celebration of his Majesty's birthday was getting under way—a bit prematurely, perhaps. But there were other disturbances as well.

Someone, somewhere, was preaching a sermon. That noise was always peculiarly hysterical on the frontiers. The minister shouted and the crowd moaned and yelled. There was evidently a "field preachment" going on in some corner of the fort. This time he had had to admit the ministers. There was no keeping them out. The heathen had been hot at their heels! He grinned. People on the frontiers lived so far apart and lonely, they mistook the excitement of a crowd when they did come together for the spirit of God. It was an old heresy. But it made it easier for the ministers. Even a bad orator could move them to frenzy. That would be the problem in America, thought the captain. How could thousands of lonely people learn to live in a town, in an army, for instance? How could they be got to submit to authority, these lonely, wild people? That was now the captain's immediate problem and he lay still pondering it.

As for the ministers—he had a genuine contempt for them. Long ago the captain had given up his Calvinistic Christianity and stopped praying. It was Voltaire and the spirit of the age. But religion was certainly still a problem in the new country. All that European nonsense had come to America, too. The captain had had a nauseous dose of it. It had followed him even to this last outpost at Fort Pitt.

Quakers, who wouldn't fight, sheltered themselves behind the ramparts they disparaged and insisted on their right to trade with the enemy. They were an obstinate and mischievous crew, harbingers of defeat. Then there were the Moravian missionaries who had dedicated their lives to telling North American Indians in Plattdeutsch their own peculiar version of the story of a Hebrew crucified in the reign of Tiberius, one thousand seven hundred years and more before. That did seem a little remote. They begged tools and goods from the king's stores to help found Christian utopias in the wilderness, and looked damned pious about it. When the other Christian settlers murdered their converts, they complained to the governor or to the general and got the captain into trouble. As if *he* could stop it!

But the worst of all these people by far was the breed that the captain understood best, since he had been brought up in their own doctrine and theology. Yes, as he once put it, he had imbibed the milk of Calvinistic doctrine at his mother's knee. But that was not to infer that the lady had had a milk leg. No, no, she was a healthy Frenchwoman. Yet what was he to do now with these Presbyterian divines who made long orations about infants born with nothing but the instinct to be suckers, whom the Master of the Universe fried in hell like so many long sausages, forever and forever. For this inspiring message they wished to be clothed and fed by general

198

contribution. To the captain they seemed to talk an enormous and ancient nonsense, a detritus of shamanism evolved at his own beloved Geneva out of ancient Carthage, Rome, and Jerusalem. A theory that insisted illogically upon the completely logical and ruthless mind of the tremendous Daddy in the sky. The Son would help you while the Father damned you on the Goddamned Pennsylvania frontiers!

Here the captain laid down Ammianus and took up Voltaire. He needed the encouragement of high sardonic joking, considering what he had to face.

There was that man Elijah Jeremiah McCandless, called the Reverend, for instance. His romances of life to come in the inferno were more than usually depressing. There was even a sort of morbid talent about them. They threatened the morale of certain tottering souls in the garrison. Something would have to be done about laying Mr. McCandless by the heels. A little competition was called for. Perhaps a "club" for dancing; whisky, Venus, and fleas. God, what a conjunction! Perhaps, though, it would help? The captain pondered the idea.

A cannon exploded violently on the music bastion and a red glare washed the windows of the room. Francis had probably poured train oil into the moat and lit it. They could pick Indians off the banks by rifle fire in the glare of the flames. The captain listened. Yes, that was it. Several rifles popped. Probably they wouldn't have to call him. It was just the routine procedure during a minor attack. He put his hands back under his head. Undoubtedly the noise tonight was unusually vociferous. Almost succulent. Terrific!

The revival was getting on. Another crowd must be baiting a bear. A pack of frontier dogs chased some loose horses across the cobbles right under his window. Wild hoofs galloped and curs yapped, others howled. The voice of a wolf could be distinguished in the hubbub. Every settler's family had brought in a dog. Large, fierce ones, like the people, used to living alone and now half wild with hysteria at being brought together in a pack. They fought, howled, growled, and whimpered. How peculiar it is, thought the captain, everywhere the English go they are accompanied by dogs and their own version of Hebrew literature. Something could be done about the dogs, however. On the flyleaf of Voltaire's works he jotted down this note to be dictated to young Albine next day for a general order:

As the dogs about the garrison make daily great disturbances, and in case of an attack might make great confusion in the garrison by their noise, so that no orders could be heard or executed, it is therefore the commanding officer's positive order that all dogs without exception that are not tied up after 4 o'clock this afternoon, shall be killed, and that a party be ordered immediately to put this order in execution. It is likewise the commanding officer's order that the wolf and bear be immediately killed or put out of the fort.

That at least was that!

But Ecuyer did not go on reading. He felt the need at the moment for a more important conversation than even the best of books and authors could provide. After all, there was only one man who fully understood the captain's difficulties, a living friend to whom he could pour out his triumphs and troubles and be understood. He got up and took down his writing board with an unfinished letter to Colonel Bouquet on it. He put his ink next to the candle, propped himself up, and began to write. The long quill waggled, throwing shadows across the papers and the bedclothes . . .

To return to that which concerns this place:

My garrison consists in all of 250 men, as many regulars as militia, all very determined to conquer or die; our men are high-spirited and I am glad to see their good will and with what celerity they work. I have little flour, the inhabitants receive half rations of bread and a little more meat, to the poorer women and children a little Indian corn and some meat. I manage as well as I can. I have collected all the animals of the inhabitants and placed them under our eye. We kill to spare our provisions, for the last resource, and in order that the savages shall not profit by our animals. They are around us at the distance of a mile . . . It is not my business to go to find them. I have distributed tomahawks to the inhabitants; I have also gathered up all their beaver traps which are arranged along the rampart that is not finished. The merchant Trent is an excellent man, he has been of great help to me. He is always ready to assist me, he has a great deal of intelligence and is very worthy of recommendation. I will say no more in his praise. Burent is always the same, indefatigable. I pray you to leave nothing undone to induce his Excellency to procure a commission for him; I do not know any man that merits it more.

Here is an abridgement of our work; I have demolished the lower town and brought the wood into the fort. I have burnt the high town; every person is in the fort, where I have constructed two ovens and a forge. I have surrounded our bastion with barrels full of earth, made good even places and embrasures for our cannon. I have a good entrenchment on the mined bastion and on the two curtains at the right and left. All around the rampart my people are covered by strong planks joined with stakes and an opening between two for firing the guns, without being exposed in any manner. If there were any open places I have placed across them bales of skins of deer which belong to the merchants. I have in the same way made galleries at the gorge of the bastion which corresponds with that of the barracks.

I have placed all the powder of the merchants in the king's magazine. I have also prepared everything in case of fire. My bastions are furnished with casks full of water, as well as the interior of the fort. The women are appointed for this service. One must take service from all in this life.

The rascals burned the houses in the neighbourhood. They have shot balls at the sawmill. If I had foreseen it I could have saved all. Burent, my right arm, does not let me forget anything. A king would be happy to have 100,000 such subjects.

I have made Trent major-commandant of the militia, but as that does not agree with my fancy, I have incorporated the militia in our companies, having given the best to the grenadiers. Being mixed with our men we can draw from them better parties. Three companies serve twenty-four hours. At two hours after midnight all the garrison is at its post or place of alarm, so that I believe we are guarded from all surprises. I have been obliged to make some outlay, but I hope his Excellency will find them just, reasonable, and necessary. My pocket is empty, nothing remains there but ten shillings. I would like very much to have a little more rum to give from time to time a drop to my brave men, they know my will and say nothing. I will be well recompensed if you approve of the measures which I have taken. I have done all for the best. If I have erred it is from ignorance. I would wish to be a good engineer to be able to do better; in short, I have neglected no care, no trouble, be persuaded of that.

I am very respectfully, Sir,
Your very humble and very obedient servant,
S. Ecuyer

The captain signed off with a flourish. It was a relief to have communicated with a friend and set down his difficulties. To be sure, the letter was not delivered yet. It might never be. But on looking it over he felt inclined to be more cheerful. A great deal had been accomplished in the last few days. There were some things and some people to be thankful for.

There was Burent, that indefatigable and ingenious little man. So far he had not received a penny for his services. He was not regularly enrolled. And, of course, there was Johnson. He would be leaving when the siege was over, if all went well. But he had been faithful and skilful beyond praise. Really, when he thought it over, few men were more faithfully served than was *S. Ecuyer*. One could not expect too much of human nature. It would be a sore blow to lose Johnson, but in this new country he, too, was entitled to get on if he could. Why not—who would be a servant forever? Even the captain did not look forward to that.

And Johnson's substitute was doing quite well. Nothing had been so great a surprise as to find certain cultivated qualities in that young savage Albine. For once a missionary seemed to have accomplished something. The boy was getting along with the paper work and copying. He had a mind! He was loyal, and how he did take to work! It will be interesting to see what we can do for that young fellow, thought the captain. There is a certain element of fate about him that I like. Perhaps I should answer more carefully the questions he asks. If I can?

Ecuyer smiled and blew out the candle. For some time he continued to look wide-eyed into the darkness. Just now the dogs had it. They were barking, wailing, and yapping at the moon. There was also the undiminished noise of the garrison and the "inhabitants." It slowly grew less in Ecuyer's ears after he closed his eyes. Deep down in himself, almost on the borders of sleep, Ecuyer knew what that noise was about. It was a protest against loneliness. The fort not only was besieged by savages, it was ringed about, positively threatened by the eternal silence of the forest. At any moment that silence might close in.

He struggled for a moment against it and succumbed.

There was no attack that night. Captain Ecuyer slept soundly. In the morning Salathiel awakened him. He was always on time now. There was a great deal to do.

19

How Salathiel Lost an Ear

IT WAS an enormously fortunate accident for young Albine that he had come to headquarters at Fort Pitt when the remarkable team of Ecuyer and Johnson were still working together at their professional best.

To the youth raw from the forest, the transition to civilized life might well have been purely aimless. It might have left him without any point of reference, lost in a chaos of new and confusing impressions. Salvation so often depends upon apparently trivial things. Salathiel was given a way of life and a direction by stepping into the old shoes of Johnson.

To be devoted to one thing and to make all other things subservient to it, to persist to the finish although not necessarily the logical end, is to become something and someone; to acquire a character adequate and necessary to master circumstances. Finally, it is to be able to steer a course through the otherwise mysterious fluid of events, because there is a constant point of reference in view.

There are, of course, minor and cardinal points of reference on the compass card of life. Compasses vary, and even strong characters can go off on a tangent. But once choose some fixed star to steer by, and talent, professional honour, experience, and imagination become levers to move and tools to reshape the world. Wander blindly, and they may well become only so much baggage to carry over the Mountains of Confusion.

Ecuyer and his valet, Johnson, afforded a nice illustration of this. They differed greatly in degree, but not actually in kind.

The captain's singleness of purpose arose largely from a simple, yet a complete professional loyalty to his chosen sovereign. Monarchy has long been an effective lodestar for individuals as well as for tribes and nations of men. It is, in fact, difficult to find a better one. To Captain Ecuyer the interests of the British crown were, while he served it, his own. He was in effect hired "valet in ordinary" to the spectral body of King George; that is, to the empire. And in thus following his profession completely he was also satisfactorily loyal to himself.

Johnson's point of reference was much simpler, but essentially similar. He aimed to be a perfect valet to the man who had hired and befriended him. Like Ecuyer, he did not have to stay permanently hired. Yet while he was serving he was completely and professionally detained.

Both of these men planned to retire later, to change their points of reference, to go in for themselves and for land. Johnson sooner than Ecuyer. But while their collaboration lasted, it was a prime example of harmony in action toward a given end. Salathiel was not the only one to feel the spell cast by its apparent magic and to profit by the results.

The three small headquarters rooms at Fort Pitt were the abode not only of men, but of the fixed purpose which they embodied. Order, neatness, and a vast organized intention lived there. To step out of those rooms was to step into a barbaric chaos frightened by its own confusion. Yet during the comparatively short time that he stayed at Fort Pitt, particularly during the days of the siege, young Albine saw order, neatness, and organized action spread from the three rooms at headquarters until they completely embraced and included all of the fort and its environs. That he had an intimate and direct part in this process was good luck in education.

For Salathiel at least, the lesson was conveyed only in personal terms. It was "Captain Ecuyer and Mr. Johnson." He was not so dull as not to understand the difference in the importance of the parts they played. But he also saw that they both played them well. The models he began copying made him ambitious to act well himself, and in that lay his salvation from savagery. Captain Ecuyer became his hero; Johnson his tutor in how to serve him. Thus the siege and Salathiel's education, the larger containing the smaller experience, went on. And it was much the same for a great many others.

The siege of Fort Pitt was what in European parlance would have been described as "a desultory investment of a fortress." There were no siege lines strictly drawn by the enemy, no scientifically constructed approaches that closed in by degrees until the wall could be breached and the place overwhelmingly assaulted. Indeed, it was that kind of attack that Captain Ecuyer most desired. But the Indians were too cunning, far too naturally informed, to provide the good captain with so convenient an opportunity for thus slaughtering them en masse.

To begin with, there were not enough of them. They produced an effect of numbers by strategy. In reality they were always much fewer than the English thought. They preferred, and they had to fight, the kind of war where every man and every shot counted. Attrition, treachery, surprise, unseen menace was their game. In besieging a fort they always awaited that not impossible opportunity, that moment of unconscious relaxation on the part of the garrison or some of its sentinels, that would open a closed way. To bring this about they perpetually resorted to incessant cajolery. The more important traders in the fort were constantly being appealed to by their ex-customers and former Indian friends. And to any trader the appeal of an ex-customer is always moving.

Scarcely a day passed when some Indian did not appear singing and without weapons, calling upon the name of

Mr. McKee, Mr. Trent, or Mr. Croghan, and claiming to bring news. Captured letters seized from murdered messengers would be brought in by them, after having been opened and read by white prisoners. For these, which they pretended to be delivering as a matter of courtesy, they demanded tobacco, bread, and vermilion. Traders' supplies were running low. Plunder from the inhabitants did not make up for the lack of steady trade. Many a petty chief came claiming still to be friendly; that he had only been coerced by Pontiac and the "bad" tribes into making war. At first Mr. McKee or Croghan would go out to meet them. At last they were admitted to see only Captain Ecuyer himself.

His stern demands that they must prove their friendship by delivering up their prisoners, his threats of the armies approaching to relieve the fort and chastise them, above all his refusal to provide them with lead and powder or weapons and food, amazed them. They were not used to being given tongue lashings by their white father, followed by no presents. To some chiefs who still demanded gifts Ecuyer passed out the blankets and handkerchiefs from the smallpox hospital.

Finally, a party paraded with English colours and a stolen drum before the fort. Then they crossed the river and kept crying out for an opportunity to talk. Two soldiers who were sent across in a boat to parley with them were attacked suddenly and knifed. They barely escaped, one nearly knifed to death. A load of grape-shot at last scattered the band.

That night several houses were set on fire up the Allegheny valley in revenge. Croghan's fine establishment some miles up that river disappeared in flames. A sentry was stealthily murdered. After that there was no further pretence of making talk.

All day, all night, and the day following, a steady stream of rifle fire from the heights and hills about was poured into the fort. It cut the roofs to pieces. Everyone, man, woman, or child, who became careless and con-spicuous, brought a swarm of bullets about his ears. The hospital began rapidly to fill up with wounded. The dead were buried at night. The garrison stood continually to arms. The casks along the ramparts were filled after dark by women. Those who would not carry water were refused rations. Fire arrows fell and were quenched. Every morning the signs of the enemy having been in the ditch and along the riverbanks, even in the Artillery Garden, were numerous. There was no relaxation. In one day fifteen hundred rounds of small arms were fired from the fort. The cannon boomed, for curiously enough the Indians still tried freely to navigate the river past the fort. The canoes and their paddlers were frequently cut in two by the round shot. Some would hastily leap into the water when a salvo caught them. Extra leggings, three pairs of moccasins, and many blankets, a sure sign of a war party, were found in one canoe that the garrison salvaged after it stranded on a bar.

Then the attacks ceased as suddenly as they had begun. The woods and hills all about were silent. At night only the owls hooted. There was not a sign of an Indian. The settlers began to drive out their cattle to pasture again. They cut spelts and even brought in unripe ears of corn from abandoned fields. Nothing happened.

Only the drone of insects and the constant lulling sound of the river water rippling along the banks made a solemn background for the sudden bursts of the bugle. The high, summer clouds drifted slowly over the Ohio valley, going east. The salmon were coming north, and some came into the moat. The quiet was menacing, but to Salathiel a relief. He began to long to go hunting. For even the people in the fort were quiet now.

A great change had come over Fort Pitt and all its inhabitants. The days of attack had enabled Captain Ecuyer to enforce the stern discipline which he professed. It was enforced even upon the dogs. Nothing sounded now but the bugles and the call of the sentinels every hour all night, post by post, "All's well."

It was during this lull that young Albine finally went across the river to get Jane.

He went alone. He could get no one to go with him. Captain Ecuyer would not permit it. He would not refuse Salathiel's plea to fetch his wife, but no one else was to risk his scalp. And, indeed, that was the best arrangement. For there might be several others with Nymwha who would wish to return to the fort in the canoe. Salathiel took a canoe. He could manage that best, and it was silent and swift.

Late on a dark night he glided out of the moat, kept in the shadow of the riverbank, and then drifted out into the stream past the point. Word had been passed, but a nervous sentry fired at him and the bullet whistled close past his head. Luckily it didn't make a hole in the canoe. Despite the possible alarm to lurking enemies he decided to push on.

There was no trouble at all. In the deep shadow of a long cloud that floated across the stars he drifted noiselessly into the mouth of Sawmill Run. The skeleton of the mill, burnt now, stood gauntly against the sky. There was not a sign of a dim fire or a sound. Presently against the stars he saw the prongs of a stag feeding upon the fresh herbage along the millrace. Certainly no one was near. Nevertheless, he took no chances.

He beached the canoe in a thicket and made a silent crawl through the woods upstream to the encampment of Nymwha. The lodges were gone. Everything, even the poles, had been removed. The ashes of the fires were many days old. He ran his fingers through them and could feel the small blades of grass coming through. Gone, many days ago! A sudden longing for Jane, stronger than he had supposed could possess him, came over him. He had a feeling she was lost.

He lay still with his cheek on his bare arm listening to the stream. It spoke sorrowfully to the forest. It seemed to lament its loneliness softly but eloquently. And eternally. He lay and listened.

A twig snapped somewhere. Now he saw the green eyes of a small night animal watching him. They caught the glimmer from the water and reflected it. He felt relieved. Then he saw something else. A white blaze on a near-by tree. He got up and walked over to it. There were marks on it but you could not read them in the starlight. And only the remnant of a moon was beginning to rise. A faint silver glow stole through the thicket. He had better not wait. Soon it would be bright on the river. Bright enough to see a canoe.

He poured some powder out on a chip of bark and snapped his pistol lock into it. There was a flash that made the shadows jump away. On the blaze he saw an arrow pointing south, four big marks and three little ones underneath. The darkness jumped back.

Almost at the same instant there was a blinding report and the side of his head seemed on fire.

He streaked for the stream and plunged in. His left ear had been shot away. He swam underwater as far as he could. When he looked back he could see the shadow of a man working himself along the bank. It would be slow going there. He dived again and swirled down the stream. He was leaving the man behind. The cold water was balm to his wound, but his head roared like a waterfall. If they had seen him hide his canoe he was done. But they hadn't. He reached it and shot out into the river. Someone came crashing through the thicket behind him. It was half a minute, however, before a shot rang out. There could only have been one, since he had stopped to reload.

He swept the canoe upstream with powerful strokes, calling out as he neared the fort. The salty blood ran into his mouth. No one either friend or foe shot at him as he swept into the moat. They let him in through the small postern. They thought at first he had been scalped. Salathiel was furious at the surgeon for laughing as he bandaged his ear.

"A close call," said the surgeon, admiring his bandages. "You're lucky."

"I'm a damn fool, sir," said Albine bitterly. "I ought to have known better than to flash that powder. Only an Indian musket would have missed me. He must have heard me and been waiting there all the time. It ain't only my ear I've lost. It's my wife."

"I still say you're lucky," said the surgeon.

Salathiel held his hand over his ear and wondered.

So Jane and the other women and children had gone south. If the marks meant anything they meant that. Probably they'd make for the settlements. Where? Virginia? Maybe he would hear if they ever got there. Maybe? His ear was gone.

He went and bundled in with Bustle. She was kind and kissed him and kept cold cloths on the side of his head. Next morning he showed up to help Johnson, as usual. Captain Ecuyer listened to his story and said nothing except "Mind you keep a patch on your ear." That afternoon Johnson let him leave work to go to sleep. Salathiel was surprised to find that he no longer missed Jane. He thought less and less about her. She was gone—south.

20

In Which a Casemate
Proves Unkind

SOME DAYS there would be no attacks on the fort at
all. A seeming peace would settle down on the whole
region. No one looking at the long line of forest-covered
cliffs marching into the distance on all sides, at the long
islands in the rivers, dressed in the green colour of amity
and the full regalia of summer could take them for anything but argosies of good will. The river rippled musically
about their prows that pointed upstream, the birds sang,
and the deer grazed. You could see all this from the ramparts of the fort. There would not be a sign of the
enemy. Not even a distant smoke plume rising above the
forests. Such appearances were indeed deceptive.

From the brick parapets on the east stretched a series
of gardens and meadows as far as the foot of Grant's
Hill a quarter of a mile away. They were full of tall
trees dotted about the meadows, of sweet English grasses
which had just begun to appear in that part of the country.
They were full of cellar holes with here and there a field
of German spelts and the remains of the settlers' corn
planted the year before.

Those east-lying meadows, and the Artillery Walk on
the north, or Allegheny, side of the fort were a constant
temptation to the confined garrison and the inhabitants
of Pittsburgh.

Let there be the slightest encouragement of the return
of peace, and they would drive out the cattle to graze in

the fields. They would scatter to gather spelts and the Indian corn for meal and roasting ears. Or in the Artillery Walk the women would be seen doing their washing about great kettles and tubs, sousing their white things in the river, making soap, and hanging up fluttering garments, while the children looked for green apples under the trees that General Forbes had had planted some years before. In the barracks the band would be practising lazily, making the same kind of noise on their brass and wood instruments that the chickens made scratching lazily in the hot summer dust. When a week or ten days of such a lull occurred, discipline was invariably relaxed. It was such times that Captain Ecuyer feared most as the opportunity for a surprise attack.

He did all he could to ward off the ill effects of false security. Those who went to work in the fields or to graze cattle were protected by a screen of troops. And these were not too scattered. After a near riot he met a committee of the women and arranged for a Monday washday, and no other. So on Monday the artillerymen stood by with lighted matches and the riflemen watched.

A parade of the troops was sometimes held in the late afternoon outside the walls. The scarlet-and-green uniforms, the weapons flashing in the sun, the roll of drums and the squalling of fifes carried defiance to ears attentive in the forests.

The effect of parade, drill, and obedience without argument had already brought about a new spirit among the militia incorporated into the regular ranks. It fell to Salathiel and Johnson's company to go out into the thickets and watch while the work went on behind them in the fields.

Albine enjoyed these occasions greatly. To be beyond the walls in the sunshine and free air, with the clouds rolling by, raised his spirits, and made him feel free again. And it was amusing then to talk to Johnson. The little valet became a different man. He would lie behind a log scanning the countryside for enemies and the near-by hills for a likely place to fix upon as his future farm.

They would talk over this farm and the kind of life to be lived there, by the hour. Johnson would contrast the ways of the New World with the Old.

Land, land! Land was the basis of everything "at home" and here too. But here a man could be his own man. He could stand up in the forest and need say thank you to no one but God and his own axe for room to stand in. Thus Johnson, who at times waxed eloquent.

Then he would suddenly fall silent, look sidewise at Salathiel, and remember presently to praise the advantages of being a perfect gentleman's servant, and the brilliance and luxury of life in England, even when seen from the servants' hall.

It was such glimpses of the great world which most interested and intrigued the boy from the forests. He could never ask questions enough. At least, at the very least, he would go downcountry and see the settlements. The thought of the ocean made his eyes widen. Somehow he envisaged it as a great river, vastly wide but with forests on either side. Here and there among them was the smoke of cities. But that men could outnumber trees never occurred to him.

It seemed as though the Indians themselves would at times come to the aid of Captain Ecuyer. Let a lull last a few days and the inhabitants would inevitably begin to grumble at the restrictions which he so rigorously enforced. Some woman would insist upon washing on Tuesday, or someone would wander too idyllically in the Artillery Walk, or stray too far after a cow.

Invariably a murder then took place. The cow and the man would be missing. A bullet would zip through a pair of breeches just washed by Mrs. Jones. And then suddenly, quietly, without any warning, the ditch would be full of devils with fire arrows all night. A fusillade would break from the cliffs. The death helloo would announce the return of a successful scalping party from the settlements.

For a week the riverbanks would be full of howling enemies waiting for a lucky shot at a sentry as he passed a loophole, or to scalp a bather. The gates would be tight shut, the forage would run low, and fuel would give out. Terror and secret despair would descend again, and with it discipline, always a little stronger and a steadier increase of discipline, enforced by the enemy more drastically than Captain Ecuyer himself could have dreamed of doing.

Those who disobeyed perished. The obstinate individual who smartly evaded some rule he felt to be beneath his dignity to observe contributed a scalp. As time went on the garrison became not only willing but even mentally smart. As their uniforms grew faded and worn, their weapons shone the brighter, their aim became surer, and their spirit more certain.

"Hammer the Americans hard enough," said Captain Ecuyer, "and you forge the best weapon in the world." The strategy of the Indians was making a keen and beautiful weapon. "The best of the provincials are better than the regular troops," wrote Ecuyer to Colonel Bouquet. "But hurry your arrival here. I boasted of provisions for three years to the chiefs instead of the three months that I have."

"Patience, in the autumn," replied the colonel. "Hold out, hold hard. I am trying to gather provisions to feed my own troops and to let the West Indian regiments recover from their fevers. The general sent me every last man he could sweep out of the hospitals. I am bringing some on wagons. Not a single one of the country people here has joined my ranks."

Meanwhile, the savages harassed the frontiers. DeTroit and Niagara alone held out, all the rest had fallen. All but Fort Pitt. And, meanwhile, there was much time to pass there, many things to be done.

For Salathiel day after day the quiet instruction of Johnson had gone on. He was now, so far as Captain Ecuyer was concerned, a satisfactory military servant and a good man. He did all the leather, looked after the captain's horse, washed, furbished the weapons, barbered, and help wait on the table. There his progress was slower.

The mystery of cooking, cooking in a civilized way, came slowly. Johnson taught him dish by dish.

It was really quite simple at first. The siege had cut them down to the plainest food mostly based on the rations. A few chickens, now and then some eggs, a rare green snatched from the neglected gardens by one of the settlers, potatoes, onions, and salted beef and pork were the staples. And there were beans, bags of them brought clear from England and hauled over the mountains on the backs of horses. The officers had a little fine flour but it, too, finally ran out. After that they lived on corn bread, johnnycake, "maize," as Captain Ecuyer called it.

In one thing Salathiel excelled. He could bake corn bread and Indian pudding beyond compare. Johnson was seldom successful there. Like most Europeans he simply couldn't take maize seriously. Or he treated it like wheat flour. Salathiel took considerable satisfaction in Johnson's flat failures with corn bread, and the captain's remarks about it, while Johnson sighed for wheat flour and wine.

Wine! How could one cook without it? This to Johnson and the captain was the chief hardship of the siege. Some precious brandy obtained at a great price from Mr. Croghan was eked out. It saved resorting to whisky. But to the inhabitants the absence of wine was no hardship. Most of them had never tasted it. There was lots of whisky, the good Monongahela corn or rye. It could be had for credit at a frightful price or wheedled from the soldiers. One way or another it was to be had. It made life tolerable, evenings merry. Many always remembered the siege as a time of plenty, that is, of whisky, and not much to eat.

On Monday and Saturday evenings the officers held a club, "The Club."

"Club" was a fresh word that held a combination of snobbery, exclusiveness, and conviviality about it. Not everyone could have a club. Not the "mob," also a new cant word. Gentlemen might form a club and invite the "ladies." They were invited at Fort Pitt, all the gay Molls.

The respectable wives of traders were not invited. Conviviality and not solidarity was desired.

The club made a good deal of hard feeling in the garrison. Most of the girls were Irish. Their finery was both weird and pathetic. Hoop skirts were decreed. No linsey-woolsey would do. The traders' stores, Indian fancy goods for vain and childish squaws, were drawn upon and selected from with considerable rivalry. A half-breed French packer bound for old Vincennes was discovered to have some lace. The chief difficulty was shoes and stockings. It was curious to see a girl with her hair powdered, rouged with Indian vermilion, "fit to kill," as Johnson said, but with bare feet. Beaded moccasins were the usual compromise. "One thing," said Captain Ecuyer, "you colonial officers will have to learn now not to step on a lady's feet in the dance."

They used the big storehouse nearly empty now of rations. It had a plank floor. There were three fiddlers, artillery lanthorns and Lieutenant Francis' candelabra for illumination. There was much stamping, much "haing" in loud explosive tones, a tall cutting of capers. Now and then came a quadrille for the sake of etiquette. These were always languid. The country dances were popular and jigs by the Irish girls, while the rest of the company sat around on bales and chests.

At midnight by special dispensation the colour guard came for the colours and the whole "rout" paraded behind fife and drum as the flags were returned to headquarters.

Johnson and Salathiel served supper there with the captain as official host. The jugs of Monongahela made up for any lack of sillabubs. The girls sat around on the officers' knees. The absence of stockings seemed to worry no one, even to be appreciated.

"We are not entirely their dupes, though," the captain wrote to Colonel Bouquet. "Poor Richards has catched the itch and seems melancholy. We hoped to be gay, now we opine it is best to be gay and careful. As for me, I have a wounded leg. I watch. What the gentlemen do

218

in their own quarters is not the subject of my curiosity, though it is the sole topic of the rest of the post, together with when you will arrive. God send that it be soon. I long to be back in Geneva."

All in all, the club was a success. Its midnight parade brought out all of Pittsburgh there was in the fort. The procession aroused venomous comments, and maledictions from the pious. Quakers pulled their hats down over their eyes. A few ministers pronounced the girls lost, in audible tones, as they made behind the drums for headquarters. Some of the older women complained. But cheers for the pretty girls from the soldiers, the asides and comment on the finery by the ladies not invited, a good supper, whisky, and ardent officers prevailed against respectability and hell's fire. Candidates for the primrose path comprised nearly every unmarried woman under fifty. Those under twenty were chosen.

What was the surprise of Salathiel one Saturday club night when Bustle McQuiston appeared at headquarters and sat on the knee of Lieutenant Francis. Somehow he felt Bustle belonged to him. Also she did not look as though she were having a child at all. She wore an old, white velvet bodice that Mrs. McKee had given her. It was trimmed with black. She managed her hoop skirt made from old flag bunting and barrel hoops a little awkwardly, but somehow delightfully. "The black is because I'm a widow," she explained. Young Albine wondered why a roar went up from the officers at this.

But she and Lieutenant Francis got on very well. Everyone congratulated him on his widow. Bustle didn't return to the casemate the night of that first dance. Salathiel slept there alone. He was enraged at first, and thought of shooting Francis with his own gun. It seemed a remarkable revenge, so good that he decided to talk it over with Bustle first. But she didn't come back the next night either. Salathiel observed that the horse on the outside had almost eaten his way inside. He missed Bustle. On the third night she returned. She sat eating the fragments of the captain's dinner he had brought her in silence. The darkness seemed a barrier between them.

"Like it?" he said.

"Lieutenant Francis has a better cook," she replied. "I'm more partial to his chicken."

"Maybe it ain't jes his chicken you're so partial to," he countered.

"Happen it ain't," she retorted.

"So all the time you were lyin' to me about yer baby, eh?" he drawled.

"All the time," she admitted.

That hurt.

"What made ye do it, Bustle?"

"Oh, I jes wanted fer to see what you'd do," she answered.

It was so unexpected and casual that he sat amazed and silent. That seemed to worry her.

"You didn't do nothin' about it," she continued afterwhile half accusingly.

"I kept my promise," he shouted angrily. "That's more 'en you did."

"I didn't promise anything. I jes hoped," she giggled.

"And got the captain's fixin's every evening and a warm sleep. I didn't think you were jes a blanket girl."

"The fixin's kinda come in handy, afore I got to know my way round the fort."

"I guess you know yer way around pretty God-stricken' well now, don't ye?" he rejoined.

"That's why they call me Bustle," she said quietly. "I bustle around and gits thar."

"Oh, you do, do yer!" His hand shot out in the darkness and grabbed her arm. She gave a frightened little shout. He drew her close to him.

"How about playin' 'Gallop the Mare to Shappinstown'?" he whispered. "How about bustlin' around with me?"

She lay quiet in his arms, her head against his breast. But he seemed to be supplying all the warmth. Not like Jane, he thought. The McQuiston was saying something. He lost the first part of it.

". . . and I don't need the captain's fixin's no more,"
was the last. A surge of fury came over him. He threw
her down on the hay.

"I'll *fix* you," he said. She laughed under him. Her
arms came about his neck.

"Wait, Sal. Wait till I kin slip out of me things," she
pouted.

That was all right. He let her go. He could hear her
rustling in the hay.

"It's me bustle," she whispered, "it's tied on." The
rustling continued. Then it ceased. He lay waiting.

"Well?" he said, and reached for her.

But Bustle and her bustle had both gone.

There was dead silence. Outside the horse suddenly
resumed champing hay. A rush of fury brought flashes
of light to his eyes in the darkness. He sprang up automatically under the surge of it and rushed out.

There was no one outside the casemate. Only the stars
overhead and the narrow brick alley down the side of
the main wall behind the barracks, with marks of Bustle's
bare feet in the puddles. The horse snorted at him. He
gave it a great slap on the behind just as the sentry
came around the corner.

"Did you see a gal pass ye?" demanded Salathiel.

"No, I didn't see no gal," said the sentry witheringly.
"An' who are you loiterin' around slappin' the leftenant's
mare on the arse. Git along wid ye, or I'll turn you in.
Let's have a look at you."

It was then that young Albine discovered that God had
given him great strength.

Without meaning to do so, he spasmodically took the
sentry by the belt and the coattails and threw him, musket
and all, clear up onto the parapet. He was a small man,
to be sure. But it was about a twelve-foot throw. On the
parapet above, the man landed with a tremendous clatter.
His musket flashed in the pan. The guard came running.

"Here, here," said the boyish voice of Lieutenant
Francis, "what the devil are you doing up here off your

221

beat, Number Four? How the hell did you get onto the parapet?"

"A young giant come out of the dark, sir, and threw me up here out of the alley!"

"He's drunk," said the lieutenant. "Put him in irons for desartin' his post. I'll prefer charges tomorrow."

The man was led off protesting; getting into deeper water with every explanation.

Salathiel stood below in the shadows, listening. It gave him satisfaction that someone was in trouble. He patted the mare's neck and laughed grimly. He wasn't the only one that could be fooled, it appeared. The sentry would get twenty-five lashes at least, maybe fifty. Good!

He crawled back into the hay and lay down in his blanket alone. Passion, disappointment, and anger made him shake as though he had an ague. Afterward a kind of torpor ensued. He slept exhaustedly. In the morning he was wakened by a whinny. The mare had finally eaten her way through. Her head protruded through the hay into the little compartment behind. Her ears waggled. She blew her nose gently. He patted her and laughed. "There's nothing here, darling," said he. "The place is bloody empty." He shook the grass out of his hair and left to start the day at headquarters. Romance had died in the casemate for Salathiel Albine.

From then on he began to acquire the fanatical devotion of Johnson to his work. The older man noted it and was pleased. As soon as Colonel Bouquet relieved the fort he was going to go and live by the riverbank and trade. The farm would come later. He could leave the captain now with good conscience. All that Albine had to learn yet was the care of digs, the dressing of hair.

For Salathiel the mystery of curling irons, the way to mix pomade with candle wax so that it would stand up in a hot climate, the nice art of powdering and tying the hair in a bag, took the place of worrying about Bustle and Lieutenant Francis.

He had given up his idea of shooting the lieutenant. One would be hanged to begin with. There was no doubt of that. Instead he was going to have the lieutenant's gift made over into a Pennsylvania rifle.

Rafe Carmichael, the gunsmith, was a powerful and ingenious man. He had never seen a "carbine gun" with two barrels before. How to make a rifle out of it aroused his ingenuity. He and Salathiel struck up quite a friendship discussing the problem. Rafe agreed finally to do the work for one guinea the barrel. That, indeed, was why he decided to keep the gun double barrelled. He found Salathiel had two guineas. He took them off the bar by which they had hung about the neck of Mawakis and polished them up. The long bewigged countenance of Charles II gleaming with a slightly red tinge from the good Guinea gold fired his avarice and ambition. He would make a good long rifle out of the English carbine piece for the "Injun boy," as he called young Albine— or he was no gunsmith.

They worked together at night after the long labour of the day was over. It took nearly two weeks.

Carmichael had to construct his own devices. He stretched both barrels nearly a foot. The gun was caught in a vice at both ends, heated, and wedges slowly tapped increasing but keeping the tension equal. The metal grew thinner as it stretched and the bore was left undisturbed, except that there had been a slight choke to it. The beautiful thing was that Carmichael eliminated the choke. When they were finally finished the two tubes seemed alarmingly thin. About the rear part of the chambers where the explosion took place the smith forged an extra thickness of steel and welded it on. Then he put counter weights near the muzzle to eliminate "upkick." He did this by hand with a hammer and a fierce fire in the welding. He made some coke in two little pots. Salathiel plied the bellows. The only part he was not allowed to see was the tempering. Carmichael had his own secrets. He retempered both the barrels and polished them.

All this was done in a common blacksmith shop. The gun was carefully remounted on a new stock to give its greater length the proper balance. Then the gunsmith himself spent a day or two on the sights. He was a majestic shot. Half the fort assembled to see a double-barrelled rifle. Rafe could snuff a candle at two hundred yards. He made a double bead on the front sight. One bead took care of each barrel.

The gunsmith was proud of his work. He insisted that young Albine must do him credit by using the gun right. They spent hours before the summer was over in the ditch of the fort shooting at a mark. Old hunters sat around drawling their advice. Salathiel became a marksman. He had a steady hand and eye. He fell in love with the gun. He was so proud of it he took it around to show to Lieutenant Francis. They became friendly again. The lieutenant was extremely decent; ". . . so I reckon I won't shoot you with it, after all," said Salathiel, grinning.

"What d'ya mean?" said Francis, who was not entirely reassured by the grin. Salathiel explained. He was now able to tell how Bustle had fooled him as a good joke on himself. The lieutenant was not entirely amused, however.

"So you left me to ride both horses, by Gad; the lady and the mare you slapped, and had the fowling piece made over into a rifle with homicidal intent. How about the sentry? He's posted for fifty lashes!" The young officer looked serious.

"That's what I really come to tell you," said Salathiel. "I wanted to get him let off, and you'd have to know why."

"Quite," sighed Francis. "Here," said he, suddenly turning less thoughtful, and pouring out a nip of brandy, "here's to a narrow escape from murder and a warning to you, you young American scalp. You're getting along in the world now, a little too fast maybe. You're the captain's man. Don't let it go to your head. Let the king's sentries alone and don't plan to murder your officers. Treason is imagining the death of the king, you know. The guilt lies in the thought."

"I've been thinkin'," said Salathiel.

The lieutenant nodded. He wanted the interview to be over.

"What I came to say is that when I heard your voice on the parapet that night I got kind of shamed and I thought I might jes say that maybe Bustle will get tired of your fixin's, too."

"Just you leave that to me," said Francis, grinning himself now.

"I'll do that, sir," replied Albine, "good luck."

"Damn his cheek," mumbled the lieutenant, and then thought better of it as he wrote out a release for the sentry. "I'll take another Moll to the next dance, though." He wrote his elder brother in England a long letter that night, The Honourable Gerald Francis. He would probably soon have the title, and it would be well to remain *persona grata* as time went on.

The incident of the young scalp I relate is typical of this levelling hemisphere. They talk to you here man to man. It somehow seems proper enough now. Just think, I've been here almost two years! Eight months alone in this howling wilderness fort! And how they do howl, dogs and Indians! Don't worry. I'll not marry the "widow." By the by, how do *you* fare with the Trefusis? Is Cornwall still kind? I hope so, my regards there. Do you know I'm absurdly superstitious about having given that young scalp your fowling piece. It's an act of generosity that plagues me strangely. Our family seldom regrets gifts. Yet . . .

. . . the lieutenant's pen ran on, discovering a rather homesick and lonely young man sitting quite solitary by a candle in a small room at Fort Pitt. An infinity of dark forests seemed to have encompassed him past redemption. London was astronomically distant. He folded the sheet, sanded the incredible address, and sealed it.

There was a tap on the door and Bustle came in. He doused the candle and took her in his arms. She lay quiet and let him do what he liked. There was some comfort in that. Maybe he'd take her to the next club, after all.

But he never had to make up his mind about that, for the last "club" had been held at Fort Pitt. Colonel Bouquet was preparing to move forward from Fort Bedford for its relief. The Indians gathered from the far west and the Great Lakes region to ambush him when he set out. It was to be another Braddock's defeat.

Meanwhile, they gathered about Fort Pitt too, and a constant day and night harassing of the garrison went on.

Salathiel was kept busy copying dispatches at headquarters in the evenings. Now and then an express would slip through from Fort Bedford and then the same man would take back Captain Ecuyer's replies. It was near the end of July. Ecuyer ceased work on his defences, which were now satisfactory even to him, and turned his attention to building boats to carry Bouquet's men down the Ohio, after they should arrive. The war was to be carried into the enemy's country. Meanwhile, they were using cannon now to keep the Indians at a distance. The gunners grew more skilful every day.

Then again there was a complete lull. Only this time people waited breathlessly for news from Colonel Bouquet. Would he be able to cross the mountains or not? That was the question.

21

The Last of the Siege

ONE FINE AUGUST MORNING a procession of Indians, mounted and on foot—there were even a number of squaws—began to pass across the peninsula between the two rivers at a safe distance from the fort. The procession continued with interludes all day long. No one had ever seen so many Indians before. Indeed, it was suspected that this was an old stage trick, that the procession was in fact continuous because it was circular.

Careful watching proved this to be so. A piebald horse that had been stolen from Mr. McKee, the trader, was seen to reappear five times. By this, and other signs, the captain concluded most of the besiegers had left the vicinity of the fort and had gone eastward to ambush Colonel Bouquet.

The anxiety at the fort was now intense. Everyone was kept at work to keep down panic and discontent. Under a screen of troops, the "Grass Guard" as it was called, the inhabitants were permitted to return to their fields and gardens. Every remnant of corn was picked, hay made, the spelts reaped, fodder and fuel brought into the fort. A small party was even sent across the river and brought back several boatloads of coal from the thick seam near the top of the cliff. They reported all quiet there, not a sign of the enemy.

Inside the fort, the carpenters and guardsmen built a bateau a day and sank it in the moat to swell. Even the children were kept busy pegging down sods and grassing the ditches. All went well. The cattle were grazing again all day in the fields. Not a shot rang out. The only discontent was from the women. Captain Ecuyer had refused to let them "smooth" (iron) their clothes, as it took too much fuel. The resulting scene he always referred to as the "female mutiny." Washing, "which," as he said, "destroyed so much wood," went on. Smoothing, however, ceased. All but his own, for he continued to appear in the starched, laced frills that became a gentleman of rank.

Johnson and Salathiel worked the little mangle with charcoal. They were engaged in just that one morning when a wounded messenger staggered into headquarters with the news that Colonel Bouquet and his relieving force were ambushed at Bushy Run about a day's march from Pittsburgh. Then there was no more news for two agonizing days.

It was the sixth of August when the first messenger came and was sent to the hospital. On the eighth a number of canoes ran the fire of the fort in the darkness and disappeared down the Ohio. Everybody had been called in. The sentries were doubly cautious. If Colonel Bouquet had been turned back, the canoes they had seen might be Indians dropping downriver to summon further numbers to surround the fort for a final onslaught. Still no word came. Captain Ecuyer, his face drawn with anxiety, which he explained as "the pain in his leg," dictated the general order as usual.

The parole was "Southampton"—"and I hope I'll see it again," said the captain. "There's no need of a countersign. Now go on, Albine, go on . . . for guard tonight, Leftenants Potts, Bollir, Price, Fleming and Milligan, six sergeants, one drummer, one hundred and six rank and file. You know the rest. Tell Leftenant Francis on the music bastion that if any Indians appear with boughs stuck in the muzzles of their guns not to fire on them." The captain stamped out, leaning more heavily than usual on his cane. The old wound he had at Quebec was beginning ~~to trouble him badly~~ again.

It was a blustering, rainy night. While Johnson put dry blankets on the captain's bed, Salathiel built a small fire in the grate with a few of the massive coals. Presently the captain returned. He smiled at the warm room and the nightshirt laid out on the bed. He had not put one on now for some days. Johnson and Albine removed his boots with great care. He took a swig of precious brandy, the last of the flask, and wrapped himself in a warm blanket. The wind and rain beat fitfully against the small, square window. Johnson departed.

"Can you play écarté, Albine?" asked the captain.

"No, sir, I don't know the cards. The Reverend Mc-Ardle forbid them. He destroyed those he found among the captives."

"They are a solace the devil has provided to comfort us for acts of God," said Captain Ecuyer, apparently speaking to himself. "Now sit down. I'll show you. This king is David, this Pharaoh, this Cæsar, and Alexander . . . suppose we try loo, it's simpler to begin with."

The world outside was forgot. Salathiel finally won a hand.

"Wrap my legs in a warm blanket," said the captain at last. "Even if I am going to lose my hair, I might as well keep my feet warm. How does your scalp feel, young man? A little itchy?"

Albine ran his hand over his growing hair now about an inch long.

"There's not much to get hold of yet," he said.

"No," mused the captain, dealing another hand. "It's going to be a close shave. Isn't that what you say?"

"Yes, sir, they do say it. But the Injuns don't always scalp you."

"We'll not go into that," said the captain. "Your play."

They went on for hours.

"Open the door," said Ecuyer toward morning, "it's stuffy in here. You're getting sleepy."

Outside lay the calm promise of a beautiful morning.

Lieutenant Francis came across the little green, his rapier clicking against his boots.

"Sir," said he, "Birnam wood has come to Dunsinane."

"What, what!" said the captain. "You're drunk?"

The lieutenant coloured violently. "I mean, sir, there's a party of Indians with branches stuck in their muskets, howling and singing in the dawn on Grant's Hill."

"Admit them two at a time," said Ecuyer, rising. "Tell the commissary to kill a bullock and start it roasting. Bouquet will have sent some troops with the news."

"Dress me," he said to Albine.

The door closed on a glimpse of Lieutenant Francis running toward the main gate.

The captain put on his best uniform and an order. He fingered for a moment in the box where he kept his few medals, some family relics, and trinkets. "Young man," said he, "there has been a great English victory. Your hair will grow longer. You are in the service of a fortunate man. Here is something to remember the greatest moment of his life." He stalked out dramatically with a peculiar French fling to his shoulders, leaving a small, silver watch in the hand of the astonished Albine. The captain had set it exactly by his other timepiece, probably to mark "the greatest moment of his life." It was 4:55 on the morning of August 9, 1763.

Fort Pitt was relieved.

To judge by the noise outside everybody in the fort including the cattle knew it already. Albine never forgot that day. In a sense time began then for him, European time on the captain's watch. The eternity of the forests and the Indians was over. He put the watch to his ear and heard it ticking. Yes, his time had come alive.

Ten friendly Indians were already in the fort shooting off their muskets and being feasted. Every inhabitant of the place had come out to take part in the general rejoicing. Men, women, and children mulled about, laughing, crying, and whooping. Indeed, the scene was one of such confusion and general abandon that Captain

Ecuyer had the drums beat and the entire garrison called to arms and sent to their posts.

In which condition of "alert," with a guard of honour drawn up before headquarters, he and Major Trent of the militia received the small advance party bearing the news of Colonel Bouquet's hard-won success at Bushy Run.

In particular the exhausted survivors of the West Indian regiments, many of them fit only for the hospital, were made much of. The news they brought was indeed stirring.

Colonel Bouquet had been attacked in a dangerous defile, where, in order to protect his convoy, he had been forced to encircle his wagons and supply train with his entire force. All forward movement had, of course, ceased. The attack went on for two days. There was no water. It looked as though the defeat of Braddock would be repeated, when the colonel ordered the circle to be opened as though part of his men were in flight. The Indians rushed in and were surrounded in turn by a ring of fire. Many warriors were shot down among the several tribes and the rest put to flight and scattered all over the country. Those scattered Indians would continue to harry the settlers, but the fort was relieved. That fact was immediately patent. The enemy had evidently abandoned the neighbourhood entirely. Scouts sent out could find no sign of him.

"Now," said Johnson, "we shall get some wine for cooking. With a little sherry we can have the Queen of Scots soup to celebrate the arrival of the colonel, and white flour!"

All that, and Colonel Bouquet himself, arrived on the tenth.

It had been necessary to rest and reorganize the troops after the battle. They came marching down from Grant's Hill over General Forbes's old road with the band playing, the Highlanders' tartans and the scarlet uniforms and accoutrements of the 76th and 77th foot making an

231

astonishingly bright show against the green of the fields and forest.

Behind them followed the dark green of the Pennsylvania provincial militia, then a long train of wagons on which rode many a drunken, friendly Indian along with the wounded, then pack horses, a herd of sheep, cattle, and hogs, finally some artillery and the rear guard of hard-bitten men in hunting shirts. Trouble, if any, could now be looked for from the rear.

The entire garrison of Fort Pitt was drawn up outside to receive them. Volleys were fired and the river valleys echoed to the discharge of muskets and salvos from the ramparts. Colonel Bouquet and Captain Ecuyer embraced, which seemed strange to all the English and Americans. Nevertheless, their hats went high in the air.

That evening the fort was full of the red glare of torches and bonfires, drums, music of all kinds, roasting sheep and cattle, Indians capering in Indian finery, fights, and official feastings. The captain moved out of headquarters to make room for Colonel Bouquet.

More important to Salathiel, the colonel borrowed Johnson from Captain Ecuyer. In two small rooms near the music bastion Captain Ecuyer and Albine now conducted their establishment alone. Johnson, in fact, had foreseen this. It would only be courtesy for Captain Ecuyer to offer to lend his man to the colonel. Johnson had simply assumed that he would, and had acted accordingly. It would in the end be an easy way to part with the captain. For after a brief service with the colonel, Johnson intended finally to depart.

It was some days before Captain Ecuyer fully realized this. He was considerably annoyed at first and sent for the chests with Johnson's valet and barber kits. They belonged to the captain, having been purchased by Johnson for him in Philadelphia.

Salathiel went for them and took them away as part of the captain's private baggage. Before the colonel, Johnson could say nothing. Later he came around and struck a bargain. He was to have the loan of what items he needed from the kits, provided he should continue to help Albine when necessary.

It galled Johnson to have to ask this and to find that his pupil was smart enough to drive the bargain. Yet in the end he laughed. It was easier than having had to give the captain notice. When Colonel Bouquet went down the Ohio into the Indian country, Johnson intended to stay behind. Already the inhabitants were beginning to plan where they should rebuild their houses when they were released from the fort. Already they were quarrelling about lots. The colonel settled that. No more houses were to be built near the fort. He had one of the royal engineers re-lay a plan for the streets of Pittsburgh. Among the first lots to be pre-empted was one for Johnson and his Amelia near the Diamond.

22

The Captain's Man

THE REMAINDER OF THE SUMMER and all of that autumn were an intensive period of apprenticeship for Salathiel. For the most part it was pretty lonely, too. More and more of his friends kept departing, while the captain remained at the fort. Captain Ecuyer was in charge of the surrounding neighbourhood and of communications as far back as Fort Bedford, while Colonel Bouquet prepared for his coming move down the Ohio into the Indian territory.

Despite the all but desperate activity of the garrison in building bateaux and collecting supplies, the population of the fort gradually thinned out. Even the personnel of the garrison constantly shifted. A few days after the place was relieved all the refugees from the mountain settlements, and the captives of the Indians who had escaped or been delivered to the fort, left for the eastern settlements under a strong escort.

Among them were Lieutenant Francis and Bustle. The lieutenant was taking her to Philadelphia. She said goodbye to Albine shyly but with a quiet triumph, for she was mounted on a good horse and in a town gown with a wimple. Uncommonly pretty, Salathiel had to admit. She secretly was in hopes the lieutenant was going to take her to England, and had already assumed a certain condescension to colonials. She said, "La, la"—and rode a sidesaddle the saddler had especially made. And she had learned to "simper under her wimple," as the lieutenant said.

"Be careful how you use that gun I gave you, Albine," he shouted, as they rode off along Forbes Road for the Alleghenies.

Most of the captives, who were being returned to the settlements, set up a great outcry of farewells and not a few lamentations. There were many orphaned children among them and they were leaving the only friends they had. The orders were strict that none should be concealed or remain behind, for the crown was evacuating all the country west of the mountains. With the exception of Pittsburgh, which was to be a trading post about the fort, that region was to remain Indian lands. With this "downcountry" party, as it was called, went most of the friends Salathiel knew.

In spite of the danger of a renewed Indian attack, the inhabitants of Pittsburgh were soon out of the fort and engaged in rebuilding their houses on the new plan provided by the engineers. They resented the plan. They wanted to put their houses anywhere. They resented the policy of the crown in retarding the growth of the region. They hid all the newcomers and refugees they could, and they insisted on carrying on an illicit trade with the savages which continued to provide the Indians with whisky, guns, bullets and powder even in the unsettled and warlike condition of the frontier.

All gratitude for the defence of the fort was soon forgot in the petty irritations of rules imposed by the royal officers. Colonel Bouquet and Captain Ecuyer remained personally popular, but the class they belonged to was more and more hated and held in contempt. Their red coats were the symbols of the crown's veto on the growth of the settlements. They and the garrisons were a dam behind which a flood tide setting westward rapidly backed up and accumulated.

For a while this tide was held in abeyance. The Indians, defeated in a pitched battle, scattered to burn, plunder, and murder; to destroy every outlying settlement and

235

lonely cabin west of the Alleghenies and to conduct bloody raids far down the eastern slopes of the mountains clear into the plains. Nothing could come west except under heavy convoy. Until Colonel Bouquet should attack the Indian villages farther westward, the war would go on.

Salathiel spent the rest of the summer at the fort. He was kept intolerably busy. That was the way he felt about it at first. Gradually he grew used to a day that was a constant round of work and routine from reveille to sunset. In fact, the evenings and nights too were frequently taken up by work for the captain. Fortunately, he soon found that he had the capacity to lose himself in his work. And the departure of his friends and companions made it all the easier. Also fortunately, Captain Ecuyer was an extremely exacting man.

Salathiel rose before the sunrise gun and groomed and fed the captain's horse. Then he took a plunge in the river or the moat and returned to quarters and dressed himself most carefully and neatly. Then he laid the captain's uniform and weapons out on a table at the foot of his bed: polished boots, knee breeches carefully pressed, a fresh laundered shirt with shirred lace neckpiece, a set of buttoned gold-lace cuffs and linen armbands to cover them.

Every button on the captain's coat and every buckle on his sword belt and baldric had to shine. The fine gold fringes of his epaulets must be methodically wiped and arranged in the correct droop. He had two pairs of pistols. One pair was always ready, perfectly cleaned. And his sword, especially the gold hilt, must be without a speck. All this, including a pair of long silk stockings that must be fresh and darned, was made ready for him, with one of his three cocked hats, kept in a press-box, laid out on the top with the gold-lace edging hooked on.

Next to the pistol holsters lay his gorget and spurs. These he put on last. The gorget was all that remained of what had once been the complete body armour of a knight.

After all this equipment was complete and every item accounted for, Salathiel brought a bucket of hot water from the kitchen and filled the captain's silver ewer and laid out the shaving kit beside his basin.

At the first note of reveille the captain sat up. He took a French book and read several verses. He looked at a locket in a small ebony box, and stepped out of bed and was shaved. He then dressed himself, had his hair dressed or he put on a wig, depending on the state of the temperature. After that, he went over to Colonel Bouquet's quarters for breakfast. This was served to both the gentlemen by Johnson and Albine together, until late in October when Johnson left. After that event the colonel dressed in his own quarters with the help of an orderly. Albine cooked and set the table.

That was the way the day invariably began. But that was only the beginning.

After breakfast Salathiel swept out the quarters, made up the bed, rearranged the captain's papers from the night before. Then he washed, starched, and ironed, curled the wigs when necessary, cleaned the pistols and leatherwork, and looked after his own clothes.

He now had two good suits, thanks to the captain. He wore moccasins whenever he could, but when he heard the captain coming he slipped into boots. Usually he was through by eleven o'clock. That gave him an hour in which to read.

The captain had a small chest of books. Some of them were in French. Others were military texts and novels in English. Before he left Fort Pitt Salathiel had read all the novels. He then took to borrowing books from Major Trent, the militia officer, who had a nice little "library," as he intended to settle in Pittsburgh.

A book called *The Anatomy of Melancholy* remained in young Albine's memory with peculiar effect. It affected his method of speech. He even confused it with the Bible. It seemed to be written with equal authority. *Robinson Crusoe* was what he enjoyed most. *Clarissa Harlowe* he pored over page by page and then read it again, since it gave him, as he thought, a complete lesson in how life was carried on in London. For the characters he cared nothing. It was what they did, and how they did it. It was their manners and what they said. Much remained in inextricable confusion but some things came clear. His curiosity about life in England and Europe was whetted keen.

At noon the captain came to his quarters for lunch. He usually brought some other officer with him. Lunch was a light meal hastily eaten, soldier's fare with a glass of wine. Captain Ecuyer then slept for an hour, first giving instructions as to what uniform to lay out for evening wear. Salathiel would rid up, lay out the captain's clothes, and go to the stables. The afternoon was his in a sense, provided he could share it with the captain's horse.

There was very little use for the horse while in garrison. He was expected to give it exercise. It gave him an excuse to return to the forests. It was not safe to cross the rivers yet. But just east of the fort between the two rivers was a tangle of high hills and ravines, glades and thickets that teemed with game. Here and there was an old clearing abandoned now. The cabins were burned.

In such a little clearing near the Monongahela he once came across the body of a child lying near a spring. The face was nearly eaten away but the fair hair remained. He could see it had been scalped.

This incident brought back to him forcibly the memory of his own early life. He began to ponder much over it. He remembered he had had a brother or a sister. A savage moodiness, part of his age perhaps, and so natural enough, began frequently to obsess him.

Sitting in a thicket once, waiting for a doe to come to investigate his lure, suddenly he thought he heard his mother scream. She seemed to scream at him from underground.

He missed his shot.

Suddenly he was furiously angry. He longed to kill somebody—Indians! How he hated and despised them

238

now! They had made him what he was. All his ignorance of what was familiar to most white children, all the enormous trouble he had had to learn to do even simple things, was their fault. The Big Turtle had carried him off. Probably it was he who had planned the attack on his father's cabin. He looked at the turtle over his own heart, felt it as though he would like to rub it away. It was there, indelible. Well, it should remind him. Remind him to kill!

He went back the next afternoon to the spring where the child's body lay, and scraping a shallow grave with his hatchet, he buried it.

There was something about this secret burial that he could not explain. There was a horror as though he were burying himself. He had a violent headache when it was over. Someone would have to pay with blood for what had happened to that dead child. It smelled. He could smell blood!

And so many a time, wandering the woods in the afternoons of that August and September, these black moods came upon him. When other young fellows were thinking of girls till grey spots swam before their eyes, Salathiel remembered, remembered, and remembered— the dim comings and goings of Indians through the dark interminable forests, the hoot of an owl by moonlight and the scream that lived in his brain. The spots before his eyes were not grey. He was waking now. He was beginning to think. Sometimes on these afternoon excursions he would find himself weeping. He loathed himself for that. Why he wept, he had no idea.

These moods gradually turned from ones of extreme feeling to a long-lasting hardness. There were rare moods but they tempered his metal as extreme heat followed by a plunge into cold crystallizes steel. It was that summer that his face began to take on the narrow planes and angles of a hard-wrought hatchet, a blade that seemed to be whetted keener and keener as time went on. Perhaps the siege had not helped to soften the metal any.

It was now more malleable, to be sure, but not exactly flexible.

No one who looked into the face of the boy who returned to Fort Pitt nearly every afternoon about five, riding the captain's horse without a saddle, and with a long double-barrelled rifle over his arm, would have described him as a pliable youth. His hair, which had curious streaks of steely grey in it from the time when first it grew out from his shaved head, was now long enough to be tied back into a queue, but it seemed to have a purchase upon, and to stretch back his forehead from his nose into a tense smoothness. The eyebrows were appropriately raised, just enough to convey a disconcerting irony of expression that went well with the piercing blue-grey eyes and eagle's beak beneath. Yet there was something decidedly humorous and pleasant about the chin, and his bright flash of a smile set off by firm straight lips and big white teeth. He wore a forage cap pulled down over the remnant of his left ear.

Salathiel seldom returned without something for the captain's pot: a rabbit, a turkey, or a young deer. His aim became more and more unerring as practice trained his eye. Twice he shot wolves. They were horribly plentiful those years. And once a young bull buffalo that had somehow wandered across the river near Croghan's burnt cabins. Buffalo were getting rare now anywhere near the eastern mountains. As for foxes, beavers, and other pelt-bearing animals—he was collecting a bail of furs for trading.

Thus during August and September he managed to lead a double life. He was the captain's man at the fort, cook and valet-secretary; in the forests and wild hills about Pittsburgh he returned to his former wilderness self.

Yet there was no conflict for him in these two widely contrasted modes of existence. They were all of a piece. Things had just happened that way.

He did discover, however, an unusual and steadily growing strength of muscle and limb. The early years in the forest of alternate feasting and starvation, of hardship and lazy timelessness, had left him with an iron frame, an unbelievable power of endurance, and a deftness of movement and keenness of sense alien to most civilized people.

In particular, he used his legs and feet as though they were meant to walk on and not as though he were lame. He could bound, leap, and turn handsprings. Few could wrestle with him. He was quick, and to lay hands on him was like grasping an eel. One after the other he threw all but the oldest and most powerful wrestlers about the fort. The favourite sport many an evening was a bout between some champion of the garrison or the militia and "the captain's man."

One older man from Devonshire, one of the grenadiers, threw him again and again. In the end Salathiel made friends with him and got him to teach him all he knew. It was the lore of a winner of the Taunton belt. It stood Salathiel in good stead all his life.

Two things troubled him: the necessity of wearing boots frequently and a sense of smell that was especially oppressive in quarters. He knew many people by their smell, and not only the unwashed. He found Captain Ecuyer's use of cologne hard to bear. The captain liked verbena in his handkerchief. It kept him, he said, from being homesick. He would often close his eyes and sniff. Why, he did not say.

Evenings were usually as busy, if not busier than the day. The horse was put up after Salathiel returned. He had to see it groomed and fed. Then he hastened to dress the captain at six o'clock. Every evening the captain dined in full-dress uniform. When it was his turn to take a parade or guard mount he did so in a wig or powdered hair. That, with pomatum, took time. Then there was supper, either to be cooked—or Albine helped Johnson serve it. Sometimes a full dinner with wines had to be prepared and served. Bouquet had brought a cart of wine along with him, including Burgundies and sherry. And on many an evening there was the captain's correspondence, which he was expected to indite or to copy,

241

and not infrequently a game of cards or chess, providing no one dropped in.

In spite of all that there were, nevertheless, many evenings free. But there was little to do about the fort. The hard-worked garrison, after labouring all day on boats, ditches, or transport, smoked, drank, and went to sleep. The drums rolled, the bugles sounded, and the beginning and ending of the day were marked by a gun. Salathiel would almost have welcomed the excitement of the siege again.

Then suddenly the whole order of his existence dissolved and took on a new and absorbing aspect.

23

The Ark

MILITARY LIFE, which so often gives the appearance of being permanent and well settled, is in reality, and of necessity, most changeable and ephemeral. Soldiers are like jinn who serve the master of a compelling cup. At any moment the new Aladdin who has the cup in temporary keeping may rub it and send them off to the world's end on impossible or even captious errands. It is the part of the jinn to salaam and obey. Young Albine was now about to learn this by experience.

He had taken the routine of existence and labour during his months of sojourn at Fort Pitt as part of the order of nature. Much of it, indeed, he had had to learn by rote, because his success depended upon imitating Johnson in particular, and others in general, in every detail. He had therefore carried on his work as a kind of ritual in which the reason for what he did was not always fully understood. He had performed as he had learned, by rote. In fact, it was this exactitude in an unvarying and faithful performance that had finally impressed even Captain Ecuyer. Consequently, when there were humorous incidents or he made ludicrous mistakes, the captain had condescended to explain. Errors were never repeated.

Now all this round of habit was completely changed. Albine was thrown on his own resources under difficult and ever-shifting circumstances, for Captain Ecuyer was ordered away from the fort and put in charge of speeding up reinforcements and protecting the transport of supplies over the difficult mountain roads from Fort Bedford westward.

The success of Colonel Bouquet's projected expedition into the Ohio country in the coming year would depend mainly on his receiving these supplies, and Ecuyer was the only officer the colonel could wholly depend upon.

So, in spite of the fact that the old wound in the captain's groin was beginning to swell alarmingly again, he left his comfortable quarters at Fort Pitt and began a kind of nightmare, gypsy existence, flitting from one small post to another through the wilderness, crossing and recrossing the mountains in all kinds of weather.

Ecuyer had intended to resign, go to his plantation to get well, and return at least for a while to Geneva. He needed a surgeon and time to recover. But Colonel Bouquet had asked him not to resign. The colonel had not hesitated in his own urgent necessity even to point out that to retire now might be construed by some, who did not know the captain, as resignation in the face of the enemy. The captain was an honourable man first of all. And Bouquet's argument had therefore been as cogent as the colonel had thought it would be. The captain had consented to remain in service. But his spirit was stronger than his flesh. He came of necessity, as he grew weaker, to depend more and more upon Salathiel. And it was literally a nomadic life they began to lead, an endless moving about in the forests upon one errand or another.

When Ecuyer finally had decided to remain, as Colonel Bouquet so much desired, he called Albine into his room one night after he had gone to bed, and had his first intimate conversation with him. Captain Ecuyer was troubled by his great responsibility and growing weakness. He needed personal help.

"Sit down," said he, "I want to talk to you. You seem to be a *garçon* of considerable natural common sense, and you have been faithful and held your tongue since you began to serve me. I have even thought you might care to go back with me to Switzerland if I resigned. It could have been arranged."—Here he raised a candle for a closer look at Salathiel's face. "Good! I see that would have pleased you. But we shall not be going to Switzerland now," he continued. "The good God only knows whether I'll ever see my own country again. The lakes with the snowy mountains floating on their bosoms! Ah, you would have liked to see them, too! It is beautiful!" Here he caught himself up rather sharply.

Salathiel was surprised at the softness that had suddenly crept into the captain's harsh features. "*My* country!" the captain exclaimed again, and went on.

"No, I rather think I'll never see it except in my dreams. Instead, we shall be traversing these American mountains, and winter is coming on. I wonder if you will care to stay with me and look after me. You are not enlisted. You have never taken the oath to the king. You do not have to follow me. Perhaps you would rather return to the forest? But I shall be needing you more than ever. My wound is not so good. Yet I would not command you to come. You understand, I think.

"I shall be needing something more than blind obedience. And much more than my personal comfort will depend upon you, because all of the success of the coming campaign will in a way depend upon me. If we can't keep the supplies coming forward over the mountains, there will be no Ohio expedition next year. So I shall need someone like yourself, someone that knows these forests, who can keep me alive long enough to do what I have to do. Yet I am wondering if the disappointment of not going to Europe will not make you feel like running away. Like—how do you Americans say it?—'going over the hill.' Isn't that it?"

"Yes," said Salathiel, unconsciously answering the literal question first. "But *no*," he cried, seeing the captain's face, "I do not mean I will go over the hill. I mean I will stay on with you. I will go over many hills with you. It is you and not the king I am serving."

"Tut, tut," said Ecuyer, "no use talking treason. There

is too much of that about in these hills now." Nevertheless, he looked pleased.

Salathiel later on was not able to conceal his own satisfaction when the captain told him that Lieutenant Francis had also asked to take him along, nor his disappointment that Captain Ecuyer was not going to Switzerland, at least immediately.

The captain understood. He knew that Salathiel was anxious to learn, and see the world. He had noted, and secretly approved, his interest in books and his struggle to learn the ritual of European ways and manners.

"I'll take you along when I do go home," he said at last. "But it is only fair to say that I may not live to get there. I am really an ill man. Yet if I do go, you'll come along?"

"I will," said Salathiel. He rose and shook hands with the captain in solemn Indian fashion. Ecuyer grinned. He knew the customs of the country, and that shaking hands after a counsel meant a solemn bargain, a pledge of friendship, something more binding between man and man than even the military oath. *"Bon!"* said he.

"Now here is what we shall have to think of first," the captain continued. "I am not going to be able to ride my horse—much. You must contrive with me some sort of wheeled vehicle, a chariot, for these hills. Not only for me, but for our supplies, papers, and medicines, and for feed for the horses. There will be five horses, four to haul and one to ride. There will be three of us. For I shall also need a man who is a good soldier, a driver, and a combined blacksmith and carpenter; a good shot, too! A man of high heart," said the captain, "and of calm courage, and patience. Do you know him?"

"Rafe Carmichael," exclaimed Salathiel, thinking instantly of his friend the blacksmith.

"Excellent!" replied Ecuyer. "But wait—the colonel will never let *him* go. He is the only competent arms smith he has."

"No," agreed Salathiel, "old Buckey would never let him get outside the fort."

"Well, then?" said the captain, overlooking the familiar term for Colonel Bouquet, which all the Americans used. "Well, then?"

Salathiel shook his head, at a loss.

"How about Burent?" he finally suggested.

"I believe that is our man, if we can get him!" exclaimed the captain, astonished that he had not thought of Burent himself. "He's not enlisted, but he's been invaluable all during the siege at every kind of work."

"Which he hasn't been paid for," added Salathiel.

"I know, I know," said Ecuyer, "but maybe I can have that rectified now. I'll take it up with the colonel tomorrow. Meanwhile, here is what I want you to pay attention to now—the *voiture,* the chariot, the wagon— what is it you call it? Maybe your friend Carmichael can help with this?"

Shuffling among his papers, the captain drew out a little sketch on a piece of torn paper and handed it to Salathiel:

"You will observe," said Captain Ecuyer, "that my machine is to be made from a heavy ammunition wagon drawn by four horses, and behind this is to trundle a chest on two wheels, a *caisson,* as the French call it, for

247

carrying extra supplies. These were first invented by that admirable warrior, the king of Prussia. I observed them first as a cadet in Silesia. However, that's neither here nor there.

"Over the main wagon is to be stretched a piece of stout canvas on a ridgepole, for shelter, the end flaps to be fitted carefully. And also observe this: the whole concern must be painted dark green, canvas and all. The gunner has that paint in stock for his iron cannon. You see, it is not my wish to be observed moving around the mountains in a white tent, ten miles away. Painted green, we shall be the colour of the forests by day and invisible by night.

" 'Tis most important that you should see that all the ironwork is doubly strong, the axles of hickory, and everything double bolted; the tires of new iron, thick, cold-shrunk on. And I shall need, too, a small stairs both to mount into the wagon and to get up on mine own horse, which is to follow behind. My leg is getting stiff. My horse can follow behind, or you can ride her.

"Now I think in this *voiture*," said he, tapping the sketch, "we can get around in these mountains. Since they have brought hundreds of wagons and heavy artillery over the new road from Bedford ever since General Forbes cut his way through, and was carried over on a litter, another sick man may follow where he went. No, it is not impossible, not with four or five horses.

"Never mind the sun and moon I have shown here in the sketch. You will not need to draw them from the quartermaster, since I have already drawn them myself. The sun in the east is to represent my rising hopes of success, and the waning moon in the west, 'tis my waning health setting behind the horizon of these Alleghenies, perhaps permanently. Who knows? The astronomy is bad, but the symbolism passable, and it has always been the prerogative of artists to express feeling by distorting natural facts.

"Well, here are the requisitions on the quartermaster and master gunner for the wagons and their parts, and

248

the supplies. And here is a list of what is to be taken along. I have already made arrangements with Colonel Bouquet for the horses. We must leave here shortly. Before the weather breaks, if possible. So see to it tomorrow, and have everything perfect. Now, good night. I'm glad you will be along."

Captain Ecuyer blew out the candle, put a pad between his knees to ease the wound in his groin, and settled himself for sleep.

Seated by the coal fire in the next room, for it was now frosty autumn, Salathiel looked at the sketch, and the list the captain had given him. Small tongues of gas flames licked out of the lumps of soft coal, flickered, and seemed to impart a shadowy movement to the wagon and its imaginary teams. He could see them jolting along the rough road through the mountains.

Captain Ecuyer's sun and moon did not surprise him. Having posed for Lieutenant Francis, he was prepared for the vagaries and vanity of artists in their own work. He smiled. The expedition was much to his taste.

Doubtless there would be trouble with the Indians. He was surprised to find how much he looked forward to stalking them. What a satisfaction it would be to have them at the end of his gun sights!

He began to turn over in his mind the difficulties that must be met, and what they would need to meet them with. The *voiture*, he had to admit, was a good plan. He turned to the captain's list. Unlike the sketch, there was nothing artistic or romantic about it. It was the neat, hard thought of a soldier, carefully set down:

Item: My camp desk with papers and writing
        materials. Pack the bottle of ink in straw.
    "   My chest of clothes and weapons.
    "   My comfortable, folding camp chair.
    "   My folding iron campaign bed like that of
        Frederick, the great king of Prussia.
    "   Six lanthorns and many candles—see to it.
    "   One dozen best English woollen blankets so

that we freeze not to death. Draw these
from the quartermaster, no Indian trade
goods.

" The charcoal foot warmer left by General
Stanwix—and the charcoal.

" The leather chests and portmanteaus containing the valet supplies and toilet contrap-
tions you received from Johnson.

" One small chest for rations and condiments,
salt, etc.

" One small arms chest with ammunition and
all necessaries for the upkeep of the pistols
and muskets.

" One chest for Indian corn for the horses,
loose and not upon the cob. To be carried
in the rear cart.

" One chest of tools, extra iron fittings for the
wagon, spare chain, spare harness parts,
bolts and sich.

" One chest upon a chest to sit at the front of
the wagon, the driver to use this as a seat
when driving from inside, the lid of the
chest to open downward and inward within
the wagon, for to be used as a desk and
table top. Leave it empty.

Item: Take notice—fasten all these chests by lashings to ringbolts ship fashion. Bateman,
the ex-mariner, will show you how. Do this
or we shall be crushed when the chests
shift on a hill.

" Two hamemucks, or hanging beds, after the
manner of sleeping picked up by the 42nd
Regiment in the West Indies. Make these
of strong hides lashed with thongs. Also
ringbolts for fixing the same.

" Rye straw deep and as many buffalo robes
as you can come by or beg for the bottom
of the wagon.

" A pot of tar and a brush for repairing the

tarpaulin. See also that the bottom of the
wagon is tight. Neat's-foot oil for the saddle and harness and boots.

Note: We shall be living in this *voiture* for months
in the winter and in the mountains. See to
it that you see to it.

Accordingly, the last days at Fort Pitt were busy ones
for Salathiel. Grateful for the hardships which Captain
Ecuyer was about to undertake for his sake, "Old
Buckey," as Colonel Bouquet was affectionately called,
gave the captain's man the run of the storehouse, the
services of the carpenters and blacksmiths, and the pick
of men, wagons, and horses. This was fortunate for
Albine, since Captain Ecuyer was now all but penniless,
not having touched his pay for over a year. And in the
English service little was done for an officer personally
that was not furthered by gold. Most important of all,
John Burent was secured to accompany the wagon.

Burent was not a soldier. He was an English master
cooper who had been brought to Pittsburgh a year pre-
viously by Bouquet. He proved to be a minor genius in
all kinds of construction. Most of the bateaux for the
coming expedition down the Ohio had already been built
by him, and in the defence of the fort his aid and ingenuity had been simply invaluable. He was devoted to
both Bouquet and Ecuyer, particularly to the captain.
But the combined inguenity of both these officers had
not sufficed to get him paid. His employment was held
to be "irregular," and the royal paymasters balked at
honouring his vouchers.

"To pay this man," wrote one of them, "it would be
necessary to get permission from his Excellency and re-
rule the pages in my book."

"Without this man," replied Bouquet, "the English
crown might well have lost the fort at the forks of the
Ohio. His ingenuity is worth thousands."

But Burent was never paid.

He was therefore ready to leave the fort and return

to Philadelphia in order to take up his trade again. But he agreed to stay awhile with Ecuyer as his "military servant." There was a page ruled in the paymaster's book for that, and he worshipped Ecuyer.

Burent was a dapper, brown little man, powerfully built. He had brown hair, brown eyes, brown eyelashes, and a brown deerskin suit beautifully made. He was all brown, even his boots. And he was unfailingly cheerful and had a carpenter's laugh, as Carmichael the blacksmith said. Burent and he were brothers in energy and in work, and Carmichael had taught Burent as he had taught Albine to be an excellent shot. With the three of them collaborating on the captain's *voiture,* it fared well.

One of the great wagons of a Pennsylvania trader who had followed the 42nd foot as a sutler was seized upon for the king's service. That wagon was rapidly made over. The huge, staunch wheels were given new iron tires and new hubs fastened to massive hickory axles where iron revolved on iron.

Upon the hubs, plates, and spindles Carmichael expended his greatest skill in tempering. Burent entirely took apart and rebuilt the wagon body so that it was tight as a boat. The whole thing was joined, dovetailed, and bolted together out of seasoned ash and oak planks.

There were no springs. The bargelike body was simply bolted to the axles reinforced by iron plates and to these plates the singletree was chained. It was long enough for the first team only. The front team was to pull against collars with their chain traces attached to a dragbar and ring on the end of the singletree. A brake, made from hickory planks sprung like a bow, and worked by a sprocket wheel and chain from the front seat, was the great innovation and was due to Burent. When the tension was released on the bow, the ends of the plank, shod with iron, rubbed against the rear tires.

It was the news of this brake "contraption" which first began to gather spectators about the wagon while it still stood before Carmichael's forge, being fitted. The smith worked late into the night. The sound of his anvil and the red glow from his door drew the crowd as though his iron were magnetized. Soldiers and settlers stood about while the chests were lashed along the sides, and their contents and storing eagerly watched and discussed. Impassive Indian faces, their owners wrapped in ragged blankets, stood like columnar shadows in the background, black eyes glinting as the flames leaped at the forge. The news went about, "The little captain's leaving, and you had ought to see the cabin on wheels he's going down-country in. It do beat the ark." And so Captain Ecuyer's *voiture* became known as "the ark."

This impression of "arkiness" was heightened when the tarpaulin was raised and flung over its ridgepole. To frontier eyes the shelter and interior of the wagon seemed luxurious.

"Whar's the windeys?" demanded one old hunter.

"Whar's the hole in the wigwam to let the smoke outen?" shouted another.

"Blow me if he hain't got a feather bed laid on that thar iron contraption!" exclaimed a militiaman. "But thar's only room on it for one."

"The captain ain't aimen to tote no trouble along with him," said Carmichael, emerging with a hot iron to fit on. "He'll find plenty along the road, and it won't be dressed in skirts neither or go to bed with him. Now get out of my way."

He began to bolt on and rivet the final iron fittings with which he had been so prodigal. Captain Ecuyer was leaving the next morning and he was putting on the last fine touches.

The "trundler," a tremendous chest mounted on two wheels with a tongue shaft, something like an artillery caisson, was trundled up and hooked on behind.

Inside the wagon the chests were already lashed firmly along the sides. A lanthorn was hung from the ridgepole, the captain's folding chair set out next to his desk constructed as he had directed, and the straw and robes spread out on the floor. The crowd peered in and grew

253

silent at so much luxury and ingenuity. All their quips by this time were exhausted. Old Buckey, Captain Ecuyer, and some of the other officers of the garrison strolled over from headquarters, where Johnson had outdone himself on a farewell dinner. They, too, were eager to inspect the wagon.

"Exceedingly snug bachelor quarters, *mon ami*," said Colonel Bouquet. "I think I'll be going along with you myself at this rate." He and Ecuyer entered the wagon and sat down. "My present to this house on wheels is a dozen of Burgundy and a jug of brandy." He sent Albine to get it. Ecuyer looked his gratitude. With a little wine, existence would still be possible. The two officers sat down under the tarpaulin and drank to Ecuyer's success.

Outside the crowd became denser. An impromptu but all the more touching farewell was being staged for Captain Ecuyer. The news and noise of the gathering spread, and a number of the settlers from the little town of huts and cabins clustered about the walls without, men and women who had gone through the siege with Ecuyer, came trooping in while the sentries looked the other way. For once the general hostility and coolness towards a king's officer was suspended, and both Ecuyer and Old Buckey received a rough-and-ready but hearty ovation.

The inevitable keg of liquor appeared. This time conveyed from the king's storehouse by command of Old Buckey himself. And good black rum it was. Hot water, hot irons, and cider and rum hissed in can and pannikin and disappeared like hot lightning down a hundred throats. Carmichael piled the entire remainder of his coal high in the forge and plied his bellows until an incandescent pyramid lit the casemate where the forge was, throwing a warm glow of heat and light about its arched door. Indians came forward rubbing their stomachs for draughts of rum. These being forthcoming, two of them began to shuffle and "woof-woof." The crowd jeered them good-naturedly. A couple of bagpipers appeared, and a fiddle with a voice like a hoarse buzz saw.

Albine and the man from Devon staged a final bout.

Salathiel understood the compliment when he was permitted to emerge on a draw.

"An' a wish 'e guid look, me lad," said the big West Country sergeant. "Don't 'e vorget they vouls a showed 'e. No vair plai vor Injun gouger. Gie une they knee in her crotch."

Johnson shook Salathiel's hand and presented him with a book of receipts copied out by Mrs. Johnson, whose heart overflowed with rum and happiness that at last Johnson would be hers and not the captain's man from now on. Her "God go wid ye" was perhaps the most sincere of all. The captain had presented Johnson with a horse. It was an old one, to be sure, but a great gift nevertheless.

Colonel Bouquet and the captain now shook hands all around. There was a cheer and a health for them, and one for the king, after which they walked off together.

Salathiel slept in the ark that night for the first time. That is, he stayed in it to watch the captain's property. The celebration about the forge went on until the small hours. It ended about three o'clock by a gouging fight in which a Welsh soldier lost an eye before the guard interfered. Then the pile of glowing coal fell away suddenly to ashes. The drink was out, and all except Burent and Carmichael went home.

Salathiel collected his own small bundle of belongings and his cherished double-barrelled rifle and stowed them in the wagon. Then he caught a wink of sleep. It was still dark when Burent awakened him.

The horses were being brought up to be hitched on.

He went and roused the captain and dressed him in quarters for the last time. They had a breakfast of sizzling rashers and fresh eggs. "The last for many a day," said Ecuyer, wiping his plate with a piece of bread as only a Frenchman can, and sighing as he rose to make ready for the road.

PART THREE

The Mountain Road

24

The Road

OUTSIDE a few snowflakes were drifting down. The dawn was breaking clear, cold, and without a breath of wind. There was a sudden heavy trampling of many hoofs and a rumble of iron wheels. Captain Ecuyer picked up his cloak and threw open the door.

The ark had drawn up before his quarters, long and dark in the half-light. The horses' breath smoked frostily. There was an occasional glint and gleam from the brazen harness mountings. Burent was riding the off wheel horse, his rifle slung over his shoulder, and the handles of two heavy cavalry pistols bulged out of a pair of holsters before him. Carmichael had come to see his handiwork and the captain depart. To his disappointment the captain did not enter the wagon but called for his horse and mounted it.

"I'll leave here as I came," he said.

Salathiel hastily fitted the last of the valet kits into Johnson's portmanteaus, took a final look about him, and then poured some water on the fire. He stowed the portmanteaus in the chest under the wagon seat and took the reins. The captain handed the key of his quarters to the sergeant of the guard as they rumbled out over the drawbridge across the moat. The gate of the stockade swung wide, giving a broad glimpse of the empty, misty fields before the fort. The chimneys of a few newly built cabins rose above the morning fog here and there, rolling out black coal smoke. Over Grant's Hill the eastern light showed a silver streak through the woods along its crest. The heavily rutted and boggy road twisted away in that direction. At a cabin on the Diamond just beyond the fort a figure carrying a jug halted them. It was Johnson.

"I wanted to say good-bye, captain, and this here's a jug of the Queen of Scots soup triple strong I brewed ye. It'll do your fixin's good. Captain Ecuyer, I'm much obleeged to you. I wish ye God's best luck."

Then to everybody's amazement he reached up to the captain on his horse and shook hands. There was no longer even the trace of the air of a servant about him. He looked like another man. Only his features were the same.

Captain Ecuyer shook hands and blinked.

"*Bonne chance,* Johnson," he said. Then he lifted his hat and rode on. The wagon followed.

"If ye ever git to England," roared Johnson at Salathiel, as the heavy wheels ground past, "tell me Lord Bishop of Exeter to go to hell." He waved his hand and strode off into the mist.

"What's come over the man?" said Burent to Captain Ecuyer as he rode up beside him.

"It's the New World running in his veins," replied the captain, and beat his gloves together to warm his hands.

Salathiel heard this reply and pondered it as they started up the breast of the first steep hill. Climbing, they came suddenly out of the mist of the river valley onto the crest of the rise, where only a few years before Major Grant and his Highlanders and some Virginians had stood to be slaughtered by the French and Indians. Their bones could still be found, if one cared to look for them, scattered through deep ravines and thickets, where the retreat had taken place from the hill to the Allegheny River. A fox barked close by, and as they stopped on the height the red sun rose smoking and curling with frosty mist out of the endless folds of the forest ahead. They stayed for a moment to breathe the horses after their short but wicked climb.

"She drags sore heavy," said Burent, patting the wagon a little doubtfully.

"It will go better when the road freezes," replied Ecuyer unconcernedly, and turned to look back at the fort he had saved for the British crown. They all looked.

The mists in the river valley were rolling. The forests all about blazed with the last strident purples and yellows of the North American fall. At the point where the two rivers met, the star-shaped mass of the fort loomed redly through the thinning mist, the morning light playing along its moats and brick ramparts.

From the music bastion the sunrise gun dirked a scarlet splash of fire and smoke into the fog and set the echoes rolling. The Union Jack rose suddenly into the upper sunlight and clear air above the fort, stood out boldly for an instant in a brief breeze, and then fell listlessly back against the staff. A fanfare of drums and trumpets began to shout the reveille.

The blood came surging to Ecuyer's face. His mare neighed, pawed the stones, and gave his wound a painful wrench.

"My reward!" he muttered.

But there were tears of pride as well as pain in his eyes. He dismounted slowly and motioned to Salathiel to ride the mare. Burent at this left the lead horse and took his place behind on the big wagon seat to drive.

"Ride forward and keep your eyes open for everything ahead. Albine," said the captain as he climbed into the wagon again. "I'll watch from behind. It's all I can do for a while. I think you'll be riding the mare most of the time this campaign, you know. Use her sweetly, mind! She takes a good grasp with the knees, and I've lost that." He sat down on his chair and began to bind himself into it with a long handkerchief.

Salathiel slung his rifle and rode on ahead. The ark, the trailer, and the four horses splashed, rolled, and jolted after him. Burent tooled his two teams along with great judgment and skill. He had driven from Carlisle to Fort Pitt several times and he knew the road exceedingly well.

261

"We'll make Turtle Creek tonight, captain," he said. "We might even get to the Loyal Hanna if we don't cast shoes."

"Good," muttered Ecuyer, his eyes glassy with pain. He wished now that he had resigned.

The wagon lurched on through Penn's *sylvania* towards Fort Bedford one hundred miles or so eastward. A light snow began to fall. The road froze and the iron tires of the wagon and the horses' shoes rang in the keen, frosty air and crunched along more easily. The captain mixed a dram of brandy with a cup of Johnson's soup, which was still warm. He felt better.

He began to wonder in what shape he would find the garrison at Ligonier. Affairs went badly there, according to Colonel Bouquet.

Well, he would see. He hoped young Albine would keep a keen lookout ahead. For his part, he would never take his eyes off the road and the hillsides as they slowly closed in behind him. If he had taken an escort they would never have got anywhere or done anything but haul food for the escort. But with a lone wagon one could not be too vigilant. Even to a small party of wandering Indians it would look tempting. That, however, was a chance he had deliberately decided to take, for with the wagon he could get around the country to some effect. No one would expect "his Majesty's inspector of outposts" to arrive that way. They would be looking, if they were looking at all, for a troop of horse at least. Perhaps there would be some surprises in store, after all. Ecuyer permitted himself to smile a bit grimly.

If, as a good soldier, Captain Ecuyer concentrated on keeping a wary eye for anything moving upon the trail as it slowly unreeled behind him, he was able to do so wholeheartedly because he had no need to worry about the thoroughness of the examination which his lone advance guard was making as he pushed on before. And yet it is not likely that the captain could appreciate to the full either the keenness or the minuteness, the breadth or the sensitiveness of impression with which the young

262

man, who was now riding his mare some hundred yards ahead of the wagon, beheld the bright new world as it unrolled before him.

Not that the captain lacked imagination. On the contrary. But he viewed the world with a sophisticated, a professional, and a civilized eye. He was in great bodily discomfort. He was middle-aged, at least in feeling, and he had undoubtedly forgot how freshly, how as with a coating of spick-and-span new varnish the landscapes, the glows and gleams, and even the rich dark depths of the universe, paint themselves upon the eager eyes of youth.

And even if he had not forgotten, it would have been impossible for Captain Ecuyer or for Burent, the brown little Englishman whose whole thought and attention was now dutifully fixed upon tooling along his four horses, to have conceived even for a moment how vividly and poignantly, with what a relish for the road itself, with what capacities for both ecstasy and tragedy—and all the gamut of feeling between—the young fellow who had been born and bred in the American forest darted ahead and waited for the slow progress of the heavy wagon. It would have been impossible for either of them to have felt as he did about a journey as they pushed eastward along the road opened by General Forbes through the fresh wilderness only five years before.

Considering the vast difficulties of its construction and maintenance, it was a marvellous good road. That is not to say that its surface was even as a ballroom floor. It was, however, quite passable on foot or horseback, and wheeled vehicles could be and had been drawn over it: artillery, baggage carts, and the heavy Pennsylvania traders' wagons from the settlements; dragged by sheer endurance, brute force, profanity, and skill.

The armies of Forbes, Stanwix, Bouquet, and various provincial detachments had now improved, drained, and repatched it as they passed over it to and fro. It was for the most part a slash through the interminable forest. The trees had been cut down, burned and dragged aside to destroy the immediate cover for ambush as far back as possible. The stumps had been partly removed. In the course of time those that remained might be expected to rot. But for the most part the way serpentined among them, since there was neither powder nor man power enough in America to get them all out.

The road skirted the edges of the worst morasses and even boasted a few embankments across unavoidable swamps. There, indeed, it was sometimes corduroyed for miles, built up on a foundation of logs with branches and earth piled upon them or upon a heavy layer of stones.

It was at such places that the worst was to be apprehended, especially if the rains had washed the clay and branches from the logs. Then horses and wagons disappeared completely into the deep swamps or mud holes, or they lay so inextricably bogged that it was impossible to drag them out.

On the steep mountainsides farther eastward, the wrecks of transport wagons, cannons, and the bones of horses, bleached and rusted in the forest, the carcasses devoured by wolves, and the vehicles visited by lurking Indians who hewed and burnt out the iron work. From Carlisle to Pittsburgh, the road ahead was strewn with such wrecks.

But the road was there now. It went on over the mountains, along the valleys, and through the pleasant open glades and natural meadows whenever possible, for forage was all-important. And in all those meadows the English grasses, timothy and "Devon hay," were beginning to drive out and replace the buffalo grass and other coarse native covering. Docks and all kinds of foreign weeds and other strange plants were beginning to creep in. The beggars' lice, which always accompanies Europeans, was founding prolific colonies of its own. Otherwise all was unchanged.

The forests and the wilderness to the far verge of the always unknown horizon stretched away, and a thousand miles or leagues away, on either side westward, northward, and southward, to the end of the world or to the shores of fabled, seldom visited oceans. Now and again some dim trail branched off the road into savage nowhere, which Europeans might take at their peril. These twilight shadow paths were best known and best followed by Indians or by traders, couriers, or old woodsmen whose knowledge and skill were to the general incoming soldier or eastern colonist a purely fantastic lore. Such professional followers of dim trails were, in fact, the eyes of the wilderness, men who had come to live by hunting or to trade for furs. They had preceded the road. There had not been many of them. But there were still a few who could yet remember when there had been no road and no white men, except themselves, at all. Before they had come there had been trails made originally by the animals, and there were also those liquid highways into mystery, the lonely gliding rivers.

The forest lay silent. A silence broken only by the rustle of leaves in summer and by the occasional voice of a rushing stream. Nothing else seemed to be in the land but trees. The war parties along the crests of the Alleghenies, where the Six Nations passed southward in single file to fall upon their distant enemies the Cherokees amid the peaks of the Big Smokies, saw no one as they passed; looked downward into blue, cloud-dappled, tenantless valleys. The forest waited as it had from the beginning.

But now there was this new military road, Forbes Road, the "Glades Road." It led from the forks of the Ohio, mounting wave after wave of the Appalachians clear back to the inhabitants, clean to Carlisle, and then on into Lancaster County and the peaceful, fruitful meadows of Penn's grant along the Delaware. To point out its more important direction, it passed in one way or another right through from Philadelphia to Pittsburgh. And it was the only road over the mountains into the west, into the valley heart of the continent. Its opening was the most important continental event that had yet stirred the colonies.

As yet only a few people fully grasped its significance. Among them was Colonel Washington of Virginia. His immense acumen which gave him the equivalent of imaginative foresight—foresaw. And he had done his best to prevent Forbes Road from being built. Instead, he wanted the road that led out of Virginia to be driven through to

265

the Ohio, Braddock's road. That road had ended with and at the place of Braddock's defeat about seventeen miles from Pittsburgh. But that seventeen miles of no road made all the difference in the world to Virginia. For the artery to the west now led out of the heart of Pennsylvania.

If Washington had only been able to get that obstinate Scot, Johnny Forbes, to listen to him! But all those determined letters about the advantages of the southern route and the arguments and intrigues brought to bear on the sick general while he lay at Raystown in '58, waiting to move on to Fort Duquesne and drive the French from the Ohio, had been useless. Virginia might have been a nation if Forbes had listened to him.

But no British general would ever take the advice of Colonel Washington. Indeed, he finally had to resort to blows, later on. Forbes had cut the road right through from Bedford to Pittsburgh, right through Pennsylvania, and had himself carried over it in a litter. Then he had returned to Philadelphia and died. In the end he had proved more obstinate than Braddock, but successful.

So the road from Virginia still stopped at a dead end on the battlefield where the skeletons of Braddock's army yet lay unburied in the thickets and forests along the Monongahela.

A great many things besides the road had come to an end on that battlefield.

As yet, however, only a few people had come over the new trail, and they were mostly the military. As Salathiel rode along it that morning on the best horse that he had ever had between his legs, it was vacant of all except a few curious or startled animals. It was just a great sword cut through the forest, a swath cut by the might of Britain's fighting arm, and the day was a beautiful winter day in the lonely American woods.

As the sun rose higher and clear of the treetops, the mist and vapours had vanished. The day grew clear and colder, calm for the most part, but with occasional gusts from the north, brisk, sudden, cold breezes that presaged bitter weather to come and sometimes rushed into miniature whirlwinds that swirled the dry, light snow across the road to smoke about the horses' feet and through the spokes of the wheels. Also the road was hard now. All the pools in it were level and as blue and hard as steel. As the light snow continued to sift down and fill the hollows and ruts, the going in many places actually became smooth.

"It will be all right for the horses as long as they're new shod and the calks stay sharp," said Burent on one of the infrequent occasions when Salathiel returned to the wagon for a while and rode alongside. "I'll git a smith at Ligonier to keep the shoes sharp," he insisted.

"Good idee," agreed Salathiel, and clapping heels to his horse, he rode on ahead again.

He and the mare were both in fine spirits. She seemed to know she was going east once more; home along the trail she had travelled before. She pawed the ground when he stopped to reconnoitre.

As for Salathiel, he was surprised himself to find how delighted he was to be out in the forest again; to be at home. A load seemed to have left his mind and even to have relieved his muscles since they had left the fort behind them. He filled his lungs with the clean, smokeless air. The intolerable stench of quarters, intolerable to one whose scent was so keen, no longer affected him. There was nothing but the smell of snow in the air, and that of the horse.

Once off the slopes of Grant's Hill, they began to move over a succession of wooded rises from the crests of which an occasional glimpse of the gorge of the Monongahela and its islands was to be had. Then the road left the vicinity of the river tending northward and emerged from an area of tangled thickets and ravines onto a plateau where there was a long vista of natural open meadows and majestic oak thickets.

No more handsome stretch of country could be imagined. There was a great bald, craggy hill to the northwest and an amphitheatre of rolling, blue hills to the east towards which the road ran. And there, dark and sombre, extending without end, the wall of the forest once more began. Those hills, in fact, were the outliers of the mountains whose main ranges lay two journeys to the eastward. But they were the highest hills Salathiel had ever seen. Unconsciously, a certain sense of exhilaration was already taking hold of him. To be high, to be up there, and away!

Enough snow had now fallen and lain sufficiently long to provide him with a printed page of the recent events of the neighbourhood. Over the open glades and under the wide even-spread branches of the oak groves, the trails of birds and animals extended in all directions. Deer, turkey, rabbits, and foxes abounded. There was an occasional wolf track, and now and then the trace of a bear or panther. But there was no sign of wheel, foot, or horses' hoof. That did not prevent him from keeping a keen watch around and ahead, but it did show him that no one had passed along or across the road for many hours at least.

There was further confirmation of the absence of men in the behaviour of the game, especially of the deer.

The wagon was now, after several hours' travelling, well beyond the range of the ordinary hunting parties from the fort. During the summer, with so many Indians about Pittsburgh, and fighting and firing going on in the vicinity, much of the game had either been killed off or scared away. But the complete solitude which had ensued after the tribes decamped down the Ohio, and the whites still remained close to the fort, together with the return of winter, had lured the deer as usual back to the open meadow country behind the two rivers to the east of Pittsburgh.

To judge by the tracks, there were more that year than usual. It had been a lush season. There was also an extraordinary number of foxes and wolves. Salathiel had never seen so many wolf tracks and he drew the captain's attention to them. They were timber wolves, evidently big grey wolves that had come down from the north.

"Battles," said Captain Ecuyer simply. "In Piedmont, after the late wars, wolves swarmed in the hills and mountains one winter, I remember. Here, too, most of the settlers' stock has been turned loose into the forests when the inhabitants fled to the fort."

It was true, thought Salathiel. There must be a good many lost domestic animals wandering about here and there. That fact, indeed, was soon confirmed and led to the only incident of the morning.

An unusual trail attracted Salathiel's attention. He recognized it as that of a pig. Following it, towards the thickets and young oaks, he finally aroused an enormously fat and ferocious old boar. With timber wolves and bears about, that boar must have been unusually able to take care of himself. There was no doubt of it, for he soon made a vicious charge at the mare's legs, rushing unexpectedly out of some scrub where he had been champing acorns. His angry squeals, the surprised snort and neigh of the mare caused the wagon to stop to watch the conflict.

The boar chased Salathiel and the mare some distance, while the captain and Burent shouted mockingly. Salathiel had never encountered a pig. He was somewhat nonplussed as to just what to do. When he chased it, it would turn on him and charge. This little game continued for some time. Finally the boar turned at bay. It meant business. Its small eyes were bloodshot. The mare was sweating. The pig charged her, slashing wickedly. Suddenly in mid career it turned and made for the wagon which apparently it now saw for the first time.

Burent now shouted in alarm. There were sixteen of his horses' legs on the road. Tired of fooling, Salathiel unslung his rifle and dropped the animal, shot clean through the head. It expired to a chorus of unholy organ-like squeals.

The captain and Burent kept laughing at Salathiel. Somehow he felt ashamed, especially when he looked up and saw on a neighboring crest a stag with a fine pair of antlers. It, too, had been watching curiously. Now it gave its white tail a jerk and left in long, soaring leaps, scared away by the rifle shot. He fired the other barrel and missed.

"Never mind," said Burent. "Pork's better nor venison any day, if you'll listen to me. And here's enough fresh pork for the trip, prime mast fed, and cold weather to keep it."

He and Salathiel attacked the carcass with tomahawk and knife. They worked as fast as possible. Head, hams, and sides were soon stowed away in some extra bags, salted, and swung high to the ridgepole of the wagon.

"The varmints will come prowling round us at night," said Salathiel. "It'll sure bring them for miles."

"We'll chance it," said Burent. "Giddap."

After an hour they were under way again. Captain Ecuyer produced a long-cherished Havana cigar, somewhat battered, but a parting gift from one of the gallant 42nd, late from the West Indies. He felt better than he had, although laughing had hurt his wound. But it was a relief to him to feel that the responsibilities of the fort lay behind him. The *voiture* worked even better than he had hoped. On a long level section the horses broke into a trot. They smoked and steamed in the winter air. The ark jounced along, curls of the captain's cigar smoke leaking from under the canvas. Burent coughed. He could scarcely abide smoke. He chewed, but secretly and rather daintily. Even the stains he made then were brown.

25

In Which Hospitality Spills Over

SALATHIEL continued to ride on ahead. It was after midday now. The snow had ceased. Presently he came on some moccasin tracks mixed with the trail of many horses. Heading through the woods, which were now beginning to close in upon them, he saw smoke rising, and then the black walls of a large cabin. There was a branch hung out on a pole over the door. A short, stout man with a rifle taller than he was himself came to the door and peered out.

This place Salathiel knew must be Frazier's tavern, or the "Bill Pens," the first tarrying east of Pittsburgh. He was rather curious to see the man he had stolen a horse from years ago. Frazier had moved since then from his old cabin at the mouth of Turtle Creek to the crossroads, where a horse trail led southeastward down a densely wooded valley towards Braddock's Field on the Monongahela. It was the same fatal trail the French and Indians had taken to ambush the British eight years before. Now an occasional trader from Virginia drove a string of pack horses over it, but only with much difficulty. Yet, bad as it was, it was the only negotiable trace between the end of Braddock's road and Fort Pitt, and Mr. Frazier's tavern had been built just at the forks of this trail and Forbes Road in order to catch all the trade there was.

At that moment Salathiel noticed a large number of moccasin tracks in the snow, converging upon the cabin from all directions, both going and coming. He reported these to Captain Ecuyer, who was evidently not pleased at the story they told.

"Frazier is an old rascal," said Captain Ecuyer in a low tone, for they were now drawn up before the door, and Salathiel had come to help him out of the wagon. "Burent, *you* remain by the wagon, and keep a sharp eye on the horses while we're here. I'm going in to have a look about and find how the wind blows. We'll stay just long enough for a bite by the fire. That'll be our best excuse."

Salathiel fitted the pair of little steps to the wagon and the captain descended with some difficulty.

"Fresh pork for lunch, captain?" asked Salathiel loudly, so that Mr. Frazier leaning by the door could hear.

"Why not?" said the captain, winking.

Up until that moment Mr. Frazier had remained by his doorway the most indifferent and oblivious of hosts. If he was consumed with curiosity and speculation about the strange conveyance which had just halted before his cabin, he was not the man to discover to others that anything could ever be new to him. However, when a king's officer in full uniform walked down out of the wagon on a pair of steps he was not entirely able to restrain a look of cunning surprise.

"How d'ja dew, captain," said he, for he had seen Ecuyer at the fort often enough. "Be ye fixin' to stay with us? Ef'n so we're pretty durned packed." With this he closed the door, that was open a crack, behind him. Then, remembering he was a sergeant in the militia, he turned and gave the captain a solemn rifle salute. There seemed to be something a mite surly or mocking in this. The captain smiled and touched his hat with his cane in reply.

"All I need, Mr. Frazier, is a bite by your fire, a touch of warmth before we drive on," he said.

"But we've no fixin's, I tell yer," replied Frazier, now leaning on his gun. "We're clean et out from crib to garret."

"I'll provide my own meat," insisted the captain, hobbling towards the door painfully, but with a determined air. "Come," said he, suddenly getting red in the face, "why do you think Colonel Bouquet granted you licence to remain and keep tavern here? Or is it only the king's officers that must stay outside in the snow?"

Frazier mumbled something that might be taken for an apology, leaned his rifle against the cabin, and with obvious reluctance opened the door at the same time roaring out, "Sabiney, Sabiney, build up the back log and put a kittle on. Do you hear, woman? It's the commandant from the fort comin' in on us!"

A complete silence followed this warning, except that the crackling of a fine fire already roaring up the chimney could be heard and its tall flames seen in the dark cavern of the place as the door swung open on squalling hinges.

"Thank you," said the captain. And he walked in, motioning Salathiel to follow him.

Once inside, it was immediately patent why Mr. Frazier's constipated welcome had been both hesitant and constrained. Eight or ten Indians—in the shadows of the long room away from the fire it was difficult at first to tell just how many—lay sprawling drunkenly about the floor in helpless and grotesque postures, wallowing in a welter of vomit-soaked blankets, bedraggled and trampled headdresses, loose feathers, muskets and tomahawks upon which some of them had cut themselves and bled freely. They were a war party, their eyes painted green with surrounding circles of red, their faces and bodies smeared black. There were blotches of vermilion designs on their naked chests. Their scalp locks nodded sickly and helplessly. Some of them gurgled and others snored. One or two, at the entrance of strangers, tried to crawl towards the door, but gave it up when that, the only entrance to the place, was banged shut and barred by Mr. Frazier.

"Take the bar off the door!" said Captain Ecuyer.

Since Mr. Frazier seemed not to hear, Salathiel unbarred the door and stood by it. As his eye became used to the gloom and shadow he looked about him in the firelight.

The captain was now standing directly before the fire, warming his back, and pulling his coat tails aside to do so or to keep his hands on the pair of small pocket pistols he carried over his hips. It was hard to tell which. There was certainly an indescribable feeling of hostility about the place, although a giant shadow of the captain was thrown across the logs of the ceiling and seemed to dominate the room.

Behind him in the chimney the long right arm of a bear with outstretched paw hung flayed and roasting, dripping grease into a pan underneath and occasionally twisting in an agonized manner in the draught of the fire.

At the extreme end of the cabin, farthest from the fire, and also in semi-darkness, the magnificent figure of an Indian chief arrayed in a scarlet, hawk-weathered bonnet with his blanket wrapped stoically about him sat cross-legged on the only table of the establishment: god-like, as it were, he sat thus superior above the prostrate forms of his fellows. He was sober, silent, kinglike. His features as though coined from bronze or carved from mahogany now and then glinted or sprang into sharp relief when the fire leaped. His silver armbands glittered, but he neither moved nor spoke. Salathiel saw that he was a Seneca, a chief of the Long House, and that the party sprawled on the floor beneath him were Delawares.

Except for a ladder, which disappeared into the mysterious gloom of the loft above, there was nothing else on that side of the room. It was into these higher regions that Mr. Frazier had ascended and he was now heard stumbling about aloft, evidently trying to arouse his wife to the importance of the visitors below. He and she soon seemed to be trying to quarrel in grumbles or whispers.

The chief on the table and the Indians on the floor were, however, not the only occupants of the room.

In that part of it which extended to the right of the fireplace, stretched out on a bench against the wall with his head on a bundle of beaverskins, lay the lanky form of a white man sound asleep. Despite the stench and foul air of the place, his mouth was wide open and he snored.

Occasionally he wrinkled a livid scar down the exposed side of his face. He had on a coonskin cap drawn down over his eyes, a deerhide shirt with filthy red fringes, and worn riding breeches of heavy English cloth tucked into a pair of cowhides provided with rusty spurs.

Judging by a bundle or two from which bottles protruded, a strong smell of whisky, and a number of bales tucked under the bench over which his lanky form seemed to be draped in sinister guard, the man might be taken for a trader or trapper, one of those inveterate purveyors of firewater to the savages whom neither proclamations nor menaces could stop.

Behind him, in sober and decent contrast, sat a quiet grey-haired man clad in butternut and a Quaker hat, the fine beaver nap of which he smoothed with a pair of fat, satisfied hands while it reposed on his knee. From time to time this rather tight-lipped individual from Pennsylvania, for he was obviously that, looked at the captain a bit apprehensively with a couple of wide-set, innocent blue eyes and smoothed the hair back from his forehead. When not smoothing either his hat or his hair, he would smooth the front of his coat.

Captain Ecuyer took both these gentlemen in at a glance, and commencing to whistle silently, continued also to twirl his stout cane. Not entirely comfortable under the captain's continued scrutiny, it was the Quaker who spoke first.

"Art thou by any chance returning home?" he asked in a tone that somehow conveyed a deal of effrontery.

"Alack for me and for thee, *no,*" replied the captain. "Art thou by any chance peddling powder and shot?"

The Quaker solemnly shook his head.

"Whisky?" persisted the captain.

"I am not acquainted with the personage asleep beside me. I am Samuel Japson of Philadelphia," said the Quaker, and moved a little farther from the man asleep on his left as though to accentuate a total disconnection with him and with the smell of whisky.

The man lying on the bench, hearing the sound of

275

voices, now opened his eyes under his coonskin cap and carefully looked about the room without moving a body muscle. Under the cap, and in the firelight, his eyes glittered like those of a hawk.

"Yer a damned, hypocritical liar, Friend Japson," he finally drawled in a southern voice, "and furthermore I kin prove it."

"*Vraiment!*" exclaimed the captain, suddenly lapsing into French at so illuminating and satisfactory a turn to the conversation. But further revelations were suddenly cut short by an outbreak, or rather by an accentuation of the scuffling upstairs.

"Stop pinching," shouted a girl's voice. "Stop it! Ouch! Oh!"—a slap followed.

"Drat ye, git yer carcass out of bed," said the husky voice of an older woman. "Git the mush kittle on. Thar's company. Up wid ye, down wid ye! Tie your hair, ye slut." Another hearty slap was followed by a sob, and at this juncture the legs and rear quarters of Mr. Frazier was seen descending the ladder. He joined the captain by the fire.

"There'll be victuals in a jiffy, yer Honour," said he, rubbing his hands with satisfaction, whether at the thought of the meal to follow or for having at last succeeded in arousing the female portion of his establishment upstairs, no one could tell.

An exceedingly good-looking Irish girl, despite the fact that her dark hair was in tangles, her face red from slapping, and her body concealed in a sacklike lindsey-woolsey, now came nimbly down the ladder and started to fill a kettle with water, corn meal and a handful of salt. There was something about her slim, young movements that reminded Salathiel of Jane of whom, to tell the truth, he had not thought for some time. The girl looked at him, the tears still standing in her large, grey eyes, and was instantly aware of his interest and sympathy.

Salathiel was not the only one whose glances followed her about the room. The trader on the bench sat up and tipping his cap back gave her a yellow-toothed grin. Mrs.

276

Frazier, who had now managed to lower her dowdy bulk out of the garret, was also aware of the glances which followed her maid. That, or something else, enraged her and she lost no opportunity to assert her authority and call attention to herself by chivying the girl about the room. Her most pleasant epithet was "Frances, ye bound-out slut."

"Aye, they'd follow ye even when ye go out to squat in the snow, she muttered.

The nimbleness of the girl in avoiding now and then a well-placed kick brought a grunt either of surprise or of disappointment from the chief on the table. As the preparation for the meal progressed, he was seen to be solemnly filling a long ceremonial pipe with tobacco and killikinick. Two red feathers and one white one hung on a string of wampum shells from its black stone bowl.

Meanwhile, Salathiel had brought in a roast of fresh pork, which he now proceeded to divide into chops, spit on a ramrod, and place before the fire. A barrel chair was rolled up to one end of the table occupied by the chief. The captain spread his handkerchief out on a corner and selected two plates from his kit which Salathiel had brought in. One of these he placed before the chief. By this time the Indian had almost completely filled his pipe. The two little piles of tobacco and "cabbage" had been well crushed between his palms and nicely packed into the bowl. He now reached down with one foot and kicked one of the sleeping Delawares on the floor.

"Go, dog," said he in the Delaware tongue, "and fetch a coal for your betters." The Delaware rolled over and belched. Salathiel seized a coal, tossed it in the air, and brought it to the chief.

"The ears of the white man are as swift as his legs," said the chief gravely in the Shawnee dialect to Salathiel. "Was it not at Logstown on the Beaver that I saw thee before?"

"At Logstown at the council fire of Kaysinata three winters ago. I am the son of the Big Turtle."

"Thou hast crawled into a larger house," said the chief,

smiling with his eyes as he dropped the coal, which he had been tossing up and down in the air, directly into his pipe.

"'I follow a greater chief,'" said Salathiel, looking at the captain significantly. "He it was who defended the fort at the forks of the three rivers."

"Is it he?" said the chief. "He's English but he talks French?"

He looked keenly at the captain, and leaning over his pipe bowl, thrust the stem in his lips and emitted a cloud of fragrant smoke.

The meat was done now and the Irish girl came forward and placed a crackling chop on the plate of the captain and one before the Seneca. A baked potato and a spoonful of corn mush followed. Captain Ecuyer made a gesture of invitation to the chief.

"Et iss de honoul to sup wid soo gleat solda," said the chief in guttural but passable English. He presented his pipe.

The captain leaned forward, and taking a long whiff, exhaled slowly through his nose. He and the chief then began to eat, the captain using his three-pronged fork and the Seneca the clean blade of a long, sharp scalping knife with equal dexterity.

"See that the distinguished company is served, Albine," said Ecuyer, looking about him with an ironical smile. "There is enough fresh hog flesh for all."

Mrs. Frazier needed no further encouragement. She seized the remnant of the large roast Salathiel had brought in and began to cut it up into a mountainous pile of chops. The trader looked towards the fire hopefully. The Quaker put his hat on his head and took a slab plate on his lap. From time to time he smoothed it expectantly with his hand.

In the chimney mouth Salathiel and Frances, the Irish girl, hung over the spit together broiling chops as fast as the pork would sizzle in the flame. Some of the Indians, smelling roasting flesh, sat up and gulped.

"The bear paw's for them," said Frazier. He took the

278

hand-like object off the hook and began to chop it up with a tomahawk. "Can't spare no hog drippin's for Injuns."

His wife sniffed her agreement.

"Reckon it was one of Bert McCallister's hogs they got," said she to her husband, and sniffed again.

"Hope it hain't been eating no corpses," said Mr. Frazier hopefully.

"Fresh killed meat at the fort last night, ma'am!" said Salathiel, lying indignantly. He was not going to let the old woman be right about anything or have the old man spoil his meal. She glanced at him and carried a chop over to Mr. Japson.

"Yer a foin lad," whispered Frances, "git me out of this for the love of Jasus."

Salathiel shook his head.

"If you can get yourself to Ligonier I might be able to help you there," he whispered.

"Ligonier!" exclaimed the girl. "And how would I be gettin' meself to Ligonier?"

"I'll Ligonier ye!" exclaimed the old woman, who had come up behind them quietly. She tossed the hair out of her eyes with the hand holding her pork chop and glared at Salathiel.

"Don't ye be foolin' with me gal, young man. She's legally bound. Mr. Frazier give six pounds for her at Lancaster a year ago come June, and she's two years to sarve yet. I'll have the lawr on ye ef ye go foolin' with her," roared she, putting her hands on her hips while the greasy chop dripped down her skirt. "I'll Ligonier ye!"

The Irish girl shrank back into a corner by the chimney, her face going pale. Mrs. Frazier's voice rose suddenly from a husky roar to a hoarse scream. But her ingenuity was exhausted, probably by anger. She could only repeat herself. "I'll have the lawr on ye," she screamed again and again.

"Speaking of the law," said the cold voice of Captain Ecuyer in the peculiarly clipped and faultless English which he assumed when annoyed, "speaking of the law—

you, madam, and your husband"——he pointed his fork at Frazier——"are harbouring drunken Indians here and selling them whisky."

"Not me," shouted Frazier. "No, sir. I wouldn't sell them a drap, nor the old woman neither."

The captain turned his fork like an accusing finger in the direction of the man with the coonskin cap.

"Right, sir! It's him. He came last night, and the ten Delawares with him," cried Frazier.

" 'Twas an honest swap," said the trader, his eyes narrowing as he looked at the captain. "Ten bottles for these hya bales of peltry." He kicked the purchases under the seat emphatically.

"What's your name?" asked the captain.

"Reynolds, Tom Reynolds of Virginia. At your service, me lud," he added surlily. "Damn the lobster backs, is what I say, says I." His hands began to move nervously towards his belt.

"I'll trouble you for the knife," said Salathiel, swooping over to the bench and sitting down beside him.

The captain nodded.

Ready for any move, Salathiel took the knife from its sheath in the man's belt and held it behind him. The man tensed. But the captain's fork was pointing at him again.

"You sold liquor to a war party," said Ecuyer. "You know what that means."

"They're going south to fight the Creeks, south to Car'lina. They're not bent for no settlements. I'd not sell 'em a drap, ef'n I knowed they was on a raid 'gin our folks. Not a bottle b'God!"

"Not a bottle!" said the captain icily. "Not if you were sure, eh? What a careful man you are. Have you a pass, Mr. Reynolds?"

"Two of them, Mr. Soldier," said Reynolds. He raised his feet in the air and wriggled them in the captain's face.

"They will pass you back to Virginia," said the captain, his face darkening. "We are keeping all the bottles. Don't come trading this way again without a licence, sir, or I'll see you hanged. I'll do that, Mr. Reynolds! This country is closed to trade and settlement by his Majesty's proclamation, and it is a capital offence to bring aid and comfort to the enemy. Tell all your friends we are having the Virginia road watched."

"That'll interest quite a few back in Virginny," drawled the trader, "especially them as give their time, taxes, and blood to make and keep the road open. I'll tell 'em! Do I lose my nags and the rest of my plunder too?"

"I said we would keep the *whisky*," said Captain Ecuyer. "You have still several hours of daylight for a good start, Mr. Reynolds," he added significantly.

"Dost thou wish to part with thy plunder for a fair price?" interjected the Quaker. "I'll give thee what it cost," said he, smoothing the front of his coat.

"And me with the trouble and danger of totin' it over the big hills! Nothin' fer that?"

The Quaker shook his head and smiled.

"I have just said there would be no trading here," remarked the captain. "Get yourself gone and be about it, Reynolds. Now, Mr. Japson, what, for instance, have you brought into this interestin' wilderness besides your pious insolence? Any powder or lead, for example?"

"No powder, my friend," replied Japson.

"Go and see what are in his bales, Albine," said the captain, "and give the knife back to the Virginian."

Salathiel stepped out and made his way rapidly to a lean-to shed behind the cabin. Mr. Reynolds was already saddling the horses, his own and two pack animals.

There were five other horses crowded into the place, milling around, and a pile of bales on which a young Delaware buck was sleeping. Salathiel rolled him over. He then took the knife and started to prod into the cloth of the bales.

"Thar's lead thar, all right," said the Virginian, grinning. "It 'ud be a shame to make holes in all that cloth with *my* knife."

"Catch," said Salathiel. He spun the knife four times in the air. The man caught it by the handle unerringly, and returned it to the sheath in his belt.

281

"Glad you and me ain't tossin' it one at t'other, Mr. Man," he said.

He swung into his saddle and led off with the two pack animals stringing behind. The young Delaware followed at a lope. The horses, Salathiel noticed, were well laden. Two of them had bales lashed in exactly the same way as the Quaker's. Mr. Reynolds seemed anxious to be back in Virginia. He took the trail south through the forest towards the Monongahela, going fast. The figures of the two men and their horses were rapidly lost amid the darker outlines of the trees.

Salathiel returned to the cabin. He noticed Burent had the wagon ready to move and the feed bags off the horses' noses.

"How long they going to be?" asked Burent. "The sun's westing now."

"Just hold your horses awhile," said Salathiel, grinning at the little Englishman, who looked cold and for once impatient. Then he stepped in through the door.

The tremendous sour smell of the cabin caught at his throat. Frances was putting more wood on the fire. The Indian chief was orating at Mr. Japson. Between sonorous periods in Algonquin he blew out tremendous clouds of smoke. Mr. Japson looked most unhappy. He had ceased smoothing anything at all. His hands lay passive in his lap. His hat sat squarely on his head, pulled down firmly. He might, indeed, have been taken as the perfect likeness of the Pennsylvania House of Assembly refusing to vote supplies on a military bill.

"There's lead in the bales, captain," reported Salathiel amidst the silence of all present. For even the Seneca had subsided at Salathiel's entrance. Everyone was waiting to see what Mr. Japson did have in the bales, and what he would say for himself. Also what the captain would do.

In addition it was certainly an uncomfortable moment for Mr. Frazier. From his standpoint Captain Ecuyer could not have arrived at a more unfortunate time. A roomful of drunken Indians, a Virginian on the loose selling whisky, and now Mr. Japson with his shot metal

—all this was not calculated to cause the authorities at the fort to renew his licence to keep tavern on a disturbed frontier. He therefore sat down heavily on a log puncheon and looked helplessly across at his wife who was wiping her hands on her skirt and standing by the fire. It was a time when a man needed an able partner to support him.

But what a fool his old woman was! She had no eyes for anything except that jade of a servant girl, who was actually going to pile more wood on the fire, and they were already roasting. God knows, he had worked like a Turkish slave building the place! He wanted it kept decent. And now look at it!

The Delawares were beginning to crawl about. Some were sitting up eating pieces of half-raw pork. One was still snoring. He would have to clean up all this mess himself. The old woman had the girl so scared she was good for nothing. He had hoped she would be a help when he bought her. Now his wife had quit everything but scolding. Six pounds for a bound lass all gone to hell—and as for his respectability . . .

The Quaker was speaking.

"As thou knowest," said he to the captain, "the Friends do not countenance the use of lead and powder in warfare. They are opposed to strife. I have brought only enough shot metal in trade to enable the savages to seek their meat from God."

"Friend Japson," replied the captain, with as near a sneer as his fine countenance could show, "your solicitude for the heathen of these devastated parts touches me to the quick." He made a motion with his hand towards his left side. "Laws, I'm desolated at having to curtail such charity. You will, however, have to leave the lead here with Mr. Frazier and return to Fort Bedford, where I shall expect you to be awaiting me when I arrive in the course of the next few days. The metal is confiscated and you are under detention. Take your horses with the remainder of your goods and start immediately. Do not fail our rendezvous. It might go hard with you." He

283

waved the man out, and Mr. Japson went meekly enough.

"Frazier," continued Captain Ecuyer, "get that lead out of the Quaker's bales and into your wagon, and take it to Fort Pitt tomorrow morning. You will be paid for your trouble. And take this note with you to Colonel Bouquet. It shall be your warrant and something more." He scribbled a message on a page of his notebook. "Now go out and see to that rascal's leaving. I have said nothing to the colonel about what I have seen at this house today," he added, "but let me tell you, you must be more careful."

"I must sarve who comes, sir," said Frazier.

"But not too well," said Ecuyer.

The man scuttled out.

"We'll be left alone with these red varmints tomorrow. Do you hear that, gal?" cried Mrs. Frazier nervously. "The maister will be off to the fort, and us here alone!"

The Irish girl continued to rock herself slowly backward and forward where she was sitting in warm ashes near the hearth. She nodded but looked at her mistress balefully.

"Ask the chief where his war party is going, Albine," said the captain.

Salathiel spoke to the chief in Shawnee, in which the Seneca replied. The Indian spoke another tongue than his own, slowly and with immense gravity. Salathiel translated literally. A short question from Salathiel brought a long reply from the Indian:

I Ganstax am of the Senecas. I am a chief of the Long House. I do not trot through the forests with these wearers of woman's clothes [the Delawares]. They are not going across the mountains to make war on the whites like brave men. They are going south to steal horses from the Creeks. It was the Long Knife [the Virginian] who has stopped them here with his firewater. It is such traders who bring firewater, new muskets, flints, axes, and powder to the Indians who make the trouble. Let our fathers, the English, listen to the wise voice of their own

284

king and make all his children listen. Let them tarry east of the mountains near the great water as they have so often promised. Let them stop hunting through the Indian lands and bringing many little horses loaded with firewater.

Ganstax has heard and seen what the white chief has done here in this house today. The great white captain has done well. Ganstax does not speak the tongue of the English nimbly, but he understood what the white chief said. It is well. He sees through the faces [masks] of liars from behind. He is inside them and hears when their false tongues strike wickedly against their teeth. He has sent the Long Knife back to his lodges. Let the friend in the Broad Hat likewise be made to return as he has been commanded. He also is a liar, a wolf with the face of a rabbit. Let all such people remain in the ploughed lands where the sun first rises. Let them come into these forests no more. They are the bringers of death and trouble.

The Broad Hats speak of the Great Spirit, shake hands and say, "How, how, how." They talk of peace and trade guns for skins. They hide behind the king's warriors when trouble comes. They stay in their cabins and squeal. Theirs is the talk of squaws by the fires of winter. It is bad medicine for men.

Ganstax is old. He recalls many winters and summers. He remembers the days before the English and French quarrelled over the Indian lands. Those were good days. The French have gone. Now the English must go, too. They have promised the Six Nations over the council fire to depart. Ganstax is on his way to the fort at the three rivers. He will bring the word of the Long House to Buckey [Colonel Bouquet]. He will say the English must leave, too.

The land west of the mountains is the Indians'. Let all white men who come over the high hills be sent back. Then there will be peace. Then the soldiers can go.

The bones of Ganstax are of the rocks of these hills, his flesh is the sand of them. The waters of these rivers are the blood of his veins. His tongue speaks for the land. In his throat is the voice of these woods and hills. He is chief of a mighty and ancient people. They are friends with the English now. But the English must keep their promises. No one can be friends long with liars. Meanwhile Ganstax will send these dogs of Delawares home. They will listen to his voice, arise, and be gone.

Many seasons ago, many, the Six Nations put the Delawares in squaws' clothes. They took away the axe out of their hands. Now the English give them firewater and guns again. Such things are shameful among men. Many troubles follow. This is the truth which Ganstax has spoken. Will the great white captain tell Frazier to let the chief of the Senecas ride in his wagon to the fort? His feet are old and the snow bites with sharp, white teeth through his moccasins.

"Tell him, Albine," replied the captain, who had learned to bargain with the savages, "that he can ride to the fort in Mr. Frazier's wagon, provided he sends these Delawares home now."

Salathiel translated, putting the matter in more flattering terms in order to save the chief's pride.

"Let the white captain also give me a writing to Buckey at the fort," countered the chief, "and I will set the feet of these drunken children upon the homeward trail."

The captain nodded and complied:

Colonel Bouquet: Be pleased to see and listen to this noble Roman. Give him my old pewter snuff-box that I left upon your mantel by mistake, and oblige your humble ob'dt servant—Ecuyer.

The chief rose slowly and stiffly to receive the paper. He shook hands solemnly with the captain. Then, equally as solemnly, he gave the nearest recumbent Delaware a tremendous kick on the rump. As the Delaware scrambled to his feet confusedly, the Seneca hoisted him again towards the door. The chief spoke harshly as the man rose and glared at him. The Delaware grunted sullenly, but finally assembled his sadly scattered effects and stood outside the door, waiting as he had been told.

The Seneca sat down again on the table edge, rubbed his foot, and then got up to continue the process. It promised to be a lengthy one, for some of the Delawares were still pretty drunk. And there were ten of them.

The chief was saved further efforts, however, by an accident at the hearth.

It was really Mrs. Frazier's fault. She had given the Irish girl a pinch on the arm to remind her to replenish the fire. It was a vicious pinch. The girl dodged, caught her skirt on the handle of the bubbling mush pot, and dumped it so that it slushed out several gallons of boiling contents into the middle of the floor.

The girl screamed and jumped. Mrs. Frazier, who found herself standing in a pool of boiling mush, screamed and jumped, with hot mush in one of her shoes. Hopping on one foot like a strange wading bird, and hobbling, she took after her servant with a stout stick, stamping upon several dozing Delawares in the pursuit. That, and a thin coating of steaming mush as it spread quietly but surely among the Indians, proved an effectual reveille.

They got up one by one and rushed out with strange guttural or whistling noises like so many large, hibernating animals disturbed and panicked from the darkness of their winter cave. In their various scrambling exits they were assisted either by the feet or the rhetoric of their father, the Seneca. Towards the last he was reduced to the use of his mouth alone, for his table was now surrounded by a film of hot mush, and he was forced to sit there, grave but isolated, looking down with grim satisfaction at the steaming confusion of the room.

Neither Ecuyer nor Salathiel had been able to restrain himself during the delayed crescendo of funny surprises, which the departure of the Delawares, one by one as the hot mush reached them, had provided.

Ecuyer had not laughed so heartily for years. Even the painful stitches it gave his wound could not prevent him from shaking with laughter. And Salathiel scarcely knew which was funnier, the Indian or the scalded spryness of Mrs. Frazier, whose pursuit of Frances had finally resulted in the capture of that unfortunate girl halfway up the ladder to the garret into which she had foolishly tried to climb.

A squalling struggle took place at the ladder, Frances trying to ascend, and Mrs. Frazier attempting to drag her down. A loud scream and a ripping sound announced and accompanied the departure of Frances' linsey-woolsey into the hands of Mrs. Frazier, leaving a rosy young figure of Mother Eve standing on the ladder.

"That's the way I want ye!" screamed Mrs. Frazier, who now seized the girl about the waist and tore her by main strength off the ladder rungs.

No one was laughing now. There was something exceedingly grim in the expression on Mrs. Frazier's blowzy countenance. Her bangs had come loose and flowed down over her face like the hair of a terrier. Behind these Medusa fringes her eyes glinted red and green. A sudden frenzy of strength possessed her. One big arm clasped the kicking girl about the waist like a child, and she was yanked to the bench by the fire and thrown over the old woman's knees like a big frog.

Mrs. Frazier then seized a short-handled, twig broom used for sweeping ashes, and began to belabour her over her bare buttocks with a merciless and iron strength.

The girl screamed and struggled furiously. Finally she went limp and simply screamed. But the old woman continued to beat her. At last, driven frantic by stinging pain, the girl managed to sink her teeth into the arm that was holding her.

At that Mrs. Frazier shrieked like a huge parrot. The screeching attained a shrill climax. Frances bit hard, refusing to let go even under a hail of blows. Finally Mrs.

288

Frazier reached for the iron poker. But at that instant the door burst open and Mr. Frazier entered.

He took in the situation at a glance, seized his wife by her front hair, and rammed her head against the wall with a *crack*. The girl slipped from her tormentor's clutches and shrank back into a dark corner, rubbing her bare flanks and moaning. Mr. Frazier gave his wife's head another solid bang.

"I'll larn ye, ye murderin' old bitch ya," he said furiously, and stood back with his arms akimbo.

His wife made no attempt to fight back. Her head drooped down on one shoulder now and she looked at her husband through her hair with one eye that had gone cold. The other was half shut and bloodshot. Mrs. Frazier drooled. A sudden silence fell on the cabin. Some of the bedraggled feathered heads of the Delawares came peering in through the door. The firelight glittered on their incurious, black-brown eyes.

"I'm right sorry, captain, 'deed I am," said Frazier shamefacedly. There could be no doubt from his expression that the man's chagrin was genuine. "It's a turrible thing to be jined with a mad thing," he muttered, and mopped his face with his sleeve.

"See to it she doesn't murder the girl," replied Ecuyer.

The Seneca grunted and spoke.

"Two squaws one lodge heap bad. Use'm big stick," he said sententiously, and smote his hands together. Then putting his feet to the floor, he felt the mush tentatively to see if it was cool enough to walk on in his moccasins.

The girl in the corner gave a shivering sob.

"Come," said Ecuyer. "Enough of this. By God, it's worse than Italy!" He walked out past the Delawares at the door, twirling his cane. Half of them were squatting in the snow.

"Get something to cover that poor wench with," said Ecuyer, pausing for a moment to look at the Delawares.

Salathiel dived into the wagon and took out a spare blanket from the chest under the seat. Then a thought struck him. He also took one of two small pistols from

289

the arms chest and loaded it. He thrust this in the folds of the blanket and returned to the cabin.

Frances was still sitting in the corner. She looked up at him unashamed and unafraid, but with so much misery in her eyes he scarcely knew how to speak to her.

"Here," he said roughly but kindly, extending the blanket.

She rose and draped it about her nakedness with great dignity.

"Thanks for that much," she said.

Then he pressed the pistol into her hands. She understood instantly and laid it under the blanket folds in her bosom.

"It's loaded," he whispered.

"I'll not be after shooting meself with it," she said. "But I'll be after you as soon as I can walk. She's nigh cut the behind off'n me."

"I know. I saw," he said.

"Aye," said she, "now that you've seen so much of me, young mon, you'll not be like to forget me soon."

"I'm not likely to," he agreed.

"Albine," called the captain sharply.

He patted her hand with the pistol in it and left. She was holding it next to her breast. The eyes of the old woman followed him witchlike as he went out.

She sat, still dizzy, with her head against the logs. As the door closed behind Salathiel she got up and with her arms hanging before her and her hands working advanced slowly upon the Irish girl.

"So you'd be leaving me after all," she muttered, keeping her eyes on her.

Frances said nothing but sat watching her intently.

"*Give* me that blanket," said the old woman, leaning forward, "or I'll strip it off yer!"

It was then that out of the folds of the blanket close to the girl's neck Mrs. Frazier saw the small round eye of the pistol looking at her. She straightened up. Her hands fell listlessly by her side. She blinked like a baboon, and went back to her seat by the fire without saying a word.

Outside, Burent had the steps of the wagon down and was assisting the captain to climb in and strap himself into his swinging chair. One of the Delawares was examining the brass mountings on the harness with a disconcerting admiration and was inclined to be surly when Salathiel crowded him towards the cabin door with the shoulder of the mare. His father, the Seneca, and Mr. Frazier took him in charge.

An harangue by the chief with a display of menacing gestures, Mr. Frazier's sturdy bulk obstinately planted in the doorway with his rifle leaning conveniently by, the fact that the supply of whisky had departed—all this at last got the badly battered and mush splattered party of the Delawares headed home. They went northwest instead of off on the war or horse-stealing path to the southeast, where temptation lay. They departed gloomily in single file, disappearing at last in a dense thicket about a half a mile away, apparently headed towards the Allegheny River.

Burent was now waiting only for the word to depart. He had already broken the wheels loose from the frozen ground, and the horses pawed impatiently. The old chief and Frazier stood looking on with lacklustre eyes. The wagon to them seemed a machine that might have descended from the skies, a contrivance whose perfection and ingenuity might at least have been the work of some minor deity. But their expressions were both noncommittal.

"Get the lead to the fort tomorrow and be sure to take the chief with you, Mr. Frazier," called the captain, who had at last bound himself with a broad kerchief and to his own satisfaction into the chair.

Mr. Frazier promised.

"I'll be passing by here now and then," said the captain significantly.

The chief grunted.

"Get on with you, Burent," said the captain.

Burent's whip cracked twice like a double-barrelled pistol. The horses threw themselves against the traces, and the heavy wagon drew away from the gloomy cabin at the crossroads at a steady trot, leaving two broad ribbons behind it in the snow. The back wheels were set a little wider apart than the front.

Half a mile ahead they began to breast a hill. Salathiel rode several circles about the slowly moving vehicle. The mare was delighted to be going again. Then the forest began to close in on them. Salathiel set himself to rein in his horse in order to keep just far enough ahead of the ark to be in sight, while as much as possible of the road ahead on both sides was in his constant and unrelenting view.

There were still about three hours of daylight left. He wondered where they would be camping that night. The shadows of the trees were long now. And the red tinge in the light began to beat levelly from the westward in open aisles of the forest, where there was a clean floor of snow.

26

In Which the Dead Arise

IT WAS uphill and downdale, about as tumultuous a bit of landscape as Salathiel had ever seen. This, indeed, was the foothill country of the Alleghenies, covered with an undisturbed forest from the beginning of time; oaks, maples, chestnuts, and ash trees of tremendous proportions. Under their boughs, now all but bare of leaves, a kind of glimmering horizon of the forest seemed to retract through the trees and to fold itself along the hills, always withdrawing before them into a darker beyond or ending apparently with the light along a crest. Then the road would swing down to follow the valley of some stream amidst sumach thickets, whose black branches, with great red torches and remnants of scarlet leaves upon them, illuminated the way.

All this was quite different from the flats, low hills, and endlessly treed plains of Salathiel's old hunting grounds beyond the Ohio, stretching west. Now they were riding great waves of land that seemed to be bearing the forest upon them as they rolled eastward or tumbled downward towards the south.

The road was in good shape here. Working parties from the fort and from the constantly passing detachments of the summer just gone had left their marks of improvement on it. The melting snows of winter had not as yet had time to gnaw at it and wash it out as they would in the early spring. Earth was still piled on the corduroy sections over swamps, and the heavy log bridges were all in place.

Suddenly they came to the edge of their hilly plateau and plunged down into the valley of Turtle Creek just as it began to grow dark.

Here the way was like a long curving canal prism through the forest, a growth so dense that Salathiel rode ahead at his ease, knowing the place was too tangled and impenetrable to provide even an ambush. The road was the only way anybody could get through. The mare trotted ahead contentedly. He could hear the wagon bumping along behind with occasional admonitions to the horses from Burent, accompanied by the scraping of brakes.

At the bottom of the long grade he splashed through a ford. His horse started to gallop ahead through the open glades of the valley, but he turned her about and waited in the twilight for the wagon on the bank of the stream near the ford. Open spaces lay ahead. The going would be good.

The wagon came over the stony bed of the creek, water rising nearly to the horses' bellies. They came up out of the flood, breasting the slope and pulling all together against their collars like one team, the water curling against their breasts and falling away gleaming. The brass points on the harness twinkled with a hundred sunset glints, and the great, dark bulk of the ark loomed behind, its wheels washed suddenly clean.

The mare snorted impatiently at her mates, and they were off again.

All at once they were out of the forest, taking a winding course through a long valley with all but perpendicular sides. There was a queer reflected light here from the bare tablelands and weathered hilltops hundreds of feet above. These bald patches were covered with snow and gleamed like glancing white mirrors in the sunset that still bathed the heights.

In the sheltered valley the stream ran in wide, sweeping curves through a succession of wild meadows where the buffalo grass was still green near the roots and stood nearly waist-high. There were green leaves here even on the bushes, as though summer lingered regretfully in this retreat. The place swarmed with rabbits and wild turkeys. The thickets were alive with crows. Long flights of these birds kept streaming down for the night. Wise birds, Salathiel knew them to be. He watched them and saw that, except for the wagon, there was nothing in that long valley of the Turtle Creek of which even a crow need take notice.

Yet they would not came here, he guessed. The horses had enjoyed a long rest at Frazier's. In the valley the road made a smooth, clear track on a gravelly soil, good clean going; and they passed on, winding in and out for miles along the meadows while the night fell, the stars came out in a cloudless frosty sky, points of steel caught in a gauzy net that shimmered like wind-ruffled water against the black vault overhead.

Yet it was a white night. The starlight alone was enough to drive by. On the heights the wolves howled. At this season the night birds were ominously still. Here and there a scream from a rabbit told where a silent owl had drifted down.

Then there was a long, heavy haul up onto the heights again.

Salathiel stood waiting again just below the crest, seated easily on the mare, his rifle in the crook of his elbow. It was a great night, he thought. A storm of high-flown and half-glimpsed happy thoughts and sensations flowed through him.

In the valley he had let himself dream. There was the unknown and alluring world of the settlements ahead of him, a desire to see and find out akin to hunger increased by expectation, yet already in process of satisfaction by his being on the way. There was also the warm glow, the pleasing pity, of having helped the girl at the cabin. He would like to take her across his knees—that way—for a more pleasant pastime. Perhaps she would get away from Mrs. Frazier? Maybe she would make it to Ligonier after all?

But he had no luck with women. It was best to let them alone. They disturbed everything else that he was doing.

Did he wish he could find Jane again?

He began to think of her affectionately with a certain sorrowful yearning. In the vast night, in the forest that ran between the rising and setting of the moon, where was she? Where was she under these stars that were sliding across heaven? But, he reminded himself again, he must *not* think of such things. He must not give himself up to these pictures that glowed inside him and seemed to have a life of their own.

The noise of the mounting wagon, still some distance below, recalled him. It brought him back to the world that was outside, that was real. It was a world so vivid and dangerous, one that needed such constant and careful attention, that to be caught "mooning," as he called it, might mean the difference between life and death. And what were dreams? What the past or the future compared to now? What was the dim inside world compared to the bright stars, the cold damp scents from the valleys, the dry crisp tang from the night breeze that drifted past him in waves of snowy and leafy smells with a far-off reminiscence of a wolf having staled somewhere—up and where the wind on the heights must be howling, too?

Aye, it was winter, and there were enemies about. His eyes must look keenly outward to fit the puzzle of the blue shadows, the trees and the snow; of starlight and the vague loom of the country into a bright, clear, true picture of the way, the way they must go!

Here were the horses and the heavy wagon now.

He gave a low call to Burent, and heard his hail in reply. Then he turned and rode on again, aware of everything about him, sights, sounds, and scents; of the mare under his bowed legs, of the weight and balance of the gun, and finally of all these dim pictures that brightened into an inner day of clear fact as he pressed on through the night.

Surely the captain would be camping now—soon. But

neither Salathiel nor Burent had yet learned the iron nature of the man in the wagon; the will in the weakening body that grew stronger as the body grew tireder. That night they rode on, and eternally on. That night they began to learn what, in the estimation of Captain Ecuyer, serving the king meant. So did the unfortunate horses.

In another hour they were up on the heights that lay between the Turtle Creek and Bushy Run, a long stretch, some of it bare and comparatively treeless from fires and weather. A wind from the northwest piped about them bitterly. It bit through clothes and slowly benumbed their feet and hands.

Burent swung his arms ceaselessly against his chest. In the wagon the captain stifled the groans that the constant motion of the vehicle was like to drag through his chattering teeth. He lit a small charcoal foot warmer and endeavoured to beat back the sleepy feeling in his leg, a numbness which threatened to ascend to his wound. He bitterly regretted now that he had set out without a sufficient escort. There should have been someone to ride behind as well as ahead. When he got to Ligonier he would rectify that.

From all accounts things were at a pretty pass with the garrison at Ligonier. Bouquet had gone into the matter with him at some length. Ligonier was important as the halfway post between Bedford and Fort Pitt. He might have to take stern measures. In this naked wilderness it was hard to be strict with the men. Poor devils, they suffered! And they seldom got paid. He would write Colonel Bouquet for the love of God to release him. He couldn't go on in this way. He needed surgeons, a rest. Geneva! How would it be to be back there next spring, drifting in a boat under the walls of Chillon? He closed his eyes to see the snow peaks mirrored in the water. Lucille, how had you found it with the reverend doctor? If you had only waited, Lucille! The campaign in Savoy had not lasted so long. But longer than your promises or patience. Alas, Lucille!

He stopped his mouth, and a groan, with his handkerchief and inhaled the verbena scent. Lucy, Lucy, how dainty you were, smelling so! Orange orchards and lemon bloom. Sicily! God, what a road! What a slide into the pit was that which the wagon had just taken! Enough to disembowel a man. They were stopped. He drew back the rear flap. A hundred yards behind, four fiery eyes were dripping molten silver in the moonlight. They stood watching with a sinister steady glare. Then two shadows faded into the brush. Wolves!

"Albine's riding back, sir," said Burent. "There's something ahead not quite right. Hosses lyin' down, it seems like."

Salathiel came trotting back rapidly.

"It's the Quaker Japson and his string of pack horses," he explained.

"He's alone, and he's made a fire in a pit to keep him from freezing. Some of his beasts can't get up. I saw the glow of his fire and rode right over into his camp. That's what bringing the wolves around. The man's scairt and wants we should camp here. He says we'll freeze if we don't. There's a blizzard-snap comin' on. It does feel like it."

The captain listened without comment. "Tell him if he wishes to come with us he may do so," he said finally. "Help him rouse his horses and let him follow behind. We'll camp at Bouquet's old battleground tonight. It can't be over an hour's going from here. There's a small stockade was built there this autumn by the convoys. It will give some shelter from the wind at least."

"And from the Injuns," added Burent, who made no disguise of his feelings. "I keep athinking of those Delawares."

"There'll be no Injuns tonight," said Salathiel. "It's now so cold they'll have stopped to make pit fires like Japson. You can't walk the ground in moccasins on a night like this. At least not in deerskin moccasins like they had."

"Maybe so," said Burent doubtfully.

"Get your horses going or they will be down too," said the captain, impatient at the talk.

They stopped again abreast of where the Quaker had camped. With great difficulty, and the use of burning sticks, Burent and Salathiel managed to get the Quaker's horses on their feet, all except one beast whose legs were paralyzed and already rigid with cold. They piled its pack into the wagon where Japson had promptly climbed. He seemed to take his welcome there for granted. One of his hands appeared to be frozen. His constant talk of the terrible cold made them all realize for the first time how extraordinarily cold it really was.

"The coldest night of my life," said the Quaker, "and I've traded through these woods twenty years come December. Thou hast caused me to lose three horses today, friend Ecuyer, two to the Virginian at Frazier's. He made off with them. And the one that can't rise."

"Thou wouldst lose all of them if Burent were not tying them behind for thee now," replied the captain. "It is fortunate we found thee here or the wolves would have by morning." He handed the man the charcoal burner.

"Aye?" said the Quaker, and began to smooth the mysteriously warm little box with his half-frozen hand. For the captain's ironical *thou*-ing of him he carried nothing.

Salathiel and Burent hastened the fastening of the string of pack horses behind the wagon as best they could. Some of the packs were loose and they had to take up on the cinches with cold-stiffened fingers. The wind was now pouring itself out of the northwest, arctic, clear, and steady. It seemed to be quieter now because it no longer came in howling gusts but in one continuous murmuring blast that drew the last warmth out of their bodies. They wrapped themselves Indian fashion in extra blankets and put the horse blankets on the wagon teams and the mare. Mr. Japson expressed great surprise at seeing the "critters blanketed." He felt the nap of the horse blankets with his unfrozen hand as they came out of the chest in the wagon, and grunted.

Salathiel took a lead horse by the cheek straps and started them off. Burent ran alongside the wagon. He could no longer abide the cold, driving and sitting still on the seat. The horses seemed to sense shelter ahead and strained forward faithfully. Luckily the string of pack horses "towing" behind was too tired to make trouble. Mr. Japson continued to ride in the wagon and let them take care of themselves, even though his precious goods were involved.

It was that which made the captain realize how cold it was, more than anything else.

Five miles, which took nearly two hours, brought them between two and three o'clock in the morning to the ford at Bushy Run. It was frozen smoothly solid. The not-inconsiderable little river had simply been halted in its bed by the sudden arctic frost. There was no sound in the valley and the still, dead cold of the place was appalling. A noise like a musket shot just ahead caused the front team to rear and everybody to handle his arms. It proved to be a chestnut tree split open halfway along its trunk by the frost. From time to time that night such reports continued to come to them out of the forest.

"Cheerily now," said Burent. "The stockade's just under the rise of yon hill ahead. Another mile will do it." He began to soothe and coax the lagging horses along.

Salathiel rode ahead for a careful look about. There was no one. The heavy wagon, its trailing caisson and string of horses came up slowly behind him. It was nearly three o'clock by the silver watch that Captain Ecuyer had given him when Salathiel saw the ark blunder through the gate into the small, entrenched stockade that had been erected for the protection of wagoners close by the battlefield of the summer before.

It lay, as Burent had said, just under the crest of the hill. The rise and the twelve-foot barrier of logs provided a grateful shelter from the paralyzing sweep of the blast. There was a rough lean-to shed and a well with a sweep.

The captain emerged from the wagon and began to call urgently for a fire. While the horses were being driven into the shed, he himself began to drag the remains of logs from old fires together, and to try to nurse along a blaze started by his flint and steel. The flame finally started up, revealing the black, log walls and frozen, mud-trampled interior of the place; the horses' rumps sticking out dejectedly under the shed.

Salathiel recalled afterward that they worked with a certain desperation that night. All were aware that in a few minutes more they would be stopped by the cold. It kept getting colder even inside the still stockade.

"Have the goodness to assist us, Mr. Japson," said the captain, "to presarve yourself."

"Me hand's frrozen," said the Quaker.

"My foot isn't yet," said Burent, and approached him menacingly.

He gave in, muttering something, and began to help drag the logs towards the fire from a near-by pile. Albine knocked the ice and snow off them with his tomahawk, cut off the dry branches, and in a short while the fire had taken hold the length of several good-sized trees. They dragged up more wood, and the sparks soon soared up towards the stars.

"That will give notice to every savage within ten miles that we're here," said the Quaker.

"They'll think there's a large force then," said Salathiel. "The more fires we make now the better."

He and Burent started another blaze between the shed and the wagon. The captain voiced his approval. The horses were fed and lay down on piles of old leaves under the shed. They fed the Quaker's horses with corn from their own chest behind the wagon, out of mercy to the half-starved beasts. Burent forced Japson to bed down in the leaves under the shed near his horses, pointing out that if the fire reached the leaves, Mr. Japson would perish along with his property. Then a few collops of meat were roasted, which all ate ravenously.

The captain cut three straws of different lengths. He and Burent and Salathiel then drew lots for keeping

301

watch. Burent drew the first watch and the captain the second. No one thought of trusting Japson.

"Two hours' sleep apiece," said Ecuyer. "That will get us under way late in the morning, but the horses must have some rest. If it comes on to snow, whoever is on watch must wake me. We'll leave, for we can't risk being snowed in here. Keep your eyes open, Burent."

The captain and Salathiel crawled into the wagon. Burent kept himself awake by keeping up the fires and bedevilling the Quaker.

"You're not to get more sleep than the captain," he said. "Lord, this is a terrible country, cold as Iceland in winter and like a furnace in summer. I wish I was back in Kent."

"I wish thou wert, too," said Japson, and then added, "Let the English stay home."

"Aren't you an Englishman?" demanded Burent.

"A Pennsylvanian, if thou *must* know," replied Japson.

Burent laughed. He continued to pile wood on the flames till the heat beat back into the shed and even through the canvas sides of the wagon.

Two hours later the captain took his watch. The fires died slowly. When it came Salathiel's turn there was a great bed of glowing coals. Japson snored. Some of the horses were beginning to struggle to their feet, although it was still dark. The wind had completely died away. A more than usual stillness reigned. The tremendous cold had laid a hand of death on the country. It was the coldest Salathiel could ever remember. In fact, it was the coldest night, save one, he was ever to know.

He built up the fires again carefully, and stood listening.

The captain had gone back into the wagon. He could hear him breathing in his sleep, and Burent too. Japson snored in the shed much like the horses. Occasionally they shifted from one foot to another. All else was silent as the stars. He knocked some lone icicles away from the horses' noses, took his rifle, and stepped through the gate.

The quiet outside seemed eternal. Once, far off, a tree split in the forest. The stars blinked and blazed a frosty carbon blue. From the gate of the small stockade, the country fell away for miles eastward, a blur of open meadows with snowy patches of thicket, followed on each side by a marching wall of velvet, black forest.

It was in this desolate, open tract of country, waterless, and hemmed in by the eternal woods, that Bouquet had been ambushed the summer before. A long line of clay scars in military order showed where his dead had been buried just off the road. The gaunt, black arms of the forest seemed to be tossing despairing hands over them towards the sky.

Despite the cold, Salathiel stepped out of his boots and hid them by the gate. His fur-lined moccasins would do, and he would be gone only a little while. He intended to fetch a circle around the stockade. It would be just as well to do so.

He faded into the shadows silent as a wolf. It was the old hunting stride, the rifle at a long trail, and he crouching a little. He went back as far as the ford, never losing sight of the stockade. There were no tracks there but their own. He felt the ground and the snow now turned to a crisp ice crust, where every track was frozen like a mark in stone. He came crouching back through the woods up onto the crest of the hill and looked down over a chaos of tumbling hills and forest.

There was a trail there that led off to the northward, but nothing but a few deer tracks were on it. Half of this scout he was doing for sheer enjoyment, half from an excess of caution. But it *was* sheer joy to be back in the wild again, to hear the silence, to be rid of smells. The cold air seemed immortally clean. He came down the hill just behind the sky line and struck the road again. Just beyond him several crescent-shaped trenches, probably the work of the embattled Bouquet, loomed lighter against the brown weeds of the fields. A faint light was beginning to dull the stars in the east. There was a hazy overcast, a kind of premonition of dawn in the air, and it was in this blue-greyness against the crest of a little rise that he saw them.

He saw them before he heard their stealthy sounds, a rustle in the weeds, the crack of a twig, or a loose stone now and then. There were only two of them, a man and a squaw, and most curious of all there was a pony. It was that which had made the noise, though the little Indian horses were taught to step carefully, too.

His first impulse was to shoot. But the thought that there might be others about restrained him. And as the grey dawn grew gradually a bit brighter, and he could see the movements of the couple more plainly, curiosity overcame him, for he could not at first imagine what they were doing.

He crawled forward to a fallen log and then down a small gully to a considerable clump of bushes. They were quite close now. They were searching for something. He saw it before they did. It was marked by a branch sticking up with a long white feather tied to it. One of the horses at the stockade neighed. The Indian grabbed his pony about the nose and looked back anxiously. He couldn't be seen from the stockade. He was just below a ridge in the hill. They waited. Morning grew brighter.

The squaw began to poke and scoop in a hollow full of leaves and pine needles below the feathered stick. She began to make a low noise of mourning. It was the beginning of the death song. The man with her struck her. She fell forward into the hollow place on her knees. When she got up a tall, rigid Indian with a chief's bedraggled war bonnet seemed to rise up out of the ground with her.

Salathiel's rifle came poking through the branches instinctively. He drew a bead on the head of the chief who had so suddenly appeared as though out of the earth. He could just see the end of his rifle well enough to aim. Then he saw that the man he was aiming at was dead, frozen stiff as a board; that his face had fallen away and the white cheekbones showed through.

For some instants Salathiel found himself looking down

the long barrel of his rifle at the two pits of darkness under the chalky brow. The dead chief was too bedraggled, too covered with leaves and debris, to tell to what tribe he had belonged. It was plain he was one of the dead from the battle of the summer before. Salathiel guessed that it must be his brother and sister who had come for him. It would not be the duty of the man's squaw. They had come from beyond the Illinois, perhaps. The western tribes made much of their dead.

While he watched the squaw, memories of Mawakis returned to him. He lowered his rifle. These were the last Indians who should ever pass safely before his sights, he vowed. But there was something moving and pitiable about the three before him. He watched them fascinated.

They took the dead chief, forced his legs apart, and bound him on the pony. One of his arms, from the hand of which the flesh had slipped like a glove, extended behind him. It seemed to move up and down in a bony farewell as the party took its way stealthily and silently towards the line of the forest below them. Above the sere weeds of the open meadows the dead chief on the pony reared stiffly as a dark drifting mast. The woman trudged before, the man behind. He stopped once and looked back. Then the forest swallowed them.

They would take some secret path westward, Salathiel thought. All these people were going that way, going towards the setting sun. And day was behind them. For an instant he had a vision of it all: the lonely battlefield, the Indians moving west, and west, and west, taking their dead and their memories along with them until the end. He saw the sea of grass, where he had once ridden with McArdle, swallowing them. They were drowning in it. For a moment, and for the last time, he felt with them and for them as his people—but his people no more! It had been only a vision in the pearl grey of the morning.

He rose, conscious now of the cold that had begun to stiffen him. The metal of his rifle burned through his jacket. All the eastern crests of the Alleghenies were outlined with grey light. The horse at the stockade neighed again. It was probably one of the Quaker's. Lucky they weren't being followed, he thought. And he was reasonably sure of that now.

The cold was colossal. Although there was no longer any wind, everything was frozen into a crisp, metallic hardness. Here and there small birds lay dead under the trees or stiffened on a bough. He started to run up the hill towards the stockade to send the blood through his numbed extremities.

In the frozen wheel-rutted interior Burent was up and had a huge fire of piled logs going. The captain, wrapped in a long cloak, was seated before the flames, toasting his shins. Japson was tending the horses in a way which met even with Burent's approval. From time to time the Quaker came over to the fire to dip his frosted hand in a kettle of hot water.

"It's a good sign if you san still feel pain in your frozen fingers," said Burent.

"Thanks for thy cold comfort," said Japson wryly. "There is much pain."

The captain looked relieved at seeing Salathiel again.

"Our friends the Delawares, for example?" he said, raising his eyebrows.

"They have not followed us, sir," replied Salathiel. "I have been out looking for them since before dawn. We'd have heard of them before this if they were on our trail."

"Thou wilt *not* be followed," said Japson emphatically, and went over to feed the horses, his own included, with corn from the caisson. Burent said nothing but looked annoyed.

"I think Japson is right," agreed Salathiel, "and the road will be like iron at least as far as the fort. We should make good time."

"I have certain plans about the road," said the captain, and smiled enigmatically. "I don't think we'll be following the road all the way. Get a file out of the tool chest, Burent," he added. "No, I'll not shave this morning, Albine. The lather would freeze on my face, I think. But the file is not for that."

They sat down and ate heartily of bacon and fried corncakes. The captain shared a dram of brandy with them and looked longingly at the mare, shook his head, and climbed regretfully into the wagon. Salathiel wrapped him up as best he could and blew into the charcoal hand stove until it glowed. Ecuyer prepared himself for the day's ordeal. Ligonier was still many hours away from the standpoint of a man in pain. Perhaps the cold would help to numb it some.

"When we come to the first crossing of the Loyalhanna Branch," he said to Salathiel, "let me know. Waken me then, even if I am asleep."

It occurred to Albine forcefully as he looked at the captain's face, which had begun to have a peaked and wasted look, that there might come a time when he would not be wakable. The captain's mouth trembled despite his firm chin.

"Never mind," said Ecuyer, sensing something of what was passing in Salathiel's mind. "I'll pull through. And there will be a good surgeon at Bedford. I hope it's Boyd."

Just then the clatter of Japson leaving ahead of them with his pack horses and the shadow of the man himself passed between the sun and the canvas walls of the wagon. The captain noticed it.

"But I think we'll get there before you, my friend, for all that," he said, signalling Albine to hasten the wagon's departure.

Burent and Salathiel linked the horses to the trace chains rapidly. In a few moments the ark rolled out of the stockade over the frozen ruts and took the road eastward to Ligonier. Japson had already disappeared ahead.

"That's gratitude for you," grunted Burent; "that's what comes when 'e gives corn to a pious rebel." He called after Salathiel as he rode off ahead, "He'll make trouble for us before we get there if he can."

"Ef there's Injuns ahead, he'll find them for us first," replied Salathiel as he galloped away. "Since we don't need to worry about the road ahead I'll be the rear guard today."

"Keep the horses at it," said the muffled voice of the captain inside the wagon. "Trot when you can. Never mind me."

Surprisingly enough, they *were* able to trot from time to time.

From Bushy Run the road went over a succession of low ridges with an occasional stretch along a brief plateau. It ran into the densest thickets, while the hills kept getting longer and steeper. Once Burent caught a glimpse of Japson and his string of horses crossing a crest ahead. He was going fast. The wagon also was making time, and quite steadily, for at least there were no ruts or holes to negotiate. The water in them had frozen level with the ground and hard. So they trotted. The cold seemed to drive the horses forward. The ark rolled and rumbled, the small caisson danced behind. They came lurching down the hills, the horses slipping and stumbling, the wheels sliding, brakes on, and Burent performing miracles with the long reins.

Then they would stop, breathe for a few moments, and breast the inevitable climb ahead with the backs of the two teams stretching out in two parallel lines, shoulders thrust into the collars.

At such places Salathiel rode forward, and passing a toggle with a canvas collar on it that had been arranged for the mare, he made fast to rings in the forward trace chains and threw the weight of his own horse into the haul upward. It was funny how soon the team horses came to expect this. They would snort and whinny for the mare to come when they started to climb. And they followed after her and her rider eagerly. In this way they would come up over the crests famously and Salathiel would whip aside as the wagon plunged recklessly down.

And so hour after hour with an occasional rest, and then the cold for a spur at the start again.

It was at one of these times of brief rest, when all was

silent, except for the breathing of the horses, that Salathiel managed to shoot a deer.

It came peering at them suddenly out of a thicket with the fatal curiosity of its kind. Then it flirted its white tail, jumped aside on a log, and was about to bound away when Salathiel's bullet struck it down.

There had been just time enough to unsling his rifle. He began to ponder that. In his estimation it had taken far too long, fifteen counts at least. He would have to learn to do better. It would not always be a deer that awaited his shot. Yes, undoubtedly, he must practice. And it was irritating how long it took him to reload too. He must change all that.

As he rode along he began to think of each motion he made in the use of the rifle, and to see if he could not eliminate some of them.

The deer was strapped on the caisson. It was a young doe and its head, that had at first flopped at him, speedily stiffened in the cold. It seemed now to be looking back at him steadily and reproachfully. *It* had not been quick enough, he thought. *He* would not like to be caught— for the same reason.

A ridge now lay ahead, the most mountainous they had yet crossed. From its summit there was a brief, splendid glimpse of the Laurel Hill and the Alleghenies far off and up, cloudy, marching parallel north and south in long, undulating solid walls of trees. For a moment Salathiel stood looking at them uplifted, astonished, and amazed. The clouds were low and the mountains seemed to drag at the bottom of the sky. Then Burent shouted something at him, and they plunged down again. He understood him to say that this was the Chestnut Ridge and that Ligonier lay on the other side.

And there were plenty of mighty chestnuts here. They and the mountain ashes stood tall and massive, often so close together you could see only a few feet off the road. At the bottom, in a wide valley, was a dense tangle of sycamores and the silent, broad, frozen levels of the Loyalhanna Creek stilled in full winter flood. It wound away like a dark, silver highway into the heart of the forest through the bottom lands.

Here they stopped and cooked a brief meal, which the deer furnished. Then they watered the horses. It was necessary to chop a hole in the river, and Salathiel noticed that the heads of the horses disappeared almost to their ears when they drank, so thick was the ice.

It was not necessary to waken the captain as he had ordered. He had emerged himself in considerable distress. The wound in his groin had broken and it was necessary to wash and rebandage it. The icy water they dipped out of the Loyalhanna, he soon discovered, gave him great relief. For some reason his fever also abated. At any rate, he now insisted upon dressing himself with some care, assisted by Albine. Except for a day-old beard, he soon looked himself again and very much the king's officer in a fresh wig and a gold-laced three-cornered hat, cockade and all.

While this combined surgery, tailoring, and toilet was going forward, the captain directed Burent to take the file and sharpen the calks on the shoes of the horses. The mare was included. Japson, they saw, had scrambled up the far bank across the ford and continued along the road, as the marks left by his horses plainly showed.

"But we will not follow him," said Ecuyer. "It is about eight miles by the road, which is quite bad here, to Ligonier, and only some three or four miles by the creek. If this little sketch map of mine is to be trusted, the stream curves here and cuts across through the forest, and you know the Ligonier stockade is on its banks. So we will take the river, since nature has paved the way. Burent, do you see that the horses do not fall."

Salathiel and Burent were both lost in admiration at this simple stratagem, particularly that even that morning the captain had remembered to take the file out of the chest. They would not have to drag the chest from under the wagon now. They might even make the fort ahead of Japson. Burent chuckled.

With a little coaxing they got the horses to trust themselves upon the ice. Then they tied the wheels together and the ark slid on its iron tires along the creek like a sleigh. The horses walked gingerly at first, but with more confidence as the iron points on their shoes continued to hold. Only once were they in great difficulty. It was where the river ran a brief stretch of rapids before a low falls. The ice was rough and wavy here and there were even some blisters under which the water could be heard rushing. Two of the horses fell, one on either side. They wrapped blankets about their heads and got them up again.

"Only the blind can be persuaded to get up and go on again, sometimes," remarked the captain. "Perhaps that is why the future is always kept dark to us? Go on! Get on with it! Don't gape. Take the blankets off!"

They dragged the ark by main force over a small rocky island at the falls whose spill made a kind of ramp. The removal of some saplings with an axe made the way just negotiable. Then they resumed, sliding ever so smoothly again. The river wound in and out like a serpentine canal. The captain lit a cigar. His wound was delightfully numb again. The discharge had seemed to improve it. At least it was no longer throbbing, and the motion of the wagon was silken. No one would be expecting him to arrive at the fort, especially when he came by "water." His welcome was bound to be exquisitely informal.

The trample of the horses on the ice made a kind of low booming sound at certain places. The absence of all other noises of any kind, except the jingle of the harness chains, showed that the cold held the whole wilderness about them in a vise. It was windless and appallingly still in the deep valley. It was many degrees below zero. The little river had been stopped, apparently arrested instantly by the sudden coming of the cold. Outside Salathiel was slapping his legs and thighs to keep the blood going. Burent from time to time beat his feet on the wagon floor.

Yes, they would certainly arrive as a surprise, thought the captain. He would be able to see what was really going on at the fort. Ligonier was such an important link, the main outpost between Fort Bedford and Fort Pitt. It had nearly been lost once last summer, reinforced just in time. Good discipline must be kept, and at all costs a strict watch, or the frontier to the west would fall for lack of supplies being able to reach it. Ecuyer leaned back for a moment, easing himself in his swinging chair, and looked up at a patch of ice on the canvas where the fire had temporarily melted the snow that morning at the stockade. The patch had frozen again like the glass of a window only semi-transparent to light. Well, when they got there he would see.

At that moment the thud of a musket and a hole that seemed to appear simultaneously in both sides of the canvas roof about a foot above the captain's head confirmed his opinion that the arrival of the wagon at Ligonier would be a "surprise." The horses reared and Burent burst into a stream of profanity surprisingly sustained for so quiet a man.

"It's the fort, sir. We've just raised it through the trees," said Salathiel. "The sentry post at the bridge across the creek must have fired at us. I can see some of them making up the road for the fort now."

"Ride forward and tell them this wagon is not a moving Indian village," replied Ecuyer, looking out at the stockade that loomed up through the forest some half a mile away across a bend of the creek. Salathiel took the west bank and galloped forward along the road to the fort, shouting and waving his cap. Captain Ecuyer dusted a little powder off his hat and looked up at the holes in the canvas thoughtfully.

A drum began to roll.

"Move on, Burent," he called. "Get the wagon up that patch of low bank at the landing, take the road straightaway, and get under the walls of the fort. They can see what we are then."

A few minutes later, and ahead of the wagon, Salathiel rode out into the large clearing before the stockade. It was high land here and overlooked the valley southward.

The clearing was large enough to serve as a rough drill ground, and for that purpose the stumps had been removed. A party of Highlanders in red kilts, evidently the squad that had been guarding the bridge, scrambled and ran before him towards the gate, which was open. Inside the fort he caught a glimpse of a frantic dashing around. The drums crashed again. Somebody was trying to close the gate. Evidently the ground was frozen under it, and it stuck. Someone else with a plumed Highland bonnet came out of a barracks door, drawing a claymore.

Salathiel rode through the gate and drew rein on a little cobbled space. For a moment all the garrison that was visible, including the sentries on the galleries, stood looking foolishly at him.

"Weel, young mon?" said a sergeant, the man in the plumed bonnet, coming towards him and sliding the claymore back into its scabbard. "Weel, what is it ye have to say?"

27

Mr. Yates Introduces Himself

SALATHIEL announced the arrival of the captain, and suggested that no more loaded salutes should be fired.

The Highland sergeant's face turned dark with anger when he heard what had happened. A furious conversation in Gaelic occurred between him and the sentry who had fired the shot. The man came forward reluctantly at the sergeant's order and gave up his musket. The rumble of the wagon was now heard coming along the walls.

In urgent haste the sergeant formed what men he could literally lay his hands on into a guard drawn up at the gate. They were a motley crew, three Pennsylvania militiamen in tattered green watchcoats and six Highlanders in red and black crossed kilts. None of them were armed except the sergeant, who still had the rifle of the sentry he had disarmed. This was duly presented as the wagon came through the gate, but not without delay. For having once been dragged half-shut, the gate was now to be opened again only by violent measures. Finally, it slipped off its upper hinge and sagged inward drunkenly.

The ark drew up before the barracks in the fort with rather a professional flourish on the part of Burent, who saw that the horses were reined in and stepping high. Salathiel fitted on the small pair of steps and Ecuyer came limping down them, his heavy cane under his arm.

A deep silence, broken only by the grunting of an extraordinary number of pigs, fell upon the interior of the outpost. The captain walked over and took a look at the "guard." He also glanced sidewise at the sagging gate. The sergeant's face turned as red as his tunic.

"You can come to the order, sergeant," the captain said. Another moment of even more intense silence ensued.

"What are these?" asked Ecuyer finally, pointing to a pile of curious, flat round stones with iron handles on them, which the guard had piled hastily in a heap behind them.

"Curlin' stanes, your Honour," gasped the sergeant.

The captain's brows went up in enquiry.

"It's a game the Scots do be playing on the ice, sir," countered the sergeant. "And it's fine curlin' weather, the noo . . ."

"So no trivial duties have been allowed to spoil the sport," concluded Ecuyer, bringing out his handkerchief with an irritated flourish, and looking the sergeant in the eye. He observed, however, that alone among the garrison, the sergeant was properly turned out. All the complicated items of his Highland uniform, although shabby, were clean, correct, and present. "And you are the only one on duty here?"

"Your Honour has stated it aboot correctly," said the sergeant, returning the captain's level gaze. "You will find the post in a dreadfu' way. You're a sight for sare eyes, sir. I'd gladly git oop and tastify so at the auld kirk. The Scots are verra loyal, but—"

"Dismiss your curlers, sergeant," interrupted the captain impatiently. "Tell them to arm themselves ready for a general muster. Post some sober sentries. And, sergeant, before you do anything else, rehang the gate and close it. By the way, where *are* the officers?"

"Lieutenant St. Clair has gone back to Fort Bedford. Him and Ensign Erskine couldn't get along, sir. The Pennsylvania officers have whusked off to Bedford, too. You see, the ensign has a king's commission whilst the two militia lieutenants were only of the provincial line. I thought we'd have had a war between them in the fort.

315

The men have a' been takin' sides. Half the Pennsylvanians are locked up the noo i' the old hay byre. Meestir Erskine is dootless aboot."

"Thank you, sergeant, that will do," said the captain. "Have Mr. Erskine report to me at once. Dismiss the guard."

"Curlers, dismissed," said the sergeant, a look of sly triumph on his face.

A cackle of loud talk burst out in the fort as the guard scattered. Hoots and catcalls mingled with the shrill voice of a woman here and there.

Disregarding this disrespectful welcome, but burning with indignation, Captain Ecuyer made for the blockhouse in the centre of the stockade from whose stone chimney, the only one in the fort, sparks were soaring high into the still air. Evidently it was the headquarters of the place.

While all this was going on, Salathiel had been looking about him at the interior of Fort Ligonier and at the strange assortment of his Majesty's subjects, armed and unarmed, male and female, who might be said to infest rather than to inhabit it.

Fort Ligonier was by no means a large one. Perhaps an acre had been enclosed by a log stockade set in the midst of much more spacious outworks, trenches, rifle pits, and artillery emplacements thrown up hastily by the troops under Forbes, and later on by Bouquet, as they had moved forward to Fort Pitt and made their base here for the time being. These outer works enclosed an area of several acres of fairly level ground lying at the foot of a small knoll upon which the stockade itself had been erected. But it would have taken a small army to man these outworks, since they had been built for that, and they were now abandoned, full of water, and lying in great raw gashes around the clearing.

In the middle of this tangle of rutted roads, camp pits, entrenchments, and various indescribable abandoned debris, the stockade of the permanent post rose on its knoll in the centre to a height of nearly forty feet. It overlooked the valley of the Loyalhanna to the southeastward and on the opposite side a fine space of unusually level greensward freed of stumps and covered already by English grasses self-planted from the seeds of eastern hay and various forage transported for the cavalry. About the whole encampment, except in the direction of the Loyalhanna Creek, and at a distance varying from a few hundred yards to a quarter of a mile, swept the black arc of the forest, peculiarly dense here, and utterly impenetrable except in single file by an Indian trail northward to Venango, or by the military road which passed immediately in front of the stockade and disappeared not far away into the rolling hills eastward towards Fort Bedford.

There was nothing remarkable about the stockade at Ligonier, except that it had been provided more than usually generously with cannon. Hundreds of hardwood trees, oaks, ash, and walnut, had been flattened on two sides by adzes, rammed into the palisaded earth, and sharpened into a point at the upper end. A ditch, now full of snow, ran around the entire circuit of wooden walls which were reinforced here and there with cobbles, loopholed, and provided at convenient intervals with an embrasure for a light field gun. There was also a small defensive tower rising a story above the gate, which could accommodate at least ten riflemen, and this, together with the more permanent buildings in the interior of the place, was roofed with cobbles and pebbles held together by puddled clay to ward off fire arrows. The last had been Captain Ecuyer's own suggestion to Colonel Bouquet, and he was very proud of it.

Salathiel was greatly disappointed as he looked about him while the captain had been inspecting the guard. He knew, of course, that Ligonier was only a way post and could not hold a candle to Fort Pitt as a fortress. But it seemed to him that he had already travelled a long distance eastward towards the white man's world, and unconsciously he was expecting that the inhabitants, if not the garrison, of Ligonier would begin to discover some

317

of those traits of elegance and refinement of which he had read in the novels of Captain Ecuyer's small library. Was he not already almost a hundred miles nearer London—at the least, fifty!

Alas and alack, there was not a single refined novelty to be seen anywhere as he gazed eagerly about him. The inside of the fort consisted of a double-storied blockhouse with overhanging, loopholed eaves and a massive door with some stone steps leading up to it. This was set precisely in the centre of the interior. Between it and the gate was an area paved roughly with large, smooth boulders from the creek, and this in turn was flanked by two long, low, windowless log barracks, slab-roofed, that looked at each other with a blind, uncompromising, bulldog stare.

Behind these barracks a foul, muddy area stretched to rough sheds and storehouses which ran along both sides of the fort close to the walls. They also were windowless, but since the area before them was enlivened by nothing but great numbers of pigs of all ages, sizes, and conditions, wading aimlessly about and floundering in the more luscious pools of frozen mire, this lack of view was perhaps not to be lamented.

Beyond the centre blockhouse or headquarters, and towards the rear of the stockade, were two lines of some twenty huts facing each other, built of logs, stones, strawed clay, and a medley of various other materials including parts of wrecked wagons, the beds of some of which had been inverted for roofs. Most of these huts had chimneys of plastered clay and sticks which smoked away abominably, filling the interior of the fort with a reeking haze through which the long rifle platform, that ran all around the place like a continuous gallery, could be seen with difficulty.

Crouched here and there along this platform was a sentry trying to warm his hands over a pan of coals or striding up and down beating his arms while his musket leaned against the parapet. These sentries, with the pigs moving below them, and the sooty folds of a flapping

318

Union Jack would have been the only signs of animation about the place had not the alarm given by the recent firing of the outpost at the bridge set the garrison to scurrying about and brought the inhabitants of the huts to their doors, where they now stood coughing and shivering, wrapping tattered blankets about their shoulders, and calling shrilly to one another.

Among the population of this miserable "village" were a number of women, as slatternly a crew as Salathiel had ever seen, with soot-smutched faces and elflocks flying in the wind. They now began to pick their way from one hut to another, driving the pigs before them up the narrow street, and lifting their skirts above their knees at the worst mudholes. Evidently the news had spread that the occasion of the alarm was not an Indian attack, but something much more serious, the arrival of a king's officer. Visits and gossip were in order.

"Hit *ain't* St. Clair; he *be'nt* back yet" seemed to be the main piece of news which they kept bawling at one another. A dogfight of major proportions, which broke out near the stables, soon drowned out any further items of human moment.

Captain Ecuyer, accompanied by the sergeant, whose name Salathiel soon learned was McLaughlin, now came across the cobbled space towards the blockhouse before which the wagon had drawn up.

"Send for the drummer," said the captain to McLaughlin; "we will have a general muster here in a few minutes. This is where you usually assemble, isn't it?"

"Aye," said the sergeant. "It's the only spot free of pigs in the establishment. Lefteenant St. Clair is verra fond of swine."

"We'll take that up with Mr. St. Clair later," said the captain. "Albine, it looks as though we'd be here for a day or two, unless Lieutenant St. Clair does return sooner. Have Burent stable the horses. Keep the wagon here, and carry in all the necessaries for cooking and comfort. Sergeant, put an honest sentry on this beat before headquarters and see that he is relieved by another honest

319

man. No pilfering from this vehicle, or out of your own pay it comes."

Sergeant McLaughlin looked serious. "There be sax Alexanders i' the coompany," he said, "twa of thim—"

"Will do," snapped the captain.

At this moment a woebegone young drummer boy of the militia appeared in a green watchcoat that stretched nearly to his heels. He had been crying, to judge by the smears on his face, and looked apprehensively about him.

"Cheer up, my child," said the captain. "Can you beat the general?"

"Yis, sor. Thot I kin!"

Tightening the snares on his drum, the boy struck an heroic stance and the drum began to roll its loud summons, filling the stockade with reverberating waves of sound. A look of rapt, urchin pleasure, of a trancelike delight fell across the boy's features, causing Captain Ecuyer, the sergeant, and Salathiel to smile. The drum ceased.

"Well done!" cried the captain. "You're a true soldier!" —and without thinking, he tossed him the next to the last sixpence he had. It fell in the snow, and as the lad stooped to pick it up, his cap, much too large for him, fell off.

"Great God!" exclaimed Ecuyer.

The top of the boy's head was one hairless, red scar. Only a fringe of hair remained like a tonsure. It also was carrot red.

"Aye," said McLaughlin, "thot's why they call him the 'Monk'."

Salathiel suddenly remembered a copper-coloured arm that had once come out of a bush and caught another boy by the hair. It might have been this way . . .

"Come on, *you*," said he gruffly but kindly to the young drummer, "lend me a hand unlading this wagon." The sergeant grinned his approval.

While Salathiel and the Monk addressed themselves to getting the captain's things moved out of the wagon and into the blockhouse, the garrison of the place was rapidly assembling in the paved area before the barracks, the Highlanders on one side and the militia on the other.

"Careful now," said Salathiel, as he and the drummer swung one of Johnson's old valet chests up the short flight of icy stone steps that led to the blockhouse door. "It won't do to stumble with these." He reached for the latchstring.

Just then the door was flung violently open, revealing a small dark young man with a pair of blazing eyes that seemed to be starting from his head. He carried a half-pike, or "spontoon," threateningly. He was dressed in filthy white officer's breeches, a pair of magnificent London boots with green tops, and a vest from which a fine cambric shirt, also filthy, protruded. In addition he had on a gorget, and the remains of a leather stock. His handsome face was flushed a dull red and subtly swollen, so that his expression was like that of a mask of extreme exasperation and sullen anger. In fact, about the short, dark young man there was an air of sleepy menace and malice, and he was now glaring directly into Salathiel's eyes.

"God damn it!" roared he. "Who's the bloody zaney gave orders for the drum to be beat?" And then, noticing Salathiel for the first time, "Who, by God, are you? What are ye trying to bring that blasted coffin in here for?" He flourished the spontoon.

"Out of my way," he screamed.

Then he seemed to be flung by some force from within him, for he cleared the doorway and steps in one nimble leap, jumping clear over the chest, and landing gracefully enough on the cobbles only a few feet behind the spot where Captain Ecuyer and the sergeant were standing awaiting the assembling of the garrison.

But something else had happened during the jump. As he passed over the chest, Salathiel had twisted the spontoon out of his hand. It had been a simple instinctive move on his part.

Disturbed by the clatter of boots behind him, Captain Ecuyer now turned around. The angry, dark young man

321

came slowly to attention, the anger in his face giving way to a blank expression of surprise.

"It was *I* who ordered the drum to be beat, Mr. Erskine," said Captain Ecuyer. "Do you usually attend formations with your coat off?"

"I sometimes attend them with nothing on at all, sir," replied the ensign.

"Losh!" exclaimed the sergeant, a look of alarmed disgust on his face.

"So I have been informed by Colonel Bouquet," replied the captain. "But it is now extremely cold weather, and I would advise you at least to put on your coat, Mr. Erskine." He smiled at the dark young man enigmatically. "And your hat, likewise."

Mr. Erskine apparently considered this advice carefully. "Yes, sir," said he at last, humbly enough, and started to return to get his missing garments.

"A sad case but a *verra* brave young mon, sir," ventured the sergeant. "His mither was a Featherstonehaugh."

"*Vraiment!*" said Ecuyer.

"Oh, aye!" said the sergeant.

"Is he always as drunk as he is now?" queried the captain.

"On the Sabbath it's much warse. He has a braw breeth on him then would be like salvation to the saints. I hae been here sax months the noo, an' I hae niver seen him sober aince."

The captain nodded impatiently. The garrison seemed to be all assembled.

"Call the men to attention," he said.

Salathiel and the boy called the Monk were now well along with unloading the wagon. Burent had stabled the horses and returned in time to give them a hand. They brought in the captain's desk, his cot, all of Johnson's valet supplies, and the cooking utensils.

The blockhouse main room was a large one. It occupied the entire lower floor of the building. It had an immense chimney at one end and was lit now by a roaring fire, three lanthorns, and a surprising number of candles stuck in an even more astonishing number of rum bottles. Except for the door, and the loopholes stuffed with rags, there were no openings. Nevertheless, with the fire, lanthorns and candles, the room was warm, inviting; bright with a pleasant glow. In each corner was a double-decked bunk and there were several barrel chairs and a ladder leading to the rifle loft.

At a table drawn somewhat back from the fire sat a dapper young man in a smart bag wig, a beautiful suit of grey clothes, and scarlet stockings. His buckled shoes were cocked up on a chair under the table, and his head was leaning on his elbow in such a manner that his hand shaded his face. Writing materials, a pile of legal papers, and a pack of cards disposed in some intricate game of solitaire lay spread out before him. There was also a bottle half-full with a tumbler turned down over its top.

When the door had first opened to admit Salathiel and the Monk with the captain's chest, and to permit the egress of Mr. Erskine, the young man had put a weight on the pile of papers with a gesture of annoyance, and one arm across the arrangement of cards.

"Shut the door," said he, with a peculiarly stark accent. "Keep the winter wind and that damned madman out of here if you can." Then he looked up, suddenly aware that strangers were entering.

Salathiel was instantly confronted by a pair of as determined and disconcerting eyes as he was ever to see. They were Scotch grey with green flecks in them here and there. A powerful but finely moulded face with a broad brow and hard pointed jaw seemed to stamp itself as if by a blow on his mind.

"Hello, Mr. Giant," said the young man to Salathiel. "Excuse me for beginning our acquaintance by offering you good advice. But, even if I were twice as big as you, I'd put that spontoon back in the rack there by the door. Its owner will be after it in a few minutes, I can promise you. Unfortunately I know him to be quarrelsome."

Salathiel nodded amicably enough. He had no objection to taking good advice. He lowered the end of the

323

chest he was carrying and put the half-pike back in the arms rack by the door, as the man at the table had suggested. Then he returned and took up the chest again. But for the first time he was suddenly aware of how very big he was. A giant, eh? It seemed to him quite suddenly that his height and his shoulders crowded the room. How could the small man at the table be so disconcerting? Maybe it was because he, Salathiel, must make a ridiculous figure, a large awkward oaf at one end of the long, black chest with the small, scalped drummer boy tugging at the other handle. The Monk's large cap had slipped down over his eyes. The man at the table was grinning. His smile was good-natured but patronizing. A wave of anger swept over Albine. He couldn't stand there with the chest forever!

"I'll trouble you to move your table, Mr. —?"

"Mr. Yates," said the gentleman obligingly, but making no effort to move. Salathiel put down the chest ponderously and took a step forward.

"Oh, very well," said Mr. Yates, "I'll give you eminent domain." He helped Salathiel to move the table to one side of the room and sat down at it again, gathering the disturbed pack of cards into one hand with a peculiarly deft motion. "Who's the nabob?" said he, nodding at the chest.

Salathiel had never heard of nabobs and he failed to reply. He and the Monk put the chest down in the corner near the fire, which he had determined the captain should occupy. He turned about . . .

"I say," said Mr. Yates, returning to the charge, "who's coming in on us? Who's your master?"

"No one," said Salathiel. "I'm neither a soldier nor a servant, my friend. The chest, however, belongs to Captain Simeon Ecuyer, if that's what you want to know."

"No offence, no offence!" cried Mr. Yates. "Ecuyer's one of the finest, even if he is a Swiss. You might well be proud to sarve him."

"I am," replied Salathiel, "but just because I'm doing something useful, I'm not a slave."

That had been one of Johnson's pet contentions, and it now came pat to his pupil's tongue.

"Demme, I like your spirit," replied Mr. Yates. "This is America and you can suit yourself." He flipped the pack of cards from one hand to another in a continuous stream. The Monk was fascinated, until his cap slipped over his eyes. "Demme, what you said is exactly the phrase I want for my letter home," remarked Yates as an afterthought. He put the cards down and made a note. "I'm much obleeged to you, Mr.—what-did-you-say-your-name-was?"

"Salathiel Albine."

"There's a fine rebel sound to that. It hath a Round-head twist." He laughed, picking up the cards again. The Monk took off his cap to watch him shuffle them. Mr. Yates started back in surprise.

"For God's sake, boy, put that cap on again," he yelled, stopping the cards in mid-air, as it were, with a skilful, nervous gesture. "I can't stand the face of a cherub topped off by what looks like an African monkey's behind!" he exclaimed. "This is a terrible country. Terrible!" he insisted, bringing his fist down on the table. "I say, boy, *put on your God-damned cap!*"

At that precise moment the door burst open again and Ensign Erskine entered and began a frantic hunt for his coat and hat. He eventually retrieved them from under piles of his belongings and the bedclothes. Then he stopped and seemed to recollect something.

"My spontoon!" said he, advancing menacingly on Salathiel. Mr. Yates pointed violently at the arms rack and managed to attract his attention.

"Hurry up, Malcolm," he said. "The commandant from Fort Pitt is here."

"Chreest, don't I know it," cried the disturbed young officer, and seizing his spontoon from the rack, he stumbled out through the door and down the steps with a curious drunken gravity and agility.

Salathiel, Mr. Yates, and the Monk found themselves laughing heartily together at this performance. Mr. Yates was full of quips at the expense of the confused Mr. Erskine, but good-natured and merry ones. He and Salathiel soon found themselves talking. The captain lingered outside, and the talk went on while Salathiel sat on the big chest, and from time to time Mr. Yates spun the cards from one hand to another out of sheer nervous energy.

It was surprising how from the time of their first meeting a definite understanding, what might even better be termed a "working agreement," came into being between Salathiel and the young lawyer, for such he was, found sitting at the table piled high with legal papers and cards before the headquarters chimney at Ligonier.

Like any other enduring alliance national or personal it was, of course, based principally upon a mutual sympathy and understanding, unconscious at first, taken for granted, and only to be tested later on by events. It so happened there were enough basic likenesses and interesting differences in the real characters of both men to provide the grist for an enduring association. It was not precisely a friendship. That woulld have been too warm and human a word to describe it. "Working agreement" is the more apt expression.

For from the very first there was something bleak and contractual in their mutual understanding. It succeeded and endured by their unfailing observance of the letter rather than by a sanguine reliance upon the spirit of their pact. From the first, until almost the very last, when they were very old men together, both of them felt that either was at liberty to withdraw from the working agreement at any time, without doing violence to the other's feelings. For that very reason they went on.

They even discovered, as time passed, a certain latent admiration for each other. But there was never much gratitude involved. And that, too, was fortunate. For gratitude is the weakest of human bonds. It can scarcely subsist between equals, and for the most part it is a disintegrating rather than a binding force in human affairs. Place a man in a position where he must be grateful, and seven times out of nine he will be lost as a friend. But between Albine and Yates there was never much gratitude passed around. They frequently disagreed. They even wrangled. Yet their differences were private and were privately accommodated, while to the outer world for two generations, or thereabouts, they continued to present a united defensive and at times an extremely offensive front of infractible unity.

Since this in the end affected a multitude of people and their descendants in diverse and devious ways, and still continues, although unbeknownst, to do so; and since it all began that evening in the headquarters blockhouse at Ligonier, it is worth discussing and recording. Many people in America came by both their deaths and their living through what can best be described as the operations of Messrs. *Yates & Albine* or *Albine & Yates*. The primacy of names shifted often in the seesaw of circumstance, but the ampersand remained in the middle as a fulcrum for the lever with which to move the world.

That evening in the room at Ligonier each of them sensed immediately and instinctively that the other was a lone wolf. Afterward they drifted into hunting as a pack of two. The dual advantages were soon obvious and enormous. They found their strength enhanced by the square. That this was the reason behind their story a great many people came to think—or was it after all something deeper, something more universal and basic, a desperate, determined, and continuous effort to attain some kind of comradeship in a continent of oceanic forests, where the social bonds had become weakened and everybody was more than usually alone?

At any rate, in the room at the Ligonier blockhouse the unloading of Captain Ecuyer's *voiture* by Salathiel and the Monk went on between remarks by Mr. Yates.

Mr. Yates continued at the table to shuffle cards with a professional dexterity punctuated by remarks of admiration at the ingeniousness of the captain's provision for comfort. As the folding bed, the chair, the neat chest of arms and wardrobe, and the cooking and valet utensils were brought in and set up one by one, his curiosity and amusement were both undisguised. In particular, his hearty approval of the preparations for supper begun by Salathiel in the great fireplace was hardly surpassed even by the Monk, and that is saying a great deal, for the boy was half-starved.

The conversation went on.

Mr. Yates presently got up and took an active and skilful part in the preparations for dinner himself, producing a large plum cake from his own baggage and anointing it with raw brandy. The fact that the cook was a giant, that anyone so large could or would cook at all, continued to intrigue him.

The young lawyer had arrived some years before in America. He had from the first made up his mind to remain permanently in the colonies and to enter into the spirit of his new environment as naturally as possible. Albine was a native specimen and a puzzle to him. Here was a warrior, almost a savage from the frontier, certainly a "giant," who was also a servant in certain skills thought in Europe to be menial, and yet he was not a servant in spirit. That was obvious. It stuck out in every motion he made. He was a free man and an equal. Here was something to be investigated. Yates began, and with great skill and tact, to cross-question Salathiel about his past. And to Yates, at least, the story was amazing. There was nothing like this in London or even in Thurso! They went on talking and laughing.

Salathiel on his part had not had a talk with anyone his own age so interesting since the disappearance of Lieutenant Francis towards Philadelphia with the ever-memorable Bustle. But this time he did not feel himself at a disadvantage. There was no condescension on the part of Yates as there had been, inevitably, from the young British officer. He had been friendly but superior. Yates was friendly, was a gentleman, and yet somehow they stood on the same floor together. If he asked personal questions, he also replied frankly when questioned himself. He helped get the supper instead of ordering a servant to bring it in. And he really helped. It was as if they had both been out hunting together and were now bending over the same campfire. Between them, in about an hour, the meal was ready. The table with the help, or rather with the disastrous assistance, of the Monk, who had now learned by all means to keep his "God-damned" cap on, was set for four.

What had become of Burent, Salathiel could not imagine. He had disappeared shortly after helping them carry in some of the chests from the wagon. Perhaps he was having his own troubles at the stables?

And in that surmise Salathiel was not far wrong.

28

In Which Poetical Licence Is Taken

THE INSPECTION of the garrison conducted by Captain Ecuyer was not, as Sergeant McLaughlin confided to one of the "sax" Alexanders, "a braw succiss."

The condition of affairs at Ligonier was even worse than Ecuyer had supposed, and he had had no roseate expectations. The company of the 42nd Highlanders were all present or accounted for, but they looked dirty and depressed, and some had "lost" their muskets, although they all still retained their claymores.

The captain was aware, however, that the Scots were genuinely relieved at his arrival and would welcome the prospect of a return of order and good discipline, if for no other reason than that guard duty would not fall entirely on them.

A certain contempt for their situation and the laxity and misery of their surroundings was in fact hopeful rather than the reverse, he felt. He therefore dismissed them with a promise to see immediately to their rations and re-equipment, together with an admonition to recollect the sovereign they were serving and to clean up both themselves and their barracks. In short, he appealed to their pride. And despite the miserable cold, that hot point in the Highland character could still be made to glow if properly blown upon.

Ecuyer, Sergeant McLaughlin, and Ensign Erskine with his spontoon—which was rusty—stood about twilight in the middle of the little paved square at Ligonier, making a gradually dimming splash of scarlet, while the Highlanders lined up on one side and the provincial militia, a thin line in ragged green watchcoats, were drawn up on the other. The dark barracks lay behind them. On the pared sapling which acted as a flagpole the remnant of a Union Jack flapped and tugged in gusts of bitter wind, as though it were trying to yank itself clear of the halyards. Without ceremony, when darkness came it was eventually taken down. The Highlanders were dismissed to their quarters and Captain Ecuyer then turned his attention to the shivering militia by the aid of a couple of smoky lanthorns that threw grim and wavering circles of light upon the unhappy scene. For it was now that the true condition of the affairs at the post began to become fully manifest. The roll was called.

"Captain Edwin Anderson."

"Died of the pox at Raystown," shouted a voice from the rear ranks of the militia.

"Lieutenant Arthur St. Clair."

A burst of laughter, catcalls, a derisive cheer, and guffaws greeted this name.

"Lieutenant Neville."

Silence.

"Ensign Willum Aiken."

"Ahoorin' at Bedford, both on 'em," shouted a peculiarly insolent voice, followed by some salty chuckles that ran along the ranks.

"Hold your lanthorn up, sergeant, so I can see these men," said the captain sternly. Silence ensued.

Then a respectable-looking man with iron-grey hair and a certain cleanliness stepped forward and saluted properly.

"Beggen your pardon, your Honour, but all our officers have left us, desarted, or gone off on their own affairs," said the man firmly but respectfully. "We've been left to take the darty end of the stick. Mr. St. Clair has been selling us rations on our pay and trading for our equipment, powder, and guns. He and his man Japson have et up the substance of all of us at the fort. It's the custom, you know, sir, but it's shameful, I say, nevertheless. So we're half-starved and naked, and nigh the quarter of us are locked up now in the stable shed next the pigpen. If I may say so, sir, those poor divils must be about perished with cold."

"Is this true, Mr. Erskine?" demanded Captain Ecuyer.

"Aye," said the ensign, "yon mon's corricht. It was Lieutenant St. Clair's orders." The captain looked at him witheringly.

"What's your name, my man?" asked the captain, advancing to the soldier who had just spoken.

"Pollexfen, your Honour."

"*Mr.* Pollexfen," said Captain Ecuyer, raising his voice so all could hear, "in the absence of your officers, I appoint you in the king's name commander of this company."

A murmur of approval rose from the ranks.

"None of that now," said the captain. He walked down the ranks rapidly, looking each man in the face and holding up the lanthorn now and then to examine a more than usually ragged individual. They all looked both starved and neglected.

"Now dismiss, go to your barracks, and see that some large logs are dragged in for fires. Sergeant McLaughlin, take five men and issue rations to Mr. Pollexfen from the king's store. Issue enough for tonight and tomorrow. There *are* rations, aren't there?"

"Aplenty, sir. Mr. Erskine has the keys."

"But these men are provincial troops, and the king's rations . . ." said Erskine doubtfully.

"Feed them for *all that*," said the captain sardonically. "And, Mr. Erskine, tell my man Albine to report to me, and do so yourself directly after you have got me the keys." He turned curtly and walked off in the growing dark in the direction of the stables, where an intolerable din of pigs', horses', and men's voices had broken out.

"Captain Ecuyer," called McLaughlin after him through the darkness.

"Well?"

"An' you let yon colonials loose from the pen the nicht, thar'll be little short of a mutiny. They're a neefarious crew."

"It's the sober truth, sir," said Erskine, who had lingered, hoping the captain might change his mind about the rations.

"What! The sober truth from *you*, Mr. Erskine?" The captain chuckled. "Give me leave to doubt it, under the circumstances."

Mr. Erskine said nothing but departed for the keys.

"Sergeant," continued the captain, "a gentleman of the Quaker persuasion may appear shortly at the gate with a string of pack horses. His name is Japson. Admit him. But under no circumstances permit him to leave the fort before I do. See to it!"

"I will," said McLaughlin. "I ken the mon weel."

The captain then limped off in the direction of the stables, where in a few moments he was joined by Salathiel. Mr. Yates, when the captain's orders had been received at the blockhouse, had obligingly promised to stay and see that the dinner did not burn.

"I've been given the lie direct by the captain," said Erskine to Yates, as he searched for his keys. "He denied that I was sober."

"You'll not call him out for that, will you?" asked Yates, laughing.

"Na, na!" said the ensign, affecting his native Scotch. "I'll no deny thar's a mite of truth in his conteention." He took a swig from Mr. Yates's bottle, and went out, slamming the door. The fire leaped, sending a world of sparks up the chimney.

Mr. Japson arrived about this time at the gate and clamoured for entrance. Presently he was admitted. Half-frozen, for his horses had given him great trouble along the road and delayed him grievously, he drove his exhausted beasts toward the stable. His troubles were not over yet. At the stables to his consternation he found Captain Ecuyer and Albine standing together just outside

333

the shed, conducting a parley with various persons inside, but invisible in the darkness. The captain had also been confronted by a surprise.

The "stables" at Ligonier was a long, slab-roofed shed. Down the middle of it ran a row of heavy, log stakes about six inches apart. These set off that part of the shed where horses were tied from the other half which had been built to contain forage and hay. The stakes had been continued all around the portion set for hay. They made, in effect, a barred stockade exceedingly staunch through which an arm, a hand, or a horse's nose could be thrust, but that was about all. This, of course, was to prevent the pilfering of hay. From their stalls the horses in the stables could snatch a mouthful through the stakes but no more.

Behind this stable and its stockaded wall was the muddy and straw-littered area in which the swine kept at the fort were supposed to be confined. Most of the pigs did go there to lie on the straw at night, although they were permitted to roam the place at will during the day. But horses and pigs were not the only animals confined in and about the stable.

The heavily barred and staked portion set off for forage had been turned into a convenient prison. The day before he left Ligonier to go to Fort Bedford, Lieutenant St. Clair had locked twelve of the Pennsylvanians into the now nearly empty forage crib. He considered the men he had thus incarcerated to be mutinous, and perhaps he had his reasons for thinking so.

But Lieutenant St. Clair had now been absent for five days. There was bad blood between the Highlanders and the Pennsylvanians, and the terrible cold had come on. McLaughlin had given them their blankets but, by instruction, scarcely enough food to exist on, and they were now desperate.

Some had frozen hands or feet. All were ready to desert at the first opportunity, and two or three were quietly determined to murder St. Clair when occasion might serve. Also there were leaders and men of resource among them. Dumb with cold, hunger, and misery, devoured by fleas from the pigpen, and in the midst of their own filth, they huddled close together as best they could with the blankets and the remains of the hay heaped over them—and waited grimly. A dark-browed and memorable Irishman by the name of O'Neal occasionally brought poetry to their relief by masterful descriptions of the details of the projected murder of Lieutenant St. Clair.

Burent, of course, had known nothing about the plight of these men. He had not even suspected their existence. And they had kept entirely quiet when he had first brought his horses into the shed. It was quite dark in the stable, and Burent could see nothing between the bars of the haymow. He had tied up his horses and returned to help Albine unload the wagon.

The prisoners, however, had watched his every move, and from the Scot who later brought them their meagre rations they had learned who had arrived at the fort.

"I'll tell you what, bhoys," said O'Neal, "the little brown booger that stabled his bastes here must be the captain's mon. Did ye notice the airs of him, the gintility of the tilet and the rubbin' doon he give the harses? Oi, there's hot mush and blankets for the Sassenach mare but niver a dacent bite or a koind word for the likes of us! It was iver so in the owld countree—feed the harses, starve the paple, and ride over them roughshod. Ef I had me knife, I'd reach through the bars and slit the throat of the mare. Listen to her champin' away at her carn, and me own belly grindin' at nothin' at all!"

A gruff growl of approval met his remarks. He rose, and going over to the line of stakes, looked out between them at the contented horses beyond. The mare snorted at him, but was presently accepting small wisps of hay from his fingers.

"Whist, bhoys," said he, "I have a foin schame, I have."

"O'Neal, ye damned fool, don't ye hurt the hoss. For-by she's the apple of the captain's eye. Ye'll only get some of us hanged belike," said one Williams anxiously.

O'Neal chuckled. With a wisp of old hay he managed to get the mare's nose in the air where the bars chanced to widen, and he finally enticed her to put her head through a space higher up. She then lowered her neck for the dainty. When she tried to back away again she was caught. The Irishman began to laugh quietly.

"I tell ye, *lay off* that horse," said one of the older men, getting up anxiously and approaching O'Neal. "Williams is right. You'll be getting your empty head in a noose for nothin'."

"So me head's empty, is it? Listen, ye poor blatherskites. Did ye raley think I'd be so wake-minded as to waste me time on the harse? It's bait I'm using her fer. And it's big fish I'm after. Now if you'll kape quiet and crooch down in the straw there, I'll get ye out of the misery ye haven't the brains to git out of yourselves. Here you, Jepford, lend me the rawhide belt off you, you fat guts. Be God, ef you aren't a fathom around, praises be!" With the man's belt he made a running noose, and then borrowed two others with the comment, "They're not so long, but they'll do." They watched him anxiously.

"Now mind ye, no nonsense," continued O'Neal. "I'm only going to taze the baste and bring that little brown booger back arunnin'. Then we'll see what we'll see."

With that he reached through the bars and lashed the mare over her back with a belt.

Unable to pull her head back, and caught as though in a trap, the mare began to kick and whinny. In a short time she had the four wagon horses frantic as well, and the stables resounded with the alarmed snorting and wild neighing of the half-crazy animals. Burent heard it at the blockhouse and came running. He thought a fire must have broken out when he first heard the horses. In the dark shed it was hard to see what was wrong. At last he made out that the mare had caught her head between the bars.

"*Soo, soo,* gal," said he, stroking her, and trying to quiet her panic. "It does beat all, lassie, the trouble you can find."

The mare finally responded and the other horses gradually quieted down. The mare quivered and waited to be released. On the other side of the posts O'Neal crouched low in the shadows. Presently Burent thrust his arm through the bars to try to lift the mare's head up. At that instant a leather noose was slipped around his neck, choking him. The world went black.

When he came to he had been turned about with his back to the posts and his arms strapped around one of them behind him. He was looking out into the stable where the dust motes danced in the air—or was it specks over his eyes? He had no idea what had happened to him or why.

"When they come to git you," an Irish voice finally explained, "say what I tell you to say, and don't say nawthin' more. There's a noose round your gullet and a sharp stake at your kidney behind." A painful dig below the ribs confirmed the latter fact. Silence resumed.

So Burent waited. It seemed hours, and he did spend a good part of the afternoon there. It was mortal cold and he shivered from chill and shock. O'Neal had released the mare's head and she now nosed Burent from time to time quizzically. The horses, however, were quiet enough now, reassured by his presence. Finally darkness fell. Shortly afterward a lanthorn approached the shed. It was Captain Ecuyer and Albine. The Monk held the light.

"Stop! Stop where you are, Captain Ecuyer. Don't come into the shed," called Burent desperately. "I . . ." his voice ended in a choked gurgle.

"Who's that?" said the captain, stopped in his tracks by the obvious urgency of the warning.

"Tell him," whispered O'Neal, loosening the noose again.

"It's me, Burent! They have me tied up here. There's a noose around me neck and a stake at me back. Don't come in for the love of God, sir. Or they'll murder me, they will!"

"Who are *they?*" demanded the captain, who had the good sense to remain standing where he was.

"Oil tell you who *they* are, ye domned lobsterback," said the voice of O'Neal, now speaking up. "Oil tell you who *we* are. We're twelve good men and true locked up by the tyranny of Liftinint St. Clair, God wither his bawdy heart, and if ye don't lave us out I'll drive this sharp stake clane through the bowels of your little brown man, captain. Won't I now?"

An agonized scream from Burent confirmed the fact that he probably would.

Just at this moment Captain Ecuyer was joined by Mr. Erskine, Sergeant McLaughlin, and Japson, who came up out of the darkness.

"You've only a short time to make up your mind, captain. It's a *nice* little mon I have here. You'd be after missin' him. And think of his wife and childer," called O'Neal.

"I haven't any," shouted Burent. "Never mind . . ." He was choked off.

"Bring the light," said the captain in a low voice to Salathiel.

"I'm coming down to parley with you," he shouted towards the shed. "I'll come alone except for the boy with the lanthorn." He and the drummer advanced into the shed.

"Stop there," said O'Neal.

In the dim light of the lanthorn Captain Ecuyer could now see the five horses, and Burent trussed up against the wall with the fear of death on his white face. Out of the darkness behind again came the voice of O'Neal.

"Let us out of here. Open the door and take us out of this dom pen. We're devoured by flays."

"Very well," said the captain, "I'll do that."

"You'll do what!" said the amazed O'Neal.

"Let my man go, and I'll let you out," said the captain.

"Will you give us a fair trial?" demanded O'Neal.

"I'll give every one of you a fair trial—and tomorrow. Do you hear that in there?" shouted the captain.

338

A number of voices began to shout at O'Neal to take the offer.

"Let us out first, and I'll let your man go," said O'Neal.

"You heard my offer," said the captain. "You'll have to take it or do murder and hang." There was a moment's silence. In the lanthornlight in the quiet stable Ecuyer stood looking Burent in the face.

"Oim lettin' your little brown man go," said O'Neal finally. "Kape your word like a mon, captain."

Suddenly Burent, who had been turned loose, fell forward on his face.

"Mr. Erskine," called Captain Ecuyer, "bring an armed guard with some lights and open this pen door. Suppose you carry Burent to your quarters, sergeant, and get some strong liquor in him. He's had a bad time."

"A verra bod time," said the sergeant, picking Burent up like a sack. "And will your Honour be sindin' the liquor over to my quarters for him?"

"*Yes!*" said Ecuyer and swore to himself. The Scotch never lost an opportunity.

Erskine appeared shortly with a portion of the guard and more lanthorns. They opened the door into the hay-pen and flashed the light on a miserable group huddled against the far wall in terror and doubt as to what might be before them. The tartans of the Highlanders and their gleaming bayonets and claymores flashed wickedly under the lights. By common consent the prisoners had all withdrawn from O'Neal, who now stood alone, armed with the sharp stake with which he had lately been threatening Burent.

"Step this way one at a time," said the captain. "No need to tie them," he added, as the first of the prisoners came up and submitted themselves humbly enough. "They're weak from starvation, poor devils. March them up to the barracks, Mr. Erskine, and give them something to eat directly, king's stores or anything else."

"This way, you," said Erskine to O'Neal, who, now left completely alone still stood fingering his club.

A panic seized the man.

"You moitherin' bastards, I'll niver submit to ye," he roared and with marvellous agility for so big a man leaped for a rafter, climbed on it, placed his back against a slab on the roof, and buckled it loose with his shoulders.

Before anyone could get to him he was through the hole and they could hear his feet padding along above them.

"Quick, Albine!" exclaimed the captain.

Ten seconds later Salathiel was out on the roof, too.

It was a moment before he could get the lanthorn's shine out of his eyes.

Then he saw that the escaped man had not really bettered himself much. The stable roof was completely cut off from all other structures and surrounded by open ground. Salathiel could see his man crouching near the edge at a far corner. The whole building was surrounded by this time, and the man was covered by the sentries standing on the galleries above him.

Mr. Erskine called to the sentries not to shoot. Evidently the ensign was just below the point where the man was crouching. O'Neal looked over the roof and began to curse him vilely.

It was now that, from Salathiel's standpoint at least, an amazing thing occurred. A figure in a pair of white trousers was suddenly seen coming down on the roof, apparently right out of the stars. It landed next to the fugitive.

O'Neal gave a howl of surprise and started running back to jump off into a strawstack in the pigpen near the end of the shed. He did not know Salathiel was on the roof and he did not see him, for he was still prone. All that Albine had to do was to reach out and grab the man's ankle as he passed. He fell with a smash and his impetus shot him off into the hands of the guards waiting below.

"You disappoint me," said the voice of Ensign Erskine, somewhat breathless. "He was mine. Mon! Did ye hear what the loon called me? Did it come to your lug?"

"No," said Albine, "it didn't."

"It's just as weel," said the ensign.

They climbed down through the hole in the roof together and dropped into the dark shed below. Outside the prisoners were already being marched away.

"Do you mind saying how you got on the roof, Mr. Erskine?" said Salathiel.

"I vaulted oop. There was a nice long pole by the wall, as God would have it."

Salathiel looked at his companion with considerably more respect. It was a tremendous vault.

"This Johnny captain of yours seems pretty sooft-hairted. Will he be coddlin' these rascals, do ye ken?" asked the ensign as they walked together towards the blockhouse.

"They'll get exactly what's comin' to 'em," replied Salathiel. "You can be sartin of that, sir."

"Aye," said the ensign, "so I thought. I am glad he's here. I'll say this to you, and you can pass it along, after you forget who told you. Leftenent Blane left this post in magneeficent order last autumn. Since then it's been in the hands of our fawncy macaroni, Leftenent Arthur St. Clair. And so—God save the king!" There was a concentrated bitterness in Erskine's tone which carried his own conviction that something was rotten in Denmark.

"Aweel," he sighed, "losh! Let's have a bite and a nip aboot the fire. That's your captain Johnny and the Monk with the lanthorn gain' intil headquarters the noo. Come on," he called.

They raced each other to the steps at the blockhouse.

29

Court-Martial by Firelight

THE LOW-CEILINGED ROOM of the blockhouse, traversed overhead by immense oak beams, provided at first glimpse something of the appearance and the same feeling of security as a large ship's cabin, except that at one end blazed the immense fire. Mr. Yates had just piled it high again, arranging the supper before it on the hearth to keep it hot. A number of candles stuck in bottles cast a wavering, saffron glow so that the apartment presented that rarest of all appearances on the frontier, a room well lit at night, at once warm and cheerful. So used was everybody to conducting existence in a deep gloom after sundown that the captain was betrayed into giving a groan of relief followed by a sigh of contentment as he sat down by the bunk in his chosen corner, looked about him, and stretched out his legs to have his boots drawn off.

"Upon my word," said he, "you gentlemen treat yourselves damned well here, don't you?" His eyes twinkled as he noticed that the table had been set for four. "I trust I shall have the pleasure of your company, Mr. Erskine, and of your friend here, if you'll be good enough to introduce him." Who the other guest was to be did not appear.

"Mr. Edward Yates, sir," said the young ensign in some confusion at having overlooked the formality. "Mr. Yates is an attorney representing the interests of the proprietary family in these parts, I believe."

At this Mr. Yates arose from a haunch which he had been basting by the hearth and bowed with the spoon still in his hand.

"Your courtesy is an honour, sir. To keep the records straight I should say that, while I *do* represent the Penns, my present business here is with the survey of certain lands that have been granted to Mr. St. Clair." He said this with a tight-lipped, legal precision which amused the captain.

"No matter who your clients are, I am quite content, Mr. Yates. Since you have saved the dinner from burning, the least I can do is to invite you to share it. My God, Albine, don't pull that boot on my wounded leg so!" The captain turned white and sick for a moment. "There, it can't be helped, I know. Gentlemen, your pardon." He slipped his feet into a pair of furred shoes and hobbled over to the table, followed with considerable solicitude by both the young men.

"Your chair, sir," said the ensign, drawing it up.

"Are you sure you will put it back under me, Mr. Erskine?" asked the captain, a mischievous smile framing his lips.

"Oh, really, I was only a bit fuddled, sir, when you first came in. It was sleep as much as anything else. And the room was hot . . . stifling, if I may say so."

"And since then the Irish mutiny has sobered us all, I am sure," said Ecuyer, seating himself. "What a leap you made onto the roof! Are you circumstanced to pole vaulting, Mr. Erskine? It seems to me to be an unusual, and yet, I have never thought of it before, possibly a valuable military accomplishment. Pray do be seated!"

The young ensign, being a Scot, was not entirely unaware of an amused gleam in the captain's eye. But he scarcely knew as yet how to take it.

"When we made the attack at The Havana," he replied, "there were a great many moats and ditches to cross. The Spaniards in Cuba go in for dirty ditches, sir. Well, some of us in the Forty-second took to jumping them on poles to get at the foot of the walls during assaults. I wasn't so bad at it. We used to do a lot of pole vaulting at Almondel in Linlithgowshire." Here Mr. Erskine stopped himself and blushed.

"But it was hotter in Cuba than in Linlithgowshire, I suppose," said the captain.

"Och, aye! Och, a fiery climate I'd call it!" exclaimed the ensign.

"Possibly then *that* was where you formed the regrettable habit of holding guard mount without any clothes on—or none to speak of," continued the captain. "You see, Mr. Erskine, that unfortunate incident here was reported to Colonel Bouquet and he has requested me, before calling a court-martial, to look into it. What is your explanation?"

At this unexpectedly serious turn to the conversation the entire room grew silent. Salathiel placed the remains of Johnson's Queen of Scotts soup on the table noiselessly, but it lay untouched and smoking while Mr. Erskine considered his reply.

"Shaw!" said the captain after an interval. "I was in hopes that there were ameliorating circumstances, to say the least. Drink your soup!"

Mr. Yates stopped a desire to guffaw by a fiery draught of liquid essence of chicken and boiled eggs from his soup plate, and choked a little. His eyes opened widely. The captain had winked at him.

"Excellent soup, sir! Very remarkable! I never guzzled the like."

The captain nodded. "I cherish the secret formula for it," he said to Yates. "Well, Mr. Erskine?"

"It was like this, sir," said Erskine, who had now recovered the use of his voice. "It was last summer when this fort was sore beleaguered. I'll no beat the deil about the bush. I was drunk. At least I had been drunk the nicht before. Airly the morrow morn there was an Injun alarm and I turned oot in haste, in turrible haste. And there I was, sir! There I was with the guard lined up by the gate, and somehow I'd forgot to fetch my kilt and jacket along. But I wasn't naked, sir. That's a gross ex-

344

aggeration. I had my boots and hat on, and I had my spontoon!"

"Your spontoon!" said the captain. "You had *that?*"

"Aweel, I *did* have it," insisted Mr. Erskine, quite shocked, for Captain Ecuyer had put both elbows on the table, his face in his hands, and begun to laugh. He laughed quite uncontrollably. And Mr. Yates joined him.

"Aweel," insisted Mr. Erskine, quite annoyed now, "I did *have* it. My friend Mr. Yates here will corroborate me—when he stops laughing."

"I'll be glad to," said Yates, suddenly turning quite sober. "I'll gladly act as a witness, but I'd rather appear in Mr. Erskine's defence and make a plea for him, if I may."

"Why," said the captain, "since you already represent the whole proprietary family I see no reason why you shouldn't represent an ensign, Mr. Yates. It's a little unusual, of course, for officers in his Majesty's service to be provided with civil counsel—perhaps you can explain that later. But—go on. Be eloquent though, be eloquent, Mr. Yates! I have no use for arguments unless they are eloquent ones."

"We have only had soup so far, captain. Excellent as it was, may I remind you . . ."

"Bring some Burgundy, Albine, one of the dark-red bottles out of the case the colonel gave me just before leaving. And put the meat on."

"Mr. Erskine, I hope you will exonerate me from any desire to prejudice your case by asking the defence to proceed on soup alone. This, I think you will agree, should inspire even a dull advocate." He held up a bottle that turned ruby in the light. "May you be ingenious as well as eloquent," said the captain, raising his glass.

They drank the toast.

"Well, sir, proceed," cried the captain, signing to refill the glasses. Mr. Yates cleared his throat:

"On the night of July the twelfth, last, the accused here was involved in a series of strange circumstances over which he had no control and which he cannot explain himself without seeming to be desirous of impugning his commanding officer. I refer to the late commander and present proprietor of this post at Ligonier, Mr. Arthur St. Clair."

"Proprietor?" said the captain. "Proprietor! What the devil do you mean by *that?*"

"By your leave and patience I will directly explain," continued Mr. Yates.

"Be pleased to recollect that up until the second of August, last, this fort was being constantly attacked and harassed. Alarms were more or less incessant. It was then under the capable command of Lieutenant Blane. Mr. Erskine here was the only officer left with the Highland detachment. He and Lieutenant Blane, therefore, were the only commissioned officers at the fort, and they defended it well and gallantly until Colonel Bouquet relieved it on his advance to Pittsburgh and reinforced it with the militia that you now find here—and the officers of the militia whom, sir, you do not find here."

Mr. Yates, now finding himself got going, drank off another glass and rinsed his mouth as a refresher.

"Colonel Bouquet, as you know, then passed on to relieve Fort Pitt, scattering the savages on the way. He took Lieutenant Blane along when he left, and Mr. Erskine as the only king's officer present was thus in command of this fort. Even after the battle at Bushy Run there was still an occasional alarm in this neighbourhood and great vigilance was necessary. And there was much trouble with the militia officers, who disputed both their rank and the command with Mr. Erskine.

"This dispute, an extremely unfortunate one under the circumstances, eventually caused factions in the garrison. Each command would obey its own officers only. The militia shirked, and all the guard duty fell upon the already overworked Highland detachment. A crisis finally occurred when, upon the occasion of an Indian alarm, the militia refused to turn out to man the rifle galleries. It was then, sir, and not before, that Mr. Erskine lost his

346

temper and attempted to settle the dispute with the two militia officers by means of his claymore."

"Was he successful?" asked the captain.

"He was. You should understand that all three of the militia officers were quartered in this room and that when Ensign Erskine entered commanding them to their posts of duty, and they refused, he drew his sword. And he was then attacked by two of the provincial gentlemen at the same time. It was Lieutenant Neville and Ensign Aiken. Captain Anderson, who has since died, sat still and looked on. Mr. Erskine disarmed Neville and cut Aiken across the forehead so that he staggered around, howling out that he was blinded. And indeed, sir, so he was, for the blood poured down into his eyes. The gentleman who was disarmed, after consulting with his gallant captain, consented to join his men on the galleries, apparently for the reason that it was more dangerous to remain here than to go there. Captain Anderson finally buckled on his sword and went out too. Now, I don't think that any of these fellows were really cowards, they were just in an obstinate and mulish state of mind. I might add that I was a witness to all this, as since my arrival here, prior to these events, I have been quartered in this room."

"What did you say the names of these two gallants were?" demanded the captain. "Albine, get your pen and write this in my red memorandum book, the one with the brass clasp."

"Lieutenant Neville and Ensign Aiken of the Pennsylvania line," repeated Yates.

Albine wrote this down and the captain signed to Yates to go on.

"It was probably a mistake on the part of my young client here to have lost his temper and to have drawn blood, but . . ."

"Tut, tut," said the captain, "during a war one is sometimes forced to resort to violence. Pray continue."

"Well, as you see, the provocation was great and the safety of the garrison had been compromised. Such considerations, nevertheless, were too subtle for the gentlemen

347

who had been worsted to concede gracefully. They obeyed Mr. Erskine, perforce, from then on, but most sullenly. And they determined at the first opportunity to complain and if possible to ruin him. And now, sir, I am forced to inject another consideration into this affair, a serious and complicated one. I refer to the arrival at this place on the eighteenth of September, last, of Lieutenant Arthur St. Clair. If things had been difficult before the arrival of Mr. St. Clair, they were thrice as confounded afterward, for he brought with him three papers, to wit:

1. A Commission as lieutenant in the 60th Regiment, your own, the Royal Americans, but that commission was resigned in the year '60—three years ago.
2. A memorandum from General Stanwix ordering that all provincial forces on the frontiers should respect and obey Mr. St. Clair as though his commission were still in force, until further notice.
3. A deed of purchase of one thousand acres of land from the proprietors of the province of Pennsylvania, transferring in fee simple, subject only to certain quit rents, the land upon which this Fort of Ligonier now stands and all the buildings and other works of man found upon it to Arthur St. Clair, his heirs and assigns forever, all duly registered and passed upon by the Land Office at Philadelphia.

"By the terms of that purchase Mr. St. Clair was also authorized and required to bring in and settle as many people as possible upon his land, and, the licence for doing so was attached."

"The damned self-serving scoundrel!" exclaimed the captain, bringing his fist down on the table. "As if things weren't difficult enough in this naked country without his trying to strip us to the bone. But the king's use and possession here is paramount, isn't it?"

"Undoubtedly," replied Mr. Yates, "but when the royal garrisons are withdrawn, captain?"

"Why, then 'all the buildings and other works of man' left at Ligonier will belong to our friend St. Clair, I take it."

"You have an apt ear for phraseology, sir," said Yates. "That is the point exactly. And from the time that Lieutenant St. Clair arrived here until the present moment, I hesitate not to say that he and his henchmen have been extremely busy and most ingenious in transferring every known 'work of man' from the possession of the garrison into the hands of the agents and to the warehouse or store of the said Lieutenant St. Clair, including firearms, powder, garments, and even the preserved rations of the garrison, which he has managed to purvey from Bedford and in some cases to trade in for the equipment of the troops stationed here. The colonials have been half-stripped. In some cases forced to trade even their muskets for food. And when they have had the spirit to complain he had them locked up and half starved. There's scarcely a man in the place, to say nothing of the women, who isn't in debt to Lieutenant St. Clair."

"I suppose he established himself here as commanding officer," said Ecuyer, turning to pose the question to young Erskine.

"It was impossible for me to stand against him, Captain Ecuyer," said the ensign, speaking up for himself. "There was that order from General Stanwix, and . . ."

"Yes, yes, I can see," said the captain.

"I did manage to keep the Highland detachment under my immediate orders, but the militia after St. Clair arrived were quite out of control. And their officers were, as Mr. Yates has explained, enraged against me."

"Was that the way you managed to lose your clothes, Mr. Erskine?"

"Yes, sir, it was."

"But you were drunk, you said?"

"I was the nicht before," the ensign hastened to explain. "You see, Lieutenant St. Clair had returned from Fort

349

Bedford, where he goes quite often. Weel, he returned thot nicht and in honour of the birth of his first cheeld, sir,—he had the news at Bedford,—he invited us all, that is, Mr. Yates and me, and the three militia officers, to a high celebration in this room. Now I don't say Mr. St. Clair planned to undo me. I think he meant his guid cheer honourably. But I was put off my guard by it, and he prevailed on us all to shake hands and let bygones be bygones on accont o' the nature of the supper thot nicht. Aweel, we did shake hands, and I meant it. And I got masel fuddled and had to be helped to bed."

"And when the alarm came you couldn't find your plaid and jacket, could you?" said the captain.

"Exactly," chimed in Mr. Yates.

"And if I hadna appeared at me post they'd have had me opp for coowardice, sir. So I went oot in me skin and took over the guard despicht the scandal."

"Were you sober then?" grinned the captain.

"Sober enough to lead a sortie and cut off some savages that had been harassing us for days," said Mr. Yates, "and very ugly customers they were!"

At this point Mr. Erskine excused himself, and walking over to his bunk, rummaged among his effects awhile and returned with four scalps nicely stretched on cord webs. These he exhibited with a certain artless pride which he could not entirely conceal.

"Some of your old playmates, Albine?" asked the captain.

"They're Mingoes I'm sartin," said Salathiel. "That's the way they braid their scalp locks, four strands to the end knot."

"You see," said Ecuyer, "there's nothing like having a well-informed valet on the frontier. Suppose, Albine, you light the brandy on that pudding Mr. Yates has contributed, and has been throwing side glances at, and bring it on. And put a finger or so of the same spirit in our glasses all around."

The pudding and its flaming halo were much admired.

"A fitting close to the feast," said the captain. "To me

at least it has been a most illuminating occasion." He raised his glass.

"Gentlemen, the king."

Ecuyer had risen with considerable difficulty. After the long day's exertion he found his wound plagued him. Salathiel prepared to dress it now while he sat before the fire.

"Mr. Erskine," said the captain, turning around to look over the back of his chair, "do me the favour of making the rounds this evening. Indeed, I'm not able. But *see* to the sentries! And there's a Quaker here by the name of Japson. He's not to leave the fort for any reason. Can you trust your men?"

"Aye," said the ensign, "the Heelanders."

"And, Mr. Erskine, consider yourself confirmed in your opinion that you are in command of this garrison. You have nothing to worry about on that score. Depend upon it."

"Thank you, sir," replied the young Scot in tones of genuine relief and gratitude. He saluted and walked out firmly—a different man.

Salathiel now prepared the fire for the night, bringing in a tremendous green ash backlog and bedding it firmly in the ashes against the white-hot throat of the chimney. Beside this at the distance of an inch or so he laid another log not quite so large. The latter was of wild cherry green, not dried. The space between the two he filled with dry oak chips, called hunks. The woodpile of the fort had evidently been cut by the colonials who knew what they were doing. There were plenty of the right lengths and kinds at hand. In a few moments, kindled by the heat of the stones, a clear sheet of flame ran up the back of the chimney, which was about nine feet wide. A long, steady sighing sound told of the strength of the draught. The room streamed with a flowing, yellow light, and a genial heat beat back along the floor and the walls.

It was still so cold outside that even the brief opening of the door for the exit of Mr. Erskine and the bringing in of the logs had thoroughly chilled the place and the captain had called out impatiently at Albine. He now sat back, however, some distance from the chimney, his wound freshly dressed, basking in the grateful warmth and relieved of his wig, stiff boots, and uniform. He was wrapped in a heavy flannel nightgown and stocking night-cap, and thoroughly comfortable for the first time in several days.

Mr. Yates, who had returned to his table after supper, and at least pretended to busy himself over his papers, was much amused by all this. It had especially intrigued him that the same man who brought in the immense logs, without so much as staggering slightly, had also bound up the captain's wounds, undressed him, and was now curling his wig and preparing deftly to put it away powdered in its right box for the night. The curling irons heating in the fire and the double-barrelled rifle leaning in the corner by Salathiel's bunk formed a variety and contrast in capacity Mr. Yates had never seen before, although he had now been several years in America. But anything can happen in this country, he thought.

"In Europe they haven't made fires like this since the Dark Ages," commented the captain. "There are chimneys like this in the castle at Blois, for instance, and elsewhere I remember. But there hasn't been the wood to feed them for generations. In Savoy I nearly perished of cold at the duke's own headquarters."

"No," responded Yates. "I never really saw fires till I came over. It's a lost art in England. They sell coals by the basket there, and bunches of twigs like bouquets. It's worse in Scotland. A peat fire, it's like trying to warm yourself before the painting of a sunset. But over here the true mark of your native inhabitant is that he regards a tree as his enemy. The more he can burn, the better patriot he is. I'm afraid the trees are doomed."

"Twenty journeys westward from here all trees come to an end," said Salathiel, who was now seated in the corner polishing his rifle. "A sea of grass begins. The sun rises out of the grass and sets in the grass. And I have seen flocks of pigeons there like great storm clouds. They

352

pass for hours, darkening the sun, and the sound of their wings is like summer thunder. All this I have seen. You can get out of the trees if you go west."

He went on polishing his gun.

Perhaps it was because he was beginning to be sleepy that he had spoken solemnly, like a voice in a dream. Something in the quality of his voice conveyed a sense of distance, of things remote.

For a space the captain and Yates remained silent. There had suddenly come over them both a sense of the illimitable vastness of the continent where they found themselves—or where they were lost. There was no end to it. No known end. Home, the familiar home of Europe, full of talk and company, from whence came help, was far away. On every side of the little blockhouse, where for a moment they were safe, warm, and comfortable, stretched the hostile forests away and away to the grass—and beyond. The room for a moment became to them the centre of their lives in a new and unknown planet.

But the American did not feel that. This largeness, this unknown amplitude was familiar to him. Each of them stole a glance at Salathiel. The fire for some reason faltered. The room for a moment darkened. In the gloom Salathiel finished greasing his gun and wiping it with tow.

"I think, sir, I'll go and have a look at Burent before turning in. He said to thank you for the brandy."

The captain gave a sign of assent.

As Salathiel opened the door the distant, savage music of a hunting chorus of wolves trailing a deer on the Chestnut Ridge to the westward yelped into the cabin. The door closed and the sound with it, leaving the two inside alone by the fire.

Outside, Salathiel stretched, pausing at the top of the steps for a moment to fill his lungs with the sparkling, bitter cold air. A draught of new life raced through his veins. There was moonlight on the snow. Even the sordid interior of the little stockade was transfigured. An occasional ripple of light twinkled on the gun barrel over a a sentry passing to and fro on the galleries, trying to

353

keep himself warm. A low hum of conversation mixed with a subdued clatter and a laugh came from the barracks.

The chorus of the wolves on the ridge to the westward suddenly attained a frantic crescendo and ceased. They have him! he thought. He could see them leaping in and worrying the kill, the flash of white fangs in the starlight. God, it was good to be alive on a night like this! He wished he were out there now, moving silently along the ridge, looking down over the black treetops into the silent valleys, gliding with his rifle from tree to tree. Well it was time to have a look at Burent and see what he could do for him.

"Nine o'clock, and all's well," sang the sentries, one after the other.

Inside the room the captain listened. There were seven sentries and they were all awake. That would do, he hoped.

"Mr. Yates," said he, "do me the favour of bringing your chair over here by the fire where I can see you. I want to talk some things over. Tomorrow I have certain moves in mind, and I should like to discuss them."

Remarking that he was flattered, Mr. Yates complied.

30
In Which Mr. Yates Draws a Bill of Credit on His Own Account

"YOU SEE, it's like this," said the captain. "I must press on to Fort Bedford as rapidly as possible. A heavy snow in the mountains might delay me for weeks, and there is much, much to do at Bedford. But this is also an important place at Ligonier. Our chain of communication is no stronger than the weakest link, and I must strengthen this one before I go. Now is it really your impression that Mr. St. Clair is the main cause of friction here? You have been staying here some time now and should know."

"Candidly, that *is* my impression," replied Yates. "Before the advent of the gentleman alluded to, Mr. Erskine had the garrison in good fettle, despite the opposition of the militia officers. But St. Clair's arrival changed all that. He brought with him some twenty-odd people, men, women, and children, as settlers, and he opened up a store for trading and supplies. These people are now quartered in the cabins which they have built as best they could. Their presence in the fort has been demoralizing. By the way, didn't I hear you mention the name of one Japson?"

"Yes, the Quaker; a pious rogue if there ever was one."

"But Mr. St. Clair's agent," explained Yates. "He it is who has been bringing goods and supplies over the mountains and even trading farther westward from here. St.

Clair and he undoubtedly have in mind a little traffic in furs with the Indians."

"It's a pretty kettle of fish, no doubt," said the captain. "And this fellow St. Clair has colour for everything he is doing."

"A specious reason for every act! You would be well advised, sir, to move circumspectly in his case. Mr. Arthur St. Clair is a man of native ability, powerful connections, wealth, and impenetrable pride. Do not mistake him for an ordinary fox. He is one of those men who, when once a thing promises to be of benefit to him, all the means to bring it about become automatically correct and in good conscience; those who oppose, unconscionable rascals to be denounced. *Dominus* is the word, sir. Nothing short of that will do for him. He has come into the wilderness to dominate, to avoid any opposition, something which he cannot understand or abide."

"You speak feelingly, Mr. Yates," said the captain.

"I have good cause to do so," replied the young lawyer. "I confess, sir, to an abiding dislike of Arthur St. Clair. I am being candid, for I know him only too well. You should know that and perhaps make allowances for the sentiment in anything that I have said." He looked the captain straight in the eyes.

"From all I can see, your feelings do you credit," answered the captain.

"I value your opinion, captain," said Mr. Yates, flushing. "I am flattered you have asked for mine. Your situation at Ligonier in regard to Mr. St. Clair is about as follows, I think: he has, as you know, only a colour, only a specious pretext for having insisted on acting as commanding officer of this post. General Stanwix's memorandum required, 'all colonial forces to recognize his commission as though still in force.' That did not and could not apply to the king's regular troops, such as the detachment of the Highlanders stationed here. Actually, Mr. Erskine, being a king's officer, was still in command. But since he was only an ensign, and, as the colonials outnumbered his men and their officers adhered to Lieutenant

St. Clair, he was in effect put down. I might say that Erskine was most miserable under this tyranny and drank a good deal even for a Scot. He knew St. Clair was writing letters calculated to get rid of him so that all would be clear sailing here for him and his missions. The colonial officers are in fact St. Clair's agents for trade, acting with Japson. They expect to settle here on St. Clair's property and prosper. Just now they are at Bedford to meet a train of pack horses bearing Mr. Japson's goods in order to guide them over the mountains. St. Clair is, of course, too clever to own these goods openly himself. They are probably the legal property of Japson. He is a trader of considerable reputation in Philadelphia, but I have no doubt St. Clair is providing the capital for this venture. Only a few years ago he married a niece of Governor Bowdoin of Massachusetts Bay, and 'tis said she brought him fourteen thousand pounds sterling in her own right."

The captain whistled. "And so," he said, "he is now laying out his wife's money in a little lucrative trade with the savages. And the caravans are on their way. Well, at least I have Japson in the net. As for St. Clair's being commanding officer here, my own commission will take care of that. It's in force, and I am a captain in a king's regiment. But what about these settlers he's bringing in? The king's proclamation, as I understand it, absolutely forbids it."

"I'm not so sure," said Mr. Yates. "A certain number of people are permitted to settle at a government post, if licensed. Just by whom is not clear. There's the rub. Also in this case Mr. St. Clair has a grant of land from the proprietors of Pennsylvania with a proviso for settlement which, of course, implies the right to bring in settlers. And under their charter, you know, the proprietors of Pennsylvania have sovereign and feudal rights, which might hold even against the king's officers. To evict these people might subject you to a civil process, and one tried in the proprietors' own court."

It was now the captain's turn to flush—angrily. If

there was one thing that as a soldier he hated, it was the processes of the civil law.

"The grant of land is for four thousand acres, the largest west of the mountains, providing settlers are brought in. If not, for one thousand on the present purchase," added Yates.

The captain whistled again.

"Just what is your position in all this, Mr. Yates?" he finally demanded. "I think it would clarify matters between us if I knew. That you don't like St. Clair is abundantly clear, but not much else."

"I was hoping you would ask that," replied Yates. "Frankly, I wish to ask a favour of you shortly, and in view of that I should like you to understand just who I am, what I am doing here, and why. May I draw a bill of credit on your patience then, in order to make myself completely clear?"

"I'll honour it," said Ecuyer, "but it must be on my own terms of discount, provided"——he smiled——"you put another chunk or so on the fire. Albine's not back yet."

"Agreed," replied Yates. "I hope we shall mutually profit."

Under his care the fire began licking up the chimney again. Captain Ecuyer drew nearer to its warmth and prepared to listen. There was a certain sincerity and matter-of-factness about the young lawyer that had greatly impressed him.

"Probably the easiest way to show you my position here and to explain a number of other matters will be to give you my brief personal history," remarked Yates, seating himself and dusting off his hands some small splinters and pieces of bark left from the firewood.

"My rightful name is Hamilton," he began. "Unfortunately I am not able to prove that. I am the second son of James, Sixth Duke of Hamilton and Brandon, by a chapel marriage with a Scotch-Irish girl named Margaret Yates. It was an early love match, surreptitious on the part of his Grace, a union which he never acknowledged for cogent reasons of his own. Perhaps, as you know, in

358

such cases neither the Church of England nor the English law recognizes the validity of marriages performed by unlicensed dissenting clergymen not holding under any of the establishments, and the duke took full advantage of that fact, in addition to keeping the proofs of his living with my mother in his own hands.

"What I say to you, therefore, rests on my own assertion alone. It is proper to insist, however, that my mother was an honest woman, although a comparatively poor girl, and that I have seen from Antrim the record of the marriage and talked with the old field preacher who performed it. The record has since disappeared.

"After the birth of a first child, my elder brother, in Ireland, the duke became more than ever anxious to conceal his adventure as he was then about to marry the present dowager duchess, a reigning beauty with a quixotic mind. For that purpose, and for various convenient reasons, largely having to do with his powerful interests and clients in Scotland—who would carry out his designs and no questions asked—he brought my mother to the town of Thurso in Caithness. Some of her maternal relations still resided there, who were ready to take their Irish relative and her little family into their care, the dull edge of their Scotch charity being no little whetted by a generous allowance discreetly bestowed on her by an agent of the duke.

"It was at Thurso, shortly after my mother moved from Ireland, that I was born. And it was in that place that I spent my infancy and boyhood. When I tell you that Arthur St. Clair was also born in Thurso, and that we were playmates and went to the same dame school together, you will no doubt begin to see that my knowledge of the gentleman is not entirely documentary." He paused a moment to glance at the captain and poke the fire.

"Go on!" said the captain. "I confess to a curiosity to know by what a ravelling of fate we find ourselves tonight in the same room at Ligonier."

Mr. Yates laughed. "It is, as you say, sir, quite a ravelling, and of many curious strands. Of course, as children neither I nor my brother had any idea of what I tell you now. My mother was known as Madam Yates— her father's name, by the way. She passed for a widow easily enough at Thurso. Her husband was supposed to have been a Belfast merchant who had died early and left her a competence, and I never heard a whisper against her. She was enormously discreet. We lived quietly and happily in a rented manse near town. The only curious circumstance being that my mother would never have me baptized. I think she feared to perjure herself on a sacred record, or perhaps to compromise my possible claims to the name of Hamilton. And, as it turned out, this was all the more important, for shortly after my ninth birthday my elder brother Ian was drowned out fishing, leaving me heir to whatever shadowy kingdom I might be entitled to.

"My mother was ill at the time my brother was brought home drowned. I think the shock of his death unnerved her temporarily, and, as a consequence of that, rather than that she thought I had arrived at the age of discretion, she called me to her and in the greatest secrecy, and with an impressive warning to be discreet, revealed to me what I can only regard in the light of after events to be the genuine facts of my birth.

"I was greatly impressed in a childish way. But I was still too young to appreciate either the dangers or the advantages of my situation, although my mother's manner did succeed in impressing something of its gravity upon me. At any rate, I had the good sense or the good fortune to hold my tongue. This was partly due to the fact that, God forgive me, I began to think perhaps my mother had arrived at the age when women have the vapours. I had been told about them. And I thought I might awaken any morning to find that she had returned to herself as Mrs. Yates and recovered from a period of romantic and hysterical imagining. But I was soon, and rudely enough, to find her story confirmed.

"For shortly after midnight of a rainy and blustering time in October fourteen years ago, I was awakened by my old nurse and told not to tarry to dress, but to go directly downstairs in my nightshirt to the study. Yet despite the hurry, the old woman insisted on doing up my hair, of which she was sillily fond. To all my questions she could only shake her head. This frightened me. I was afraid my mother was very ill or had died, and I descended the old twisting stairs to the study, where there were lights and strange voices, with fear at my heart and tears in my eyes.

"When I flung open the door I was greatly relieved, however, to find my mother, dressed as I had never seen her before, seated in her winged chair and entertaining two gentlemen with hot possets. Both of them seemed enormously at home and quite familiar with my mother. One of them, an affected dog with a keen face, sat in the deep embrasure of the study window, fondling an eyeglass that dangled down onto his peach-coloured waistcoat. The other, a plump, blond gentleman with kindly blue eyes and straw-coloured hair, stood before the peat fire dressed in the extremity of fashion, wearing a short sword with small diamonds in the hilt. I am bound to say he was most handsome and most affable and smiled at me quite tenderly.

"All this I saw later, for on first entering the room I had run with a cry of joy to my mother and thrown my arms around her, weeping with relief at finding her still there and well.

" 'A bonny lad, me lud, one her Grace might be proud to know you'd got. What did I tell you!'

" 'Hauld yer clack,' said the gentleman by the fire, with some indignation and alarm. 'Did I no tell you Farguson, to keep your feet oot of your ain mouth! And now you've stepped into it with both of them. Whist,' said he, holding his hand out in my direction somehow impressively, 'come hither, me laddie. I want to see you.'

"My mother pushed me gently away and I went over and stood before him.

" 'Now, what's your name?' said he as though to start a conversation.

" 'Edward Hamilton Yates, sir,' I replied—'but I was never baptized.'

"He laughed at my mother. 'You *are* a discreet woman, Margaret,' he said. 'I shouldn't have thought of that myself, and I'll no forget that you took the precaution.'

" 'Do you know how you came by the Hamilton in your handle?' he asked me next quite suddenly.

"I glanced at my mother and saw that she had turned pale.

" 'Not exactly,' I said fibbing on the instinct that it would help my mother. 'I've been told, sir, some of my father's grandfathers were in the Hamilton line.'

"The gentleman did not seem displeased.

" 'You are quite right in that,' he said archly. 'Quite!'

"I heard Mr. Ferguson in the corner snickering appreciatively.

" 'Lord!' said he, 'the boy can lie like a nobleman already.'

" 'It's a talent you much overvalue, Harry,' said my lord testily. Then he reached down, took my face between both his hands, and after looking at me so intently that I blushed, he kissed me on the mouth. I was greatly confused by this and was much moved to see that he had tears in his eyes. I withdrew in embarrassment to my mother's chair and found her weeping.

" 'Zounds!' snorted Mr. Ferguson. 'Sink me, if I am not overcome myself.' He popped his eyeglass into place after wiping his eyes with a fine lace handkerchief. And I was horrified to see the eye behind the glass give me a solemn wink. But I was also made aware by this of the fact that both my mother and the gentleman by the hearth looked so miserable that they were positively funny.

" 'For shame,' cried my mother indignantly, wiping her eyes. 'It's natural for a man to yearn over his own flesh and blood.'

" 'It's natural, madam, but in this case it's not legitimate,' replied Mr. Ferguson. 'And that's the nice point that I have been trying to make with my lord here for some years past. The time has come when this kind of thing can no longer go on. You must both be aware of that, unless you have lost your senses. The duchess will get wind of it, and then there'll be the very deil to pay. The heirs to the title will not disinherit themselves in order to soothe your domestic yearnings, Mrs. Yates, nor my lord's. All that is necessary to acknowledge this boy is to prove my lord a bigamist at least. What do you think the duchess and her extremely cautious family would say to that? And she is a barren woman, too, Mrs. Yates. It is her much-admired story that 'tis my lord here who is impotent. Should ever a natural son turn up, my lord would find himself taking tea with a tigress. My dear madam, you have no idea what would inevitably happen to you then. Being turned out to beg would not be the half of it. Am I not right, James?'

" 'Cousin Farguson has put it plainly, Margaret,' said his Grace, shifting awkwardly from one foot to another. 'I know I promised you, but conditions have changed.'

" 'I gave you one bonny bairn that's gone down in the deep,' cried my mother. 'Now this one is all we are left with, and you'll no acknowledge him. He's yours! He's your son, James! I've been true to you, and I gave you all.'

"Now, my lord was much moved by this. His hands shook, and I saw that Mr. Ferguson also was alarmed. His hands shook too, and his glass fell out of his eye again and dangled about on its string.

" 'Faither,' I said. 'It's true, then? You're my faither!'

"His Grace wiped his eyes.

"At that Mr. Ferguson did the crucial thing. He came over, and leading me to the window seat, set me on *his* knee.

"I think if I had run to my father before Cousin Harry got me—well, who knows what might have happened? The duke was at bottom a truly sentimental man.

" 'Now, Edward,' said Mr. Ferguson, holding on to me firmly, 'you're a sensible lad, I can see. I'm your friend, if you only knew it. And I'm trying to save your mother from destroying herself and your own bright prospects.

363

And that is God's sacred truth.' There was something so vehement, so urgent and sincere in the way he spoke that we were all compelled to listen to him.

" 'Mrs. Yates,' he continued, 'for God's sake give up your mad ambition. It can only ruin yourself and your young son. James,' he cried, 'if you continue to persist in the impossible course you outlined to me this morning, you'll bring ruin on every soul in this room. I will not be able to help you. Now be sensible. There are other people, other things to consider, besides your own tender feelings. I have a proposal to make, a sensible and rational one. Something that will bring as much happiness to all of you as, under the circumstances, any of you can expect. Will you listen to me?'

"My mother lifted her hand to protest. There was a wild look in her face. But his Grace motioned to her to be still.

" 'There is much truth in what Cousin Harry says, Margaret. I am afraid we shall have to listen to him,' said the duke.

" 'Aye, aye, that there is!' cried Mr. Ferguson. 'Listen to me I am afraid you must.'

"At this my mother put her hands over her face and sank back into her chair. I felt she knew she had lost, and I ran to comfort her. Mr. Ferguson made no effort to detain me.

" 'Now, then,' I heard him saying while I hid my head in my mother's lap, 'here's the plan, and it's a good one. It's the kind of plan that will work in *this* world and not a mad scheme meant for some world not yet discovered. Do listen to me, Mrs. Yates, for it concerns you and your boy very nearly!"

" 'I hear you,' said my mother, choking. Taking her hands from her eyes, she looked at him intently. I sat looking up into her face and listening. Expressions seemed to flit over her countenance as though some strange disconcerting instrument were being played.

" 'What I propose,' said Mr. Ferguson, 'is that his Grace settle a sufficient sum on you, Mrs. Yates, to keep your own house comfortably here at Thurso. This can be done by giving you for the term of your natural life the rents of certain tenements and messuages in Edinburgh. Then, no matter who inherits as the head of the house of Hamilton, these moneys will be collectible by you or by your agent. This will not provide quite so generous a sum as you have been receiving as an allowance from his Grace for some years now, but one of your boys is dead, and this other one will be well looked after, so that both their expenses will be off your hands. And these rents will be secured to you whereas, if his Grace were to die, the allowance that is now your only income would immediately cease and you would have no recourse.'

" 'I am not so sure of *that*,' said my mother, biting her lip and tapping her foot on the floor.

" 'I am *very* sure of it, Mrs. Yates,' continued Mr. Ferguson, 'for I have in my possession all the papers concerning your Irish marriage, and I have caused the chapel register at Antrim to—shall we say?—disappear.'

" 'It is admirable of you to triumph thus over a lone woman, my lord," said my mother bitterly. 'James, James, how can you!'

"It was now my lord's turn to look confused. He hurriedly waved to Mr. Ferguson to go on.

"It is not admirable but it is quite essential,' continued Mr. Ferguson. 'And all this is conditioned on the supposition that you will keep your own counsel about these matters and never hereafter write, try to see, or attempt to communicate with his Grace again under any circumstances whatever.'

" 'I'll no promise sic a thing for my bairn,' cried my mother, reduced by excitement and emotion to her native Scotch. 'I'll no do it for him.'

" 'But you will for yourself, Mrs. Yates?' suggested Mr. Ferguson, trying to see just how far he could venture—and where to stop.

"My mother clasped me in her arms and, seating me on her knee, seemed to face the two men as though she were at bay and defending her young.

" 'Before God, it's your own begetting that sits here. What will you do for him? Will you cast him off to beg?' she cried.

" 'Tut, tut, madam,' said his Grace. 'You *must* know me better than that.' He came over and took my mother's hand and my own in his and squeezed them together. 'It's a grand plan we have for the laddie too, the verra best under the circumstances. And do you really think I want to part with you the noo, Margaret? Na! Na!' said he, shaking his head violently. 'But ye dinna ken the troubles would come upon ye if I owned ye and the bairn before a' the world. Ye dinna ken her Grace! Would ye proclaim yourself the dupe of a field marriage at best and hae the lad here harried oot o' the land? Much, much better to listen to reason than to have all the Hamiltons and Dooglases in the twa kingdoms bayin' at your heels. Whoosh! It's not to be thought of! I'll cherish the boy here. I'll keep him in interest and affection. But the secret can never be let out. Don't you see, if it ever does get about, I can't do anything for either of you?'

" 'Don't be obstinate and cruel, Mrs. Yates,' said Mr. Ferguson. 'Be sensible. His Grace is absolutely right.'

" 'Aye,' said my mother brokenly, 'I suppose he is.'

" 'Come here, Edward,' said Mr. Ferguson, after a little.

"I went over to him.

" 'Tell me now, what is it you'd want to be when you're a man?'

"Now, I had never thought much of my future. To be the captain of a fishing smack had been my highest childish ambition. Yet I understood that night what was going on well enough, and I had been trying to think how I might help my mother.

" 'I'd like to be a lawyer,' I answered glibly enough. 'Someday then maybe I'd know enough to make my mother a duchess.'

" 'By God, Harry, there's rhyme, reason, and policy in the infant,' cried my lord, laughing. 'At least he might learn enough if he reads the law to know he never could inherit.'

" 'There's much to be said for your idea, my young friend,' replied Mr. Ferguson, looking me over appraisingly. 'Do you think you can stick to it?'

" 'If you stick to me, I'll stick to you,' was my pert answer, a phrase the children used much about Thurso.

" 'Very well,' said Ferguson. 'You can entirely depend upon me.'

"It was not for many years that I fully appreciated both the honesty and the literal sincerity in that remark. For after that evening I never saw his Grace again, but I was to see Cousin Harry Ferguson often and under various circumstances and to get to know him well. His foppery was only a polite screen. He was one of those amiable Scots who would rather be taken for a fool than risk the expense of permitting it to be discovered that he had a kind heart."

Mr. Yates paused and looked into the fire as though its flames were of the substance of memory. Either he was looking into the past—or was he looking into the future? At any rate, it was some time before he recollected himself and looked up apprehensively at Captain Ecuyer. "But I have been tiring you!" he exclaimed. "All this is personal, naturally of great interest to me—but to you?"

"Go on," said the captain. "It's as curious a tale as I've heard for years, and I am one who likes to finish what's been begun. Besides, you may have a special reason for telling me."

"I'm not so sure of that now," replied the young man. "I'm afraid most of all I just needed someone to talk to. It was to have been about St. Clair, of course."

"Never mind him," said Ecuyer, smiling. "I'm more interested in you now than in St. Clair. And besides, who am I to interrupt the rightful Duke of Hamilton?" He laughed slyly but good-naturedly.

Mr. Yates winced.

"Now, now," said the captain, observing the young

man's confusion, "do me the credit of believing me sympathetic; interested, at least. Go on. What happened?"

Seeing the captain was quite in earnest, Mr. Yates took heart and continued:

"Well, it was all settled in the room at Thurso that evening. Once having capitulated, my mother made the best of it, more for me than for herself. It was arranged that I was to be tutored by one of the clergymen in the neighbourhood and to go up to St. Andrews when the time came.

" 'After that,' said his Grace, 'we'll see whether it will be the English or the Scotch practice you'll want to follow, my boy, and what can be done for you when the time comes. It's all some years away. You will have to prove yourself a worthy little man first.'

"He then took me aside and spent some time impressing upon me that I must obey my mother, be a man, and a protector to her, and keep my mouth shut. I understood, and I promised with a childish gravity that seemed to please him, for he put a small ring on my thumb to remind me of all he had said. Finally he embraced me. Nor was he entirely able to control his emotion.

"Meanwhile, Mr. Ferguson had been arranging matters with my mother. Certain papers passed between them and I overheard him once cautioning her against the sin of female vanity.

" 'For it is that,' he said, 'which will most likely undo ye. 'Twould be a rare thing to whisper to your best friend what's at the foot of your rainbow. You'll have to be marvellous circumspect madam, or the pot o' goold will vanish. And you're a handsome widow, Mrs. Yates. There'll be many a mon, ye ken . . .'

" 'I'll be looken after me ain,' said she. 'And you'll have to leave that to me.'

"By this time the duke had finished talking to me and an embarrassed silence fell in the room. The full realization came over my mother and father that they were seeing each other for the last time. It was my mother who finally rallied herself to pass it off with gaiety.

"She went to the door and called to old Jenny to bake some scones. Then she served some basins of steaming Bohea, with a wealth of chatter about the comic incidents of the neighbourhood and of the good times she and my lord had once had at Antrim. Only the high colour in her cheeks and a few tears his Grace dropped into the tea, which he tried hard to hide by laughing at her quips, showed which way the wind blew. And for that matter the real wind was blowing hard enough outside and a violent wash of cold Scotch rain could be heard running off the eaves and gurgling down the stone gutters. That, too, made the gentlemen linger longer than they otherwise might have, I suppose.

" 'But it won't be so gay here at Thurso, for the rest of my lifetime,' laughed my mother. 'Aye, it will be drab enough,' she sighed. 'And no loved visitors again!' She choked over her tea.

"The gutters outside went on gurgling.

" 'Maybe a wee horse and a carriage would help a bit,' suggested Mr. Ferguson, who, I could see, by now admired my mother immensely. 'Don't you think we could manage that, your Grace?'

" 'Certainly! By all means,' said the duke, looking miserable. 'And a pony for the boy.'

" 'Oh, faither,' I cried, 'not a pony! Not a pony for me! I'd always love you for that.' And I rushed over to him.

"Luckily the old woman had not yet come into the room with the scones. Nevertheless, I had greatly alarmed the gentlemen.

" 'Come,' said Mr. Ferguson finally, 'at this rate the toll bridge at the foot of the glen will soon be washed out, and we must be at Wick the morrow nicht. Come, James!'

"My mother rushed over and locked the hall door to keep out the servant. Then she threw herself into my lord's arms. She wept on his shoulder. And I could hear him choking trying to comfort her. I know from what they said that they loved each other.

"I was shocked by all this, puzzled at seeing my mother

369

in a stranger's arms, even if he was my father, and torn by a hundred conflicting emotions.

" 'Good-bye, Cousin Edward,' said Mr. Ferguson to me. 'I'll be seeing you soon again. You're to write me. And remember I am your friend. Your mother has the address.' He looked at the two standing together miserably by the hearth and shook his head. Then he took my lord by the hand and almost forcibly led him to the door.

"I can never forget that moment. He pulled the door open violently and the wind and the rain roared in. Outside I could just see the outlines of a coach and the horses prick-eared against the sky. The two gentlemen threw their cloaks over them and ran for it. The coach door banged, a whip cracked, and they were off down the valley and lost in the night.

" 'James!' called my mother frantically. 'James, James!'

"I thought she would run out into the storm after him. So I closed the door and put my back against it.

" 'He's gone, mither,' I said. 'Don't you see? My faither's gone!'

"She gathered me up in her arms and sat down before the fire and began to chafe my feet that were red with the cold stones of the floor.

" 'Puir bairn,' she kept saying. 'Puir little mon.'

"Afterwhile Jenny came trying the hall door, and I unlocked it.

" 'I've the fresh scones for ye, madam,' she said. And then, 'Aroosh! The gentlemen have gone!'

" 'The deil take your scones,' screamed my mother at the old woman. 'And if I ever hear your tongue waggin' aboot the gentlemen here the nicht, may the deil fly away with you too.'

"Old Jenny dropped the dish and ran. Neither she nor I had ever seen my mother like that, and we were never to see her that way again. For from that day Mrs. Yates became the model of all widowlike virtues and female patience at Thurso. Neither complaint nor reproach was ever heard to escape her lips.

"As for me, the years passed like a flock of birds,

swiftly. Yet each seemed to sail slowly by me at the time. I had my friends in the town and in the country about. The Reverend John McTavish came to teach me four times a week, Latin, mathematics, and the Old Testament —he seldom dipped into the New—driven home with a ruler. My hands and my tail were often sore. But I'm indebted to that man. I can navigate, and I can read Cicero with pleasure. The truth is that I had little trouble at the university when the time came to matriculate.

"But it's the old town of Thurso and the life about it that I love most to recall. 'Twas a fine place for a boy. Many a time we made trips out to the islands in the fisher boats, although my mother was always uneasy about that, having lost one lad at sea. It is a grey, foggy, rocky country with something out of the past, golden and mystic, breaking through the clouds here and there in streaks of sunshine in summer. Hard and cold in winter, full of the sound of the tides and the sea and with great birds passing over it. It is a good place for a man to come from who expects to settle here. I had my pony, as I had been promised, and my mother her hooded cart and a little mare. And a faithful old gillie to drive and look after her.

"I would ride alongside of her in the summer days and the long, twilight evenings when we drove over to Wick to visit Great-aunt Tabor, who kept a fine little house and a couple of neat maids and lived in worldly style for a Presbyterian lady.

"It was at Wick that Harry Ferguson would come to see us. I gradually came to understand that he was the duke's secretary, a cousin of some kind, and that he managed the whole estate and all the interests of the house of Hamilton, which was the god he served with no small idolatry. He would examine me every year in the progress I had made and seemed satisfied for the most part. The last two summers we went off shooting together and stayed at Castle Sinclair, the seat of the lairds of Assury, and the great place of all Caithness. My mother was proud to hear of that.

"It was at the castle that I really came to know Arthur St. Clair. We'd gone to school at Thurso together, but at the castle we met as youths. There was a merry crowd of youngsters there, both boys and girls. Arthur was a cousin of the lairds' family. He's changed his name a bit since coming here. 'St. Clair.' It's a more aristocratic spelling, I suppose. Arthur was the son of William Sinclair, a merchant at Thurso. And his great-grandfather was the second laird, so that's how it was.

"From the first we never got along well at the castle. He professed to regard me as an inferior, and a thorough taking down given him by Harry Ferguson did not help to mend matters.

"About this time my pony was getting much too small for me. He borrowed it and broke its leg one day racing in the stony pastures. And then he had it shot without telling me. I never could forgive him for that.

"Then we both became soft on Agnes Sinclair at the castle and the quarrel finally came to a head one day when Arthur came with his cool insolence to borrow my horse, for Ferguson had got me a good nag after the pony died. I refused him, and he challenged me to a duel. We were both just sixteen. Ferguson and the old laird got wind of this affair, with the result that both of us were packed off and Agnes was given a sound whipping by her father for being a flirt.

"I found myself at Cambridge instead of St. Andrews, for it was thought best to get me clean away from Scotland. Arthur was sent off to Edinburgh to Dr. William Hunter, the anatomist. But I heard he liked medicine very little; was more curious about the anatomy of wenches than of corpses, and that his mother, who was a Balfour, eventually bought him a pair of colours in a British regiment. That's how he happened to come over to America with Jeffrey Amherst. And it's strange I should be running across him here in Pennsylvania. But that's the way the world wags. People meet!

"As for me, I did nothing particular at Cambridge. Harry gave me a generous allowance, but I was a Scot and made few real friends. It would have been better at St. Andrews, I think. I got through the tripos tolerably and went down to London and was entered at Lincoln's Inn to read in the chambers of Francis Buller and George Wood. I liked the law, and Mr. Buller took an active interest in my progress. At this time my mother died and I was left with nothing but professional interests, for the London life irked me after that of Caithness. When I was called to the bar I received a gold watch from Mr. Ferguson, which he said was sent me by my father. It had the arms of Hamilton with a bar sinister engraved inside the case and there was a Latin motto underneath:

The disinherited succeed in time

"My allowance was increased out of the rents my mother had been drawing, and I took chambers at Thare's Inn. All now seemed settled for my career as a London barrister.

"As a beginning Harry Ferguson quietly threw some of the family practice and patronage my way. While I had been reading with Mr. Buller and George Wood I had also helped prepare certain briefs and petitions for Thomas Penn, one of the proprietors of Pennsylvania. I thus became familiar with the proprietary interests and difficulties, and when I set up for myself more and more of Penns' minor affairs were placed in my hands.

"I was also lucky enough to be successful in a matter with Lord Baltimore, which greatly pleased Thomas Penn. He came to know me personally, and through him I became known to the rest of the family and was made welcome in their houses. In short, we became friends. That was the pleasantest thing that had happened to me in London.

"Prospects widened—when all was quite suddenly changed by the death of the Duke of Hamilton in 'fifty-eight, my father. His Grace who succeeded was a proud man. He was also head of the house of Douglas and not inclined to listen to Mr. Harry Ferguson, who was now retired to a small estate in Argyllshire, my late lord had left him. My allowance ceased. And I was wholly reduced to such small practice as the patronage of the Penns might provide.

"It was in these circumstances that Mr. Thomas Penn first began to discuss with me the advisability of my going to Pennsylvania to represent certain interests of his family in that province.

"I was not averse. Arrangements went forward for my going to Philadelphia. But letters across the Atlantic took time, and meanwhile I determined to see the new duke, tell him my story, and try to prevail upon him to do something for a cousin of whose existence he would at least be surprised to learn.

"Naturally, I was aware of the dangers as well as of the advantages of my situation, and I acted with great care. Since the duke was a proud man, I determined to appeal to rather than to threaten his pride. I wrote to Harry Ferguson, asking him to give me the papers and proofs concerning my mother's Irish marriage to the late duke, which he had once shown me. He refused. But he wrote me a letter saying that he had them, and relating the circumstances. He was also careful to say that he would never surrender these papers to anyone as long as he lived. Knowing his fanatical loyalty to the house of Hamilton, I was sure that this was all that I could expect of him.

"With some difficulty I then managed to obtain an interview with the duke whilst he was in Edinburgh. I was able to convince him of the truth of my story. And I am bound to say that he was most decent and courteous about it, although greatly shocked and disturbed. He questioned me about my life and prospects, and seemed both relieved and pleased to find me the kind of man I was.

"'Well, Cousin Edward,' he said towards the end of our talk, 'I shall have to see that you are retained in some of the legal work for the estate and that retainers reach you from time to time. You can count on that. But you will not thrust yourself upon me personally, I trust. That, as a man of sensibility and honour, you can see would be painful for both of us.'

"I agreed, and I took the occasion to explain that Mr. Penn had in mind to employ me in America. His Grace made no comment but I could see that he was turning this over in his mind.

" 'The Penns owe me a neat sum of money,' he said at last. 'A debt from the time of their father, the old Quaker proprietor. I'm glad to hear his sons have given up old Fox's nonsense and are in communion with the Church of England. Will you not become a Quaker yourself, Mr. Yates?' he asked hopefully. 'They hold that all worldly titles are vanity, you know.'

"I assured him I would never share such unworldly philosophy and opinions.

"He laughed a bit ruefully and bowed me out. I returned to London.

"I was greatly surprised about a month later to receive a letter from the duke in his own hand. But on maturer reflection, and in view of the events that followed, I came to see that he had taken the wisest course in writing me as he did.

"He said that he had been thinking over the matter we had discussed and had arrived at the conclusion that I could expect nothing directly from him now or in the future. If, however, in the quite *near* future Mr. Thomas Penn should make me a peculiarly advantageous offer, he should expect me to understand, as a man of the world, that it was not personal merit alone which had detained the glance of Fortune.

"Shortly afterward Mr. Thomas Penn did come to my chambers one afternoon. He told me that he had always had confidence in me since I had first begun to handle some of his affairs. 'But,' he said, 'I had no idea you were a young man with great influence.' He looked at me somewhat quizzically. 'However, that's not going to do you any harm,' he added after a pause. 'It will merely hasten what I had already proposed tentatively. That is, that you should go to Pennsylvania to represent the interests of the proprietary family. Nevertheless, there are certain conditions to which you must agree beforehand. Allow me to explain:

" 'You will go to Philadelphia as a special messenger, taking along with you the appointment of James Hamilton as lieutenant governor of the province. Under the circumstances, he will be glad to see you when you arrive. And in the instructions which accompany his appointment we have required him to name you as our special legal agent for the survey and patenting of land grants and the collection of quitrents for the proprietors. You will report directly to me as the head of the Penn family here in England, and you will not be responsible either to the governor or to the Assembly, since the moneys you collect are the private revenues of the Penn family. Your fees will be ten percentum of the total amounts remitted to London. A tidy salary if you work hard. In addition you are to be paid a lump sum of one thousand pounds within three months after you arrive, but in Pennsylvania currency. Out of that I shall advance two hundred pounds sterling to you before you leave here. The conditions are that, if at any time hereafter you leave America, the one thousand pounds so advanced will become your debt collectible in England by us, and your employment and emoluments in Pennsylvania will immediately cease. In other words, Mr. Yates, you have exceedingly influential friends in England who will be quite happy to advance your prospects abroad, so long as you remain there. What do you think?'

" 'I shall consent, Mr. Penn, provided you do not regard me with aversion for having the payment of an old debt thus forced upon you in my person. As your agent in Pennsylvania I must be assured of your genuine support and respect, and that I shall be continued in office. Otherwise, I should be a fool to go.'

" 'You can be assured of that,' he said. 'I will give it to you in any form you desire, a letter patent if you will. As a matter of fact, you can be at ease about our opinion of you. We have compounded an old debt quite satisfactorily, and'—he reached forward and plucked my sleeve—'I think the Penns have secured themselves an honest and able servant. Do you see?'

" 'I think I do,' I said, 'and I'll go.'

"Mr. Thomas Penn spent the rest of the afternoon in describing the difficulties of his family in getting any revenues out of their lands in America and instructing me in the paths I should follow. We parted, I am quite sure, warmly, and in good understanding.

"So that is how and why I came to America.

"I sailed in October, 'fifty-nine, and the only person in the world to see me off was old Cousin Harry Ferguson. He came down all the way alone from Edinburgh. It seems the duke had admired the way he had handled my affair and he was in good graces again with the head of the house. At least I had been able to do that much for him. It was the restoration of the sunshine by which he lived. He embraced me warmly when we parted and told me to write him, and he wept. He is the only human being in Europe that I can say I love, and he's probably dead now, for he was an old man, and that was all of four years ago."

Mr. Yates paused and looked gloomily into the fire that was beginning to burn low again.

"And so we find ourselves at Ligonier," said the captain. "Well, the colonies are full of strange stories. Take this fellow Albine, for instance, you must get him to tell you his tale. It *is* curious that you should run across your friend St. Clair again, and here of all places. Isn't it?"

"Damme if it isn't," said Yates. "I *am* a bit superstitious about it. And he isn't happy about my being here and surveying his land. He has received his one thousand acres and *no more*. I've seen to that. And I've made him pay up. He was willing to compound matters to gain a little time. It's a pretty kingdom he's got with his wife's money, the lucky dog! I envy him. I would like to do likewise, I admit."

"Land?" said the captain.

"Land!" said Mr. Yates. "Precisely that."

"So you'll be staying on in the colonies, will you?"

"Permanently," replied the young lawyer. "I am going to find my ideal spot and seat myself there. But I shall look far and carefully first. It must be like Scotland in some ways. Something that will remind me of home."

"Your lost dukedom regained?" laughed the captain.

Mr. Yates smiled but did not reply.

"Bouquet and I both have some land in Maryland," continued the captain. "The colonel has built him a house and found a nice wench to put in it, too. That makes a difference, you know."

"I suppose so," agreed Yates apparently indifferently. He looked up in surprise as an odour of verbena came to him. The captain was using his handkerchief. The perfume was faint but it was almost as though the ghost of a woman had walked into the room.

"Well," said the captain, "since we've eventually got round to the wenches, I suppose bed is next in order. After your confidence, Mr. Yates, I'll be inclined to consider the favour which you have forgotten to ask me. It's been an interesting evening, and in these parts one should be grateful for finding an enemy of *ennui* to be one's friend."

"The compliment is delightful from you, sir," said Mr. Yates. "May I return it only in part by not asking you my favour until later? It is too late tonight for further explanations."

"It is," exclaimed the captain, "a half after one o'clock! That rascal Albine must be making a night of it with Burent and his friends in the barracks. I don't blame him. What humanity needs is an innocent debauch about every ten days. But will you give me a hand to my bunk, sir? *Bon Dieu!* I'm stiff. It's been a long journey and a devilish hard day."

Mr. Yates helped the captain to his bunk, threw a chunk or two in the chimney, and after hastily undressing climbed into his own corner. The candles had long ago burnt out. In the headquarters room at Ligonier, the steady breathing of the sleepers blent regularly with the soughing of the mighty logs in the fire. Salathiel entered noiselessly towards morning, and wrapping himself in a fur rug, lay down near the hearth and slept like a panther on the warmed floor.

31

In Which Friend Japson Returns

THE PROFOUNDEST SCHEMES of statesmen and the high strategies of soldiers are at the mercy of such things as fatigue and temperature. The truth is that humanity is frail and functions well only within a narrow range of heat and cold. The sodden breakfast of a bodyguard may account for the carelessness that leads to the unexpected murder of a sovereign. Empire itself is a quarry hunted forever by miserable and tiny things. Here and there, over a hemisphere, rains and field mice gnaw it away. Confusion and revolt patiently await the rotted palisade, the rusted cannon, or the dried-up well to come crashing and roaring through into the citadel: Because there was a log of wild cherry in the chimney at Ligonier, and because it burned warmly and long, trouble came upon that humble outpost of the king's dominions while Captain Ecuyer slept.

But it was no wonder that he slept. The sheer exhaustion of the day before had reduced him to a state of coma in which even his will power, which usually aroused him automatically, lapsed. His tired body lay recovering itself, trying to heal its wounds; and Colonel Bouquet's plan for an advance down the Ohio in the early spring hung in abeyance. In fact, although nobody knew, it quietly slipped over into the late summer or autumn of the next year, while the captain softly snored.

Mr. Yates, too, was doing full soporific justice to the

soft occasion, after a certain relief of mind and frame that had followed his "confession" to the captain of the night before. The room was delightfully warm. Just the right temperature for late sleeping. The gradually penetrating cold of the early morning hours, also conducive of sleep up to a certain point, had suddenly been dispelled when the green cherry log, dried out by hours of baking, had burst into a vigorous flame towards six o'clock in the morning.

And it was about this time that Mr. Japson, released from durance vile by some of his many friends in the garrison, quietly loaded his pack horses and drove out of the gate of the fort headed for Fort Bedford.

A glorious sunrise greeted him an hour later as he pressed on smartly, using switches and a certain strained vocabulary of Biblical language to hasten his horses. These, if they had been theologians, might have been surprised to note that the pious testimony of Mr. Japson in Friends' Bank Meeting, Front Street, Philadelphia, seemed, in the wilderness, to be turned into a loud altercation with two members of the Trinity at least, in which horses figured.

However that may be, Mr. Japson was joined about five miles from Ligonier by two Indians who appeared from nowhere quietly, and were trotting beside him before even he was aware. He drew up in a small valley near a spring from which his horses drank, while he and the two Indians went into council. Tobacco and one small flask off Mr. Japson's person were exchanged and the business at hand was soon settled. The Indians might easily be recognized as old acquaintances of Mr. Japson by a film of mush which still clung to their blankets and trousers from the day before. To tell the truth, they were also customers of Mr. Japson, and a short conversation in muskrat-Delaware soon served to conclude the business at hand. What this was, was soon quite evident, for as Mr. Japson pressed on merrily in the direction of the Laurel Hill Mountain, the Indians left his company and disposed themselves thoughtfully behind a log on a small eminence which overlooked a considerable stretch of road to the westward. At the same time they carefully reprimed their muskets and adjusted their flints.

Back at the fort Salathiel had been awakened by the cherry log not long after it had burst into flame. The heat had nearly blistered his shoulders and brought him up standing, shaking some running sparks out of the smoking fur rug he had slept in. A glance showed him that both Mr. Yates and the captain were still sound asleep, and he saw no reason to disturb them. In fact, after the evening of the night before with Burent he had no idea what time it was at all. Going quietly to the door, he stood outside on the stoop watching the slow approach of dawn and chewing a piece of dried beef from his pouch. He washed it down with a handful of fresh snow. This preliminary "breakfast" was scarcely swallowed before Burent and Ensign Erskine came hurriedly around the corner of the militia barracks to say that Japson was gone.

A hasty conference took place on the steps as to the best measures to take. O'Neal and some of his friends had been released at the same time by the sympathy of the militia. They had overpowered the Highland sentry posted to watch Japson, managed the man at the gate—and the bird had flown. The curious thing was that O'Neal had undoubtedly remained in the fort.

"He's loose now down in the inhabitants' quarters, no doubt hidden in one of the huts waiting to make further trouble, and it's that which worries me," said Erskine. "St. Clair, you know, was expected back last night. That's what the fourth chair was set at the supper table for. He'll probably be along today and the two militia officers with him. All hell my break out when they ride in. I hate to take this to the captain as my reveille report. He'll wonder if I was drunk again."

Salathiel shook his head. "I doubt that, Mr. Erskine," he said; "at any rate, you were sober up to two o'clock. Both Burent and I can testify to that." He smiled slowly at the nervous young Scot. "I'll tell you what we'll do. I'll take the captain's horse and set off after Japson. Rely upon it, I'll bring the varmint back. And you can tell that to the captain when you report. Give me a few minutes now until I can get me gone. A little more sleep won't do the captain any harm. I'll not exactly dally."

He strode back into the room and silently gathered up his pouch and rifle. He also snatched a piece of bread and cold meat from the supper remains of the night before. Two minutes later he was feeding and saddling the mare. That took a bit of time. Both Burent and Erskine were still standing on the steps as he rode for the gate of the fort. The ensign saw him out.

"*Habeas corpus*," he called after him and waved hopefully.

Salathiel had no idea what that meant, but the tone was cordial and he waved young Erskine an encouraging good-bye. There was a clear run through the forest near the fort and he clapped heels to his horse. Japson had a little over an hour's start of him, he figured. A few moment's later the sound of the reveille rolled through the woods and told him that Captain Ecuyer and the fort at Ligonier were awake.

The trail of Japson's horses led like a plain line of print straight-away into the dawn, telling the intricate but precise story of his every move. Here at one place one of the horses had stumbled. At another Japson had dismounted and cut a good-sized hickory switch. From there he had gone on faster. Two Indians had joined him at another place. Their pointed moccasin slots accompanied him along the road ahead and on around a curve. It was precisely at this point that Salathiel pulled the mare aside and skirted through the forest. Thrice he crawled back to read the record on the highway. The third time, he came to the place in the little valley where Japson had held his hasty conference near the spring.

It was all quite plain. There was even a little tobacco spilled on the ground. Best of all, there were only the same two pairs of moccasins.

So Mr. Japson had then gone on without them!

Salathiel paused to consider. Presently he tied the mare

383

near the spring, scraped some snow away to give her a brief patch of forage, and took up the trail of the moccasins carefully, holding his rifle handy, and gliding from tree to tree.

The Indians had made no attempt to conceal their trail. Once they had run along some logs and leaped sidewise off into a patch of snowless ground. But it was all sufficiently plain to the eyes of the Little Turtle.

He had forgotten everything now but the joy of the hunt. He laughed silently.

It was quite light now. The sun came streaming over the ridge to eastward. A faint, slow breeze drifted with it, slightly warmer, carrying a message to Salathiel through the silent forest. He sniffed it eagerly. Away off somewhere a branch cracked. It was a magnificent day. He shivered slightly, not from cold. It was the shiver of a hound absorbed in and thrilling to its life's business. In the breeze was the faintest but absolutely unmistakable tang of tobacco smoke.

They must be crazy to smoke now, he thought. And they must be someplace fairly near. He had his plan. He must shoot one of them first. That would inevitably bring out the other. Most guns had only one shot in this country. He smiled and instinctively patted his rifle. It mustn't miss. Presently he came to the sharp declivity of a deep ravine.

He crawled along the edge stealthily and came to a clifflike formation topped by a thicket. He wriggled through this, covered his face by a branch with brown leaves on it, and peered out.

A considerable panorama lay stretched out before him. The road crossed a stream in the valley just below and then wound upward through a tumble of small foothills to the shoulder of the high ridge beyond. Then, almost at the same instant, he was rewarded by a glimpse of exactly what he was after, both Mr. Japson and the "moccasins."

A succession of small black dots began to crawl up the mountain road over a bald patch about three miles away;

384

and on the hill immediately below him, and directly across the valley, he detected a faint blue disturbance in the air. It was just at the crest, an ideal place from which to overlook the road. Innocent travellers could be shot beautifully at the open ford below, without their even knowing it. But to think that the "moccasins" were still smoking! That *was* luck! Delawares, he guessed, careless, eastern redskins who despised their fathers' lore. And Mr. Japson was alone. He saw him, the one dot bigger than the others, following along behind until a twist of the ridge took them from view. Japson was going slowly up the mountain, but he would have to act quickly if he was going to overtake him before noon. The smokers, of course, must be disposed of first.

He crawled back from the edge of the ravine and then ran along it rapidly. He went noiselessly, although he had no fear of being seen. He skirted the edge, going north, for nearly a mile. Presently the land levelled out at the headwaters of the little valley. He took a drink from the spring there, and still in good cover, crossed around it. In another half hour he was on the other side of the ravine, coming up on the watchers of the road from their rear.

The last quarter of a mile was a brief masterpiece of stalking, a flitting of one shadow into another from tree to tree. At last he could hear them talking, a guttural remark now and then. But it was some time before he could see them. They were just over the ridge of the hill, looking down on the road.

Another ten minutes of inch by inch movement and he could see them. From behind a log they were both intently watching the road below. Someone must be coming, for their muskets were both brought to the ready. Then he understood. He heard the mare neighing at the spring, where he had tied her, a mile away. Probably she was lonely by this time and was trying to pull off her bridle. It was a bad habit she had when left alone, but the acme of fortune now.

The two Delawares waited tensely, all their senses and

attention directed towards the road. One of them had a good rifle, and he drew a long, careful bead on the ford. His head slowly came up above the log to do so.

Salathiel shot him through the back of the neck from behind.

It was a windless straightaway over brown leaves and snow at about one hundred yards. He had meant to catch him between the shoulders. So the right barrel fired a little high, eh? That was what he thought as he watched the other Delaware roll over and down the ridge, clutching his musket, and out of sight instantly. There had been no time to draw a new bead, and it would never have done to risk an unaimed shot.

Instead, he leaped back into a dip in the ground behind him, away from his own powder smoke, and crouched down. At that instant the surviving Delaware came racing back over the slope.

Why he did that Salathiel was never able to figure, except, perhaps, that he was very young and probably foolishly brave. Or maybe he hoped to catch his enemy before he could reload. At any rate, there he stood for a couple of seconds perfectly silhouetted against the sky.

Salathiel shot him through the heart.

He fell, and his musket went off with a dull bang that echoed in the valley. Just for old times' sake, for several minutes Salathiel kept absolutely still. After a while he heard the mare neigh again. She seemed nearer now. Very carefully he ascertained that both the Delawares were really dead, but only after he reloaded both barrels and before crawling too near.

Then he went over them both rapidly. He took a fine French knife, five louis d'or, and a rifle from the first Indian. He also took a letter from his pouch, and his powder and shot and tomahawk. Then he scalped him with the French knife neatly and quickly. The scalping opened the dead man's eyes.

There was nothing on the body of the second Delaware. He looked to be scarcely sixteen years old. He had a copper medal of George I around his neck, six cartridges in his matchcoat pocket, and a small flask of whisky nearly empty. Maybe that was why the boy had been so careless, Salathiel thought. He took the medal for good luck—and the scalp.

He dragged both the bodies back into the underbrush and covered them over in a hollow with leaves. The wolves would attend to them promptly. No one would ever know who they were if they did find them. There was no use starting a blood feud with the Delawares, he reflected. He obliterated the traces of where they had been lying, picked his way carefully down a rocky spine where he left no tracks, and threw the young Indian's musket, and the rest of the useless articles, into a deep hole in the stream.

A noise of hoofs on the road startled him and he looked up to see the mare coming trotting around a bend in the road as though she were going somewhere. She stopped at the ford and whinnied at him. One of the cheek straps of her bridle was broken and the bit hung loose. Probably she had broken free when she heard the firing.

Here was a sorry complication. He might not be able to catch her, and he didn't want to have to wade the ice-covered stream. It was too swift to have frozen over hard. There were only floats of ice on it.

He stood up, let her catch the scent of him in the wind, and then moved off up the road calling and holding his hat out like an oats bag. She dashed about for a while doubtfully. Once she started back. Then she thought better of it and came dashing right through the ford, whickering and blowing her nose after him. Yet she was shy and would start away when he came near.

It took him a good quarter of an hour to catch her in a kind of exasperating game. He finally got near enough to vault into the saddle. He sat on her while he mended the cheek strap with a thong from his moccasin. Then it struck him that it was the fresh blood on the scalps that must have made her so shy of him. He had forgotten.

Indian horses along the Ohio had been used to fresh scalp locks dripping at their riders' belts. He observed that his were already frozen.

A few minutes more and he was galloping after Japson as hard as the mare could go. He left the Indian rifle hidden by the ford. He was irritated with his horse and made her go hard. Japson would now be from five to seven miles ahead, he supposed. If he had heard the firing, he might be making a run for it. But he thought he hadn't. Musket shots didn't carry far in hilly wooded country, and there would be the clatter of Japson's four horses on the stones.

The way was stony enough; jagged, conglomerate boulders with frozen gravel over them. Here and there mica glittered in them like a streak of silver. He had never seen stones like that. He let the horse pick her way here. She was beautifully sure-footed and sharp-shod. After a while he came to a long stretch of corduroy covered by clay. The engineers had laboured sorely here. It was the approach across a mile of high-lying swamp to the main ridge beyond. There was a bridge near the end. He galloped over that and just at the edge of the rise, where the road soared upward in a series of scored zigzags on the mountain, he overtook Japson.

The meeting was quite casual. Japson had dismounted and was tightening the girths and lashings on his pack horses in order to make the climb.

"You don't need to worry about that now," said Salathiel, drawing up.

"Good morning," said Mr. Japson, glancing up from an obstinate buckle that had detained him. "Ah, my young friend with the ragged ear." Then he saw the scalps at Salathiel's belt. "Well," he added, "thou art a determined young man!"

"Back to the fort, Mr. Japson," insisted Salathiel, pointing towards Ligonier with his thumb. "I'll trouble you for your pistol—and your knife."

"Thou may'st have the knife," said the Quaker, drawing out a smooth, long-handled table knife from a case that held, besides, a pewter fork and spoon. "I have no pistol. I never go armed."

"Keep your table gear," said Salathiel. "Ain't you afraid of wolves, or bars at least, that you carry no fire-arms?"

"I'm afraid of nothing," said the Quaker quite simply. And Salathiel saw that it was true.

"In that case I shall have to tie you on your horse," he said, and prepared to do so. Obviously there was no use pointing his rifle at such a man.

"No, no," said Mr. Japson. "I won't resist thee. I'll go."

"Git then," said Salathiel, "and remember, I kill. That may at least be of interest to you."

Mr. Japson turned his pack horses back the way they had just come, started them off, and rode quietly behind them. Salathiel followed him a few yards farther back, silent and watchful of both his prisoner and the road. They continued without speaking back to the ford, where he stopped and retrieved the Delaware's rifle. Mr. Japson recognized it. It was one he had traded for a mass of magnificent beaver pelts four years before at Harris's stockade. The rifle was a fine one, a German gun. Japson said nothing. They rode on again slowly. The horses were beginning to tire.

"Art thou a king's man, Salathiel Albine?" asked the Quaker suddenly without turning his head.

"No," answered Salathiel, instantly suspicious and more watchful. Yet somehow the use of his name had molli-fied him. It was as though Japson, despite the circum-stances, was simply talking with him man to man.

"No," he repeated. "I serve Captain Ecuyer. And I try to serve him well. But I have no oath to the king."

"Swear not at all: neither by the earth, for 'tis his footstool; nor by heaven, for 'tis God's throne," said Japson, smacking his lips appreciatively at the taste of words.

"You are mistaken, Mr. Japson," said Salathiel. "The

two verses go this way in the fifth of Matthew"—and he quoted them correctly.

Mr. Japson now turned around to look at Mr. Albine.

"Keep going," said Salathiel. "Here's some Scripture to go on: 'And their laws are diverse from all people; neither keep they the king's laws: therefore it is not for the king's profit to suffer them.'"

The Quaker bowed his head thoughtfully and smiled. "Certainly not for the king's profit," he said. "Thou art learned in the Word. And thou wast born in this country, and west of the mountains?" he asked.

"Aye," said Salathiel—and the words of the Seneca chief came pat to his mouth, "the water of these rivers is the blood of my veins."

"Well said, my friend," answered the Quaker. "I also was born in this country, by the banks of the Delaware. It is *our* native land." There was a pride in the Quaker's voice which Salathiel had never heard there before. He found himself responsive to it.

"It is a good land," he muttered, "good!" He almost added "mine."

"There is none other like it on the face of the earth," insisted Mr. Japson. He paused for a moment. "Does it not strike thee, friend Salathiel, thou may'st be serving Captain Ecuyer too well?"

"What do you mean?" demanded Salathiel, surprised and indignant, but mostly surprised.

"The captain is a sworn servant of the king of England," said Mr. Japson. "England is not here. This is God's country. It and the people of it lie in the fold of His hand. Dost thou think these hills and forests are the king's?"

"No," said Salathiel, "I do not. They belong to no man. I have heard say they were here before even the Injuns came. Even papooses know that."

"Yet the king has said we must not come here. And that those who have come must go back over the mountains. He has said we must not trade here. People like thee and me who were born here are not allowed to come into this land. It is the king's—and the Injuns'. Dost thou believe that?"

"It is a hard thing to believe, if you come to consider it," replied Salathiel. "I had never thought of it that way before."

"Thou shouldst begin to ask thyself who this king of England is," continued the Quaker. "What wilt thou do for thyself, Salathiel Albine, who art not permitted to stay in the land in which thou wast born?"

"I'll go east to the settlements. I want to see the wide sea water and the world."

Mr. Japson grunted like an Indian and said no more. As for Salathiel, he rode along thoughtfully. He began to have a secret respect for the Quaker. He seemed to know what he was about and why. There was much to be said for such men. Kaysinata had always admired the Pennsylvanians. He remembered that. Presently they came in sight of the fort again and rode for the gate.

"When thou dost get to Philadelphia," said Mr. Japson while they were waiting for the gate to be opened, "thou hadst best come to see me. We might have some more talks, and we might find each other helpful. I live on Fourth Street betwixt Chestnut and Mistress Nicholls's racing stables. Fourth Street, Fourth Street, the house farthest in. Canst thou remember that?"

"I'll write it down," answered Salathiel. "What does 'Fourth Street' mean?"

Mr. Japson gaped at him.

Just then the gate swung open.

32

In Which Soft Bargains Make Hard Feelings

THE INTERIOR of the fort was a busy spectacle. The Highlanders were assembled in full equipment and at rigid attention before their barracks. Sergeant McLaughlin was walking up and down before them looking exceedingly grim. Facing the Highlanders, and likewise drawn up before their barracks immediately opposite across the cobble-paved area, was the company of Pennsylvania militia with their non-commissioned officers in charge. They were laughing and carrying on.

From time to time some of them, who were evidently on detail, came from the storehouse or from the direction of the huts and laid down articles of various kinds—clothes, arms, blankets, and equipment—on a large pile immediately in front of the company. For some reason not apparent to Salathiel the appearance of many of these articles was greeted with bursts of laughter, catcalls, or ribald remarks. It was that which seemed to be annoying Sergeant McLaughlin.

This undisciplined confusion was bad enough, but it was many times magnified and twice as noisy in front of the stone steps that led up to the headquarters blockhouse.

Before the door of that building was assembled a crowd of women, some of them so ragged as to be half-naked, several with babies, and all clamouring aloud with curses, imprecations, and the brandishing of fists for admission. One old woman prowled about the block-house like an ancient mangy lioness, looking as though she would spring on the roof and tear the shingles away.

"God damn the lobsterbacks" and "Ecuyer is a bastard thief from hell" were among the more delicate of their screamed assertions. Around the edge of this crowd of loose-haired furies stood some of their men, looking sullen enough, but for the most part silent.

"It's the owld English game," shouted one vixen with fiery red hair, "drive us from the land and starve our childer. Divil a sop have I had for me tiny darlint these two days." She held up a baby in a filthy shawl and fairly waved it at the crowd. It howled obligingly. Moved by this appeal, the women gathered apparently to storm the steps en masse, when the baby began to vomit copiously a spray of sour pap that scattered the forming cohorts. Some wry laughter mixed with restraining remarks from the men served to calm matters down. The two Highlanders standing with fixed bayonets by the door now managed to make themselves heard.

"Bide a wee, haud yer hoorses. You'll be heard when your toorn coomes."

As if to confirm this, Mr. Erskine appeared and called from a list, "Mr. and Mrs. Turner." The woman and her husband pushed in through the door eagerly.

What this was all about, Salathiel had no idea. It looked like the mutiny of the washerwomen of Fort Pitt all over again, he thought. Suddenly he became intensely aware that several hundred eyes were turned on him and Japson while they sat their horses with the gate being closed behind them. A curiously boastful and savage in-stinct overpowered him when he found himself the centre of so much attention. He snatched the scalps from his belt, held them up dangling for all to see, and gave the death helloo twice.

A roar of appreciation came from the colonials. Many of them now began to make sport of Japson for having been caught and brought back. Then Mr. Erskine came out again to see what was the cause of the new uproar.

As soon as his eyes lighted on Albine and his prisoner, he smiled delightedly and beckoned for them both to come in. After turning over the pack horses to McLaughlin, Salathiel took Japson over to headquarters. The Quaker sat down in a corner, keeping his hat on and seemingly quite at ease.

Captain Ecuyer was seated near a table behind which Mr. Yates was ensconced with plume pens, an inkpot, and several long lists both of persons and of things neatly written and laid out before him. Ensign Erskine stood near the captain with his stocking dirk drawn, and there seemed good reason for this, since the captain's face was scratched and bleeding, and his wig, which had evidently been torn off, still lay before him in a badly trampled condition on the floor.

Despite that, the captain was patiently explaining something to the couple that stood before him, while from time to time he daubed his face with his handkerchief.

"Whatever has been taken from you will be returned, Mrs. Turner," he was saying. "It is only the articles which belong to the king that will be kept by the quartermaster. What is it in this case, Mr. Yates?" asked the captain. "Turner's the name."

"One musket and a forage cap, sir," said Mr. Yates, checking his papers.

"All the rest will be *returned*, Mrs. Turner," repeated the captain, "and before the day's over."

"Ike here, that's my man, bought thot shooten iron from St. Clair's store and guv good Portygee joes for it," said the woman. "Hit's ourn!"

The man nodded emphatically. "Thot's truth," he said.

"I've no doubt of it," said the captain, "but you see, Mr. Turner, the musket was stolen. It has the crown mark on it. We know the soldier who sold it to the store."

A torrent of abuse broke from the woman's lips so virulent as to startle them all.

"Hold your horrid tongue, Rachel," cried her husband. "Can't you see the captain's a gentleman and will deal honourably wid ye?"

"How will ye be gitten' any meat in the woods withouten your gun, ye fool?" his wife spat back at him.

With one hand Mr. Turner made a motion of respect and despair towards the captain and led his wife out with the other. She was still cursing.

There was a pause for a moment as the door swung open on the yelling mob of women outside and then banged to again. The captain ran his hand over his wigless pate and looked at the Quaker smugly sitting in the corner with his hat on.

"Friend Japson," said he, "blast me, if I'm not much obleeged to you for your work here! You can see," he added, pointing to his bleeding face, "that I am not the only one who feels deeply about it. Perhaps you can explain how so much of his Majesty's property seems to have passed over the counter of your store into the hands of these miserable inhabitants."

"It's quite simple," replied Mr. Japson, apparently not at all put out. "It happened in honest trade. The garrison has never been paid since they came here. They need things desperately. The soldiers traded what they did have for what I had to offer them at the store. In some cases the people friend St. Clair has brought to settle here had certain coins. They in turn bought what the store had to sell them."

"Which seems to have been, as near as Mr. Yates and I can make out, about half the equipment of the garrison," replied Ecuyer. "While you were taking your early ride this morning, I took the liberty of temporarily impounding all the property in the fort. We are now in the midst of sorting out the king's and returning what is legally theirs to your late customers. Since you think this is 'so simple' I suggest you take my place here and oversee this process yourself. Your wig is a natural one and will not be pulled off quite so easily as mine. And you will find an able and accurate assistant in Mr. Yates. All you will have to do is reverse the process that went on over the counter of your shop; to wit, purchase back the king's property. Mr. Erskine will see that it is returned to the members of the garrison to whom it belongs, item by item. Quite simple, friend Japson, does thee see?"

"Thou *canst not* mean it, Captain Ecuyer!" cried the trader, for once jarred out of his habitual pious calm. "Why, it will cost me two hundred pounds sterling at the least!"

"What do you think it would have cost if this fort had been lost, Mr. Japson?" enquired the captain. "Let me remind you: all the treasure the crown has lavished to extend and defend these frontiers for years past, the lives of soldiers, and houses ablaze from here to Carlisle. Women and children in the flames . . ." Ecuyer halted, trying to control himself.

"I know nothing of all that," replied Japson. "Such things belong to the princes and powers of this world to decide. All I know is I have to make my living in this wilderness. And I am a man of peace."

"Who buys and sells the muskets out of the hands of his Majesty's troops," interrupted Ecuyer. Salathiel had never seen him so angry.

"Swap for swap," interrupted Japson, not a whit daunted.

The captain rose from his chair and picked up his wig from the floor. He dusted it off and looked at the Quaker in complete amazement. For the first time it came to him fully that the man really believed in and meant what he said. Christ deliver me, he thought, and it is for this kind of a swine-louse that Bouquet and I have poured out the blood within us and the talents of our souls.

"Mr. Japson," he said, "I owe you an explanation. I did you the honour to think you were a villain. I see now that you are only a dangerous fool. Now come and sit down here and take the consequences."

The Quaker paled, shifted his hat onto his knee, and hesitated.

"See to it that he goes through with it, Mr. Yates," said the captain, walking over into the corner by his bunk and sitting down weakly. "Albine, come here and do what you can for me. I'll need all your skill. That woman nearly tore me apart. Hang a blanket over a string, will you. Demme, if I want any more of these viragos to gaze on my battered charms."

Salathiel strung the blanket across the room behind the captain's chair and went to work on him. He was shocked to find Ecuyer dangerously exhausted, and for the moment unmanned. He was about to have a chill. The experience of the morning, contending with violently hostile people, which had culminated in an assault upon his person by an hysterical woman, had shaken him more than all the difficulties of the journey and the hardships of the day before. It was at this juncture that it was borne in on Salathiel that Captain Ecuyer was not getting better; that he was slowly dying of his wounds and exhaustion, and that it was merely a case of how long he could last.

"I must see it through until next spring. I must. I can't disappoint Bouquet," Ecuyer kept muttering.

Brandy, hot applications, and a rest lying down brought him back to a semblance of himself in an hour or two.

He then insisted upon sitting up in his chair and being refurbished from head to foot. A fresh wig and some black patches on his pale face, where it had been scratched to the quick, gave him a peculiarly rakish and dissipated look like that of an old courtier who had quarrelled with his mistress. He looked at himself in his pocket glass and laughed. Salathiel's account of the capture of Mr. Japson and the taking of the two scalps was then listened to intently and with approval.

"But you must give up these savage customs," said the captain. "I was particularly shocked to hear you give the death helloo. It seemed to me you forgot yourself there."

"I'm afraid I remembered my old self—and didn't know it," replied Salathiel.

"That is even more serious," replied the captain. "You must try to remove such impulses from your soul. Now— my boots. I think I can bear them again."

From behind the blanket curtain Mr. Japson's difficulties could be heard going on. It was only when he realized that Mr. Yates would turn him loose into the mob assembled about the door that the Quaker had finally consented to "take the chair." The news of what had happened had gone around outside. It was regarded as an excellent joke and poetic justice for the trader, and every individual or couple admitted to see him made the most of it.

One by one Mr. Japson, under the relentless prodding of Mr. Yates, whose lists of each person's property as found that morning invariably contained the items belonging to the equipment of the garrison which had been bought and sold—one by one, these were ferreted out and returned. And the trader was left to do the best he could in each instance about returning the cost to his late customers.

The muskets and powder horns were the most costly. No less than twenty of the former had been "pawned" by the militia, and the squabbles over returning them were long and acrimonious, in some cases verging on violence, for St. Clair's settlers' were reluctant to give up their purchases.

As the day lapsed towards evening, however, all this came to an end. The last of the inhabitants were finally appeased, if not wholly satisfied. Mr. Japson, pale and haggard, had paid up. What belonged to the garrison was returned to them by Ensign Erskine and Sergeant McLaughlin. The property of the inhabitants which had been seized for inspection was given back, and the last check made against the final articles by Mr. Yates.

All were now inclined to put an end to what had been a laborious and nerve-racking day. Nevertheless, at five o'clock Captain Ecuyer had the garrison assembled, the quartermaster's store shack opened and every missing item of equipment down to the last button inspected, and when missing, replaced.

For that purpose the prisoners of the night before were released, paraded, and after a short reprimand returned to ranks without further punishment. One of them, the

Irishman O'Neal, was not to be found. But McLaughlin informed the captain that he was undoubtedly in the stockade and probably hidden in one of the huts.

The release of the militia gave considerable satisfaction to the Pennsylvanians and all hands were pleased at having their outfits and equipment renewed. For that reason both the militia and the Highlanders stood without a sign of impatience for three mortal hours in the bitter cold, while Ecuyer's Prussianlike inspection and re-equipment went on.

Darkness fell, and torches were brought out. The stockade swam in a kind of lurid, smoky glow, while boots, coats, muskets, belts, and new blankets were issued man by man and every item checked and signed for. From time to time, to keep from freezing, the men were put through the manual of arms.

By nine o'clock a new garrison seemed to have taken over the post. The late ragamuffin militia had disappeared and a formidable company of completely armed and quite soldierly-looking men stood in their place. The Highlanders once more resembled themselves in every particular, except a broken bagpipe which was beyond repair. Sergeant McLaughlin was ready to weep with joy.

Ecuyer then took them over, put them through some movements ending in a hollow square, and made a brief appeal, quite unexpected, in a strong, soldierly voice. He ended by remarking that the pay chests were expected at Bedford by December at latest, and that it was his and Colonel Bouquet's intention to have every man on the frontier paid before Christmas in good, round English pieces.

"Men," said he, "return to your quarters, cleanse your persons, your habitations, and your arms like soldiers and Christians. What infractions of discipline have occurred here I shall overlook. But from now on I shall punish relentlessly. Cut your hands off rather than part with your rifle guns. Your lives and the defence of this province depend upon them. In a short time you will be relieved here"—he paused as a rustle went through the ranks—"and you will be sent forward to Fort Pitt to go down the Ohio next spring with Colonel Bouquet. With the help of God it is his intention to force the savages to return their captives. Prepare yourselves to liberate your countrymen and restore them to the arms of their families, prepare to meet a cruel enemy that you already know so well. God save the king. Dismissed."

Ecuyer turned and staggered up the steps, with the help of Mr. Erskine, who now regarded him with a veneration impossible for him to express. The men scattered to their barracks, supper, and an extra tot of grog. A new kind of rational and disciplined noise filled the stockade. Only in the direction of the huts the quarrelsome grunting of hogs or an occasional human altercation broke out.

"There must be liquor loose over there, Mr. Erskine," said the captain, pausing to catch his breath at the top of the steps. "If we have any more trouble tonight I shall make an example that will long be remembered. Perhaps I have already been too lax. There comes a time when mercy to one may be cruelty to all. I dislike such moments."

They went into the blockhouse together, where a leaping fire and a smoking supper promised both cheer and surcease. The table was set—with four places again.

"Mr. St. Clair seems to be perpetually expected and always absent," remarked the captain as he sat down and drained a glass of wine to the dregs.

33

Another Side to the Same Question

THE MEAL BEGAN. A few minutes later St. Clair and the two militia officers rode into the fort, half-frozen and hungry as wolves. St. Clair was greatly worried at not having met Mr. Japson at an appointed rendezvous at the old Shawnee Cabins east of the Allegheny Mountain. He had waited for him there until a shot fired from ambush had ripped up the back of Lieutenant Neville's saddle and caused them all to take cover. This had given them pause, for it was hard to tell how many Indians might be about. Altogether, it had taken them nearly three days to ride over from Bedford, about fifty miles away. St. Clair cursed the Highland sentry heartily for his delay in opening the gate and the precision of his challenge in receiving him.

"By God, you ought to know us by this time," said one of the militia officers. "What's all this hifalutin' nonsense about?"

"Strict orders, sir," replied the sentry.

"Ensign Erskine's?" St. Clair snorted.

"Aye," said the sentry, "his verra ain, sir."

"I'll soon take the feathers out of *that* young coxcomb's bonnet," grumbled St. Clair to the militia officers, as they dismounted before headquarters.

"Let that arrogant bastard find out how things are for himself," remarked the sentry under his breath, as he closed the gate. "I'd give a month's pay, if I had it, to see his face when he walks into yon room."

The three officers began to bellow for someone to come and take their horses.

Inside, Captain Ecuyer laid down his pewter soup spoon and listened.

"His Highness has undoubtedly arrived," said Mr. Yates. "He and his tactful myrmidons."

"Do not rise or pay any attention to them when they come in, gentlemen," said Ecuyer to Yates and Erskine. "I'll do all the necessary honours. Albine, put another bowl of soup on the table for Mr. St. Clair. See that the two colonial officers are fed in the corner with Mr. Japson. They're close friends of his, I understand; or should I say customers?"

"Thou wouldst make the distinction," replied the Quaker, and went on eating his supper of which Salathiel had served him a generous portion. He had already resumed his complacence, and the fact that he was a prisoner scarcely seemed to annoy him at all.

St. Clair and the two militia officers now came storming up the steps with a loud scraping of boots. Considerable hard swearing marked their appearance, for Lieutenant Neville, having had his saddle practically shot from under him, had consoled himself with enough rum to restore his nerves and partially paralyze his legs. He had to be dragged along, and the whole party now precipitated themselves through the door with a crash. St. Clair was about to call angrily for assistance in getting the lieutenant to a bunk, when the words were stricken from his lips by the sight that met him.

Captain Ecuyer, wig, scarlet jacket, epaulets and all, sat at the head of the table, facing the door with the fire burning behind him. Yates and Erskine sat on each side of him, and a vacant chair with a bowl of soup smoking at the empty place was awaiting someone. Mr. Japson was in the near corner of the room, where Salathiel, towering six feet four, stood beside him. His head was near the rafters and his hatchet face and cold grey eyes appraised the newcomers quietly item by item.

St. Clair and Ensign Aiken stood stock-still, while Lieutenant Neville slumped casually to the floor and sat there. The two who remained upright seemed to be standing at bay. There was a moment of complete quiet broken only by the crackling of the fire.

"Good evening, *Mr.* St. Clair," said Captain Ecuyer at last. "We have been expecting you here for some time. In fact, a place at the table has been reserved for you at the request of your friend Mr. Yates." Here he indicated the vacant chair. "Won't you sit down?"

"I'm certainly greatly obleeged to my friend Mr. Yates," drawled St. Clair.

"You are more in his debt than you know," countered the captain. "Pray join us. Your soup will soon be cold."

St. Clair removed his greatcoat, gloves, and muffler. "And these—*er*—other officers here?" he asked, waving his hand loftily towards the colonials.

"I'm afraid we shall have to forgo their fascinating company this evening," said Ecuyer, "inasmuch as they are both under arrest. Mr. Erskine, suppose you take his hanger from the officer who is still able to stand. Albine, put the gentleman on the floor into a bunk. Or, if he be able, he can join friend Japson in arrest in the corner. All of you will remain here until further orders, of course."

"Am I to consider myself under arrest, too?" demanded St. Clair, his face turning scarlet.

"Not unless you insist upon it, sir. Since you are no longer in the army, I should prefer to settle what mutual business we have here as man to man. You can, of course, join Mr. Japson if you desire."

"Oh, the devil take it all!" exclaimed St. Clair, flinging himself into the vacant chair at the table. "I might as well acquiesce, I suppose. No doubt I'm indebted to Mr. Yates for more than a place saved at the table. Mr. Yates is an extremely old friend of mine," said he bitterly. "It takes one Scot to ruin another, you know."

403

"You do Mr. Yates an injustice, St. Clair," said the captain. "Recollect please, I'm not a schoolmaster who goes about gathering tales in order to inflict punishment. It is what you and your agent there in the corner have been doing here at Ligonier, and elsewhere, that has forced me to take certain measures. And what you have been doing here is notorious. It has disrupted the discipline of this fort and threatens to interfere with Colonel Bouquet's expedition. I refer to the supplying of the savages with arms and ammunition, besides other things, and the consequent encouraging of them. To further that and your profits, you, sir, tried to impose yourself on this young officer, your countryman, as the commander of this fort. And you have stirred up strife in the miserable militia here, and at Bedford, I am told, by involving them in your trade and interest. Now, this is all true. Deny it if you can. I can see it with my own eyes. It is not a mere jealous tale by Mr. Yates or anybody else, I can assure you. It is a fact. And at this time with the frontiers hanging by the thread of one road, and this place like a bead upon it, your conduct is tantamount to treason. My own duty is clear and I propose to see it done."

"And just what do you consider your duty to be, Monsieur Ecuyer?" demanded St. Clair.

"Your attempt to settle people here at Ligonier must cease, St. Clair. Your people must go back to Fort Bedford with me. And I will permit no trade to go on west of the Allegheny Mountain for any reason whatever. You have probably heard of the royal proclamations about trading with the savages, Mr. St. Clair?"

"Yes," said St. Clair. "I've heard of 'em."

"I trust I have answered your question plainly, then," added the captain.

"You have made yourself painfully clear. But man cannot live by proclamations alone, you know, captain."

"Mr. St. Clair," said Ecuyer, "I have answered your question. Now I wish you would answer one of mine. It is this. How is it that a certain British officer I saw only a few years ago in Canada leading his men gallantly against Montcalm is now, at a time when his sovereign needs his services more than ever, engaged in trading enterprises that amount to giving aid and comfort to the enemies of his king? Certainly they are seriously interfering with the desperate efforts of Colonel Bouquet and myself to defend this harried frontier. At least I thought I might expect a certain *sympathy* for those humble efforts from a former comrade. But I find the opposite. Frankly I am perplexed. It is this contradiction in your conduct which astonishes me. Is there an explanation, and what can it be?" Ecuyer leaned back, putting the tips of his fingers together while he sat gazing at his guest interrogatively.

St. Clair stirred uneasily. He poured a glass of rum and water, drank half of it, and still hesitated. Then he began in a low voice, without a trace of his usual pomposity or easy arrogance. For a while he managed to be simply and naturally impressive.

"Candour is the most costly of all virtues," said he. "Yet I shall be frank with you, Captain Ecuyer. You are known to be a man of honour, one with clean hands." He raised his glass, looking at the captain, and drank it off. "Your very good health, sir. I confess that under other circumstances I might envy you. But other climates other customs. If I make you my conscience now, it is because I think you will not abuse the confidence." He paused.

"Proceed, sir," exclaimed Ecuyer. "You are advancing your works by slow stages. I demand only the honours of war."

St. Clair laughed.

"With me it is like this," he said. "I am a Scot. I came to America to make my fortune, and for nothing else. When I found I could not do it in the army, I resigned. I married me a wife born in the colonies, and my children are and will be natives of this country. I shall remain here the rest of my life, and hence the interests and advantages of this place are hereafter and forever my

405

own. Against all other interests, captain, even against the crown and its officers—when they conflict."

He paused, and Captain Ecuyer leaned forward. In the corner Japson gave Salathiel a dig in the ribs, as much as to say, "Listen, young man."

"Now what you and Colonel Bouquet, and a great many other Europeans and Englishmen, do not realize," continued St. Clair, "is, that the interests of the crown and of us Americans are not always the same. No, sir, they are frequently at variance, and I venture to say that they may become increasingly so if the crown continues its present policy towards the western lands. For instance, you and Buckey—pardon me—wish to defend the frontier for the king. But the best defence of the frontier is to permit the people to settle here and exterminate the Injuns. There would then be no frontier to defend. In the end it would be better to let me settle the poor people I have brought to Ligonier, at great personal outlay, than to maintain a garrison here at greater public expense. And for how long? For forever, if you had your way. No, sir, it is to my advantage, to Mr. Japson's and his kind, to the advantage of everybody except the king and his ministers and his officers, to open up this country across the mountains to settlement, trade, and a vast continental prosperity that surpasses and overleaps the island imagination of all at home. In this adventure for profit, but also for better and for worse, I have cast my lot and set my compass, lead where it may. I have not sold out, as you may think. Think so if you will. I have simply transported my vital interests to this place and against all others they are now my own." St. Clair brought his fist down on the table.

"Land?" said Ecuyer, drumming his fingers on the chair arm. "Land, Mr. St. Clair?"

"That is one way of saying it. *Yes*, if you will, land, in America!"

The captain nodded and smiled. He looked tired and said, "I've heard that before. But not quite so well put. Well, you have been candid and eloquent in your own

406

cause, St. Clair. You will go your own way, I mine. But since you have so declared yourself, there is one thing it is my plain duty to demand of you. That is the paper given you by General Stanwix, reviving under certain conditions the lieutenant's commission you have resigned. It was yours on only one supposition of course; that you would use it to further the interests of the king as a loyal officer. And you have been using it not for that, but for your own purposes, as you admit. I must, therefore, demand the surrender of that paper, sir. And I shall return it to the present commanding general with your own explanation substantially as given to me tonight. Do you have the paper on your person?"

"Perhaps, and perhaps not. At any rate, you will not commit highway robbery to get it, I take it?"

"No," admitted Ecuyer, "you are going to give it to me."

"Yes, but only under certain conditions."

"*Mon Dieu!*" cried Ecuyer. "Is there nothing you won't bargain about?"

"Between a Scot and a Frenchman, what can be exempt?" laughed St. Clair. "I will give the paper to you —it is at Fort Bedford—if you will let the people I have brought here remain. Even Mr. Yates will tell you there is a good legal argument for that, and . . ."

The captain held up his hand.

"Agreed," he said unexpectedly, "provided you and Mr. Japson will return with me to Bedford without making any further trouble here."

It was now St. Clair's turn to hesitate. He did so for a minute or two, looking over at Japson, who finally nodded.

"Very well," said he. "I agree. My word upon it. Well, you *did* get your honours of war, captain."

"But that is about all," said Ecuyer.

He rose and bade them good night, almost as though he could not see or that they were not in the room at all. The three Scots, St. Clair, Yates, and Erskine, made their excuses and went over to the Highland barracks for draughts. In that pastime all rank was forgotten in a commonwealth of skill. Japson and the two militia officers finally retired to their bunks.

"Now help me to bed, too," said Ecuyer to Salathiel. "I've done all I can today—and a little more. Bedford tomorrow! Tell Burent to be ready. I wonder how long it will take? The mountains will go up and down and, O Lord, so will I!" He sat down with his hand to his forehead. Salathiel started to help him to bed.

"I have a plan for you, Albine," he said later, as he crawled under the covers. "I've been thinking something over, and we'll discuss it with you at Bedford. We'll see. No, don't press me about it now. Tomorrow I want you to take full charge of the trip. There will be quite a company, not all as friendly and helpful as they might be. I'll not be able to do much more myself, I'm afraid, until I see a surgeon. So you'll be in charge. I'll depend upon you. You did well with Japson today—and the two scalps." He extended his hand out of his bunk.

"And so, good night."

34

Fire

BUT THEY were not able to get off next day as the captain had hoped and planned. Ever afterward it seemed to Salathiel that the stop at Ligonier had provided a climax of trouble and annoyance even in that troubled time. Captain Ecuyer was not able to move. Even he himself had to acknowledge it. He lay in his bunk and slept from pure exhaustion. Salathiel made it easier for him by explaining to everybody that a wheel had come loose from the wagon; that Burent's back was still too stiff to drive, etc., etc. The captain was grateful for this—and so were all the others, for a damp snow began to fall early that morning. In the mountains it would be miserable. The Monk came in and built up a huge and comfortable fire, ate a flooring breakfast, and sat down like a tailor to watch Salathiel pamper his gun.

At the table Yates sat with St. Clair and went over the survey and the papers for the grant of land which the Penns had sold to him. For a while there was a hot dispute. To St. Clair the boundaries as described by Mr. Yates seemed, as he put it, to have "attenuated his parcel."

"And look," he cried, "look how the Loyalhannon sweeps around on me and cuts all the meadows out."

"You can hardly expect me to alter the course of the river just to suit you, Arthur," suggested Mr. Yates.

"Arthur me no Arthurs," exclaimed St. Clair, his face

blazing. "B'Gad, I'll have to be made surveyor here myself to get my rights. You haven't taken in either the pond or the spring west of the fort. I must have them for the site for the manor house. 'Tis just there I intend to seat myself."

"We can probably manage the pond by altering this west boundary angle just a little."

"But the spring, the spring!" insisted St. Clair.

Mr. Yates leaned back in his chair and looked across at his companion with a smile in his eyes.

"Do you remember a dappled pony that broke its leg—and you shot, *Mr.* St. Clair?" demanded Yates, leaning forward suddenly and looking his companion in the eyes.

"Why, that was years ago, years ago, at home in Thurso! I'd forgotten it. I swear I had."

"But I haven't," said Yates.

"And so I am to pay for it now, Mr. Attorney?"

"You should at least have offered to do so years agone."

"How much will the spring cost me—Edward?" said Arthur.

Mr. Yates held up the fingers of both hands. "Guineas," said he.

"I thank God you're not like that bairn o' the widow by the owld toll gate at Thurso. Do you mind it? A sax-fingered freak," chuckled St. Clair. "I'll pay."

Not without a certain thought of admiration for his boyhood friend's being a true Scot, St. Clair counted out ten gold pieces and returned his lightened purse with a sigh.

"You might consider coomin' oot with me here and managin' things aboot this settlement, Edward."

"I might," said Yates. "I might. I've been thinking of seating myself in the wilderness sometime."

"*Arr,*" said St. Clair, "you'd do weel! Think it over. And you a surveyor, too." He chuckled again.

Yates nodded. He now began to alter the plats and the descriptions in the deeds and grants to take in the spring and the pond. St. Clair sat smoking before the fire, his feet high on the back of another chair.

While this was going on Salathiel had been marching silently up and down the room, going through motions with his rifle. He unslung it, rammed home a make-believe cartridge, primed, and presented it a hundred times. The ceiling was just high enough not to interfere with these exercises. The captain's silver watch by which he was timing himself ticked in the hands of Monk, who called off the seconds as he had been told.

"You could handle it faster standing still, couldn't you?" asked St. Clair, who was watching the performance with interest.

"Yes, but I want to learn to reload it on the run," said Salathiel.

"Sort of a running fire," grinned Yates.

"Exactly," said Salathiel.

St. Clair took the rifle and examined it with great interest. A double barrel was new to him. He made some valuable suggestions as to firing and inspected the set of the flints. "One would do," he said; "a double lock seems unnecessary. If you get to Lancaster, take it to Jacob Ebey, the old clockmaker near Manheim. He's ingenious. He'd be able to fix it."

Salathiel stored this address away in his memory, along with Mr. Japson's on "Fourth Street."

Ecuyer was awake now. He felt greatly refreshed and insisted upon getting up and going out, despite their united protests.

"The king's business and invalidism are enemies," he said and smiled. "There's that fellow O'Neal. He's loose yet. Or did they find him, I wonder?"

He and Salathiel went out into the snow which had about stopped falling. There had not been enough of it to close the roads. It was a bright day, but it was getting colder again. Ecuyer gasped in the cold as they walked over to the barracks.

O'Neal had not been found. Mr. Erskine was now red-faced about it. He and Sergeant McLaughlin had hunted the fort through like two terriers after a rat that morning —but no O'Neal. Yet he had been seen only a few hours before at one of the huts owned by a McClanahan, one with a grievance.

"Let him alone," said Ecuyer. "He'll give himself away shortly, I'll wager my last sixpence. The McClanahans all smelled of whisky. Did you notice it, sergeant?"

"I did. They're a family with braw breeths," said Mc-Laughlin.

A good deal of the breath-sweetening beverage was loose in the village, evidenced by a gradually growing delirious noise about the huts. They were celebrating the return of Mr. St. Clair in some of Mr. Japson's whisky.

Nothing much could be done about that, Salathiel supposed.

The captain all but exhausted himself by taking the garrison out and putting them through a mock Indian combat. He enlarged on the new drill and tactics for fighting the savages that he and Bouquet had devised. He was most careful in instructing the leaders in this native mode of warfare, which most of the men, understanding the reality of it, took to naturally.

On the whole, things were much improved with the garrison. A cheerful discipline reigned, and the captain returned to his quarters considerably encouraged. The rest of the afternoon was taken up in an enquiry he conducted into the conduct of the two militia officers. They were both so sullen, and the testimony against them was so grave, that he suspended them from active duty and ordered them to return to Fort Bedford for a general court-martial. Mr. Pollexfen was confirmed in command of the militia and appointed his own officers.

How the fire started no one ever found out. Probably O'Neal started it out of pure drunken mischief. Increased pandemonium at the huts and a terrible fuguelike squealing of swine provided the first alarm.

Smoke was rolling from the east end of the stables and the litter in the pigpen was seething in flames almost before the startled sentries on the platforms could announce it. Burent rushed down to the stables to rescue the horses, and it was he who first reported the presence there of O'Neal.

"He's standing on the roof now," he gasped. "He threw a knife at me through the hole from under the rafters. And he's pitching pieces of burning bark from the slabs into the straw pile. It's the pigs what's spreading the fire," insisted the excited little Englishman, "the pigs!"

This sounded unlikely, but those who rushed out of the blockhouse soon saw what he meant.

The walls of the stable and the pigpen, where the unfortunate animals had been carefully confined by the captain's orders, had become crackling sheets of flame. The swine were fat, and between two blazing walls they were literally cooked alive. In the intolerable heat they became living torches of roaring flame, screaming like a thousand organs played by maniacs and rushing about at furious speed.

It was at this juncture that someone, either out of mistaken mercy or quite deliberately, opened the gate of the pen. Flaming and shrieking confusion started galloping about the fort, rushing under the miserable huts and driving forth their shouting and fear-stricken inhabitants. One of the huts took fire and another column of flame began to crackle and roar at one end of the village. Half-crazed dogs fell upon one another. People began to shoot at the pigs and a child was wounded.

Meanwhile, O'Neal pranced up and down along the stable roof, overlooking his enormous success and spouting a drunken ode of blasphemous triumph. In the lurid light of the flames now beginning to take hold on the Saxon roofs, he saw reflected the refulgent glory of the O'Neals and ten thousand other thatch-firing ancestors. Poteen, a keg of which he had dumped on the pigpen and set fire to, was also seething through his veins and brain and loosed in his mouth the tongues of bards and devils. It was a moment great enough to justify his being born. It seemed to him he had turned the world into a volcano, and that it would run off in molten lava, leaving him godlike and alone—on a burning stable roof.

The long roll of the drum at headquarters put an end to a period of delirium which had lasted exactly seventeen minutes, but which secretly pleased everybody, except the little boy who had been shot in the hip, the burning pigs, and a few officers. It was a relief from the dreadful monotony and menacing silence of the forest that for years now had encompassed them all with gloomy taciturnity, night birds, and leafy rustlings. That natural siege had temporarily been lifted. For five minutes everybody screamed his head off or roared. And then—the drum.

The garrison fell in; order resumed. From the top of the steps Captain Ecuyer gave his directions and in half an hour the flames were washed out with water, wet bags, mud, and snow. Half the stables were burned, one hut— the McClanahans', and the stockade wall was scorched. O'Neal had been rescued, overpowered, and put in irons.

Seated at supper an hour later, Ecuyer looked about him and at the grimy and soot-smirched company in the blockhouse. All of them had a certain chagrin and surprise fixed on their faces that seemed to peer through their grimy masks in a kind of dumb, ineffectual protest against the anarchy of unexpected events. The captain began to laugh at them and at himself. How smug and secure it had seemed in this room only the evening before!

"I hope you are enjoying this roast pork, gentlemen," said he. "It is the banquet of a king. In fact, I judge it must have cost his Majesty nigh three hundred pounds." Then he began to quote and translate:

" 'The bridegrooms of Folly make merry with torches.
They lie down upon the couches of discord
With cups of confusion in their hands.
All the imaginings of their hearts is unexpectedly evil.
The granting of their prayers is the revenge of the gods.
Destruction covers them, and they are heard no more.'

"I remember," said he, "that was in a grammar we

used at Geneva. It's surprising how you can recall things when you have once had to parse them. Grammars are like fools and children. They contain wisdom without knowing it. Don't you think so, Mr. Erskine?"

"I can't say, sir, that I ever reflected upon it," replied the surprised young officer uneasily.

"I suppose not," said Ecuyer. "But did you ever chance to reflect, Mr. Erskine, upon a convenient place about this stockade for hanging a man?"

There was a moment's abysmal silence.

"Yes, sir, as a matter of fact I have thought about that several times," said Mr. Erskine more cheerfully. "There are three beams which stretch out from under the gate-house floor just as you go out of the gate, for instance."

"One will do, Mr. Erskine."

"The middle one, sir?"

"Why go in for symmetry at a time like this?" said the captain, looking annoyed. "See that the rope is stout and have the decency to inform the man. O'Neal, of course."

35

Rope

SO THEY HANGED O'Neal next morning at sunrise.

The entire garrison was out, drawn up in the little square between the barracks. And every other man, woman, and child in the fort was looking over the backs of the soldiers at the one man standing on the cart under the gatehouse.

"Summary"' was hardly a swift enough term to describe the briefness of the court-martial which had been accorded the Irishman in the dark of the early morning, when the officers had hastily assembled by candlelight. He had been allowed his say, which consisted of a defiant statement that he was mortal sorry he hadn't been able to burn the fort to the ground, and a demand for a priest. There being no priest nearer than Maryland, and the offer of Protestant prayers having been indignantly rejected, he was sentenced, driven standing up in a cart under the beam projecting above the gatehouse, and the noose fitted about his neck.

There was a curious convention about hangings in all English-speaking lands. A hanging was at once a spectacle, a moment of moral edification, and legal vindication. He who was hanged was also momentarily distinguished; felt to have arrived at a parlous but eminent end, no matter how humble his beginnings. Indeed, it was one of the few ways in which a common man might hope to transcend the common oblivion of commoners, and his fitness for

416

having done so was judged largely by the eloquence of his own statement at his final taking off. It was considered to be the right, even the duty, of the condemned and the privilege of the spectators to participate mutually in a moving and admonitory farewell.

But the poor Irishman, when he was driven out under the gate and the rope put around his neck, could at first say nothing at all. He could only stand in the cart, weep, and look towards the officers, who were standing in a group at the top of the stone steps leading up to the block-house.

"Speak up, Shamus, now gie us a word, mon! The sun will soon be oop, and it will be all over wid ye," called one of the men from the crowd.

"Oi," said O'Neal, "it will be all over wid me. Oil go down into darkness. Oil not be seein' the sun!" He kept muttering.

"Captain Ecuyer," he called suddenly, "*must* I wait till the sun rises?"

" 'Twas the sentence of the court," said the captain.

In the growing light the figure of the man in his shirt with the collar turned down, and his hands tied behind him, shivered while his teeth chattered. There would be no eloquence. A grim, disappointed, sodden silence fell on the assembly. The captain could hear his watch ticking in his own hand. In another minute the sun would be over the mountain, he figured.

"It's the cold makes me teeth to click, good paple. Not me heart. I'd have you remember thot. Me heart is a ragin' lion," cried O'Neal at last.

"I'll have a mass said for you, O'Neal, when I get home," called the captain, touched by his courage.

The sun seemed to be deliberately delaying.

"You're a gintleman, captain. I'm sorry I cursed you, I am. Do you forgive me for it?"

"I do," said Ecuyer.

"Give me bundle of plunder to Mrs. McClanahan. Do ye be hearing me, Maggie?" Somewhere in the crowd a woman sobbed. "You're the only charitable hoor in the stockade. It's me all I'm lavin' you."

A golden radiance beat on the man's face, suddenly transfiguring it. The glistering edge of the sun's rim looked over the Laurel Mountain and filled the valley of Ligonier with light. The sunrise gun crashed. The drum rolled, beaten frantically by the Monk with tears streaming down his face. The gate swung open and the cart drove out— leaving the body of O'Neal swinging darkly like a pendulum in and out of the shadow of the gatehouse.

He raised his feet, which were tied together, once or twice, flexed his legs frantically at the knees, and then was still, except that he slowly spun around. A woman screamed. Then the drum stopped. Its echoes died, rolling away up the valley of the Loyalhanna into ghostly silence. No one moved. The troops blinked in the sunlight . . .

"Mr. Erskine," called the voice of Captain Ecuyer very clearly, "cut the body of that man down in half an hour after I leave this fort and give it decent burial. Raise the flag after the body is down. I'll be back here in two weeks' time, and I shall expect to find a strict watch kept and good discipline." He raised his voice slightly so all could hear. "And I leave *you*, sir, in command of this fort."

With that the captain walked down the steps and climbed into the wagon, which had been ready and waiting for him for an hour past.

"Gentlemen," said he, turning about on the little ladder to address a small group of horsemen, some of whom were already mounting, "you have your instructions. Be good enough to follow them to the letter. Move off, Albine."

Salathiel rode ahead on the mare. He had to lean aside to avoid the hanging body as he rode through the gate. The garrison came to present arms as the wagon rumbled out of the stockade. O'Neal's heels dragged along its roof, scraping the canvas gently. The captain looked up until the shadow of the dead man passed. "I'll remember the mass," he said aloud. There were others who more richly deserved hanging, he thought. He went

418

on tying himself in the swinging seat with his long, silk kerchief. It was over fifty miles to Bedford and two ranges of mountains to cross between.

36

Owls at Ray's Dudgeon

ST. CLAIR on a raw-looking gelding, the two sullen militia officers, Mr. Japson with his string of pack horses, and three inveterate deserters from the militia being returned to Fort Bedford for discipline, rode about fifty yards behind the wagon. They were all armed but had no powder. If there was an Indian attack the captain would serve it out to them then and let them defend themselves. They could probably be counted on to do that. Otherwise he was not taking any chances. This arrangement had been made at Salathiel's suggestion.

Another fifty yards to the rear rode a party of four of the Pennsylvania riflemen under the temporary command of Mr. Yates. These men were frontiersmen from the vicinity of Bedford and Wills Mountain, excellent shots, and were to be trusted according to Captain Pollexfen, who had vouched for them. Their cabins had been burned out by the Indians the summer before, and they therefore had a natural dislike for redskins and for all traders who supplied "the varmints" with clothes and ammunition.

Mr. Yates was the best mounted of anyone in the little procession. He rode a fine grey "loaned" him from the governor's stable and the Penns' own stud in Philadelphia, and he rode well. He had no rifle, but two immense horse horse pistols in holsters, and a short sword. He was a cheerful companion, joked a great deal, and the four Pennsylvanians had soon accepted him as their leader in fact as well as at the captain's command, when they found he was neither a soldier nor an Englishman. A rumour had gone about that he was a cousin of the Penns who had come out to settle.

"You had oughten to seat yourself in this ya kyounty, Maister Yates," suggested young Tom Pendergass, whose family had long been settled near Bedford. "My dad did mortal well with carn, whisky, and tradin' fer pelts before the Injun troubles begun. He has a big store and tavern at the fort now. All of us boys has been driv off our land. But we'll be back, we'll be back and the axes ringin', soon as Buckey burns the redskins out on the Muskingum. He's got the knack of whippin' them at their own game. Him and the little rooster up ahead in the wagon air the boys for we'uns, even if they do be king's men. Thar's no shenanigan about 'em. Now I'll pint out some right desirable bottoms to ya while we ride along."

"Girls' or farm lands?" demanded Mr. Yates, a repartee so much appreciated that he was forced to remind them that loud whoops must be subdued to chuckles in the enemy's country.

This merriment of the rear guard was in stark contrast to the silence and occasional remarks exchanged in a bleak undertone amongst the party nearer the wagon, headed by St. Clair. He himself was for making a bolt for it. But he could get no encouragement from Japson, who would not abandon his pack horses, nor from the deserters, whose spirits, never too high, had been entirely cowed by "having been rid under a hanged corpse." This, they contended, was a portent of imminent disaster.

"Be damned to you," said St. Clair, "for a parcel o' yellow dogs!"—and confined the rest of his growls and steaming invective to the ear of Japson. These were none the less effectively interrupted, even in their low undertone, when Ecuyer occasionally looked out the rear of the wagon.

Meanwhile, and so far, they were making pretty good time.

To Salathiel riding forward, and ranging ahead sometimes as much as a quarter of a mile, the country un-folding before him was a continual delight, and his minute examination of it for possible lurking foes a positive pleasure.

The damp snow of the morning had now frozen into a fairly solid surface crust, giving the horses good footing and just permitting the wheels to break through and roll without bogging down.

The road east of the fort led over a series of rolling hills. It was half-open country with clumps of woods on the heights and a dense, winding thicket that marked the course of the Loyalhanna leading off towards the south. There was not a sign of anything except elk, whose tracks every few miles crossed the road in con-siderable numbers, headed south, as though the animals were retreating from the tremendous cold towards the sheltered valleys in the pathless peaks of western Vir-ginia. Forward lay the long god-ruled edge of Laurel Hill, undulating slowly in a single line of unbroken mountain almost due north and south, white with snow and dark with vast forests, a wall that looked impenetrable, glitter-ing with winter light. It was at the top of this mountain, and beyond its crest at a wayside entrenchment and stock-ade, that they intended to spend the night.

They were soon up and out of the rolling hills and crossing a comparatively bare plateau of mountain mea-dows in which lay the little stream and valley where Salathiel had taken the scalps only the day before. He rode back here and brought up two of the Pennsylvanians from the rear to help him in scouting ahead. They knew the country intimately. And, if anyplace, it would be on some of the dense reaches of the mountain wall ahead that they might be ambushed.

A surprise of a different kind did, in fact, lie ahead of them, for Salathiel at least. It was the abrupt end of the plateau and a sudden drop into a great wooded valley a good thousand feet below, beyond which the Laurel Hill rose towering, seeming to be a stilled wave threatening war against the sky. To a man from the low-river lands the unusual sensation of height was overpowering. He stopped for a moment in his tracks, and the two Pennsylvanians, realizing the reason, laughed.

"Hit hain't nothin' to what's beyont," said young Pendergrass. "But this here *is* good bar country. Thar's caves in the bottom o' the branch." They stopped the procession to examine the road and the country ahead with extreme care. Some miles away a slight mist rising from the valley attracted Salathiel's attention.

"I was wonderin' ef you seen it," remarked Pendergass. "Hit hain't Injuns. Hit's a warm spring. Leastways hit's warmer than this hyer winter air, and she fumes. Me and par spent a hul day sneaking up to surprise 'Injuns' thar some years ago. Par was right mad when we found what it was. Thar's a salt lick near by."

Indeed, after some minutes they could see a movement of something making that way through the woods.

"Elk or buffalo cattle," grunted Murray, the other Pennsylvanian, after watching for some time. "And I can see another passel on 'em goin' south 'long the mountain."

"The wind's from the ridge," said Salathiel, holding up a wet finger.

"You're right, friend," agreed Pendergass, "and them critters is handy shy and spry these days. Looks like if thar be any Injuns, thar way down on t'other side o' the mountain."

"Liken they be," said Murray.

So they agreed to move forward—and their troubles began.

The road down into the abyss ahead was icy in stretches where springs had burst out across it. They had to let the wagon down inch by inch with the pack horses toggled on behind and holding back desperately step by step over such places. One of the beasts slipped, rolled; was cut loose by St. Clair with splendid agility; crashed with a scream into the forest below. He was hung there, transfixed on a giant dead oak tree.

"You'll be paid for that one, friend Japson," said the captain. "He was lost in the king's service."

423

"But not for the others?" asked the Quaker.

"Not for the others," said Ecuyer.

"I will sue thee in the provincial courts," called the outraged trader. "Thou shalt see!"

"There is a Scripture against going to law one with the other. Shall I quote it?" asked Ecuyer.

Mr. Japson turned purple, and St. Clair laughed—but at that moment the caisson skidded and threatened to pull the whole outfit over the edge after the lost horse. The Scriptural banter ended in a chorus of profanity and frantic "whoas" apparently addressed to various divine persons.

It took them over two hours to reach the branch near the bottom of the Laurel Hill. From there the road soared up over that mountain in a series of zigzags and banked curves directly into the sky. And the mountain was a wall of solid maple forest.

They stopped here and broke fast in the valley in a thicket of ancient but huge and hollow sycamores. Two or three of these trees gave the whole party shelter, while the horses were tied to the wagon and overlooked by two men with rifles, sitting high in the branches. A wolf loped off among the big trees.

"No one here," said Salathiel. Young Pendergass nodded. "Wolves here is a comfortin' sign," he admitted.

Ecuyer laughed to himself at the horrid comfort of the wilderness. He asked St. Clair to eat with him, and that ex-officer and up-and-coming gentleman looked pleased in spite of himself. They built no fires. The horses were rested, watered, and fed. Shortly after midday they forded the creek that lapped the foot of the mountain and began to climb.

It was desperate work.

"Only a Switzer like Ecuyer would try to take so heavy a wagon over the mountains in winter," remarked St. Clair. Japson agreed. But they all threw themselves into the task. As many horses as possible were made to draw. All minor differences were forgotten in the little party, for if they were attacked now it might be a close thing. It might go hard with them. No rescue would be coming. The captain issued a charge or two of powder to those without it. The Pennsylvanians ranged the woods ahead on both sides of the road as best they could. They were certain no one would try to desert here. Their attention could be turned all outward to scouting.

The wagon came up and up. At the worst places Ecuyer got out and hobbled along. He was obviously in great pain, yet his practical suggestions for making progress were constant and skilful. They stopped, breathed the winded beasts, and went on.

The afternoon passed away. Just before sunset they came out on the top of the ridge.

To Salathiel's surprise it was not like the top of a mountain at all, when he looked eastward. The valley was behind, but a broad tableland undulating easily and sprinkled with dense thickets and snowy open spaces lay before. The mountain was actually several miles broad at the top. Beyond in the sunset glimmer lay a welter of peaks seemingly incredibly distant, and wrapped in a glowing, translucent haze of fading scarlet lights and deepening blue shadows.

"Them's the Alleghenies and the peaks beyont," said Murray. "God send we're in the Shawnee Hunting Grounds tomorrow night. We kin take shelter in the valley. Hit's cold enough here to freeze a jug o' whisky. Push 'em on, friend Salathiel, the harses ul git the heaves standin' steamin' in this hyer thin, cold air o' the mountain-top." A blast like the intimate breath of winter roared across them at this great height, piping eerily.

So it took little persuasion on Albine's part to get them under way again. The horses fairly stampeded for shelter. The wagon rolled, bumping along the rocky road, rumbling, and striking fire from the stones and tires in the twilight.

Just as the stars began to come out and a new moon was sinking, they turned off the road into a clearing rutted by innumerable wheel marks, in the centre of which was a dark mass of low entrenchments and the sawtooth rim of a stockade lonely and dark as a castle left from other ages.

Owls had nested in its abandoned cabins and these withdrew reluctantly, hanging about with dismal cries and the snapping of beaks until a great fire leaped up into the night and set the sinister shadows of the place dancing to a cheerful, rosy light.

Now was the hardest time of the day for Salathiel. Everybody was exhausted and was for standing around near the warmth of the logs. There was no preventing such a fire being made. The men simply built it. As soon as it was going he had to drive them from it and to work. There was a good deal to do to make the place safe for the night. The powder issued to the deserters, to Japson, and to St. Clair was taken from them again.

They propped the big gate in place and wedged it. Salathiel asked Yates and two of the Pennsylvanians to watch on the galleries. The rest, even the "gentlemen," he insisted should cut wood, start the supper, and prepare generally for the night. Ecuyer came out and set an example, axe in hand.

Burent and Japson with two of the deserters put up the horses under a lean-to shed half collapsed with deep snow on the roof, as best they could. Blankets went on the wagon teams and mare after they were rubbed down and stones dislodged from their hoofs. The old sheds were many feet deep with rotten straw and leaves. Water was drawn from the garrison well after smashing in the head ice with a boulder. The giant sweep was soon creaking and passing about overhead through the stars.

Salathiel brought the remains of the pig, shot the morning before they reached Frazier's out of the wagon and grilled and roasted them over the fire. Potatoes were baked in the coals, and hominy cakes fried in the dripping grease from the shoulders and hams. Some of the men produced loaves of bread baked at the fort. A handful of brown maple sugar cast on the sizzling hog meat caused such an appetizing odour to arise that the sentries on the galleries called out with impatience. They began openly to envy the deserters. Promises of special cuts scarcely bribed them to remain on duty. Captain Ecuyer emerged from the wagon with a small puncheon under his arm and served out a good glass of black, fiery Jamaica rum to all present in grace or disgrace.

"Lum, lum, him heap good," cried young Tom Pendergass, rubbing his stomach and doing a shuffle about the fire like an Indian. "What kind of country must it be that grows juice like this here?" he demanded after downing his share.

"Rum is a little essence of Paradise squeezed out of hell, young man," said Japson, who had once been to Jamaica.

"Attar of nigger sweat," suggested St. Clair, also inspired.

"Gentlemen, you libel my contribution," said the captain, driving the bung home in the puncheon with mock indignation. "Rum—'tis the courage of fighting Dutchmen and the main brace of the royal navee, a potable charge for explosions of friendship—wings on the slippers of Mercury! Gentlemen, your health." He downed an entire glass at one gulp without a shudder, while St. Clair regarded him with admiration. A ragged cheer greeted the captain's noble defence of the white man's solace and his command to fall to on the victuals.

"Here, Murray," said he, heaping some pine slabs high with smoking cuts, hominy and potatoes, "carry these to the unfortunate sentries on the galleries and tell them to watch while they eat. Many an Englishman has lost his scalp for dessert at an American dinner. It's a barbarous end to a meal. And see that the rum gets to them too!"

Laughter followed Murray, who obviously had his plans for an extra sip at the expense of those on watch. Mr. Yates was soon shouting down his thanks and reporting that the place was about to be taken by storm by owls. Nor was this entirely a joke.

The old stockade called "Ray's Dudgeon," built by Forbes in '58, swarmed with owls since its garrison had departed, and the birds kept swooping about, their eyes glittering, beaks cracking, until blinded by the great fire they would make a pass over its heart and fall snapping on the ground to lie on their backs with their claws drawn up threateningly. Callahan, one of the deserters, was badly bitten when he snatched one up to "take home to his lil gal." His thumb spouted blood and he threw the bird into the fire where it shrieked like a lost soul, roasting.

"That's *you* in hell, Callahan," said St. Clair, who thought he knew how to deal with what he called "frontier cattle." "You've walked under a hanged man, and now you've roasted an owl. I doubt you'll last till morning. It's bad, *bad* luck!"

Callahan was visibly shaken and went off to bind up his thumb and sulk.

"God damn a brute like that," continued St. Clair.

"You ben't used to roastin' yet, Maister St. Clair," remarked young Nat Murray. "Me grandad, an old white-haired man, was tied up by a passel o' Shawanees in 'fifty-seven and had his legs burnt off to the knees with me grandma watching. Then they—"

"None of that," said Ecuyer sternly. "Every man here knows what we're fighting, devils that live in these hills and haunt the forests."

A growl of assent went around the circle. Only Japson seemed silent.

"Give us a song, St. Clair," exclaimed the captain, "a good rousing one."

"*Lillibullero, bullen a la,*" sang St. Clair in an unexpectedly fine tenor.

The rest joined in, for among the Scotch-Irish Pennsylvanians there was scarce one that did not remember the good Protestant chorus of King William's days, the anthem of Orangemen—and:

> To loyal hearth and hall
> Came King William's royal call
> To his golden standard flaunting by the Boyne,

And Boyne waters they ran red,
And King James he up and fled,
While the crown dropped from his head—
Up Orange, and up Orange, and huzzah!

Then would come the chorus in which all joined mightily:

King William was King James's son
And of the royal race he sprung—
Aha, aha, aha!

The mocking laugh drove the owls back with its hearty shout.

After which Ecuyer gave out the watches for the night, and cautioned them with an earnestness that went home to be mortal careful and stay awake. "For one slumbering sentry is the death of us all." The men around the fire scattered to find what places they could to sleep in among the half-ruined cabins.

In the lean-to and among the horses Callahan, the deserter, sat sucking his bleeding thumb and cursing. He was from old Irish Baltimore, a good Catholic, and the Orangemen's songs made his heart turn black with hatred. He determined to make another break for home. "And this time," he said half aloud, "I'll get over the hill, owls or no owls!"

The night and time wore on.

It was soon Salathiel's turn to go on watch. He had the second, and later the last watch in the morning. He and Murray and Pendergass went up and relieved Yates, and the other two Pennsylvanians on the galleries.

Quiet settled down on Ray's Dudgeon, broken only by the gurgles of owls and the screams of a panther hunting in the ravines lower down beyond the crest of the mountain.

"Hit's high heaven for painters up here," remarked Murray. "God, how they kin yell when they be coortin'. Listen to *that*, will yer!" After which no more was said.

The three passed to and fro on the platforms, keeping

429

themselves warm, awake, and peering out of the loopholes on every side. The stockade was built at the bottom of a saucerlike depression, and it now struck Albine why this was a good plan.

The rim of trees all about stood out against the sky. From the stockade you could see through them at the crest, and you could see anything that moved there against the stars. And at the bottom of such hollows there was usually water. That accounted for the copious well.

It was another exalting night. The high mountain air was a new sensation and experience for Salathiel. He was not tired, he was even glad he was up on the platform overlooking everything. Sleep could come later. The mountains were surpassing his expectation. He felt the rum in him and the good supper. He laughed quietly to himself.

Outside the stockade the wind swept through the bare branches of the forest and sang like a sorrowful squaw. Inside, all was still. The fire burned down to glowing embers. The oblong of canvas over the wagon shone dull yellow with candlelight from within. The captain, St. Clair, and Yates were having a round of loo. Occasionally their conversation and a laugh sounded distant and muffled. A light flickered here and there in the windows of the huts and went out.

The card game in the wagon broke up. Albine heard St. Clair and Yates saying good night and walking off into the darkness. Soon only the horses were stamping now and then, apparently in a vast solitude. The noises of the forest prevailed. Over the stockade the stars slowly wheeled and marched to the westward, glittering in clear frosty multitudes, white shimmering clouds of them such as he had never seen before. A fox barked and sniffed along the gate. It would soon be time to change the watch. He saw the animal sneaking off through the trees, a grey, shadowy outline of nothing. He watched it through a loophole—and then he saw something else.

It was a man gliding from tree to tree. He was going away. Salathiel watched the line he was taking. It was

430

towards the road. Presently he would be on the rim of the "saucer." There was a patch of snow there. The way he was going, he would have to cross it. Salathiel could see the sights of his rifle only against that snow. He aimed there and waited. Suddenly the end sight was blurred by a shadow on the snow. The two sights came in line. He fired. He peered out again. Either the man was down, or he had missed his shot.

Then he saw a figure bound down over the rim of the "saucer." It was running across through the trees and against the stars. There was an agonized scream out in the darkness. Salathiel fired his other barrel, aiming at the same place he had fired at before. He had almost forgotten that he had another barrel! Outside there was silence complete and unbroken. Even the owls had ceased.

The fact that Murray and Pendergass were good men was proved when they faced out and watched at the loopholes when Salathiel fired, instead of running to him with questions.

But there were plenty of questions from below. The captain was out, demanding what the firing was about, and St. Clair, too. Some of the others came tumbling out with their rifles.

"Who fired?" demanded Ecuyer.

"I did," Salathiel answered, still keeping an eye on the section of view through his loophole. "There were two of them, captain. I think I got the first one. Then an Injun came to scalp him. I don't know whether I got him too, or not. I think the first I fired at was a white man. Maybe one of our own people. He seemed to be leaving the stockade."

"Where's Callahan?" asked the voice of Japson suddenly.

Several voices began to call "Callahan" in vain.

"Guess he's made a break for it," remarked O'Toole, one of the deserters, "and that big renegade bastard on the platform's shot him. I ain't goin' to lave him out there to be scalped," he whined. "He's me nevvy. Me sister will go woild."

431

Considerable stir was going on down in the darkness. "You men go back to your huts," said Ecuyer. "I'll shoot the first one of you that moves towards the gate, myself. You can see what happens to you outside."

The glint of a pistol in the firelight confirmed the captain's sincerity. The bereaved uncle of the late Callahan and his companions departed, cursing under their breaths.

The captain doubled the watch on the platforms. Everyone, including Japson, took a turn. But nothing more was seen or heard.

Towards morning Albine and the party first on watch got some sleep but not much, for soon after dawn they cooked food and prepared for an early start. It was the captain's intention to reach a place called the "Shawnee Cabins" on the other side of the Allegheny Ridge before evening.

He called Albine aside and cautioned him to push on without regard to the fatigue of those following. "And keep a good watch in advance, for I wouldn't be surprised if we meet a train of pack horses and drivers. I think Mr. St. Clair and Japson have long been expecting them. They have not been able to send back messengers to warn them not to set out. I rather think that's why Callahan was so anxious to escape last night. He could have deserted more easily when he got to Bedford. It is my intention to turn this caravan of traders back," said the captain significantly. "Ammunition to the savages now might be the ruin of Bouquet. If we can catch these people redhanded, it will put a stop to the trading business at least until the campaign's over, I feel sure."

There was only one incident that marked, and that with quiet chucklings on the part of several, the departure from the Laurel Hill stockade.

The men under charge of attempted desertion were put to drawing water that morning from the well for the horses. As Salathiel passed them, he recognized the voice that had called him a "renegade bastard" only the night before. It belonged to the uncle of the deceased Callahan, a large, loose-jointed, carroty-looking fellow with

432

red hair and bristles bursting from his ears. As the man was without weapons, Salathiel laid his own rifle and long knife aside and walked up to him. The man seemed inclined to dodge what was evidently coming his way. As he did so, Salathiel jammed the captain's little water bucket down over his head, not gently. It proved quite difficult to get off, and the sepulchral remarks of the man in the wooden hat were appreciated even by his friends. The two militia officers stood by laughing heartily.

"Served thee right, O'Toole," said Japson, "thou art a disagreeable fellow with thy tongue. And thou art now muffled."

This man with no head walking about, talking like a voice down a well, put everybody but himself in good humour. The wagon and its attendant cavalcade got under way that morning to the tune of considerable laughter, despite the tragedy of the night before. Merriment, however did not travel with them more than a rifle shot from the gate.

In the snow patch on a small rise where they turned off on the road, the body of Callahan was found half scalped and shot through the back. There was no sign of the Indian, who must have sprung up and fled before Callahan died, except a scalping knife dropped in the snow near the dead man, and a trail of blood as far as the road. It ceased there or it could be traced no farther. Just how the Indian had got away was not plain. It was a source of great satisfaction to Salathiel none the less that both his shots of the night before had evidently found their mark. He patted the butt of his rifle affectionately and saw that Murray and Pendergass and the others regarded him with increased respect.

They stopped long enough to tie the body of Callahan over the empty saddle of his horse, which Japson was now leading in his string, and went on. A little farther along they buried it some distance off the road.

"Owls," said St. Clair to his small group of followers, "owls! What did I tell you last night?" He enjoyed their consternation and winked at Japson, who could not see the joke. O'Toole and his friend began discussing in an undertone what they were going to do to Salathiel. "Wait," said they, "wait till we git to the fort. We'll stop his time."

It was now getting sensibly warmer. Captain Ecuyer made that his excuse for demanding extreme exertions from everybody to push forward. If it came on to thaw, the road would be little better than a bog. They came down the eastern slope of the Laurel Hill without any mishaps and in good time. Halfway across the valley to the Allegheny, Salathiel and his advance guard found a letter stuck in a cleft stick by the side of the road. It was addressed to Mr. Samuel Japson in a sprawling hand:

Friend Japson—Me and Lt. St. Clairs nigger Jed come as far as this lookin out for you. Thought you and him was coomin back to gyde us over the hill west. Not finden you we stopped here half a day and then took back to Chowanee Cabins where is the men and harses and goods waiten in the big grove tol you come. Seen no redskins nor sines on em. Came an express Fryday from Harriss on Susaquahannok sayin sum pay chists was on the way from Carlysl with starlin. Looks like brisk trade at Raystown soon promises. Prendergass in high hopes hez tooken 5 kags offen you for his place and promises coin. Hope you find this. Will wait at cabins while vittels holds out.

Your obgt. serv.
T. Wilcox.

So that was why Japson had been so anxious to get ahead of them, and why the captain had been so determined to hold him. This would simplify matters considerably. Now they would know where to find the traders. And from what Wilcox said it looked as though there were no Indians about.

Of course, he could not depend upon that, Salathiel pondered. There was no date on the paper. And some of the Delawares who had been following Japson might turn up. It was probably one of them who had scalped Callahan last night. All at once Salathiel remembered the letter he had found in the pouch of the Delaware he had scalped. How could he have been so forgetful! Well, he would give both the letters to the captain now. He folded it up in the letter found by the road and sent both back by Murray with an explanation to the captain, after cautioning Murray not to be seen giving it to Ecuyer. Also Murray was to tell Burent not to spare his horses at all. Then he took up the march again and pushed on towards the mountain confidently and swiftly. Murray overtook them only with some difficulty on his return.

"The captain says, 'that's good'—and he wants to see Albine at the noon halt."

They had begun the ascent of the Allegheny Mountain and were a quarter of the way up when the halt came. Salathiel found Captain Ecuyer quite elated over the finding of the letter.

"It puts these gentlemen in our hands," he said, "if we play our cards right. Now I've altered my plans a little. We'll camp tonight at the top of the Allegheny in the entrenchment at the crest, instead of pressing on. After the camp is asleep I want you to take the four Pennsylvanians, go down the mountain and make an attack about dawn on the traders camped in the grove. *Panic* them back to Bedford. Don't kill anybody, if you don't have to. But don't hesitate to kill if you must. Make them think you're Indians if you can, but see to it that all the trade goods are left behind. They can take their horses, arms, and personals if they wish. Arrange it, if you can, by making terms, or any other way. Do you see? Burent and I and Yates will keep Japson, St. Clair and Company in hand till morning. You can wait for us tomorrow till we get down the mountain. Now I told you at Ligonier I had something in mind for you. Well, this shall be your test for fitness for certain other things. Don't tell your men anything of this until just before you leave. Not an inkling or suspicion must get about. Be especially careful of the two militia officers under arrest. They are St. Clair's friends. Japson, too, is keen as a fox. Wait until they are all asleep tonight. I leave the details to you. See to it!"

"See to it," Salathiel kept repeating to himself. It was the captain's favourite phrase. Well, he would *see to it*, he promised himself.

They resumed the ascent of the mountain, but more slowly. The captain even managed to trump up some plausible delays. It was not difficult to find good reasons for stopping. The climb was a killing one, the road a series of dismal tunnels through an oak forest whose branches met overhead. On the higher slopes the embankments of Forbes's engineers had in some places washed out. Burent was much admired for his skill in getting the wagon up at all. Men and horses were exhausted more easily on the heights. It was twilight when they arrived at the "Allegheny entrenchment," and the captain's decision to spend the night there almost met with applause. Watch was set, supper prepared, and the captain pleading his great fatigue as a reason for retiring early, all settled down for the night.

"No owls here," said St. Clair to Albine. "Not a one."

"I take that for a *good* sign, sir," Salathiel replied, and grinned in the dark as St. Clair went off to smoke a pipe and go to bed.

37

Panic as a Cathartic

IT WAS ABOUT eleven o'clock of an extraordinarily clear, moonless night when Salathiel gathered his four Pennsylvanians together and explained what was in view for the next morning.

They had managed to leave the camp in the little entrenchment without anyone but the captain being aware of their departure.

It was quite simple. Half of them had been on guard for the first watch and the other three had been detailed for the second. No one thought anything of that. But when the relief showed up, Salathiel, after cautioning all to maintain complete silence, had simply marched all of them out of the entrenchment, which was near the crest of the mountain, and then down the road for half a mile. The captain, Burent, and Yates took over the task of guarding the camp while the others slept on. A flask carried by Lieutenant Neville and generously shared with his friend in misfortune had more than guaranteed the sound sleep of the two militia officers.

Salathiel brought with him a bag of shot, powder, some boiled meat, and hoecake sufficient for one meal, also several pieces of the captain's charcoal. Well beyond hearing of the camp, he now halted and made his plans known while everyone blacked both hands and face with charcoal.

The four Pennsylvanians entered into the scheme to

turn the traders back, with grim enthusiasm. All of them had been driven from their clearings and forced to take refuge from Indians at Fort Bedford, consequently their opinions of "Injun peddlers," as they called them, required invective to express. Murray and Pendergass had both been born near Raystown. So they knew the country about Fort Bedford as only young hunters could. The grove on the knoll above the Shawnee Cabins was quite familiar territory to them, and it was understood they should act as guides.

Several other suggestions having been discussed and rejected, it was finally agreed that they should attack about an hour before dawn and try to palm themselves off as Indians on a raid—"which won't be no hard stunt, neither," asserted one Harry Banner from the Juniata water gap—" 'caise the mostest of these here packhorse drivers and men is from the German settlements, and all them Dutchmen knows about Injuns is that they yells like hell fustest, and then scalps ya."

"Well, we'll yell like hell," said Salathiel, "and I'll jabber real Shawnee at them, and a few shots might help. Time to git on now. Watch we don't meet some of the real article layin' for us as we go down."

A growl of approval met this caution, and they swung off in single file with Murray leading at a good pace.

The road began to tend downward rapidly. They had reached the eastern slope of the Allegheny Ridge at one of its highest elevations and passed over. It was suddenly much warmer on the eastern slope. The cold northwest wind which had plagued them for days was suddenly cut off. The road swung unexpectedly outward around a great shoulder of shaly rocks. Towards the east the mountain here fell almost sheerly to the broad floor of the mighty valley below. There was the feeling of being high, and alone among the stars. All felt this, and they stopped for a moment as if by common consent.

"Come over here, Albine," said Murray. "I want to pint out the lay o' the land to you."

Salathiel approached the unprotected outer edge of

the road on cat's feet. To him at least, the sensation of height was tremendous, not to be entirely denied. Just ahead of him it seemed that Murray was about to walk out on invisible levels of atmosphere and swim among the stars. They stopped, of course, at the brink.

"Wal," drawled Murray, "what do ye think of our country? God, y'oughter to see hit by daylight!"

But the night was quite enough for Salathiel.

Immediately beneath him was the roof of a dark forest that undulated over the swelling floor of the valley in a tumult of hilly waves, ending eastward against a far-flung, black mountain wall whose edge was hung like a great floating ribbon along and across the stars. Beyond that, seemingly beyond the confines of the night itself, great masses of fleecy white clouds staggered up into heaven with black windows through which appeared glittering, familiar constellations and the dim eyes of unknown stars. And against the cloud curtain, lower down, seeming to be afloat on the breast of darkness, was a jumble of dark peaks, domes, and profiles of mountain crests, high, disconnected, and lonely; the mysterious midnight country of a beautiful, terrifying dream.

"Ain't no Injuns goin' to drive us out o' this," commented Murray, after respecting Salathiel's silence for a proper time.

"Nor no traders neither," he added. "Man! Ya oughten to see the harvests hereabouts. The black loam's two or three feet deep even on the hillsides, oncet ye git the trees down and let the light in; carn, punkins, wheat, taters, and you kin grow tobacker ef'n yer want to. And thar's sweet springs and the music of livin' streams. Hit's God's gift to them that kin keep it."

"Looks like it's worth fightin' fer," admitted Albine, who could not tell what his eyes saw and how he felt about it. "If we can once git things settled, looks like thar's homes for all of us somewhar"—he flung his hand out with a sweep as generous as the landscape itself.

"You're right, friend," agreed Murray. "Reckon we've come fer to stay. But look," said he, lowering his voice.

"Do you see that ring of little lights twinklin' away north there? Thought they was stars myself at fust, but they be too low down. They're on the valley floor, and that's the fires o' the peddlers waitin' in the grove fer Japson, And thot's whar we must be, come mornin'. And it's a many a mile away."

They returned to the trail to report to the others what they had seen.

"No more haltin' now," said Albine. "Keep going down, Murray. When you git pretty nigh tell me and I'll give you my scheme for drivin' these fellers back. Git your packs and your straps set now for a long swing down the mountain."

"It looks farther than it is," said Murray encouragingly, and struck off downhill in a steady hunter's stride, half trot and half swift walk, that ate up the miles.

The road was like a narrow cleft through the forest here, hugging the long surging folds of the "Allegheny Hill," making halfway down a wide half-spiral to the east which they realized only because the stars seemed to swing overhead through the branches and the Dipper could be dimly seen through the trees. All of them knew "Charles's Wain" and the polestar. The rest of astronomy had been forgotten under a sea of leaves.

When the night birds ceased towards morning they halted by a spring, ate hastily, and looked to the fresh priming of their pieces, wiping the flints and flash pans clear of damp.

They had now reached the level of the valley floor.

"It's about two miles to the grove now," said Murray. "They must have let their fires die down, or we'd see the glow over yon hill. Shows they ain't keepin' much of a watch after all. Well, Mr. Albine, and what now?"

Salathiel was tickled. It was the first time anyone had "mistered" him as a superior.

"Here's the scheme me and the captain agreed on," he drawled. "Thar's five of us, and I hear thar's open space all around the grove which is kind o' set out and bare like on the top of a hill."

"Thot's right," agreed Pendergass. "Hit's the very picture."

"Well, we'll spread out all round it in a ring. You'll have to jedge your places pretty nice. Each man about the same distance from t'other. I'll give you half an hour fer that. Then, jes when the first grey shows in the sky, I'll hoot like an owl goin' home. Like this . . . You can all reply one by one a few minutes apart. When it gits round to me again I'll know we're all set, and I'll 'whahoo' twice. That'll be the signal fer all ready. I'll fire, and then we'll all begin to yell like Injuns and let the rifle fire go round and round the ring. Let 'em think thar's a hundred Injuns in the grass. And move about a bit so they can't fix on your gun flash. And mind you, keep firing one after t'other with about a minute between. That'll give you all about four minutes each to reload, and mind you keep it going. Make them keep their heads down, and if they fire back, fire at the place the flash came from. If they holler for terms, let me do the talking. And if they make a break for it, shoot 'em down when they gather. Each one of you will have to make enough noise fer a hul tribe. Now everything, firin', yellin', and talk will go round from left to right, sunwise turn. Kin you remember it?"

A chorus of reassuring growls from the darkness was the encouraging reply.

"Wet your whistles now at the spring and don't forgit to wipe your rifles again, if ye crawl through the grass. I'll allow fer that. Ready?"

"Let out," said Pendergass.

They swung off silently as animals, scarcely making a rustle in the leaves with their moccasins. Another half hour and they came out under the stars into a wide-open meadow. In the middle of it, and to the left of the road, was a moundlike hill with a dark grove on the top. Here and there a bed of ashes glowed faintly when a breeze blew, marking the place of the now-neglected fires. A dog began to bark up among the trees.

"Dang it!" whispered Murray.

"Won't make no difference," murmured Pendergass. "He maunt be barkin' at a coon."

Salathiel gave the signal to fan out. One by one, with a wait of a few minutes between, they began to feed themselves out into the darkness and to surround the hill. Salathiel stood where he was. He would wait and then crawl forward himself. In half an hour all should be ready. The people on the hill apparently slept on undisturbed, although the dog came rushing down the hill barking violently. Then he turned tail and went back again. Nothing else happened. Three-quarters of an hour went by. Over Will's Mountain to the east near Bedford a grey pencil of dawn made a stroke in the sky.

An owl hooted.

Slowly, a few minutes apart, four other owls replied. They seemed to be nesting all about the hill. The "bird" to his right Salathiel judged to be about three hundred yards away. "More than a rifle shot."

The dog was becoming frantic. Someone at the grove got up to quiet him violently. For the first time Salathiel saw the figure of a man moving among the trees higher up. He could now begin to make out the white roofs of several wagons up there, and piles of bales spread about in a rough circular barricade. The man walked along the top of the bales evidently hurling things at the dog.

"*Du Gottverdammter Hund, du.*" The dog gave an agonized yelp. A rifle cracked. Salathiel had shot the man.

His scream rang a terrible reveille through the grove. Salathiel emitted a horrid, bloodcurdling, gurgling wail.

The man on his left took it up and passed it on. Around the hill rifles exploded. Little spurts of red-blue powder flame and wisps of cottony smoke dotted the grass, half visible in the morning fog. A sound like a parliament of souls in hell wailed, and ululated, and re-echoed all about the grove. The wounded man kept on screaming. The dog was apparently going mad. Horrified roars and shouts arose among the horribly awakened

442

traders. Bullets droned over their heads and smacked amongst the trees. Three horses tore up their pickets and galloped wildly away. A ghastly early dawn dissolved into infernal pandemonium.

"Injuns, Injuns!" shrieked the German pack drivers. "*Wir sind verloren. Herr Maxwell, wir sind verdammt.*"

Maxwell, Mr. Japson's trusted clerk, awakened with a spasmodic jerk out of a calm depth of winter slumber, where he lay wrapped in five trade blankets in the middle of a pile of soft bales. He sat up and looked about him in a shrieking inferno of terror.

He felt this terror before he could even begin to think of its cause. His body stiffened like a spring. Then a reflex of unlaxing began as he caught his breath. It hit the pit of his stomach and relaxed his bowels into his small-clothes as easily as though he had been an infant.

It is a terrible thing to have no control of your body; to find that it has mastered you. He loathed himself. He smelled fearfully—of panic. And death would find him like this! he thought. And if it didn't, the others would find him, and he would be a sight. All the respect and influence of a lifetime that he had built up by constant, faithful toil would be gone. He would be an eternal laughingstock.

The Indians had come! The worst had happened! Soon he would be roasting tied to a tree! A terrible groan escaped him. He tried to pray, but all he could see was a vision of his cubicle of an office in Philadelphia, the peaceful, high, three-legged stool he sat upon there with a quill behind his ear and the two big ledgers open before him. The company account of *Marvin & Drexel* was open before him with a mistake of subtraction in the third column—£1—2*s.*—6*d.* They must be completely surrounded. My God, what *was* a man to do?

He got up on his hands and knees and began to crawl towards the outer ring of bales which had been piled like a rough circular breastwork about the grove of trees on the knoll. He peeped through between them. There were rifle flashes in the grass! Around and around the grove went the rifle fire. Hoops of cruel triumph and a wailing death dirge made him sick. A bullet passed him with a banshee howl and dropped a horse that began to kick, holler, and squeal. Someone fired a pistol from between two bales, the sole reply to the attack.

Then a complete silence ensued, except for the struggles and moans of the dying horse. Outside, and down the hill somewhere in the grass, Maxwell gradually became aware of a voice calling to him in Shawnee.

"Take your horses and your saddlebags and go. Go back to your own country, paleface," called the voice.

So it *was* a war party from beyond the mountains, thought Maxwell. Shawnees! He had traded with them often.

He replied. His voice quavered. "Friends here. Friends! We bring rum and powder. Blankets, bullets for you."

"What say, what say?" demanded the voice.

"Bring heap rum, heap bullets, much blankets for you."

"Leave um lum, leave um blanket. Take um holses go, go," shouted the voice in English. "Us no shoot."

Maxwell explained this offer to his men. A babble of Plattdeutsch ensued from the terrified drivers. The rifles began to crack and bullets to smack against the trees again.

"We'll go, we'll go," shouted Maxwell in a lull of the firing, a glow of hope giving his voice some confidence again. "They'll let us go if we leave the goods," he shouted to his men.

"You go?" demanded the voice.

"Yes, yes," screamed Maxwell. "You no shoot?"

"No shoot," said the voice.

A rush took place for the horses. Two got upon the back of one and galloped off into the grey of dawn. The rest waited to see what would happen. The sound of hoofs died away up the Bedford road. Reassuringly not a shot followed.

There was a wild saddling and scramble. A couple of bales were tossed aside and a torrent of men and horses

tore down the hill. As they scrambled up the road to the
east a couple of bullets droned after them. They plied
thongs and spurs. It was five miles before they drew rein
and waited for the stragglers to catch up. Mr. Maxwell
was one of the last to arrive. He had stopped for ele-
mentary reasons farther back. He began to curse them for
cowards and poltroons.

They took it quietly until someone suddenly shouted,
"Who shit his breeches?"

A roar went up at that. It was true. Everyone now laid
the blame on Maxwell. He was obviously, nervously
helpless. They heaped curses on his head. Then someone
shouted they were being followed. A second but quieter
panic overcame them and they rode on towards the fort,
drawing closer together as the sun rose and revealed them
to one another, haggard, for the most part unarmed, and
surrounded on all sides by the snowy wilderness. They
were hungry too. Someone had a bottle of schnapps and
they drained that. There would be nothing to eat till they
got to the fort that evening.

Maxwell groaned as the liquor took hold of him. He
began to think of the goods he had abandoned. He began
to think—that voice, had it really been that of a Shawnee?
Black, sullen hatred filled his mind. Somehow, somewhere, he would get even with somebody for this.

Back at the grove sunlight was beating goldenly all
along the east flank of the Allegheny Ridge, and Salathiel
and his four Pennsylvanians were enjoying a breakfast
of unlimited rashers of bacon and piles of johnnycake
from a bag of meal that lay slashed open and streaming
out onto the grass.

Bales of loot lay piled all about them, at least a
thousand pounds' worth of trade goods: blankets, matchcoats, small kegs of powder and rum, rolls of lead, bags of
flints, beads, small mirrors, brass jewellery, and a deal
of salted and preserved provisions; flour, sugar, bolts of
English cloth, kegs of wrought nails, hatchets and knives,
pieces of iron, unfurbished and old-fashioned pistols and
muskets, a chest of curious seashells, wampum, and toys.

All this the Pennsylvanians hunted through with more or less contempt, breaking into small chests with their tomahawks and slashing open bales with their knives out of pure wantonness and curiosity. Nor could Salathiel stop them. His insistence that no kegs of rum should be broached, and that one good tot apiece must suffice, was as far as he cared to go—and that met with some grumbling.

A somewhat tense situation was saved by the discovery by Murray of Mr. Japson's Negro Jed hidden under a pile of bales.

He was hauled out praying. Fear had turned him a kind of grey color. His surprise at finding his captors were "buckras" instead of Injuns was only equalled by his relief. He jabbered the lower Gold Coast dialect of his youth, having been scared clean out of English for the time being. He kept close to Salathiel, because he was the biggest man present, and he had assured himself he was white by rubbing some of the charcoal off his cheeks. "Him buckra massa," he shouted. "Him no yam niggah." And he began forthwith to cook piles of link sausages snatched from one of the Pennsylvania Dutchmen's saddle-bags, sprinkling them with brown sugar as a peace offering.

All this, and the rounding up of several stray pack horses, consumed considerable time. A huge fire was built before which everyone dried himself out and several went to sleep. After some persuasion Salathiel finally prevailed on young Tom Pendergass to carry back a message of their success to Captain Ecuyer.

"Reckon you'll meet him about halfway down the mountain," said Salathiel, "and mind you don't shout out the news but just drop it quietly in the captain's ear. The loss of these goods will be a sore blow to both Japson and St. Clair. You can't tell how they might take it."

"Who cares how they take it now!" exclaimed the young Pennsylvanian, and slinging his rifle, he set out at a trot.

446

Salathiel swarmed up one of the taller trees at the top of the grove-crowned mound and took a look over the wide landscape that now lay unrolled beneath him.

A wide undulating valley stretched endlessly north and south as far as he could see, low hills covered with dark, bare forest interspersed with patches of open snow-covered glades through which the road to Bedford cut a yellow scar. It could be traced eastward over the low crests for many miles, twisting and turning. On it already some miles away the frightened traders must be making for the fort. But they had already made such distance that he could not catch sight of them, although he watched for some time. Westward the tremendous wall of the Allegheny Ridge marched down into Virginia, apparently an unscalable barrier, and toward the east, topped by even higher ridges and pinnacles beyond, lay the parallel barrier of Will's Mountain. Over there somewhere was the Juniata, and Fort Bedford.

He hoped the captain would be coming along soon, for the place where they now were, the mounded grove called Shawnee Cabins, lay in the midst of natural open fields with the forest enclosing it. And if they were really attacked here by a wandering war party Salathiel felt he could no more hold out than the traders had. Perhaps he should also send a messenger on to Bedford? But the arrival of the traders there with their story would probably bring a large party to rescue their goods. And the traders would arrive at the fort before his messenger could. No, on the whole, he had better not send another man away. He was shorthanded enough as it was.

He wrapped his blanket around him and continued to sit in the crotch of the tree, keeping a careful watch. In the camp below, the remaining Pennsylvanians were now asleep in various soft nooks amongst the bales. Jed was keeping up the fire under the pots and a big lazy plume of smoke rose and drifted off bluely among the trees. He could hear the darky humming a monotonous, contented song with something of relief in its tone. The silence of

447

the wilderness seemed to close in on the slow movements of the Negro, to surround him and the others, and to take the place of time. Besides Jed, there was nothing else to be seen moving or to be heard in all that snowy, sunlit valley except some lonely flocks of crows flying from hill to hill, and the shifting cloud shadows on the roof of the forest.

Towards noon Salathiel's treetop speculations were put an end to sooner than he had expected by the emergence of the wagon and its escort into a bare patch near the foot of the mountain. In another hour they would be safe in camp. Captain Ecuyer must have got under way in the early watches of the night. At any rate, he had timed things nicely, Salathiel thought, and he would by now have received the news from Pendergass.

Not a little numb from the cold, Salathiel climbed down and began to urge Jed forward in the active preparation of the approaching midday meal.

38

In Which a Compromise Is Reached

BURENT'S SKILL in driving horses was not the only reason why the wagons had arrived safely at the foot of the mountain. It had also taken a combination of force and diplomacy on the captain's part, for both St. Clair and Japson had suspected the reason for the absence of Salathiel and the Pennsylvanians, when they awoke that morning and found them gone. But they also realized Albine and the others must have left the night before, and it was now much too late to warn the traders or to try to prevent what must, if it had happened at all, already have taken place. Besides, St. Clair and Japson were once more minus their weapons, and the captain, Burent, and Yates were more than usually watchful.

The two deserters were trussed up in a way which precluded their offering resistance even if they could have been approached and persuaded to try to do so. Japson did try to speak to them just as they left the entrenchment at the top of the mountain, but he was warned off by Yates in a manner which caused St. Clair to describe that little attorney as a "truculent, young bantam" from whom nothing but trouble was to be had.

Mr. Japson agreed, but at that moment he was called to join the captain in the wagon. His string of pack horses, hitched on behind, were left to St. Clair, who rode his mount behind them in a rather dejected way, making an ineffectual signal now and then to the Quaker to *do something*. But the Quaker declined.

Their remaining hope was that Maxwell might have put up a successful resistance, or that he had either returned to or had never left Fort Bedford.

That the traders would be waiting for them somewhere along the route, they both felt fairly certain. Yet neither of them could be sure exactly where it would be. In fact, all was uncertainty and surmise. They scarcely knew what to do until the situation should unfold.

St. Clair therefore resumed his usual cheerful manner and continued to exchange pleasantries with the captain through the back of the wagon, while Japson sulked inside. Mr. Yates brought up the rear of the procession with the two militia officers, the deserters trudging ahead, roped together effectively, but in such a way as not to interfere with their marching along.

Burent exhausted his skill in preventing any untoward slips or slides down the mountain. He was successful. And it was in this order, and in this way, that the somewhat constrained company finally reached the spring over halfway down and stopped to water the horses.

Here they were met by young Pendergass who brought news to the captain, which St. Clair and Japson would have paid sterling to overhear. Naturally they were not enlightened. Indeed, they were left even more than ever in the dark.

But Ecuyer was not able entirely to conceal his satisfaction at what he had heard. His relief at learning that Albine had been successful was immense. He became more cheerful, even animated. And it was characteristic of him, since he guessed what must be going on in the minds of Japson and St. Clair, that he should make the most of the situation and strike while the iron was hot to shape his future plans.

"Mr. St. Clair," said he, poking his head out through the end curtain. "Be good enough to join me and friend

Japson here for a moment. I have some news for you. Perhaps we had best discuss it now and arrive at an understanding."

Digesting this as well as he could, St. Clair turned his horse over to young Pendergass and climbed into the wagon, which he overtook only with some difficulty through the mud.

They proceeded for quite a distance before the captain saw fit to enlighten him further. Ecuyer sat strapped into his swinging seat with a large, black silk handkerchief. He and the two lanthorns swung together with the motion of the road, suspended from the ridgepole. Mr. Japson sat on a chest, looking grim, with his hat drawn over his eyes. The broad back of Burent loomed through the canvas ahead. After some consideration the captain began.

"In my situation," he said, "and in these heathen parts, it is not always possible to enforce the letter of the law. I must make arrangements to carry out my instructions as best I can. I am even inclined to make a bargain if possible, when, under happier circumstances, I might be bound to make no concessions whatever." He paused and looked at St. Clair and Japson, his hands resting on his knees.

"A sensible conclusion, I am sure, captain," interjected St. Clair. "I was certain when you encountered our—er—trading caravan on the road—quite a considerable force, isn't it?—you would be willing to concede the point that business and trade must go on; since all that it is necessary to do is to wink at the proclamations as you pass by. Now, I confess I have considerable interest in friend Japson's venture, but . . ."

The captain held up his hand.

"I thought as much," he said, "and I also thought that, since your traders have seen fit to abandon your goods and retreat to Bedford, leaving them in the charge of Albine and his men, this might be an auspicious moment, from my standpoint, to talk things over." He paused for a moment to let the full import of the news and the situation sink in.

Mr. Japson stirred uneasily. St. Clair's cheeks flushed with a sudden choler that gradually ebbed away to leave him paler than before.

"There's a thousand pounds sterling laid out in those goods, thou must know," said Japson, smoothing his coat thoughtfully. Whether he spoke to Ecuyer or to St. Clair or was just thinking aloud was not plain.

"A staggering loss for our Quaker friend here," said St. Clair. "I think you should consider carefully before you ruin a man for a mere point of duty, captain."

"Doubtless the title to the goods *is* in Japson's name," continued Ecuyer. "No doubt *you* would see to that, St. Clair. But I also imagine the man who is backing him did not wish to lose so large an amount, even of his wife's money, at one stroke. Am I right?"

St. Clair winced.

"What is it you propose?" he demanded. "All that I ask is that you don't call in that infernal little stickler Yates to drive your bargain with me."

"You may well be thankful you are not called upon to deal with one of your own countrymen, St. Clair," said the captain quietly. "As for me, I am not inclined to be so hard as you may think. I wish to ruin no man. I am not likely to be among men much longer and, although they do not understand it, I really wish them well." He paused for a moment. "Yet I still have my duty to do."

His two listeners sat looking at him with astonishment. Somehow they both felt humble and quite suddenly and curiously in sympathy with the man in the swaying seat.

By God, I believe he *is* in a bad way! thought St. Clair.

"Thou wilt be merciful, then?" said Japson. "If so, I will no longer oppose thee."

"You can put it that way if you like, friend Japson," said the captain. "It is rather the way I wanted it. What I propose is that, if I return these goods to you and Mr.

St. Clair after we reach the fort, you will undertake—you, on your word as a gentleman, St. Clair, and you on your affirmation as a Christian, Japson—not to trade in any manner with the savages until Colonel Bouquet returns from the frontiers with his men. What I cannot abide is that you, or any other white man, should be the cause of his undoing or the death of any of his men, Nay, I confess that I cannot even understand how you can do anything to hinder him."

"And you would let me furnish forth my settlers at Ligonier, then, captain?" asked St. Clair in frank amazement.

"Certainly, but with nothing to supply trade to the Injuns."

"And thou wilt ask no bond of me?" demanded Japson.

The captain shook his head. "I will take either your goods or your word, Japson. I can keep your goods. But you can also keep your word. Which shall it be?"

There was a moment's complete pause in the negotiations. Both St. Clair and Japson were trying to think where the trick lay, or whether the captain was baiting a trap. But for the life of them they could find neither. And it gradually dawned upon them and then burst into their minds with the full light of day that an honourable spirit proposed to treat them as equals. The captain understood this and said nothing more. He was even amused by their momentary silence. At last Japson motioned his acceptance to St. Clair.

"You have my word of honour, captain," said St. Clair. "I understand, and accept your proposition."

Ecuyer touched his finger to his hat in acknowledgement and looked at Japson.

"It will cost me a pretty penny," Japson sighed, "but thou hast my promise not to trade with the savages till Bouquet's return."

"Good!" exclaimed Ecuyer, assuming at once an easier and friendly attitude. "That will save us all a world of trouble. From now on we understand one another. We are all free to act now. The goods are at the Shawnee Cabins. I suggest we do all we can to press on there. I sincerely trust not too much mischief has been done."

Both Japson and St. Clair left the wagon with a feeling of release rather than chagrin. St. Clair was given his weapons again without comment. The Quaker took his pack horses in hand, and with the united urging of all hands it was only an hour past noon when the wagon and its escort reached the grove, where all sat down together to devour the stew prepared by Jed.

That individual gave a curious manifestation of joy at finding his master again. Every now and then he flipped off his feet and walked in a circle about St. Clair on his hands. Even the two deserters who sat roped together on a log had to laugh. A general feeling of relief and good nature took possession of them all. The sun was pleasantly warm and the stew comforting.

"It is at times like this," said the captain to Salathiel, whom he had called into his wagon, "that the enemy falls upon one and the massacre is complete. Beware of being at ease and comfortable."

It was a timely remark. There was not a single sentry posted and, for the time being, not even the captain did anything about it. He sat and listened to Salathiel's account of the "spoiling of the caravan."

"You have done well," he said finally. "When I get to Bedford, I shall go ahead with the plan for you that I had in mind. It will engage what I believe are your more important talents. That is, you will not be curling wigs much longer, I fear. But let that go for the time being. I mean to camp here for the night, or until help comes from Bedford. No doubt Captain Stewart, the commandant will be sending out a party to reconnoitre this scene of carnage at least. It will be a strong party, if even half the story of the fugitive traders is believed."

"That is what I figured," said Salathiel. "But I'll post a sentry or two while we wait."

"Do so by all means," laughed Ecuyer. "I am glad you

remember my hint. Remember it in the future too. And, by the way, I might mention that you no longer need to keep an eye on either St. Clair or Japson. We have arrived at a certain understanding."

Salathiel could make nothing of that, but he had long learned now not to worry about what was satisfactory to Ecuyer. He went out and posted his sentry in a tall tree and kept an eye on the deserters himself. Then he sat down with Murray and had a good smoke.

Japson was wandering about bemoaning the condition of his burst bales. Jed was shaving St. Clair. The horses ate eagerly and lay down to sleep or to roll in the leaves.

The afternoon passed slowly, seeming to die away into the blue shadows of the smoke of the campfires that curled away lazily through the bare branches of the grove on the knoll. The sun dropped behind the western wall of the Allegheny. Cold and the earth shadow swooped. The wide cheerful valley was suddenly chilly and lonesome. Everyone hastened to gather closer to the fire. Mr. Yates, who was by this time regarded as the greatest wit in the world, by the Pennsylvanians at least, sensed the occasion and the opportunity to relate an anecdote.

There was something curiously magnetic about the little lawyer when he began to speak on his feet. He had the broad brow and the mobile mouth of an orator. Nature had compensated for skimping his bulk by giving him an outline at once dapper, swift, and effective. And he had also received a gift of gesture that was like a second tongue of accompaniment to what he said. He now stood before the fire with his coat drooping about him like a gown of precision. His voice reached out and arrested attention. Even St. Clair, who had always been annoyed by his existence, was forced to listen and reluctantly admire.

"Did you ever hear about the cross-eyed judge and the three cross-eyed prisoners?" began Yates, as the silence which he had somehow conjured cleared the stage for his voice, and he looked about him entirely seriously.

"Ain't never heared on them, never," said Murray obligingly.

"My friend Murray reminds me of the description of Paradise in the Saxon poem," said Yates. "It was a place where 'not any lions never ate no lambs'—but let me go on with my story. It is a famous one, the chief precedent out of *Blackstone* for a case lost by malprision of vision, a peculiar cast, as it were, in the eye of the law—the case of the cross-eyed judge and the three cross-eyed defendants. It was like this:

"The three cross-eyed prisoners were lined up before the cross-eyed judge, right to left as usual. And the judge looked on the prisoners, and the prisoners looked at the judge—and their mutual confusion was considerable. In fact, his lordship couldn't quite tell which prisoner was which, or just where they began or left off. So he said to the one that looked to him like the first prisoner, 'What's your name?' And the second prisoner answered and said, 'John Hobbs. But *I'm* not quilty.' And the judge looked at him and said, 'I wasn't speaking to *you.*' And the third prisoner said 'I knew you weren't. I didn't say anything at all.' At this point the judge declared a mistrial."

Mr. Yates stood entirely still, quietly looking at his audience. Their appreciation was by no means simultaneous. It spread slowly from one person to another. But both the deserters seemed to get it at once. Perhaps because they were still tied together and seated on the same log.

Salathiel let the gentlemen continue their conversation around the big fire, where he was glad to see the captain had felt able to emerge from the wagon and take part. With the more than willing assistance of Japson, he put the rest of the men onto repairing the damage of the morning and getting the bales and chests ready to go back to Bedford. By evening they were ready to move again as soon as horses could be obtained. Nor did they have to wait long for them.

Shortly after nightfall three scouts from Fort Bedford rode in with the news that a troop of mounted rangers was on the way. Murray was sent to hurry them along, and about eleven o'clock they came threshing into camp. It was now too late to move, however. But Ecuyer gave instructions to have all in readiness for leaving as soon as it should be light enough to see.

Yet in spite of an early start before him next morning, and the long, strenuous hours immediately past, Salathiel did not fall asleep easily that night. Perhaps it was a natural elation over his first success as a leader that made him wakeful; the thought of unfamiliar difficulties ahead that kept him pondering. Tomorrow, he knew, would take him across the threshold of the wilderness into the more complicated surroundings of a large town. For Bedford was to him a "big town." Counting troops and transport, the usual inhabitants, and refugee families who had crowded into the fort and village, there must now be several thousand people at Bedford, all told. That *would* be something to see. And he was eager to see it—full of curiosity and anticipation. But he was also aware of possible pitfalls in unknown ground.

Turning over in his mind the past and future, he lay on a pile of the captured trade blankets, looking into the clear, white heart of a dying ash-wood fire. For a while he let his eyes and fancy shift from scene to scene amid the slowly changing frescoes of its golden caves. What a filigree of fact and hope was there!

He shifted uneasily as the fire fell.

Shucks! A man could see anything in a fire—the past, for instance. Nynwha said *he* could foresee the future there.

He smiled dreamfully to himself. Poor Uncle Nymwha!

How those old days in the forest, and the boy he had been there, how they had all passed away suddenly—gone like a hunter's dream when he wakes from some half-enchanted nightmare to the wild, cheerful sound of horns in the morning.

457

That was it! That was what had happened.

Somehow with good luck, and despite the bad, he had been wakened from that long, green sleep of the forest, the forest that was alive, but didn't know it was there. He knew *now!* Not that he knew all about himself yet. But he was going to find out, to measure himself against other men and things. That was what it meant to be looking into the fire as a white man instead of an Indian. You knew what you saw there was a piece of your mind. Only when you were half asleep could you think it was real.

He laughed, half doubtfully, half in triumph, and settled down under his blanket for the night. The new rangers had the watch to keep. Tonight he would not be responsible for everybody's safety, not even to Ecuyer.

Now there was a man it was hard to serve! Your best, even when it *was* the best, was only just good enough for him. But who could equal Ecuyer? There would never be another man like the little captain; no one else would ever be able to say to Salathiel, "Albine, *do it*"—and the thing would be done. Why, that was almost like the centurion in the Bible! Certainly it was the same kind of thing. But he would never be able to trust another man so as to serve him like that. He would not want to find another master, even if he could. Once, and once only, a young man found his perfect warrior. Even among the Indians that was so.

And then—Ecuyer was passing on. He, Albine, knew that. There was a way you could tell. A certain farewell look that came into a man's eyes. Malycal, the white witch, had told him.

And so Albine would be on his own soon!

That was a sobering thought—and yet he faced it with certain eager anticipations. A free man, a young man, might leave some sorrows behind him—and go on. Why, that was inevitable! Time would tell. And meanwhile a man must sleep.

He closed his eyes against the glare of the fire that

was somehow just bright enough to have drawn moisture from them.

Now he was quite alone inside himself. For a moment there was nothing but the smoothness of the dark and the vast contentment of rest. His fatigue seemed to flow out from him. His body was long, but strong, and a comfortable thing to be one with. Presently, it seemed to be floating away from him towards the far-off voices of the wind in the treetops. And yet he could see again, see without opening his eyes, something that brightened inwardly and went on before.

A sunny section of the familiar forest road winding through a country of comfortable hills with bright patches of new snow on them stretched far into the distance. The wagon was ahead of him just going over a crest. Oh, yes, he remembered now. They were going somewhere, he and all the others, on a long journey. There was a town, a wonderful village just over the hill, they said. He couldn't see it yet. He must press forward eagerly—tomorrow—

Tomorrow he would be riding over the old Shawnee Hunting Grounds, that lost country he had heard the squaws sing about in sad, homesick dirges, around the Shawnee fires. He could hear Mawakis chanting:

High are the stars above the long mountains,
So far away are we who behold those hills no more.
Too long have we waited, fooled by white winter,
Birds that would fly back in autumn,
Black swans with frozen wings.

Yes, Mawakis would be there—tomorrow—lingering about the site of the village, where she had played as a little girl. The marks of her tired feet were in the forest. She would run after him but the wind would fill her footsteps with sand. Only the leaves would whisper where she passed. And he would ride by. He would see and understand like the Little Turtle. But nevertheless he would pass by now.

There was a town just over the hill where the wagon was going, and he was no longer the Little Turtle. He was—He listened, while the green light of the forest seemed to close about him. He listened. Someone was calling him.

"Salathiel—*Salathiel Albine*, you come out of those woods!"

Why, it was his own mother, his mother calling him! Of course, he knew his name. Sal Albine—*that's who he was!* And his mother had never died, after all. She was not going to scream—not this time. No, no, she was just calling to him to come out of the woods.

Suddenly he was a little child again. He dashed forward, how smooth, warm, and beautiful she was! She was leaning over him. She was going to tell him now that . . .

"Sal, Sal"—he could hear her voice. Oh, if he could only hear what she was going to tell him. The words. Then everything would be . . . would . . . be . . . all —

Darkness ensued, complete, lasting, and deep . . .

. . . and what was that now? Sound again? Noise obstinate and disturbing. Something must be wrong . . .

Danger!

He sprang to his feet in one motion, grasping his rifle instinctively, ready for anything, completely and fully awake.

The fire was out, fallen into grey ashes. At the top of the mound, standing tiptoe on a bale, a young trumpeter of the rangers was sounding over and over again the piercingly clear notes of the English reveille. It was like a hunting horn. Behind his small figure the eastern stars hung burning like clear lamps in the first grey of morning.

The camp began to stir. Horses neighed, and were saddled. Cooks blew impatiently on dull embers to kindle their breakfast fires. Ecuyer emerged from the wagon, calling out crisp, brisk orders. His breath smoked in the frosty air.

Albine stood for a moment, looking into the swiftly growing day over the mountains toward Bedford.

"Lord," he said aloud, "what trouble a man's mind can

460

get him into at night! The only way to see the future is to march into it and find out."

He tossed his hair out of his eyes, and ran forward to help Burent harness the teams to the wagon.